VEIL OF KINGS

MICHELLE KIRBY

MICHELLE KIRBY BOOKS LLC

ISBNs
Paperback: 978-1-972159-00-2
Hardcover: 978-1-972159-01-9
Ebook: 978-1-972159-02-6

Published by
Michelle Kirby Books LLC

*For my dad, who shared fantasy worlds with me and made
sure I never left them behind.*

PRONUNCIATION GUIDE

Names carry power in Mystralos. If you wish to speak them as they are meant to be heard, a few are noted here.

Gisela — Gii-suh-luh

Noah — NOH-uh

Elysande — eh-lih-SAHND

Orion — oh-RYE-uhn

Ivy — EYE-vee

Vivianna — vih-vee-AH-nuh

Tristan — TRIS-tuhn

Cillian — KILL-ee-uhn

Selene — seh-LEEN

Thorne — THORN

Silas — SIGH-lus

Marina — muh-REE-nuh

Adrian — AY-dree-uhn

Eva — EE-vuh

Bjorn — BYORN

Ravenor — RAV-eh-nor

Crag — KRAG

Eira — EYE-rah

Ignitus — ig-NIGH-tus

Ondine — on-DEEN

Aerion — AIR-ee-on

Tempest — TEM-pest

Pyraxis — py-RAK-sis

Mystic — MIS-tik

Mystralos — mis-TRA-lohs

Terranox — TEHR-uh-nox

Vespera — VES-peh-ruh

Frosthaven — FROST-hay-ven

Rockridge — ROCK-rij

Aquamere — aa-kwuh-meer

Sunhold — SUN-hold

Windspire — WIND-spire

Thunderpeak — THUN-der-peek

Tevrin — TEV-rin

Mount Kharos — CAR-ohs

Hylja — HILL-yah

MYSTRALOS
FROSTHAVEN
THE SNOWDRIFTS
THE NIVA
MT. KHAROS
THUNDERPEAK
TEVRIN
ROCKRIDGE
THE ZEPHYRAS
WINDSPIRE
THE STONE RIFTS
INFERNO RIDGES
THE FLARES
SUNHOLD
AQUAMERE
LUNARA SEA

CHAPTER ONE

I t wasn't a coincidence.

Gisela Valor knew better than to believe in chance on days like this.

The storm had arrived with the King's guard, black clouds clawing across the sky, thunder growling its warning. Rain hammered the earth, soaking the roads to muck. It was the gods' judgment. Their fury exposed. Every drop of rain was a curse, a reminder of what the kingdom had become.

Of what it did to its own.

"Strip down to your undergarments," King Ravenor's guard barked, his stare cutting through the crowd, daring anyone to resist. "Eyes forward."

Rows of young men and women huddled at the village center, arms wrapped around themselves, shivering. Villagers lingered at their windows and doorways, silent, as it happened again.

Gisela peeled her dress over her head, the soaked fabric clinging stubbornly to her skin. There had been a time when this exposure made her want to curl into herself and vanish. Now, she locked her fear away, standing rigid beside her brother as the guard scanned her.

A scream cut through the rain. The kind that silenced everything else. The kind that hollowed the air.

Gisela's head snapped toward it.

A guard had a woman pinned in the mud, his fist tangled in her hair. She tried to erase the elemental mark on the base of her neck, but it remained.

"Please . . . for the love of the Six, have mercy," the woman sobbed, her hands clasped in prayer. One moment she was kneeling there, and the next, she lay slumped on the ground as a sword sliced through the air.

They had found a Mystic.

And the gods were watching.

Gisela's stomach lurched at the sight of the lifeless body, the metallic scent of blood stinging her nose. She forced herself to block it from sight, fighting the scream rising in her throat.

She could stomach the death; she'd been forced to. What she couldn't bear was the silence.

Mystralos didn't just execute its Mystics. It trained its people to look away, to accept. She had once felt that same quiet compliance.

But not now. She refused to turn from it.

Her hands flexed at her sides.

Noah stood beside her, posture stiff, flinching as the guards dragged the body away.

"Clear out," the guard ordered, wiping his blade on the dead woman's dress.

No one moved until the final bootstep faded and the last of the guards passed through Frosthaven's gates.

Only then did the air return to their lungs.

Gisela's muscles still resisted, as though they hadn't yet thawed from the inspection. She reached for her dress, pulling it on with trembling limbs.

"Another one," Noah said, tugging up his pants.

"Another one," she echoed.

Their father, the new Village Lord, waited beneath the archway, his expression carved from stone. The gates groaned shut, and he brought his fingers to his temples before striding away, councilmen trailing at his heels.

"Should we go to him?" Noah asked.

Gisela shook her head. "No. Let him be."

He had enough on his plate.

They trudged home in silence, shoes squelching in the mud. The sun broke through the clouds as if signaling the departure of the King's guard, warming her skin, though the chill in her bones lingered.

Gisela rolled her shoulders, trying to shrug off the tarnish of spilled blood that wasn't on her hands, but on her soul.

Villagers waved, and some bowed, carrying on as though an execution hadn't happened down the road.

How could life continue so casually after such cruelty?

"I wish they would wave at us like they used to. The bowing makes me feel awkward," she muttered, watching a villager in tattered clothes nearly lower his head to the ground. "It's not like we're royalty now."

"I think they're all grateful Cillian isn't Village Lord anymore," Noah said with a shrug. "They have hope."

The villager stumbled up the step to his crooked timber house, sending a box of odds and ends teetering toward the ground.

Gisela darted forward, catching it before it could make contact. She handed it back with a quiet smile.

"Well, I take that back. Not all of them," he added, nodding toward a group of young men.

Their laughter was jarring after what had happened.

At their center stood Thorne Alderose.

She'd learned how to spot him in a crowd as a child. He was tall and broad shouldered, with dark hair that fell above sharp eyes. His smile was a flash of white but entirely devoid of warmth.

A woman had died, and he laughed.

Something sour coiled in her gut. No matter how many inspections passed, they never stopped feeling like survival was a mistake. For most, these rituals were routine. For Gisela, they were beginning to feel personal.

Thorne's gaze snapped to hers. The laughter died, extinguished like a flame touched by frost. His smile vanished, replaced by that look she'd grown used to.

Since her family had risen, his stares lingered longer. His words had sharpened as if he wanted her to feel responsible for Cillian Alderose's fall from power, for every whisper of gratitude at the change.

She met his stare.

Their new home loomed ahead. Stone walls, slate roof, a door that never swelled in the rain.

Gisela slowed, taking in the structure. It was everything she ever wanted. And now, it didn't make her feel the way she thought it would. The house didn't feel damp, and rodents weren't a problem anymore, yet the guilt crept up on her like a draft under the door.

"I'll meet you at home. I'm going to check in with Elysande," she said.

"See you there," Noah called, hand lifted in a lazy wave.

Gisela climbed the front steps of the village scribe's house, the sound of wind chimes jingling in the breeze. The wood creaked beneath her feet. She raised her fist to knock, but the door opened first.

Elysande gasped. "By the Six, you're soaked!" She shook her head, ushering Gisela inside. "Come in, dear. I've got tea ready."

Warmth greeted her at the threshold, the scent of parchment and chamomile wrapping around her, familiar and steady. Elysande's home was a refuge.

Scrolls and worn books lined the walls. A long table stretched across the center of the room with tools and parchment scattered across the top.

"I'm sorry, Ely, I'm all muddy," Gisela said, easing into one of the kitchen chairs with stiff limbs.

Elysande waved her off. "It's fine, dear. How was the inspection?" She handed Gisela a towel and set a hot cup of tea in front of her.

"A woman," Gisela replied, drying herself off. "Vaughn's older sister. She tried to cut her mark off."

"Maya?"

Gisela nodded solemnly.

Elysande winced and ran a hand through her ivory-white hair, the furrows in her brow carving deeper.

"It's impossible to remove the mark of the gods. No matter how hard you try," Elysande said. "There was a time when it was a gift, you know. Not something to hide . . . to be hunted for." She lowered herself into the chair across from Gisela with a long sigh. "I was a young girl when King Thraxus was crowned and began the executions. I had hoped once the tyrant croaked, his son would see things differently. But evil doesn't die easily. It breeds."

And breed it did. Gisela suspected King Ravenor didn't have a kind bone in his body. His mother, Queen Marcella, died in childbirth, leaving King Thraxus alone, though neither was known for benevolence. Thraxus later died from a heart condition. Ironically, given what Gisela had read about him, she was surprised he had one at all.

"It's all about fear," Gisela said. "Fear of the unknown . . . fear that what happened in Thunderpeak could happen again."

The Mystic from the Elding bloodline—a family name spoken in hushed tones across the realm.

A crater still scarred the center of their village. Proof, the kingdom claimed, of what Mystics were capable of.

"Yes, that incident . . . it happened at the right time, didn't it? But it isn't only fear. There was a prophecy." Elysande's face shifted, a shadow of regret crossing her features.

Gisela paused, fingers tightening around her cup. "Prophecy?" Her voice was soft yet demanded an answer.

Elysande sighed, her grip mirroring Gisela's. "One given to Thraxus. Right before these executions started. But it's—" She shook her head. "Forget it."

"What do you mean?" Gisela leaned forward slightly, pulse ticking up.

"Don't mind the ramblings of an old woman," Elysande said, waving her off. "My mind isn't what it used to be."

Gisela set her cup down. "You never *ramble*."

For a beat, Elysande didn't answer. She swallowed like the words had physical weight. "Forget it, child. Please. Some things are safer unsaid."

Silence stretched between them.

Gisela wouldn't pry, though she ached to.

Instead, they turned to safer things. Village gossip, complaints about the new baker's prices. Gisela let herself soften. Despite the years between them, Elysande had always been more than a neighbor. More than the village scribe.

She'd become a friend.

As a young girl, she sat in this very chair with her feet dangling, watching Elysande work. Her parents trusted Elysande to watch over her when their duties kept them away. Somewhere along the way, Gisela never stopped returning.

"I have to get home for dinner soon," Gisela said, disappointment lacing her voice.

"Ah, yes, tell your parents I said hello." Elysande gathered the cups with gentle efficiency. "Not going to Tristan's?"

She scowled. "No. I didn't tell you? That's over."

A half-dramatic gasp left Ely's lips. "What happened?"

"Found him in a barn with Elowyn last week."

Elysande shook her head. "That boy. What a shame."

Gisela reached for the door, her cold, damp dress still clinging to her body. "I'll see you at the Imbuing Day celebration?"

Elysande's smile came easy, but something in her eyes lingered a beat too long. "I wouldn't miss it."

She stayed submerged to the neck until her skin wrinkled. Steam curled around her ankles as she stepped out of the tub, her hair hanging to the small of her back. Drying off, she pulled on a fresh dress and braided her brown hair with quick, practiced fingers.

As the last strand was tucked into place, she let her fingers drift across the oak dresser, tracing the grain. Evening light spilled through the leaded windows, a luxury she hadn't grown used to yet. Plants along the windowsill drank it in, their leaves reaching skyward. Tapestries of mountains and trees hung along the walls, grounding her in the places she'd always felt safest. Her bed, freshly made with crisp linens, beckoned her to disturb its neatness. The room was peaceful. Serene.

It was a lie.

She laid back on her bed when her mother, Ivy, called, "Dinner!"

Gisela entered the dining room. The calm, familiar rhythm of the house only made her skin crawl. Her father, Orion, moved with his usual composure, laying out slices of meat with a steady hand. The servants hovered quietly, their presence almost invisible, like her parents preferred. Doing the small things kept the Valors grounded in who they were, even under the weight of a new title.

"Another Mystic was found today," Orion said, remarking on it like it was the weather. "Her family . . . unless they can prove ignorance, will be sent to the King's prison."

"Has that ever worked? Do we know what happened to the last family?" Noah said, earning a glare from their father.

Gisela dropped a piece of bread onto her plate harder than she intended.

"You're quiet today, Gisela," Ivy said.

"I don't have much to say after watching a woman die by sword."

Her mother's gaze sharpened. "Gisela, your sister is at the table. Spare her the details."

"Why hide the truth from her? She'll be out there one day too."

"There's nothing for us to worry about. We have no Mystic lineage," Orion said, calmly cutting his meat.

"How do you know?" Vivi asked.

She was years away from the violent reality of inspections. In school, they learned about the Six gods of Mystralos and the villages tied to them: Frosthaven, Sunhold, Rockridge, Thunderpeak, Aquamere, and Windspire. Yet the Mystics themselves went unmentioned, save for the incident in Thunderpeak—the family the kingdom pointed to whenever fear was needed.

Names carried power.

The true names of the gods themselves had been long erased. Time and fear suppressed them—the world itself refused to remember.

"No Mystic in our bloodline. Not that I've ever known," Orion explained.

Ivy gave Vivi's hand a soft squeeze. "The gift is only passed through bloodlines."

"Far from a gift," Orion muttered.

Ivy gave a stiff nod as he went on.

"We do the inspections every six months to find the small marks. Mystics receive one anywhere between the ages of eighteen to twenty-one. When they're discovered, they . . . well, they're dealt with. It's harsh, Vivi, but we can't risk their powers threatening Mystralos."

Gisela shifted in her seat, tension coiling in her shoulders. "Isn't it a little hypocritical, though, Father? Killing Mystics blessed by the gods while we keep using the Life Stones they gifted us?"

"Gisela," Ivy warned. Her hand gripped the arm of her chair.

"How do you think the King sleeps at night?" Gisela pushed. "Knowing he kills innocents?" The words slipped through her mouth so fast; they burned her tongue.

"Like a baby," Noah mumbled.

Orion's scrutiny pinned her to the chair. But curiosity slipped through.

"What you speak of is treason, and you will not ask such a thing again," Ivy scolded, more gently than her words allowed.

"The King doesn't forgive questions like that. Think of your sister, your brother . . . our family," Orion added.

"I'm not hungry," Gisela said as she pushed her chair away from the table.

Wood screeched across the floor. She let the door slam behind her as she left the dining room.

Her pulse raced. Confronting her father at dinner was uncharted territory. Orion didn't relish violence. The inspection left a shadow across his shoulders, even though he tried to hide it. Perhaps he was torn, trying to reconcile the man he'd always been with the man his new position demanded he become.

When the sounds of dinner faded into the evening quiet, footsteps approached her door. Noah knocked and pushed it open. "Can I come in?"

Gisela nodded.

"What was that all about?"

She sat up in her bed, leaning against the headboard. "I don't know. Today rattled me."

"I get it," he said, voice low. "But speaking like that in front of the new Village Lord . . . reckless."

She sighed. "I know. But right before Imbuing Day? The Six gave us the Stones to keep our land alive. And we just kill their own and call it justice."

Noah sat beside her. "Between you and me, I don't disagree with you. But this is the way of things." He draped an arm around her shoulders. "I want you to be safe."

She pressed her lips into a tight line and leaned against him.

"Father's doing what he has to," Noah added. "Cillian let everything fall apart. Little salt from Sunhold, no stone from Rockridge, not enough fish from Aquamere. It's a mess. He'll fix it all."

She stood and paced in front of her bed. If anyone could assess Frosthaven and actually fix it, it was Orion Valor.

"There has to be another way," she said. "Fear isn't meant to be answered with cruelty."

Noah stared at her. "We've seen executions before, Gisela. Since we were kids. But this . . . this is different. You're different. What changed?"

Nothing had changed.

She had always hated it—every inspection, every death—but what was normal had to be endured. She'd buried the anger and the horror for years. Today, though, the shame of that endurance threatened to claw its way up.

She froze mid-step. "Nothing."

Gisela waited until the last candle in the hallway surrendered to darkness. The inspection had come sooner than it should have. She wouldn't trust the guards' timing again.

Her daytime foraging trips to the Snowdrift Forest for the family herbalist shop were routine, but this time, in the protection of the night, she needed materials of her own. She was running low; this trip couldn't wait. Wearing a black cloak, she grabbed her satchel and slipped out the front door. She navigated the dark alleyways and weaved through the shadows, keeping her senses heightened. From the corner of an abandoned building, she spotted a group of drunken men stumbling out of a pub. The ale in Frosthaven was weak. They must have been drinking for hours.

Gisela waited for the men to clear the alley and hurried into the field that led to the forest's edge. A chill ran down her spine and she spun. She scanned the darkness.

There was no one there.

The Snowdrift Forest changed after dark. What was a sanctuary in the daylight now felt like a gauntlet she had to navigate. She kept her steps light. Shadows twisted between the trunks, and every rustle of leaves made her pulse jump. Someone could be watching. If they were, it would be the end of her.

She needed ingredients that came from the same ancient tree, solitary and hidden deep within the forest. Gisela discovered it years ago, and since then, it had been hers—as much a part of her as the secrets she kept. Bark, root, aether leaf, silver sap, dreamberries. Together, they formed a pliant putty.

She learned how to make it not long ago as an unknown rebellion against the world that sought to control. She'd called it The Guardian Tree long before she'd fully understood why. And now, it stood as her only ally in this twisted kingdom.

In the heart of the forest, where the moonlight barely touched the earth, the tree was unmistakable. Its height stretched far beyond the eye's reach. Long vines draped down from its limbs, swaying in the cool breeze of the night. Clusters of violet dreamberries decorated the branches. The iridescent leaves never fell, even in the harshest of winters.

Gisela approached the tree trunk carefully. She dug the root from the soil, broke off a piece of bark, and coaxed the silver sap out. The sap glistened like liquid stars, each drop precious as she caught it in a small jar.

She scaled the tree, gripping the rough bark, and plucked a handful of dreamberries. Their violet hue glowed faintly in the dark and pulsed with energy between her fingers. She descended the tree with precision, jumping when she was close enough to the ground. The forest floor crunched beneath her shoes.

Another chill ran down her spine as she studied the forest. Movement in the bush to her left. She tensed—

A rabbit.

She exhaled, relief escaping her throat. But the tightness in her chest remained.

The putty shimmered with an impossible translucence as she ground the ingredients in her mortar. She rubbed a small amount behind her ear, freshening a coat she never let fade, and stored the rest safely in a new jar.

Gisela returned to her room, closing the door with a soft click. She pressed her back to it, letting the solid weight of the oak hold the rest of the world at bay.

The jar of hylja, her small miracle of concealment, was safely hidden beneath her bed. She changed into a silk nightgown meant for nobility. Comfort brushed her skin, but the weight of every coin it cost sank in her gut.

At her mirror, she brushed her hair aside to check the area behind her ear. She smiled. It was as if nothing had ever been there. No amount of water or scrubbing could wear it down. It simply faded over time. She could only pray to the Six that the tree remained there, because if it didn't, it wouldn't take long for the village to discover her secret. Three months ago, on her twentieth birthday, she had become a Mystic.

Chapter Two

Orion and Gisela woke before sunrise on practice days, the sky still heavy with night. Her father, a skilled swordsman and former master-at-arms for the village, never taught her to wield a blade but passed down his knowledge of combat in a way that felt like a quiet rebellion against village customs. Women were expected to focus on proper duties like gardening, cooking, cleaning, and bearing children. But Orion wanted more for her. He wanted the security that his daughter could protect herself, and she had embraced his teachings without hesitation.

As dawn's first light crept over the horizon, Gisela and Orion were at the practice field, a secluded spot away from the village and prying eyes.

"Remember, being smaller doesn't make you weaker. It makes you quicker and more agile," he said. He demonstrated a swift block and counterattack. Orion's body moved with grace, like a hawk circling its prey. His navy-blue tunic hugged his form, accentuating the muscles that flexed with each movement. The breeze lifted his long brown hair across his face, while his eyes narrowed in focus.

They shared the same scatter of freckles across their noses and the same light brown eyes—proof she was her father's daughter in many ways.

But not all.

"Keep your stance strong, focus on your opponent. Find their tell," he instructed, circling around her. "Some shift their weight slightly forward; others flick their eyes to the spot they plan to strike. Watch their facial expressions. A slight smirk, a narrowed gaze."

Gisela nodded, absorbing every word.

Orion demonstrated a lightning-fast jab and a low sweep.

She observed him and her body mirrored his movements instinctively. Quicker now than it had weeks ago.

"Again?" he asked.

She nodded once and settled into a defensive stance, her eyes locked with his.

Wasting no time, he charged.

She feinted left, her dress swirling around her legs in a fluid, precise blur. But triumph was a dangerous distraction; a moment's loss of focus was all he needed to strike her shoulder. The force swept her feet out from under her. As she hit the ground, pride bruised faster than her skin. Cold air pierced into her lungs in a ragged gasp.

"Damn it," Gisela muttered, lying on her back.

Orion stepped over her and shook his head. "See? A second. That's all it takes." He extended his hand.

"I'm tired. We've been out here for an hour already." She grabbed it with a smirk. With a foot to his chest, she pivoted her body and pulled him down to the ground beside her.

He stared, stunned, and they both burst into laughter.

"Cheap shot on an old man."

"Oh, is that right? You're an old man now?"

"I am when you best me." He laughed.

"Then I guess you should quit being a Lord and join the Village Elders," she teased. "Sitting around all day, giving wise advice, sounds like an easy life."

He scoffed. "It would be less work, that's for sure."

"Thank you for doing this still. I know your days have gotten busier." She rose to her feet and extended her hand to him.

He took it and brushed the dirt off the back of his pants as he stood. "It's important you know how to defend yourself. Noah has told me that you have been taking some heat from the Alderose boy," he remarked as they walked back to the village.

"Thorne? That's nothing new. He's always tried to bother me since we were kids, but I don't let him anymore."

"Maybe he feels threatened?"

She scoffed. "Well, he should."

Orion's soft smile gave way to a serious expression. "This village is run by the Valors now. I won't stand for it."

"I can handle it," she reassured him. "I'm not a little girl anymore."

He nodded, draping his arm around her shoulders and kissed the side of her head. "I know."

Walking down the main street of the village with a full basket from the bakery, Gisela breathed in the sweet scent of fresh bread. The lively hum of Frosthaven in the mornings was a comforting melody to her ears. Children's laughter rang out as they darted through the streets, creating toys from sticks, rocks, and burlap sacks. Villagers greeted her from both sides of the road. Frosthaven wasn't the most luxurious village in the realm, but it was home.

Home didn't mean perfect. It breathed in silent contradictions. The same people who smiled at her now would bow to the King's men another day. She'd learned long ago to read more into what people *didn't* say.

Further up the street, Selene Alderose tended to plants on her porch. Her light blue dress fluttered in the breeze, and her shiny black hair cascaded down her back. Her wave was quick and tense, gone before Gisela could wave back. It was no secret that Cillian wasn't a gentle husband; the whispers followed Selene wherever she went. Despite this, Selene was sweet in the small ways she had interacted with the Valors. Still, she kept to herself when it came to village politics.

A burst of movement broke her thoughts. Children ran past, singing a rhyme, voices laced with excitement and fear.

"Grimthorn Bramble, fearsome sight,
Its thorns will catch you in the night.
Stay away, don't dare to tread,
or find yourself in a deadly bed."

Gisela smiled faintly.

Everyone in Frosthaven grew up on the tale of the Grimthorn Bramble—the same worn story her mother placed in her hands on long winter nights to keep her and her siblings entertained. She and her mother had studied every herb in the forest, yet the Grimthorn Bramble remained nothing more than a name, its fearsome reputation far larger than any proof of its existence. No one she knew had ever actually seen one. A myth, meant to scare children from venturing into the forest alone.

"Good morning, Gisela!" a little voice called.

She turned, and there was the baker's son, sprinting her way.

His foot caught on a stone, and he tumbled forward, skinning his knee. "Ouch," he winced.

Gisela knelt, rummaging in her bag for a bandage. She cleaned the scrape, dabbing some healing salve on it. "There, all fixed," she said.

"I don't have any coin."

"Don't be silly, Roy."

"Are you working today? Maybe I can come help with something?" The dimples in his cheeks deepened.

She smiled at him. "I'm off today. Maybe tomorrow, but you'd have to ask your mother first," she said, ruffling his curly blonde hair.

He giggled, wrinkling his tiny, upturned nose.

Distant shouting cut through the hum of the village.

Gisela shaded her eyes, searching for the source of the commotion. "Go on, now. The men are training."

Roy nodded and ran off to join his friends.

A nervous chill ran down her spine when she spotted a man in a blaring red tunic, the color worn only by the King and his guard. Cillian, now the master-at-arms, was instructing the men in combat. Her father's previous job.

Gisela scanned the men and spotted Thorne circling Tristan, sweat gleaming on their bare backs. Jabs snapped through the air, fists and elbows trading in a blur. Thorne's gaze never wavered. Tristan stumbled, his hair falling into his eyes as he missed his mark. Thorne saw the opening and shoved him to the ground.

Gisela smirked. She would never root for Thorne but watching him rough up Tristan was . . . satisfying.

Maybe it was wrong to enjoy, but she refused to feel guilty about it.

They paused and Fynn handed Thorne a towel. As he wiped his face, his eyes flicked to her. She shivered at the glance, the faintest sense that he'd noticed her before she'd stepped fully into view. Without looking away, he whispered something into Fynn's ear.

She lingered at the edge of the ring, half-hidden behind the press of bodies, before pivoting away from the crowd. Gisela straightened her spine and kept moving. She hated that Thorne could still make her feel small—not with words, but with that look. Like he knew something she didn't.

She sensed someone creeping up behind her. The fine hairs at the nape of her neck lifted. Reflexively, she shot her hand out, seizing his arm and twisting sharply.

Fynn yelped, but she didn't relent. With a strong step forward and a pivot of her hips, she used his momentum to flip him over her shoulder.

He hit the ground hard, her bread scattering across the mud as laughter erupted behind her.

Thorne leaned against a wooden post, a faint, mocking curve to his mouth.

Gisela narrowed her eyes.

A voice called from the crowd, "Maybe you should join the ranks, Gisela!"

"I'm s-s-sorry, Gisela, I was just messin' around," Fynn stammered. "Thorne told me to . . ."

"You ruined all the bread I bought! Aren't you tired of being told what to do for Thorne's entertainment? Grow up already, Fynn."

The sound of approaching footsteps made her turn as her gaze locked onto Cillian, the last person she needed to see this altercation.

"That's quite the skill set you have there, Miss Valor," he said, walking over and helping Fynn to his feet.

Fynn hurried back to the group of men.

"Call it instinct," she replied, picking up her basket. She lifted her chin and willed her breath to steady.

"Hm," Cillian mused, his scarred face studying hers with curiosity. "Perhaps it runs in the family. Although now that I think about it, I don't believe Noah has that trait at all," he added with a sneer.

"I know a trait that runs in your family too, Mr. Alderose," she shot back icily.

Cillian's glare hardened. "Oh? And what would that be?"

Before she could respond, Thorne approached with his usual confident stride, placing a hand on his father's shoulder. He glanced between them, his expression neutral. "Come, Father. Let's leave Freckles to . . . whatever this is."

Cillian nodded, studying her. "Have a nice day, Miss Valor. Give Orion my regards," he said, brushing Thorne's hand off his shoulder with a dismissive flick.

Gisela's nostrils flared as the two of them walked away. She couldn't stand that man.

Tristan was approaching as he called out, "Gisela, wait up!"

She veered away, quickening her pace towards home.

Gisela flung the door open and slammed it shut behind her.

Ivy spun at the table, alarm flashing across her face. "What happened!?" she asked, dropping her herbs and grabbing the empty basket.

Vivi looked up from where she was playing on the floor, her wide eyes softening the storm brewing inside Gisela. Despite her frustration, she managed a warm smile for her little sister.

Gisela exhaled slowly, facing Ivy. "They're jerks. Why do the Alderoses hate us so much?" She flattened her palms on the table.

Ivy turned away, bringing the basket to the table to clean. She adjusted her bandana, a strand of her light blonde hair slipping over her delicate face. "Cillian has his trousers in a bunch for losing his position. Selene has always been kind to us, at least. Although she clearly has poor taste in men," she remarked, raising her eyebrows. "Here, have some frostbites. I made them this morning."

Vivi jumped up from the floor and rushed to the table, eagerly grabbing a small, wrapped bundle. Each frostbite was encased in a delicate, ice-crusted shell, with a creamy, honey-sweet center that melted smoothly on the tongue.

"I love the berry ones," Vivi said, savoring the sweet cubes.

Gisela scoffed, slumping into a chair and popping a frostbite into her own mouth.

Cillian must have felt the sting of losing the assembly vote to her father, but his demeanor had shifted into something filled with hostility. When he served as Village Lord, Frosthaven was listless, cut off from the other villages, messages arriving in dribbles of ravens. Now, men were beginning to repair the trade routes, ravens were starting to come more steadily, and the village's Ice Stone glowed brighter than she had ever seen it.

The low rumble of drums sounded off in the distance.

Ivy and Gisela exchanged confused glances and hurried out the front door, Vivi trailing close behind them.

Villagers poured from their homes and into the square, following the sound of the rhythmic beat. The gates to Frosthaven groaned open to reveal King Ravenor himself, riding astride his horse, flanked by his mounted guards.

Gisela caught her mother's worried expression. "What's happening? Did Father know about this?"

Ivy watched as the King drew nearer. "No, he didn't."

The citizens of Frosthaven gathered in the village center, murmurs of confusion rising as they awaited the King's word. Tension hung thick in the air, threaded with smoke and livestock. A personal announcement from the King himself was unprecedented.

King Ravenor ascended the dais, long, jet-black hair brushing his shoulders. His eyes, dark as a bottomless void, swept over the crowd, unsettling even the bravest of villagers. He wore a crimson robe adorned with intricate gold embroidery.

Orion leaned in to whisper something, but King Ravenor ignored him, staring straight ahead.

At the bottom of the dais, Cillian leaned against a post, arms crossed, fingers drumming on his sleeve. A cruel smirk tugged at his lips, an unspoken taunt to anyone watching.

"Good people of Frosthaven," King Ravenor's voice echoed through the village center. "I am here today to deliver an important announcement. From this day forward, the executions during inspections are suspended."

Whispers spread among the villagers.

Gisela's shoulders eased, but a quiet hum of suspicion lingered.

The King had enforced the old laws of execution for Mystics, and nothing about him suggested genuine mercy.

"Suspended? But they're dangerous!" someone shouted.

The King raised his hand, and the crowd fell silent.

"In addition," he continued, "I'm temporarily removing the Life Stones from each village. For the good of the realm."

Gisela clutched her chest as gasps echoed around her.

A young girl whimpered and pressed against her mother's side, while an elderly man muttered a curse. Even Orion, standing nearby on the dais, wiped a bead of sweat from his temple, eyes wide with worry.

The Life Stones sustained Mystralos, their energy threading through every corner of the kingdom—nourishing crops, feeding lakes, and sustaining the forests. Without them, the land itself would suffer.

"Temporarily? What does that even mean?" another villager asked. "Right before Imbuing Day? How do we celebrate without the Stone?"

"*Silence!*" King Ravenor's voice boomed.

The chaos subsided and the village center fell into a stunned hush, broken only by the rhythmic snap of the King's banners in the wind.

"Difficult decisions must be made for the kingdom," he said, his tone leaving no room for argument. "The Life Stones, while vital to our villages, hold greater potential when they are united. This counsel comes from an Ancient Elder. By gathering the Stones temporarily, we will harness their combined power to ensure greater protection and abundance across Mystralos."

Parents tightened their hold on children, exchanging wary glances with neighbors.

Ivy shook her head, Vivi clutching her arm like she might disappear.

The King's voice reverberated around the center once more. "The Ancient Elder has informed me that Mystics are to assist in this task. They will be brought to the castle and rewarded generously for their service. This decision is not taken lightly, but it's a necessary step toward securing our realm's strength and security."

With his final word, unease spread through the crowd. Some recoiled at the thought of sparing Mystics. A few seemed relieved—but they were in the minority.

None of it made sense.

King Ravenor descended the dais, crimson robe trailing behind him, and strode directly into the Temple of Vitality, where the village's sacred stone was kept on its pedestal.

The crowd whispered amongst themselves until he emerged, cradling the Ice Stone in gloved hands. The large gem gleamed white and translucent, otherworldly in its radiance.

Gisela could feel its pulse from afar, a subtle thrum that resonated with her own heartbeat. When touched with bare hands, it was said to exude a chill that penetrated straight to the bone. At least, that's what the villagers claimed. Gisela had touched it once during prayer at the Temple of Vitality. Instead of chilling her, its icy touch was strangely comforting.

She had avoided it ever since.

After the announcement, the villagers dispersed back into their homes, spirits heavy with uncertainty. The King never explained how temporary these changes would be. No one knew what would come of a realm without Stones. He moved as though the villagers had no right to question him, departing in a rush that left Orion bristling.

Her father's jaw was stiff as he watched the King leave through the gates.

Gisela didn't move.

She looked toward the Temple of Vitality, where the Ice Stone had rested for generations. The air already felt different—thinner, as if the breath of the village had been sucked out with the Stone. A cold wind rattled the shutters of a nearby house, and it didn't feel like the seasonal chill setting in.

The Valors gathered around the dinner table, treading carefully on the topic in front of Orion.

"Father . . ." Gisela began.

"I had no idea, but Cillian . . . he was ready for this," he said, brushing sweat off his brow.

They nodded but stayed silent.

Orion sighed heavily. "I don't know what this means. I tried to speak to the King before and after his announcement, to no avail. I'm the Village Lord, and he couldn't spare a moment to tell me what the hell is going on?"

"Orion," Ivy said gently, putting a hand on his forearm. "I know you're angry, but you need to be careful—"

"Ivy, please. You know nothing of these matters."

Noah, Vivi, and Gisela exchanged stunned looks, their mouths slightly agape at Orion's sudden harshness toward their mother.

Ivy lowered her chin, taking a bite of food.

"I apologize, Ivy," Orion muttered after a long pause, his voice quieter now. "I'm a little agitated. That's all."

She inclined her head and laid her hand on his.

"Stopping the executions makes little sense. I need to look into that. But . . . perhaps uniting the Stones truly could strengthen the kingdom," Orion added, his thoughts spilling out in a rush.

Gisela wasn't convinced.

"Maybe I need to speak to Cillian. Find out what he knows."

Noah and Gisela exchanged a knowing look across the table.

"Good luck talking to that asshole," Noah mouthed.

She lifted one corner of her mouth, despite the tension. A shadow of unease hung over the table as they finished their meal. The King's announcement changed everything and explained nothing. She couldn't shake the feeling that this was only the beginning.

CHAPTER THREE

The mist-shrouded forest enveloped her, fog curling around her ankles like fingers of shadow. The wind carried the damp, earthy scent of rot and moss. What once was a second home had become unrecognizable, the familiar comfort of it stripped away. Joy had fled this place, leaving only dread clinging to her. Gisela's feet carried her without thought, every instinct screaming to stop, but the pull was stronger than her fear. Shapes flickered at the edge of her vision, but she couldn't tell what was real. The crunch of leaves and sticks sounded unnervingly loud, echoing in the stillness.

At the center of the clearing stood the Guardian Tree.

Gisela approached, goosebumps prickling along her arms.

The leaves no longer shimmered. They drooped, withered, wrong in the moonlight.

The berries had shriveled, their violet hues drained to a lifeless gray.

She squinted through the dense fog and inched closer.

A strange figure crouched at the tree's base, dressed in obsidian robes. Bony fingers twitched along the roots. Black tendrils snaked from its hands, wrapping around the tree like living chains. A wet hiss escaped its mouth.

She gasped and stumbled backward. The beat in her ears surged, loud enough to drown out everything else. Her foot caught a hidden root, and the world tilted beneath her. She imagined shadows swallowing her whole.

Crimson orbs glowed beneath the figure's hood.

Her mind screamed to move, to get up, but her body refused. Something about the figure pinned her where she'd fallen. With a jarring, unnatural motion—like a puppet on tangled strings—it hovered over her.

Its skeletal hand reached out, brushing her cheek.

A searing burn flared across her skin. Her rational mind whispered it was only a dream, but another, louder part insisted it was far too real.

Gisela jolted upright in her bed, panting as sweat dampened her face. Goosebumps covered her flesh as the memory of her dream lingered. It was so real, so vivid. Even in the comfort of her own room, as she reoriented herself, the phantom touch burned her skin. The acrid scent of the forest was still sharp and alive in her nose. She knew she had to visit the Guardian Tree tonight.

Nestled in a quiet corner of Frosthaven, the Valors' herbalist shop exuded a homey warmth. Its weathered wooden planks, partially hidden by dark green ivy, gave the cottage a secretive charm. The scent of dried herbs permeated the air as Gisela stepped onto the porch.

Unlocking the heavy wooden door, she was greeted by the familiar creak of the hinges.

Setting to work, she arranged jars of dried herbs and vials of colorful liquids on the wooden shelves.

Now that her father had become Village Lord, her mother was occupied with the transition, which meant Gisela had to spend more time working here. It was an outcome she welcomed, though she missed Ivy. The shop was too quiet without her mother's soft humming of a familiar, wordless tune. The stillness left her too much room to think—and too much thinking was never a good thing.

Ivy was the village's revered herbalist, known for her gentle bedside manner and her ability to heal with nature's bounty. She tended to wounds and illnesses with calm expertise that earned her a cherished place in the villagers' hearts. Many came to the Valors' shop not only for herbs and remedies, but for the comfort of Ivy's presence alone.

Gisela had grown up watching that trust take root—now, it reached for her too.

As Gisela adjusted a crooked shelf, the door swung open. She spun around and her heart sank at the sight of Tristan. "I'm working."

"Please . . . hear me out," Tristan said, shutting the door behind him.

"Oh, I think I heard plenty, coming out the barn."

Tristan's face reddened. "It was a mistake. I had too much ale, and—"

"Oh, piss off, Tristan."

"I regret it. Gods, I regret it. I love you. I—I wanted to marry you," he said, voice trembling.

"Clearly not," Gisela snapped. "Now leave before I lose my patience."

"You're supposed to be my date for the Imbuing Day celebration tonight." He reached out to brush her cheek. "I miss you, Gisela, I miss—"

Her patience shattered. She slapped his hand from her face, seized his arm, and ripped him toward the door. A final shove hurled him into the street, and he stumbled to catch himself before falling.

Noah, walking up to the shop, froze mid-step at Gisela's vigorous push. His smile faded.

"Don't bother showing up here again. You'll need a new herbalist once that rash of yours inevitably flares up, asshole!" she shouted, slamming the door with a finality that echoed through the shop.

Moments later, the door creaked.

Gisela whirled, her glare sharp enough to cut glass.

Noah held his hands up in mock surrender, an amused twitch lifted his lips. "It's me . . . good morning to you too."

"Sorry," she muttered.

Noah leaned against the counter, watching her work. "Why didn't you come to breakfast?"

"I woke up early. Had a nightmare," she said, grinding the herbs with a little extra force. "Needed to get out of the house."

Noah nodded. "You good?"

"Yes, I'm fine. It was only a dream."

Noah wandered around the shop, his focus shifting between the shelves.

Gisela, observing him from the corner of her eye, recognized his nervous habits.

"So," he began, and she braced herself for what he was about to say. "I hate to ask, after your rough night and Tristan but . . ." He gave her a hopeful look, and despite herself, her lips curved slightly. "Can you cover for me for a few hours? Tell Mother I went to the Snowdrifts for plants, maybe?"

Gisela eyed him suspiciously. "Why?"

He hesitated, wringing his hands. Another nervous tick.

"Are you meeting Ruby?" she asked teasingly.

"Yes. How did you—?" He sighed. "You know everything. Only for a little while."

She cocked her head at him. "Why are you hiding it? Ruby is lovely."

"Her family wanted to keep Cillian as Village Lord."

"And? Are they giving you trouble about it?"

"I don't want her to have tension with her parents is all."

Gisela rolled her eyes. "That's ridiculous. They need to get over themselves."

"Well, if you must know, they want to betroth her to Thorne."

She shot him an incredulous stare. "For the sake of a family alliance? Certainly not for his personality."

Noah laughed. "Probably. They have ambition. They know Cillian is close to the King. She wants nothing to do with Thorne and her family knows that."

Ruby's family, the Blackwells, always had their eye on whoever was in power. It puzzled her that they still wanted Ruby betrothed to Thorne after Cillian was forced to step down. She wasn't sure she wanted the answer.

"Well, if she's seeing you, she must have a better head on her shoulders than her parents do. I'll cover for you."

"Thanks," he said, rushing over to give her a quick hug.

"Here," Gisela said, grabbing a small bag. "Give her some of Mother's frostbites."

"Good thinking," he said, taking the bag from her and heading out the door.

Villagers trickled in for their various needs: tinctures to uplift their mood, ointments for minor burns, and oils to encourage respiratory health now that fall was coming. More of them had been asking for tinctures for anxiety lately. She couldn't blame them. Everything was uncertain, and Gisela wasn't sure it was as temporary as they hoped.

As she sharpened her knives under the desk, the door burst open.

Her head snapped up.

Thorne and his companions, Fynn and Zane, stepped inside, smirks curving their lips.

"How can I help you?" she asked through gritted teeth.

Zane hopped up on the counter, leaning far too close. "Just checking if you're still whispering to the weeds."

Gisela slammed the desk drawer shut. The crack echoed through the room.

Fynn shifted uneasily, shooting Zane a warning look.

Her lips curved at the memory of tossing Fynn over her shoulder like a sack of potatoes.

Zane snorted. "Easy there, Valor. Thought you might get jumpy again with all those new storage crates stacked by the pub. Tight fit, those things, huh?"

Thorne's hand paused halfway to the shelf.

She stiffened as the memory surfaced, unbidden—wooden walls closing in, the scrape of a lid sliding shut, breath thinning to nothing.

Gone as quickly as it came.

Her expression cooled. "You know, Zane, it's bold of you to barge in here to pester me. I know why your mother comes by so often. Still dealing with those boils you have on your ass?"

Zane's eyes bulged.

Thorne casually picked up vials, hiding a grin.

"You wouldn't want me to . . . hmm . . . accidentally put something else in that vial, would you? To make your cock shrink even smaller than it already is. Considering your personality, you've got to be overcompensating for something."

"You bitch," Zane's voice cracked, his hands twitching.

Gisela's hand moved before her mind did. She grabbed her knife from under the table and pressed it to his throat. "Get. *Out,*" she demanded, her voice deadly calm as she held his furious stare.

Fynn grabbed Zane's arm and pulled him away. "I told you this was a stupid idea. Why do I even hang out with you guys . . ." he grumbled, dragging Zane out the front door.

Thorne approached the counter, ignoring the threat of the knife.

Gisela's grip on it tightened.

"How are you and Tristan?" he mused, as he idly inspected a vial from the counter. "I saw him chopping wood with a little extra fervor."

"We aren't together. Not that it's any of your business."

His mouth twitched.

She lowered her knife, but her grip didn't loosen. "What is your problem? You can't bully me at school anymore, so you find new ways to get under my skin?"

He crossed his arms, the movement pulling the fabric of his shirt tight across his chest. "I've never laid a hand on you."

She scoffed. "*You* haven't. But you make your friends do your dirty work. Always a coward."

For a fraction of a second, something softened his eyes, regret maybe, but he quickly masked it with his usual nonchalance. "I am no coward."

Gisela shook her head. "Well courage doesn't need friends to back it up."

He stepped closer, and she raised the knife, pressing it lightly to his chest.

He didn't flinch. Instead, he leaned into the blade, lowering his head to her level. His voice dropped, gravelly. "Whatever you think you know about me, Freckles, you don't."

He was close enough for his heat to reach her.

"Yes, I have freckles. Impressive observation," she said, voice unwavering. "And I know plenty."

They held each other's stare, the silence between them heavy and suffocating. After a heartbeat too long, Thorne backed away, holding her gaze before turning to leave. He moved to the door, paused, and with a deliberate glance over his shoulder, whispered:

"Not yet."

The door shut behind him. Gisela's hand lingered in front of her before she let it drop. Her body trembled—not with anger, but with something unfamiliar.

The intensity of her encounter with Thorne faded as the hours slipped past. By the time Noah sauntered in, his face flushed and framed in tousled hair, the shop had settled into a quieter rhythm.

Gisela noticed his red, swollen lips and stifled a giggle with her hand.

"Shut up. Is Mother here yet?" he asked, urgency undercutting his usual teasing tone.

She let out the giggle. It was impossible to hold back. "No. She's been at home with Vivi this afternoon. But you need to get yourself situated. You look like you just stepped out of Ruby's bed."

He hushed her, putting a finger to his lips. "We weren't in her bed."

Her eyes landed on a stick poking out of his hair. Her lip curled. "You have no idea how much I *don't* want to hear that about my little brother." She took off her apron, draping it over a chair. "You can take over for the rest of the evening. I need to visit the tailor to pick up my new dress for Imbuing Day."

"Fair enough," he agreed. He ran his hands through his hair and found the stick.

Gisela shook her head at him.

With a playful flick, he tossed the stick toward her, and she caught it midair.

"Good idea with the frostbites, by the way," Noah said, grinning.

Gisela smiled. "I know the way to a woman's heart. Men think it's jewels or fineries . . . but it's always sweets."

She turned to leave, but Noah stopped her. "You should know, while Ruby and I were in the forest, we noticed some of the plants we use in the shop are wilting."

"Wilting?"

Anxiety prickled her skin.

"Yeah," he said, furrowing his brow. "You don't think it's because the King took the Ice Stone, do you?"

"I don't know," she admitted, her voice uneasy. "But if it is, that's not a good sign."

The rich scent of wool, dyes, and faint beeswax met her at the tailor's door. Warm light spilled across the room, glinting off threads and catching the folds of colorful fabrics that hung from racks and hooks. She approached the wooden counter, cluttered with scissors, needles, and spools of thread.

"Hello?" she called, glancing around.

She waited until their Village Elder emerged from the curtain behind the counter. Hunched, he shuffled forward with a pronounced limp, each step labored and slow. Elder Aldric's clouded eyes stared ahead, his leathery face etched with deep wrinkles. His frail body was draped in clothing that now hung loose on him.

"Gisela?" he called out, his weathered hands hovering over the counter, searching for hers.

"Yes. It's me, Elder. Where's Mrs. Fisher?" she asked, extending her hand to his.

His frail hand clamped onto her wrist in a death grip that made her gasp. His head jerked toward her, his clouded eyes turning to her with unnatural certainty.

"Elder Aldric? Please, let go," she said, her voice shaky as she tried to free her wrist, but his fingers wouldn't budge.

His words rolled out in a voice not entirely his own, strange and resonant. It echoed as if carried from somewhere beyond.

"I know what you are, Gisela Valor." He paused, closing his eyes to gather strength.

"I'm sorry?" Her breath shortened as she spoke.

His eyes opened again, glowing faintly in the warm light.

"In times of dire, the balance shall break,

Six elements lost, a world at stake.

To mend the divide, the willing must find,

The six who unite, in heart and mind.

By trials endured and elements' might,

The Great Guardian Tree shall rise in sight.

When darkness looms and hope is thin,

The power within shall new life begin."

Every nerve in her body went taut.

He trembled, his eyes fluttering closed. The strange force that had seized him released its hold. The grip on her wrist loosened, and he shook his head, blinking in confusion, like he was waking from a deep sleep.

She pulled her wrist back, nursing it against her chest.

"Gisela," he said, his voice now gentle and familiar, "Mrs. Fisher has your dress in the back room. Did you need anything else from us?"

She swallowed hard, trying to steady her racing heart.

"Uh . . . no. No. I think I'm good. Are *you* okay, Elder?" she asked with hesitancy, trying to compose herself.

"Never better, my dear."

Chapter Four

The Imbuing Day celebration was a thrilling affair in the villages of Mystralos. Villagers prepared food for a grand feast and decorated the village center and council building with colorful banners and streamers. Lively sounds of bagpipes, lutes, and tambourines filled the square as people danced and sang. Children sprinted through the streets, their giggles blending with applause for magicians who performed enchanting shows. Hollowed gourds carved with the sigils of the Six were hung from every post, their firelight meant to ward off misfortune for the year to come.

Fires blazed in stone braziers, their warmth cutting through the night chill. The aroma of spiced meats, fresh bread, and ale mingled as laughter and cheers drifted from the square's edge. It was usually Gisela's favorite day of the year, when the village felt like one beating heart. She could almost forget, for a moment, that the Stones were gone.

Almost.

This year, without the Life Stone on its pedestal, the mood was more subdued. Though the music played and food was abundant, villagers exchanged wary glances. Their hands gripped walking sticks tighter than necessary. Even the air was heavy, as if the land itself hesitated to celebrate.

When the Valors entered the Council Building, they were met with a warm reception.

Ivy and Orion moved toward the council members, who appeared relieved to have Orion there instead of Cillian as their Village Lord.

Vivi hurried off with her friends, twirling and giggling in the great hall.

Gisela lingered in the doorway, a step behind her family. She wore the new gown she'd picked up from the tailor—a pale pink dress with an intricately embroidered bodice that hugged her figure and flowed into a full, elegant skirt. She ran her fingers over the smooth fabric, allowing herself a rare moment of satisfaction. She wasn't used to wearing luxurious fabrics and had never cared for such things. But tonight, she felt beautiful in them.

Beside her, Noah stood, glancing between Gisela and Ruby across the room.

"Go on," Gisela said. "She's waiting for you."

Tristan appeared next to Ruby, tracing her line of sight to Noah. But his attention was drawn to Gisela, and he moved toward her with a face of determination.

"By the Six," Gisela muttered.

"I got him," Noah said, giving her a nudge. "Run."

Gisela ducked behind a group of villagers deep in conversation. Tristan wove through the crowd, but Noah intercepted him.

"Hey, man . . ." Noah said, steering Tristan back toward Ruby.

Gisela couldn't help but smirk.

She slipped down a hallway lined with doors and leaned against the wall, wondering how long it would take Tristan to stop trying. As she collected herself, one of the doors burst open and Thorne stumbled out, looking disheveled.

Cillian stormed past him, shoving him roughly, his face twisted in a scowl.

"If you dare question my authority again, you will regret it, boy," Cillian spat. "Pain is how you'll learn."

"I've learned enough," he bit back. "So has Mother."

The two of them were nose to nose.

Gisela tucked herself into a shadowed alcove a few doors down. She pressed into the stone, holding her breath as Cillian turned and marched down the hall to rejoin the party.

When his footsteps faded, she exhaled slowly and stepped from the shadows.

Thorne's shoulders dropped, his hands running through his hair. He went still when he saw Gisela, his eyes dragging over her for a beat too long before he turned and walked away.

Thorne's pain was evident in his shoulders and the look of embarrassment that flashed across his face. She could almost feel his pain, her own shoulders tensing at the sight of his discomfort. She wondered what it would be like to be raised by a father so cruel. Someone who strikes first and asks questions never.

Gisela hesitated a moment before continuing down the hallway in the direction Thorne had gone. Her footsteps were light as she approached a door she'd never been through before. She pushed it open and stepped inside.

It was the Village Lord's chamber, cluttered with crates stacked in the corner. The room smelled of old parchment and dust. Gisela hesitated at the threshold, biting her lip before deciding to sift through the contents of Cillian's old documents.

She glanced around, taking in the heavy curtains meant to shut out the sun—curtains Orion hadn't yet replaced.

Moving to the desk in the back of the room, she skimmed through the papers strewn across the surface—council records, supply tallies, and petitions from the villagers—finding nothing of note. She tried the drawers one by one, but the bottom refused to budge.

Gisela braced her foot against the desk and yanked. The drawer gave with a sharp crack. Inside lay a letter sealed with the King's black seal.

Without hesitation, she opened it to find a map of Mystralos. But as she studied the map more closely, the name of a neighboring realm caught her eye. To the North was Noxis, a realm that had never appeared on any map she'd studied at school. The land was marked with dark shading. A thin white line encircled Mystralos, separating it from the unknown realm.

She ran her finger across the area, wondering why it was never taught. She folded the map and tucked it into her bodice.

Gisela left the chamber and returned to the grand hall, darting her eyes around the area to ensure she didn't run into Tristan again. Her attention fell upon Selene Alderose, standing slightly behind her husband, Cillian. Selene's posture was stiff, her stare locked on the floor, a bruise darkening the corner of her eye. The Alderoses were speaking with Elder Aldric, who made eye contact with Gisela and sent over a small wink.

She scanned the room further, finding each of her family members engrossed in conversation.

As she eased through the door, she nearly bumped into Elysande, who was stepping inside.

"Going somewhere?" Elysande asked with a smile.

"I need some fresh air."

"Already?"

"Yeah, it's crowded. I'm feeling a little short of breath."

Elysande's smile softened into a concerned frown. "Hmm, well, be careful out there."

Before Gisela could respond, Orion's voice cut through the crowd. "Well, if it isn't my favorite Frosthaven scribe," he called out with a playful grin.

Elysande turned her attention to Orion, hand on her hip. "I'm the only Frosthaven scribe," she said, shaking her head.

Their easy banter brought a smile to Gisela's lips, but an urge pulled at her, and she slipped into the night.

Gisela's journey into the forest filled her with dread as she neared the Guardian Tree. The forest was quiet, save for the faint rustle of trees swaying in the breeze. Some plants were wilting—not terribly so, but enough to unnerve her. It had only been a couple of days since the King had taken the Ice Stone from its pedestal. She would have to inform her father. They could send a raven to warn the King that the land was already suffering.

A jagged branch caught the hem of her new gown and the silk tore. Gisela glanced down at the embroidery, now split at the seam. She clicked her tongue against her teeth. Moments ago, it had been precious. Now, it was only fabric. She pulled it loose and kept moving.

When she reached the clearing, the Guardian Tree stood as beautiful as ever. Unchanged. Unharmed. Relief escaped in a soft sigh as she laid a hand on its trunk. A subtle warmth spread through her fingers as if the tree recognized her.

She spun at the sound of brush rustling behind her.

A figure emerged from the shadows, and she squinted, instinctively reaching for the knife strapped beneath her dress.

"Always with that knife," Thorne said, rolling his eyes.

She drew it anyway. "What're you doing here? Did you follow me?"

He advanced with an air of annoyance. "Don't be afraid. I'm not going to hurt you."

"I'm not afraid of you." She tightened her grip on the knife.

"Then lower it."

She paused to wonder if that would be a mistake. With fragile trust, or perhaps misjudgment, she lowered her arm, letting the blade drop to her side, and shot him a warning glare.

In the Council hallway, she hadn't taken him in properly—but now, in a velvet doublet and silver-clasped cloak, he was striking. He looked every bit his family's heir.

Her gaze lingered longer than she meant before she forced herself to look away.

Thorne studied her face intently, a slow smile spreading across his lips. "I know what you are."

She huffed, the words of Elder Aldric echoing in her mind. "Doesn't everyone?"

He opened his mouth to speak but she cut him off with a mocking tone. "What is it you said to me earlier? Whatever you think you know about me, you don't."

Thorne laughed, a genuine sound that caught her off guard. "Clever."

It was an endearing laugh, and she hated that it made her soften.

He inched closer, and she took a cautious step back.

His laughter faded and his expression narrowed. The arrogance he usually wore like armor peeled away, revealing something different. Something she had never seen from him. Away from the scrutiny of his friends and family, he was stripped of his edges, unrecognizable.

"You really think I'm a monster, don't you?"

"I know you're a monster, Thorne."

"If I were a monster," he said, stepping closer, "you'd already be dead."

She glared at him. "What the hell does that mean?"

"I've seen you come here," he said. "You make that mixture."

Gisela stiffened, her fingers curling into the fabric of her dress.

He knew.

Cillian had always advocated for executing Mystics, she assumed Thorne was the same. But Thorne had known about her—and she was still standing here.

"I've followed you here before," he admitted. "Couldn't let you see me until I was sure."

"You followed me?"

"I saw you making it a few months back. Tried my hand at it afterward. Not as good as yours, I'm sure but . . . it worked."

Gisela stared at him, watching him shift his weight. The words landed in her ears, but her brain refused to accept them—impossible.

"I'm a Mystic too," he added casually, shrugging like it were the most mundane of admissions.

Gisela covered her mouth as the reality of his words sank in. Then, to her own surprise, she burst into laughter, clutching her stomach. "You're full of shit," she said between gasps.

His face fell flat. "I wish I was. You think I want this?" he said, crossing his arms.

"Prove it," she said. "Show me your mark."

He smirked. "You'd like to see where it is wouldn't you? Mind if I—" His hands moved toward the waist of his pants.

"Stop," she interrupted. She wanted to test him, to call him on his potential bluff but her cheeks flushed. "Even if you were a Mystic and you're using the putty correctly, I wouldn't be able to see it anyway."

She paced the mossy ground, fingers rubbing her temples, debating whether to believe Thorne. Why should she? He had never given her a reason to trust him in all the years they had known each other.

Crossing her arms, she eyed him warily. "But your father . . ."

"Doesn't know," he cut in. "No one does. Other than you, now. I don't want to risk anyone going down for me."

"Oh, so you tell me instead?"

Thorne's expression softened, and he sighed heavily. "Like I said, I wasn't going to involve you at all until I was sure you were one too. I started noticing a strange feeling when you were around. After the mark appeared."

"A chill?" she asked.

"No," he replied. "A burn."

She blinked, struggling to process it all. The icy chills down her spine suddenly made sense. Thorne had always been nearby, except during some of her secret trips to the forest.

"Why haven't you turned yourself in?" she asked, her voice laced with sarcasm. "Do your duty to the King?"

"Because I'm not an idiot." He ran his hand through his hair, eyes flicking toward the tree. "Something's wrong. There's more we don't know."

"Isn't your father the King's best friend? You're telling me you haven't heard him talk?"

Thorne hesitated and dropped his eyes to the ground before looking back at her. "I've heard enough. He was furious when he lost the assembly vote. Thought the King would never let it happen."

Gisela frowned. "But he did."

"Yeah," Thorne said. "And then the King came for the announcement. After that, my father stopped raging about it. Now he says it's for the best. And maybe it is. Maybe now he'll stop taking it out on my mother and me."

She clasped her hands together to fight the urge to reach out and comfort him, cursing the nurturing instincts she'd inherited from her mother. "What else do you know?"

"Other than my father not caring at all about the Stones being taken . . . nothing."

Gisela recoiled, her face scrunching in confusion.

Cillian's indifference suggested a level of trust or knowledge far beyond what she could fathom. Whatever the reason for his blind faith in King Ravenor, it made the situation even more curious.

Her thoughts wandered back to Elder Aldric's strange encounter. "The plants are wilting already," she said, breaking the long silence.

Thorne glanced around, brow furrowing. "What does that mean?"

"You know . . . wilting. Like dying."

He shot her a flat look. "I know what wilting means."

She bit back a smile, though the weight in her chest didn't lift. "It's the Stone . . . its absence is already showing. The land isn't right. The balance has been disrupted."

"Balance . . ." Thorne echoed.

Gisela turned Thorne's words over in her mind, unease tugging at her ribs. Telling him about the Village Elder would change things. There would be no taking it back.

She studied him, searching for something solid to hold on to, but trust didn't come easily.

They had grown up in the same village, attended the same school, yet she could barely remember a conversation between them that wasn't edged with teasing. She'd spoken to him more today than she had in all the years she'd known him. Whether that made him an ally—or a complication—she couldn't tell.

If he trusted her enough to tell her his secret, she supposed she could share hers.

"I went to the tailor to pick up dresses today, and Elder Aldric . . . he . . . he stared right into my eyes and rattled off some message, but he didn't sound like himself. It sounded like some sort of prophecy, or maybe not. I don't know."

"Only a Seer can give a prophecy. What did he say?"

Gisela closed her eyes, recalling the Elder's voice clearly. She recited the words from memory.

> "In times of dire, the balance shall break,
> Six elements lost, a world at stake.
> To mend the divide, the willing must find,
> The six that unite, in heart and mind.
> By trials endured and elements' might,
> The Great Guardian Tree shall rise in sight.
> When darkness looms and hope is thin,
> The power within shall new life begin."

She caught Thorne staring at her like she'd grown a second head.

"Are you sure that old man isn't off his rocker? He's on death's door."

"Thorne, I'm serious. It was really weird."

He smirked in acknowledgment and crouched on the forest floor in thought. "Alright, I'll play along. The six that unite. Is that the Stones?"

Gisela shook her head. "I'm not sure. It all felt like a warning."

"And The Great Guardian Tree . . . is it this one?" he asked.

"Maybe? I thought I made up the name," she replied, more to herself than to him.

Thorne sighed and stood up. "Well, this was enlightening." He turned to leave the clearing.

"That's it? You're leaving?"

"Yeah, I have to get back before my father notices I'm gone."

She muttered to herself, annoyed at Thorne's abrupt departure. She had been vulnerable, and he treated the conversation as ordinary. "You're just going to pretend this conversation didn't happen?"

"Shouldn't we? Things are stable right now. Plants wilting could easily mean winter is coming early. I'll keep your secret if you keep mine."

She nodded and bit back her argument. The Stone kept the crops alive through harsher chills than this. If they were failing now, it wasn't the weather's doing.

Before he left the clearing, she called out, "Thorne!"

He paused and turned around.

"Do you have Mystic lineage?" she asked.

"Not that I know of. I can't ask anyone though. What about you?"

She shook her head. "No."

He disappeared between the trees, leaving her alone in the clearing.

In the quiet that followed, a single aether leaf drifted from the Guardian Tree and landed silently at her feet.

Chapter Five

Thorne was a Mystic. And somehow, his father was involved in whatever the King was plotting. Gisela contemplated this as she wiped the sleep from her eyes the next morning. She slipped on one of her new dresses and braided her hair.

Muffled voices drifted from the kitchen, along with the enticing smell of breakfast.

Her stomach grumbled in response, and she left her room.

Her father, mother, Noah, and Vivi were already at the table eating breakfast. The clink of cutlery and hum of conversation filled the room.

Orion sat at the head, his focus lifting from his plate as she entered. "Good morning, Gisela. Nice of you to join us," Orion said with a hint of sarcasm.

She offered a nervous smile.

"Morning, love," Ivy said, giving her a curt nod.

The kitchen felt smaller, the usual warmth replaced by an uncomfortable tension between her parents. Wary glances passed between them.

Vivi played with a doll, ignoring her meal.

Gisela second-guessed bringing this up here but proceeded anyway. "Father, there's something you should know."

Orion's fork paused mid-air.

Gisela's palms prickled, and her stomach twisted with nerves.

He raised his eyebrows. "Go on."

She swallowed hard. "The medicinal plants we use from the Snowdrifts . . . they're wilting."

Ivy's eyes flicked to Orion, widening slightly.

Gisela's focus shifted between them, puzzled by the exchange.

"Well, yes, that's to be expected," Orion said. "Temporary effects, I'm sure. Until the King unites the Stones. Just make sure we have enough supplies for winter."

Bewildered, Gisela pressed. "I—but Father, aren't you concerned that these changes happened so fast? The Stone hasn't been gone very long."

Orion slammed his hands down on the table, the sharp crack making everyone jump. He clenched his eyelids shut, drawing in a long inhale. "Gisela, this is not your concern."

"With all due respect, Father, it concerns all of us," she said, her finger tracing a circle in the air. "If the plants die, we can't treat the villagers. We won't have food. And we certainly can't heal the starving."

Ivy's look was a silent warning, but Gisela ignored it.

Noah held his breath and watched.

"You need to send a raven to the King. Notify him of this."

"By the Six," Noah muttered, pressing a hand to his forehead.

"My advisor now, are you?" Orion said. "Leave the table, Gisela. Remember your place."

Her father's voice, hard and unyielding, didn't belong to the man she knew. This was a man stretched too thin, trying to hold the weight of an already struggling village, each word laced with stress he could not hide. Still, it didn't excuse the dismissal, the coldness. The urge to argue rose, to make him see reason, but the words died in her throat.

She exhaled hard and turned away, looking anywhere but at him.

Her mother cast a knowing glance toward her father, frustration and concern pinching her expression. She imagined her mother's plea that morning, her hushed, urgent voice trying to pierce through Orion's stubbornness. Her soft touch, attempting to ease his strain. The tension at the table was proof it hadn't worked.

Gisela slammed the door behind her, the sound reverberating through the quiet street. Her thoughts whirled as she tried to grapple with her father's sudden hardness. Orion had always been stern but fair. Perhaps becoming Village Lord weighed heavily, but this was deeper.

The Stones had never been removed from their pedestals before. They were sacred gifts from the Six gods, ensuring the land thrived. According to the teachings, the gods bestowed their power upon the lands so the people could prosper despite harsh conditions and the unpredictability of nature. These Stones were living symbols of their protection and favor.

Gisela wondered if the King's actions reflected a growing scorn for the divine power he once claimed to honor.

Gisela passed familiar faces whose worry mirrored her own as she walked through the village. Dread thickened with each step.

The village center came into view, a royal carriage flanked by guards waiting ahead.

Thorne leaned casually against a building off to the side. His gaze found hers.

She walked toward him but halted after two steps. Being seen together could draw unwanted attention.

A woman's voice rang out, "Our son, Vaughn, received the mark of a Mystic yesterday evening. We are honored to allow him to do his duty to the kingdom and assist the King in his endeavor to strengthen our realm."

Gisela's heart sank. "What the hell are they thinking?" she muttered under her breath.

The guards handed Vaughn's mother a large bag of coins. She and her husband rejoiced, their faces glowing with relief.

Gisela's blood ran cold as sweat beaded along her hairline. She pushed through the crowd, throwing caution to the wind. Before she could get close, a hand caught her arm and pulled her into a narrow alley.

Thorne's face was inches from hers, but the world around her was shrinking. The rough brick was cold against her back, but in her mind, it was timber. The smell of the damp stone became the scent of trapped air and sawdust. Her chest constricted, the walls closing in until the alley was no wider than a wooden crate.

The noise of the crowd dulled, voices fading into a distant hum, a backdrop to the ringing in her ears.

Thorne guided her into a wider path.

Gisela braced herself with her hands on her knees, gulping air.

With a hesitant look, he reached out to touch her shoulder, but she shoved his hand away.

"I'm fine. I don't like tight spaces."

Thorne's brows flicked up. "I didn't know."

"Didn't you? Back when we were kids—you all used to throw me in wooden crates and sit on top."

"That was *not* me," he said, sharper now.

"Of course it was, I saw you."

"You saw me open the box and let you out."

Gisela recalled the memory, but the details were hazy. She pushed it back down, where it belonged.

"Why did you stop me? They're going to hurt Vaughn. They just lost Maya. What are they thinking—"

"The guards are following orders. If you reached him, they'd have arrested you. Or worse," he said sternly. "I saved your ass."

Tears burned her eyes, and she looked away. She pinched the bridge of her nose and slid down the wall, still trying to catch her breath.

Thorne lowered himself a few feet away, mirroring her posture.

"Why isn't anyone asking questions?" she said.

"Half of these people are morons. The other half are afraid."

They sat in a comfortable silence. Her pulse slowed, and she drew her knees closer, curling inwards.

"My father completely dismissed me this morning. I told him about the forest, about the plants."

"There's more than that now," he muttered. His midnight eyes carried a grayish, smoky hue. Mysterious yet oddly comforting. "There was a letter on my father's desk. Black wax. The King's seal." He rubbed the back of his neck. "He was offered a position in the King's guard. I should've seen it coming . . . but there was something else. Something about the Trials of Kharos and putting castle guards there."

Gisela frowned. Cillian cozying up to the King made sense. But the Trials of Kharos was a mystery. "I've never heard of that."

"And it's not just the plants," Thorne said. "The animals in the forest . . . they're different. Aggressive. Their eyes, Gisela, they're . . . blank. A deer charged me this morning."

Her pulse jumped. Not only because of the revelation about the animals, but when he used her real name. He never had before.

Thorne hesitated before continuing. "Maybe it really is connected to that message from the Elder. We need to do something. Before it gets worse."

She snapped her head up. "Do what, Thorne? Go to the castle and beg King Ravenor to return the Stones? I have a family here. My parents, my brother, and my sister. I have people who rely on me for healing. I can't abandon them. And I certainly can't tell them all what I am."

Thorne clenched his jaw.

"And we? When did this become a 'we'?"

"It became a 'we' when *we* became Mystics," he said, his tone low. "You think you're the only one with something to lose? I have a lot at stake here too. But sitting around waiting for the King's next move won't save anyone."

Her expression hardened, but beneath it, fear and doubt pulsed. She crossed her arms, struggling to hold onto her resolve. "All I have are the words of a vague prophecy and a secret that could kill me. You are the *last* person I could ever trust enough to—"

"To what?" Thorne cut in. "To understand? To help? You may not trust me, Gisela, but I know what it's like to feel helpless, like the world is closing in on you."

Gisela pressed her lips together to keep from screaming. She wanted to lash out at Thorne for pushing her when she was already so confused, so vulnerable. But his words resonated within her, although she was reluctant to admit it. "Trust is earned, Thorne, and as of right now, you haven't done much to earn mine." She stood and walked away.

"Gisela."

Her steps faltered when he said her name again, but she kept going.

Confusion flooded her mind like poison, corroding every other thought. The forest, the animals, and the Stones were all pieces of a puzzle she didn't understand. Taking care of people was in her blood, in her bones. Her hands itched to move, to do something, but how could she act when she didn't know where to start?

She clenched her fists so tight her nails left little crescents in her palms.

Every instinct told her to run, to hide, to pretend nothing was wrong, to cling to the mundane as she always had. Villagers waited to be treated, her family needed her, and lives depended on her keeping it together. So, she would. For now. She'd keep pretending the world wasn't slowly unraveling like a loose thread around her.

Chapter Six

Honey and crushed herbs thickened the air as Gisela cleaned a villager's wound.

"Those animals ain't right," he said.

"When you were hunting?" she asked, wrapping his arm in a bandage.

"Right. And it ain't just the beasts," he said. "The greens . . . they're dyin' faster than they oughta."

Gisela bit her lip, narrowing her focus on her task.

"I'm tellin' ya, I've never seen 'em actin' like this, and I used to hunt in Rockridge. Makin' me question if we should be eatin' 'em anymore."

"What'd their eyes look like?"

The man cocked his head. "You've seen 'em too?"

Ivy poked her head out of one of the treatment rooms at the shop. "Gisela, we're out of hearthsage and dewdrops. Can you go to the Snowdrifts? Noah can take over."

A small boy groaned from inside the room, shivering and clutching his stomach.

Gisela's gaze softened. "Yeah, I got it. I'm about done here anyway. You're good to go, Sal."

Noah walked up from the back of the shop, scratching his head. "I swear we restocked last week."

"I thought so too," Gisela said, grabbing her foraging bag from the hook. "But fall is here. You know how many kids come in with illnesses this time of year. I'll be back as quickly as I can."

"Thanks again, Gisela," Sal called. "Stay near the edge. It ain't safe in that forest anymore."

Gisela hurried down the street, toward the edge of the forest.

Days had passed since she had last seen Thorne. Days since Vaughn was taken by the King's guard. Days in which the Elder's prophecy gnawed at the edges of every waking thought.

Vaughn's family paraded their new wealth through the village in new cloaks with brighter dyes. Others offered themselves up, desperate to prove they bore the Mystic mark. It made her sick.

The farms were failing. Frosthaven's soil only produced hardy crops like turnips, beets, potatoes, and rough grains. They relied heavily on the other villages for salt, fish, and the delicate fruits and vegetables Frosthaven could never grow. If their farms were already dying, the thought of the others failing too stabbed her like the edge of a dagger.

A farmer smacked his shovel against the dirt, cursing.

She lifted her gaze to the sky—no raven in sight.

The Stones were truly bound to the realm's balance. If it was ever a question, that doubt could be put to rest.

Tristan jogged up, brushing leaves from his tunic. "I'll go with you. You shouldn't go in there alone. We're bringing the recommendation to the council—to your father."

"I think I'd much rather encounter a rabid animal than be anywhere near you."

Tristan sighed, shoulders dropping. "I know. But really, Gisela—the forest is changing."

"I'll take her from here," Thorne's voice rumbled behind them. He stepped in beside her, and the urge to tell him to leave didn't come. There was relief, both alarming and welcome.

Tristan looked at Thorne with disdain. "Why? You hate each other."

"And I still prefer him to walk me there over you, Tristan. Would you look at that," she said, voice laced with venom. She turned and continued walking, feeling Thorne behind her.

Tristan stomped away, grumbling.

Gisela hid a smirk behind her frown.

The forest air was damp with the scent of rot. Where Gisela once found green leaves and blooming herbs, only brittle brown remained. They moved on hesitantly, scanning the path beyond for any sign of animals. The crunch of dead leaves beneath their feet was loud in her ears. Her eyes swept the usual patches of dewdrop ferns. Gone. All of them. Ashen soil crumbled between her fingers as she knelt in the dying patch.

"There's a sick child back at the shop who needs these," she said. "It's too early in the year for this. They won't make it through winter. How are we supposed to heal our people when the world itself is dying?"

Thorne bent down beside her, voice low. "This is what the Elder meant. The Stones . . . without them, everything we rely on is dying."

Her eyes flicked to him, searching.

"What's the point of being a Mystic then?" he asked and stood up. "I don't even feel anything. No power. None of the shit they tried to scare us with. Maybe if we felt something, we could do something worthwhile."

Gisela tapped a slow, rhythmic beat on the dead earth. "Maybe it's not about feeling it yet. Maybe it's about knowing we could do something . .

. and being willing to try." The words left her lips and lingered, echoing the prophecy:

"*. . . To mend the divide, the willing must find . . .*"

Thorne turned toward her. "Poetic." He walked a few paces down the path, a branch crumbling at his touch. "My father and the Blackwells are leaving Frosthaven. He took the position."

Gisela stood up. "Ruby too?"

He nodded. "Her and her mother will leave eventually. My mother is staying. She somehow found a way to convince my father that she'll come after he's settled. But he wants me to go with him."

"Are you going?" Her stomach dropped and she flinched at the feeling.

He studied her for a moment, like he was weighing something. "I don't want to."

"They just get to leave and not deal with what's happening here?"

"Looks that way."

Gisela took a deep breath and ran her hands down her face. "I need to get back. Maybe look around and see if I have dewdrops somewhere else."

"I'll walk you." He didn't wait for her answer, falling into step beside her.

She returned to the shop. The emptiness in her satchel mirrored the hollowness in her chest. She'd gone searching for herbs and brought back proof—proof that Frosthaven was running out of time. Fast.

Noah glanced up from the counter, concern widening his eyes.

Gisela entered the room where the boy was now sound asleep in his mother's arms.

"We were able to cool him off and stop the vomiting," Ivy said, gathering up cool towels from the child's body. She turned to the boy's mother.

"Keep him cool. Small sips of water, nothing heavy. If the fever spikes again, bring him back."

"Thank you, Ivy, thank you." The mother dressed her child and slipped out of the room.

Ivy turned to Gisela expectantly.

"Nothing, Mother. There is nothing left in that forest."

Ivy brought her hands to her temples as she paced.

"We can't treat the villagers. Pretty soon, we won't be able to eat. The farms . . . have you seen them?"

Ivy stayed silent, wringing her hands.

"Mother!"

Ivy looked up, her blue eyes flaring. She took her apron off and threw it over her shoulder. "I'm going to the Council. I'll be back."

Gisela stood rooted to the spot. She had never seen her mother panic like this. Ivy understood how dire this was, even if she didn't yet know what to do. But there was one person in Frosthaven who might.

"Elysande?" Gisela's knuckles rapped against the scribe's front door.

When Elysande opened it, her face went from pleasant surprise to concern.

Gisela hurried inside and shut the door behind her.

"Are you okay, dear?" Elysande asked, resting her hand on Gisela's back.

"The herbs are gone. We won't have what we need for winter," Gisela said.

Elysande's face went pale as she guided Gisela further into her home.

"We can't survive without the Stone, Ely. The King—"

"The King has summoned all of the scribes," Elysande interrupted.

Gisela froze. "Why?"

"The letter didn't say. I'm supposed to leave in a few days."

"Please, don't."

Elysande hesitated before pulling a book from her shelves. She ran a finger along the cover, as if weighing the burden it carried. She handed it over with a heavy sigh.

"I worry for *your* safety. Not mine," Elysande whispered. "I fear for the future. Things are changing quickly. This is what he wants. Chaos. It makes it easier when the people are distracted. But this . . . this may help you understand your path, but it may reveal things you're not ready to face." Her eyes met Gisela's, shadows of worry evident in their depths.

Gisela took the book and sat down in her usual chair at Elysande's table. "My path?"

"I'm going to the market. I'll be back in an hour," Elysande said with a pointed look. She opened the front door and stepped out, leaving Gisela alone with her thoughts and the mysterious book.

The house was impossibly silent once Elysande left. A draft stirred the candle flames, casting shadows across the walls. Gisela immediately opened the book and skimmed the pages. Faded ink and blurred lines made some passages nearly impossible to read. One line, darker than the rest, caught her eye.

"*. . . for what lies within the god-marked is not power alone, but aware.*"

Another passage, smudged but legible, followed beneath it.

"*. . . those who endure the trials of the hidden cave of Kharos shall awaken what slumbers within . . .*"

The Trials of Kharos.

Thorne had mentioned them that day in the alleyway.

She pressed a finger to her lips, heart fluttering as she continued reading.

"Mount Kharos waits for the willing, yet the path is fraught with truths too difficult to bear."

Mount Kharos. It was southeast of Frosthaven, forbidden territory.

Then there was The Niva. The woods before Mount Kharos. It was dangerous, full of wild animals and treacherous paths even in normal times. Now, knowing of the Trials of Kharos, she wondered if the mountain's forbiddance was less about danger and more about keeping people away from it.

All her life, the warning was the same: Mystics were a blight, dangerous by merely existing. Yet here she was, wondering if ignoring her power would kill more than using it ever could.

She never felt the dangerous power they spoke of. But if she could awaken it, maybe she'd have a chance to protect her village and stand against what was coming.

When she finally closed the book, a fragile sense of direction stirred to life within her. It felt like the beginning of something profound. Something that might demand everything of her.

Soaking in her basin, perhaps for the last time in a while, Gisela leaned back and shut her eyes, letting the water cradle her in its quiet stillness. By morning, she would be miles beyond Frosthaven's gates. She had finally stopped weighing the cost and started looking toward the answer.

She dried herself off with a plush, probably too expensive towel, and slipped into a fresh dress. She moved through the house with light footsteps and a heavy heart, her travel bag waiting behind her bedroom door.

When she reached Vivi's room, she paused at the doorway, taking in the sight of her little sister nestled under the covers, clutching her wool doll. Gisela walked to her bed and leaned over to kiss her on the forehead. "I'll see you soon . . ." she whispered.

As she turned to leave, she nearly collided with her father.

"Oh, I'm sorry," he whispered. "I was coming to check if you were still awake."

Gisela collected herself, wiping her clammy palms on her dress. "I couldn't sleep. I was checking on Vivi."

Orion's eyes narrowed but he continued. "I haven't seen you all much and I'm sorry for that, it's been hectic. But I wanted to apologize to you. I was not myself that day at breakfast. Being the new Lord has been a huge adjustment with all the changes. You didn't deserve my outburst."

Her face softened. "It's okay. I'm just really worried."

"I sent ravens to the King, Gisela. They've all gone unanswered."

"What are we going to do?"

"I don't know yet. Supplies are running low. Frosthaven will always feel it first, being so far north. We haven't seen a trade cart this week."

She bit her lip. "Do we send men out? Rockridge is closest."

"We may have to. But I don't like the idea since it's so close to winter. I'll have them ration what's left for now, focus on the stores we know will last. And I want hunting parties checking the forest."

"It's a good plan."

He nodded, but the lines in his brow deepened.

"I love you," she said.

"I love you too, Gisela." He pulled her in, holding her tightly against him. "I'm off to bed. Your mother will be waiting for me."

"Yes. I should sleep too."

Orion paused at his door when she stopped him. "Father . . ."

He looked back, his hand resting on the doorknob.

"You're a good man," she said, fearing she might not have another chance to tell him.

He smiled and lowered his head. "And you're growing into a fine young woman."

Gisela went back to her room to wait, hoping the house would soon be asleep. She grabbed her bag with essentials for the journey: herbs, plants, and potions from the shop, extra dresses, her knives, and provisions.

When enough time had passed, she crept out of her room, closing the door as quietly as she could. She made a quick stop at Noah's room. The door creaked open, revealing him sleeping peacefully. Gisela reached into her bag and placed a small bundle of wilted plants on his bedside table—a silent message he would understand by morning.

She stared at her brother. Noah was her best friend and leaving him felt like a betrayal. A lump rose in her throat. She swallowed hard, fighting the urge to wake him, to explain. But she couldn't. If he woke now, she'd never make it out. He'd talk her down, remind her of duty and safety. But her home was exactly what she was trying to save.

He and Ivy would take care of the shop.

Tears blurred the world as Gisela stepped onto the porch and into the night air. She glanced back once, then turned away before doubt could take hold. A few paces in, the back of her neck prickled. She turned—just in time to see a window curtain snap shut.

For a moment, she paused. But no one came running out. No one called her name. The coil of dread in her stomach unspooled, leaving a lightness that felt like a blessing.

Permission to leave.

With a newfound purpose, she approached Frosthaven's front gates. The guard was asleep at his post, as expected. No danger ever came to these walls. She reached for the lever when a familiar chill crept down her spine.

She closed her eyes. "Thorne."

He emerged from the shadows. "Going somewhere, Freckles?"

CHAPTER SEVEN

"Are you going to let me go, or do I need to force you out of my way?"

Thorne tilted his head, amusement flickering in his dark eyes. "How would you force me?"

Gisela hesitated.

A low laugh slipped from him. "I'd pay to see that." He shifted his bag and stepped past her. "It won't be necessary. I'm coming with you."

She scoffed. "No, you're not."

"I am." He didn't look back, his stride lengthening. "You can complain the whole way. I'm still coming."

She caught sight of the sword strapped to his back, a beautiful red gem glinting on its hilt. "What is it with you and following me everywhere lately?" She hurried to catch up as they approached the gate.

He reached for the lever before she could, his smirk catching the faint light of the moon. "Call it instinct."

The gate groaned shut, the finality of the sound echoing in the open air. Before them, a field of dead, brown grass stretched toward the east where The Niva rose like a dark wall. Ancient oaks tangled with thick underbrush, narrow paths vanishing into shadows.

Farther still, Mount Kharos loomed in the distance, its jagged peak shrouded in mist. The field would offer little cover, but The Niva promised both concealment and challenge.

Her dress was a delicate, impractical mistake, clinging awkwardly as she surveyed the land.

"What's the plan?" Thorne asked.

"We're going to the Trials of Kharos."

His head whipped her way. "So, you *do* know what it is?"

"No. But I read about it . . . sort of."

"Sort of?"

"I can't say where I read it, but I know Mystics can awaken their powers there. That's where we should go before they put guards at the mountain."

"Awaken?"

Gisela hesitated, thinking of the faint, water damaged words from the book. "I think the trials are meant to push Mystics to their limits . . . and whatever's buried comes out."

Thorne looked at her curiously. "You're saying we need to be tested?"

She nodded. "I believe so."

Silence hung between them.

"You can turn back now if you want." She put a hand on her hip and waved back toward the gates of Frosthaven.

Thorne kept walking. "You're not getting rid of me that easily."

Gisela caught herself smiling and a tiny bit of warmth ignited in her core.

"Have you even been outside of the village before?" Thorne asked.

"No. We never really needed to. Have you?"

"A few times. I went to Tevrin, the castle town, with my father as a boy."

"There." She pointed to the formidable mountain ahead. "Mount Kharos. That's where the cave is. We'll walk as far as we can through The Niva and camp for the rest of the night."

Thorne nodded. He moved ahead, forcing her to keep pace.

They walked for hours. Doubt clawed at her, burrowing under her skin. What if she wasn't strong enough? What if she died before she was able to help her people?

The Snowdrift Forest had always felt like home to Gisela, but The Niva was completely foreign, with its unfamiliar trees and sounds. A feeling settled deep in her chest. Homesickness.

Was she pathetic? She had been gone for mere hours and already longed for home, for comfort and certainty. But this is what the prophecy demanded. Willingness.

And she was willing. Fear and discomfort weren't enough to make her turn back.

Oddly enough, the decay hadn't reached this far into the forest. At least, not yet.

Thorne let out a breath and turned to her. "Let's stop here for the night."

They found a small clearing where the ground was flat, blanketed in a layer of moss and fallen leaves that crunched under their feet. Thorne unpacked his bag, unrolling a simple tent beneath the canopy of towering trees.

"Who's sleeping in there?" she asked.

"We are," he replied, not looking up.

"Together?"

He stilled, then lifted his gaze to hers. "Unless you'd like to sleep outside alone?"

She did not.

Thorne gathered dry twigs and leaves and arranged them into a small pile. He struck a flint against a piece of steel, sending sparks flying. It took a few tries, but a spark caught and he blew on it, coaxing the flame to life. The fire grew steadily, spreading warmth around them. His eyes reflected the fire as he fed it with larger sticks, a satisfied smirk growing as the flames danced higher. He looked mesmerized.

The sight stole her breath.

The question she had been wanting to ask bubbled to the surface. "Why did you come with me? Trying to avoid leaving with your father or a betrothal to Ruby?"

Thorne sat there, gaze fixed on the fire. "How do you know about—ahh, Noah." He laughed. "Neither. I didn't like who I'd be if I didn't." He hesitated before adding, "My mother will be safer without him there. And it's not like he'll miss me."

She tilted her head at him, waiting for him to say something more.

Thorne wasn't known for doing the right thing. Growing up, he was usually in the middle of all the trouble or at least on the sidelines orchestrating it. She didn't recognize the boy, now a man, sitting beside her.

"You've always done the right thing. You don't think I see you?" Thorne said. "I've always seen you. Healing villagers. Helping the farmers herd the sheep when they get out. Always the first to step in when someone needs it."

She smiled faintly. His words made her body relax in a way it hadn't all day. She was seen—not as a Mystic, not as the child he grew up with, but as the person she had worked to become.

"There were plenty of times you stepped in and defended kids I was cruel to." A hint of remorse laced his words.

"I *was* that kid most of the time. How quickly you forget," she said, rolling her eyes. "You were an ass."

Thorne's lips thinned, accepting her criticism. "But that's not who I want to be. I came with you because I needed to do something right for once. Something that might actually help. And whether you like it or not . . ." He turned his head toward her, the fire still dancing in his eyes. "You need me."

She scoffed, glancing away. "Yeah, well, excuse me for being shocked at all of this. You haven't exactly developed a reputation for being helpful."

The light in Thorne's eyes dimmed.

"It hasn't even been a month since you sent Fynn to try to scare me," she added.

Thorne chuckled. "I knew you wouldn't get scared. I wanted to see what you were capable of. And you delivered."

Gisela's eyes narrowed, her face flat and unamused.

"Look, I know I was never nice to you. I always felt the need to impress my father," he admitted, his voice trailing off. "He's not particularly impressed with kindness."

Gisela's brows knitted together at his confession.

"I thought cruelty was the way to get him to notice me." He dragged in a breath. "I'm really not like—" The words died on his tongue. "Did you hear that?"

She paused, listening intently. A faint growl echoed from beyond the trees.

They stood.

Her hand instinctively gripped the hilt of her knife, while Thorne shifted to a defensive stance.

In the darkness, an animal emerged from the shadows. Its movements were slow, deliberate . . . malicious. Its eyes glowed with a predatory gleam. The forest grew silent and still, not a leaf stirring.

"What the hell is that?" Gisela muttered.

What looked like a wolf was not a wolf at all. The creature's eyes were a swirling white haze. Unfocused and wild. Its whole body quivered and its coat, grey with black-tipped fur, stood straight up, stretching its skin taut over protruding bones. Every breath it took was labored, rattling in its chest.

With a guttural snarl, it sprang forward.

Gisela ducked and attempted to roll but the beast's claw cut her side, slicing through flesh. A scream tore from her throat. The pain of the wound was searing, burning her from the inside out.

The creature hovered over her, its vicious mouth snarling and dripping saliva all over her face.

"Gisela!" Thorne shouted. He barreled into the creature's side, distracting it enough for her to scramble out from under it. Thorne grappled with the beast, desperately trying to avoid its snapping jaws and raking claws.

Pain blurred her vision, but firelight caught on something metal near the tent's entrance. Thorne's sword.

She seized it and, with a fierce cry, plunged it between the creature's shoulder blades. The blade's tip protruded through its chest. The squelching sound of pierced flesh made her stomach lurch.

The beast collapsed.

She ripped the sword free and let it fall as she dropped to her knees.

Thorne sat up abruptly, his eyes wide with fear and maybe reluctant admiration. "By the Six," he whispered. Thorne got to his feet and walked over to the creature, nudging its lifeless head with the tip of his boot. "It's definitely dead," he said, glancing back to Gisela.

She gave a faint nod, still too shaken to speak.

He extended his hand to her, and she hesitated before taking it. With a gentle pull, he brought her to her feet and drew her in, one arm steady at her back. They stood together, their chests rising and falling from the shock of the encounter.

"Impressive," he whispered in her ear.

His tone brought her back to her senses, and she pulled away.

"That was no wolf," Gisela said.

"No, that was something else. I've never seen anything like it."

"I've never left the village, so I don't know if that's normal out here—" she rambled.

"That was not normal, Freckles. I can tell you that much."

She glared at him. "I just saved your life and you're back to calling me Freckles already?" She walked back to the log to sit down.

"To be fair, I saved yours first." He smiled, sitting down next to her. "That creature looked possessed. Like the deer I saw in the woods that day."

The adrenaline left Gisela's body and the pain in her side intensified. She hissed, looking down at the blood pooling under her dress.

"Let me see that," Thorne said, reaching for her dress. "May I?"

"No, I can take care of it," she replied. She turned away, lifting her dress over the wound. She winced at the sight. Three long claw marks ran across her abdomen. It wasn't fatal, but it needed to be tended to immediately.

Thorne had already grabbed Gisela's bag for her, knowing she would have brought supplies for this.

She pulled out a jar of silver sap, scooped up a generous amount and applied it to the gashes to prevent infection. Rummaging through her bag, she found her jar of hylja putty. Suspicion etched across her face. "You don't think . . . maybe?"

"It's worth a shot," Thorne replied with a shrug.

Gisela dipped her fingers into the jar and pressed a small bit of putty lightly over the wound. They watched in silence as it warmed under her skin. For a while, nothing happened. Then, slowly, the skin knitted itself together.

"No way," Thorne said.

Gisela let out a small laugh, continuing to spread it across all three gashes. The pain was easing, the wound wasn't bleeding anymore, and three light pink scars formed. "Incredible," she said. "It's like the tree is helping us somehow."

They sat in a comfortable silence, the night's events replaying in her mind. The strange creature, the hylja's healing properties, and the mysterious Guardian Tree were woven together into a pattern. The removal of the Stones had triggered a series of strange occurrences. Their absence stirred something ancient and powerful, suggesting their purpose extended beyond simply sustaining the villages.

"We have to eat," Thorne said, breaking the silence. He retrieved one of the dead squirrels he'd caught earlier in the night with his bow and arrow and placed it over the flames to cook. The scent of smoke and roasting meat curled into the night sky.

As Gisela watched him work, the gap between them was obvious—she didn't know how to do any of this. Her decision to venture out alone was a reckless gamble.

Reckless . . . or stubborn.

The night's dangers made her shortcomings painfully clear. She'd never pitched a tent or learned how to hunt. Without Thorne, she wouldn't have made it through the first night. The thought made her question her own judgment. Inadequacy stung. And maybe a touch of embarrassment.

"Thorne," she said.

He turned to look at her.

"Will you teach me?"

"Teach you what?" he asked.

"Everything."

CHAPTER EIGHT

Gisela wouldn't have called the night restful, not by any means. In truth, she hadn't slept at all. She and Thorne took turns keeping watch, wary of another ambush by a possessed animal. Fear kept her from the deep sleep her body begged for. As the first light of dawn broke through the trees, they hastily packed up their camp for the long day ahead.

"If we leave now, we can reach the mountain today," Thorne said.

Gisela nodded, grabbing the last of their things.

"And I'll teach you how to catch our lunch today," he added with a smirk.

She'd admired archery, the precision, the focus. Maybe now she'd actually get to learn. "Who taught you archery?" she asked.

"I'm self-taught. My father never really taught me anything. Other than how to take a beating."

She froze, unsure how to respond, but he laughed it off.

"I actually learned the most from your father when he was master-at-arms."

Her heart warmed at the mention of her father. Then quickly iced over as they would have noticed she was gone by now.

By the grace of the Six, they found a stream by midday. The water reflected the light that shimmered through the canopy above them. Serene. A welcome change from the journey so far.

"You think this water is safe to drink?" Thorne asked.

She studied the water, kneeling at the edge. "Should be. It's fast-moving. No surface scum." She dipped her fingers in. "We should still boil it though."

Gisela leaned back on her palms and closed her eyes, soaking in the calm she hadn't felt in gods knows how long. When she opened her eyes, Thorne was watching her. She looked away, pretending not to notice, until his gaze shifted past her shoulder.

A squirrel scampered up a nearby tree in the oddly quiet woods surrounding them.

Thorne caught her eye with a mischievous smile, and she couldn't help but smile back.

"You hold it like this," he murmured, stepping in close behind her, his voice low in her ear.

A shiver traced Gisela's spine, goosebumps trailing down her arms.

His frame blocked out the light behind her as he adjusted her grip on the bow. The brush of his rough fingers against hers made her pulse quicken. Each instruction came with the press of his hand, his patience disarming her more than his teasing ever had.

She tried to focus on the bowstring and her aim. Anything but the nearness of him. She'd never imagined willingly standing this close to Thorne Alderose.

"Focus on your target," he whispered.

The world narrowed to the line of her arrow. His breath brushed her ear.

For a heartbeat, she couldn't tell if the tremor in her hands came from the bow—or from him.

She released.

The squirrel fell with a satisfying thud. Their eyes met. Triumph sparked first, then something deeper neither dared to name.

Thorne's gaze softened before he turned away. "Good shot," he said, his voice flat as he retrieved the kill.

Her shoulders sank as Thorne inspected their catch. The praise was real, but the way he turned back to the squirrel so quickly left a small ache beneath her ribs. She busied her hands with the bowstring, letting the sudden quiet stretch between them. The warmth of his closeness faded, leaving behind a hollowness she didn't know how to fill.

Thorne glanced up at her. "You barely hesitated," he said. "Most people do."

She gave him a gentle smile. "Thanks."

The sun hung low in the sky, painting it with hues of pink and orange as they reached the base of the mountain. They ascended, and the rugged terrain challenged Gisela's every step. She pressed forward, pushing her body to its limit. Her legs strained against the incline while Thorne trudged on like it was the start of a new day.

"Do you think our families are looking for us?" Gisela asked.

Thorne scoffed. "My mother is probably the only one who cares, but not enough to press my father about it. I know your family is probably worried."

She knew they were. Her mother and father were probably worried sick, Noah heartbroken, and Vivi confused. She bit her lip. Better to talk about him instead.

"So, what's the deal with you and your father?" she asked, hoping she wasn't crossing a boundary.

Thorne shook his head. "There was never any real love there. He's a complicated man. I tried for a long time to win his favor, but nothing was ever enough." Thorne walked a few steps ahead of her. His demeanor shifted, a hardness settling around his eyes when he spoke of Cillian.

While her home was filled with laughter and care, Thorne had grown up with a father whose temper left scars, both seen and unseen. She'd met Thorne as a child, known him for years—but had never truly known him at all.

"You've spent a long time trying to earn something he never intended to give."

He whipped his head toward her.

Gisela slowed to a stop. Her face softened as their eyes met. "You don't need your father's elusive approval. Despite it all, there is goodness in you, even if you don't like to show it." She raised an eyebrow at him. "Be better than him and *show* him that you are." She turned and started walking again, passing him.

When she glanced back, he was still standing there. "Take the compliment. Don't make it awkward."

The trail curved ahead, narrowing between stone and brush. Gisela took one more step—and stopped.

Nestled in the rocky outcrop stood a small wooden house. Its pale wood was unweathered, newly raised on the mountainside. Men's clothing hung neatly beneath the covered porch, drying in the breeze. Nearby, a vegetable garden pushed stubbornly through rocky soil.

Gisela crouched instinctively over the crops, brushing her fingers over the edge of a leaf. A slow smile crept across her face—not at the vegetables themselves—but at how they grew. Whoever tended this knew how to coax life from poor ground.

She glanced at Thorne. "Someone lives here."

"Only one way to find out."

They approached the house cautiously.

Thorne paused at the porch, peering through a window.

Gisela walked up the steps, hand raised to knock when the door creaked open.

A brawny man stood in the doorway, his head cocked, waiting for her to speak. He was exceptionally tall, with short, white hair and deep blue eyes. His skin was a smooth shade of brown, with subtle wrinkles creasing his eyes and forehead. He looked to be around her father's age, possibly older.

Gisela found herself speechless, and the man noticed.

He smiled as a powerful, masculine voice called from behind him, "Let them in. They're one of us."

Thorne took a startled step back, and Gisela stumbled down the porch step.

A hearty chuckle left the man's lips, and with a warm baritone voice, he said, "You've come to the right place. You're safe here. Now come inside, I have fresh venison."

Thorne and Gisela exchanged a curious glance.

They stepped inside and warmth entered Gisela's soul. A peculiar sense of safety blanketed her, though she couldn't say why.

The house smelled faintly of wood and smoke, simple yet undeniably welcoming. A small dining table sat by the window, chairs tucked neatly beneath it. The kitchenette held a tiny counter with a basin. Even the small hallway leading to the bedrooms was calm and inviting.

The man turned, and a translucent figure rose out of him, taking shape at his side. An earthy brown shimmer cloaked a broad, stone-muscled form, neither human nor beast. Deep amber eyes glowed, pulsing with the rhythm of the earth itself. The man regarded the figure with familiarity, as if it were an old friend.

"Welcome, fellow Mystics. The name is Silas Donolo. This is my Primal, Crag."

The figure bowed.

Gisela tried to take it all in, but her vision went black.

Chapter Nine

"Does she have a habit of falling over?" Silas's muffled voice drifted through the haze as her consciousness returned.

"No, definitely not," Thorne whispered.

Her eyes fluttered open, and she found herself lying on an unfamiliar bed.

Thorne and Silas hovered over her, amusement tugging at their mouths.

"Are you okay?" Thorne asked.

"Yeah." She blinked rapidly. "I'm sorry. I don't know what happened."

"Don't apologize. It's a shock when you first see one," Silas said.

"See one . . . ?"

"A Primal," he answered. "They're the essence of our power."

Gisela looked at him, bewildered. "You're saying we have one of those?"

He chuckled, the lines at the corners of his eyes deepening. "You absolutely do. Crag sensed you both coming from beyond the mountain. You two must have strong ones, usually we can't do that."

Her hands shook and sweat beaded on her forehead. They'd been given only fragments of information about the Mystics. A sentient being . . . inside her?

Silas handed her a piece of bread and set a warm cup of tea on the wooden end table. "I've got clothing for you that'll be more practical for your travels, if you don't mind pants and tunics. Why don't I fetch those for you, and then we can all sit down and have a little chat. Crag will be able to answer more of your questions."

Without waiting for a response, Silas left the room.

She sat up to lean her head against the headboard. "I'm so embarrassed."

"Don't be." Thorne sat down next to her and handed her the cup of tea. "I'm not gonna lie . . . I was pretty close to fainting myself. I thought I was hallucinating."

"I don't know if I'm ready for all of this," she admitted, shaking her head. She took a sip of her tea, and the warmth of it traveled from her mouth to her core.

"Me neither. But we're already here."

Gisela's thoughts crowded in, loud and relentless. With no Mystic lineage, she wanted to believe the mark was somehow a mistake. Aside from feeling drawn to the Ice Stone, there was nothing to suggest she was anything more than an ordinary girl.

Silas returned to the room with a tunic and pants for Gisela, as well as new clothes for Thorne. A soft smile lingered on his face, his expression gleaming with excitement, as though this simple task brought him genuine pleasure.

Silas and Thorne stepped out, giving Gisela space to get dressed. The tunic and pants felt strange on her, though they were almost a perfect fit. She tugged at the waistband, adjusting it slightly. The sturdy fabric was a far cry from her dresses, but for the first time, she felt like she could actually run if she had to.

When she stepped out of the room, Thorne and Silas were seated in the main area.

Thorne's eyes roamed from her head to her toes and the corner of his mouth lifted.

Gisela shifted her weight, tucking a piece of hair behind her ear. "Thank you for the clothes, Silas," she said. "If I may ask, why do you have women's clothing? Do you have a wife here?"

Silas grimaced, his face flashing with pain. "No, my wife is with the gods now."

"I'm so sorry," Gisela replied.

"It was a little over a year ago. Those clothes were my daughter Marina's." He sighed. "We had an argument. She left after we completed the Trials. I haven't heard from her since."

Gisela nodded. He was alone here.

Except for Crag.

"Have you always lived here?" Thorne asked.

"No, we're from Rockridge. We left after the kingdom executed my wife, Helena. She made it through the inspections as a young lady, only to be discovered later anyway."

Gisela's mouth fell open. *Helena was a Mystic too.* "How did you make it through the inspections?"

"Helena was born in Aquamere," he said, voice rough. "That's where it happened. She'd gone back to visit friends." He swallowed, then cleared his throat. "Growing up, her best friend there was an herbalist. Taught her how to make something to cover the mark." He looked away, eyes dark with memory. "After the execution, Marina and I didn't wait to see if the guards would come for us. We fled that night."

"What she made . . . was it like a putty?"

Silas shrugged. "Yeah. Is that what you two have done?"

They both nodded.

Silas looked contemplative, lost in thought.

Thorne leaned back, a shadow of a smirk on his face. "I didn't know what I was going to do when I found my mark. I followed this one into the woods one night. Saw her making something and putting it behind her ear. Figured if she could do it, I could too."

Silas raised an eyebrow, half-amused, half-sympathetic. "Resourceful, but why did you have to follow her? Aren't you two married?"

Gisela flushed. "No, we're . . . old classmates. Friends."

Thorne's smirk widened ever so slightly at the faint pink tint creeping up her face. "Friends," he repeated, as if testing the word.

"I learned how to make it years ago," Gisela said. "Before I knew what it could do. When my mark appeared . . . I don't know what made me try it. I was desperate."

Silas rubbed his chin. "Trust me, I know desperation. And loneliness. Thought we'd never meet another Mystic. We would have protected more of them, but you know how it is. We never want to reveal ourselves. It's hard to trust people."

Gisela nodded, her eyes flicking to Thorne.

"Do you mind if I allow Crag to join us?"

"No, not at all. And I promise I won't faint this time," Gisela smiled sheepishly.

Crag materialized next to Silas, who straightened with pride, a broad smile spreading across his face.

Thorne stiffened, his grip tightening on the armrests of the chair.

Gisela's lungs refused to expand as she studied Crag. Though she had only glimpsed him earlier, his presence was mesmerizing.

"I will not cause you two any harm," Crag's voice resonated through the room. "Destiny has brought you here. It is vital you complete the Trials. And accept your fate at the end."

Thorne kept his gaze steady on the Primal. "That's exactly why we're here."

Crag hummed in agreement.

"What are the Trials of Kharos, exactly?" Gisela asked.

"They're what Mystics endure to awaken their Primals," Silas explained. "It's a knowledge lost to many of us. The Trials aren't easy, which is why most Mystics here don't have their Primal."

"You mustn't succumb to your fears during the Trials," Crag added.

The butterflies in Gisela's stomach fluttered at the thought.

"The main entrance to the cave was destroyed when King Thraxus started killing us," Silas continued. "But there's another way in."

"How did they manage to execute those with awakened power?" Thorne questioned. "Couldn't those Mystics have just . . . destroyed them?"

Silas furrowed his brow at Thorne. "Contrary to popular belief, son, it's not in our nature to wield our powers for harm," he said firmly. "The guards are following orders from tyrants. But there weren't many awakened Mystics. Most of them fled, and others were taken by surprise. I was but a baby when it started."

"What's your power exactly?" Gisela asked.

"I'm an Earthshaper," Silas said with a touch of pride in his voice. "My power channels through Crag, who's an Earth Primal." He gestured toward Crag, who gave a slight bow of his head.

"Do you know what Thorne and I are? Can you tell?"

"No, we're not able to tell. Though, I have my suspicions about this one here," Crag said, nodding toward Thorne.

Thorne leaned forward, elbows on his knees. "What's that supposed to mean?"

Crag crossed his arms over his chest, and a light smirk appeared on his face.

Gisela glanced back and forth between them. Her heart quickened ever so slightly as she sensed the tension building around them.

Silas broke the silence, giving Crag a pointed look. "He's the reason I can call upon the Earth and use it to cultivate and grow my crops, but it's been difficult lately."

"The Stones," Gisela said. "King Ravenor took the Life Stones from all the villages. In Frosthaven, the forest is dying, and the animals are changing. We encountered a vicious beast on the way here."

Crag and Silas exchanged concerned glances.

"I suspected the balance was disturbed," Crag said, nodding. "I could feel it. Though, whatever is happening to the animals has not reached the mountain yet."

"What does that mean exactly, though? The balance?" Thorne asked.

"The Stones do not only sustain the villages. They are the very essence of our world. The Stones and the Guardian Trees work in tandem to maintain the balance and protection of our realm."

Gisela blinked. Guardian *Trees?*

"The Trees draw the gods' power and hold the realm in balance," Crag said. "The Stones absorb that power and return it to the land. Remove them, and that balance breaks. What follows . . . it has never been done."

She'd climbed the grand tree in the Snowdrifts for years, never knowing it was holding the realm in balance. "You said The Guardian *Trees,*" Gisela mused.

"Yes. One stands in each village of Mystralos."

Gisela's brows lifted, mind churning.

"Why'd the King remove the Stones?" Silas asked, shaking his head in frustration.

"He said they would be stronger united. Said an Ancient Elder told him so," Thorne said.

Crag fumed. "He dared take them from their rightful place on the word of a false prophet?"

"Crag . . ." Silas warned.

"He continues to insult the Six, executing those granted with their gifts and now he's defiled the very bond they gave this land."

The house rumbled violently, the floor beneath them shuddered. They all grabbed their chairs, bracing themselves. The walls creaked as though the house might give way.

"Crag, please," Silas said. "I worked hard on this house."

As fast as Crag materialized from Silas, he disappeared, and the house steadied.

Thorne and Gisela both let out a breath as their eyes met.

"Apologies," Silas said, tensing his body. "That won't happen again."

"It's alright." Gisela forced her fingers loose around the chair.

They told Silas everything they knew: the sudden halt of the inspections, the King's announcement before he took the stones, and the warning Gisela was given by Elder Aldric. Silas confirmed it was, indeed, a prophecy. He listened intently as they spoke, his brows furrowing with concern. When they finished, he revealed his Mystic mark on his thigh—a swirling circle with extended vines.

Silas moved to the kitchen and set plates on the table. He arranged dishes of freshly cooked venison, colorful vegetables, and a small dessert of nuts, seeds, and honey with a light dusting of cocoa.

Gisela went straight for them, giving in to her sweet tooth. She crunched into one, savoring the perfect blend of sweetness and hint of cocoa bitterness. She couldn't help but let out a satisfied moan. "What are these?"

Silas chuckled. "Crumble Clusters. They're famous in Rockridge."

"It's delicious," she said. "I love sweets."

Thorne glanced up at her from his plate, his eyes softening with a smile as he watched Gisela's joy radiate off her.

Silas cleared his throat, shifting the mood reluctantly. He set down his fork and looked up, face firm. "The Trials are different for everyone. There's no way for me to prepare you, and nothing truly can. You'll each face your worst fears, be broken down completely, and essentially, your old self will perish. A new self will be reborn with your Primal. It's the only way to secure a lasting bond with them," Silas explained.

Fear settled in Gisela's stomach, turning sour. Despite it, a tiny spark of resilience ignited.

Gisela glanced at Thorne. Emotions flashed across his face—fear, apprehension, acknowledgment, and then strength. The two of them caught each other's eye. Neither looked away.

They were tethered on this journey, whether they liked it or not.

Before they settled for the night, Gisela stood by the window in their room. She stared at the horizon, ruminating on all the possibilities that awaited her.

Tomorrow, everything would change.

"I'll sleep on the floor," Thorne said, breaking her away from her thoughts.

"No, it's fine. I sleep curled up anyway. We can both fit." She moved to the bed, claiming the side closest to the wall. Thorne wasn't sleeping on the hard floor the night before the biggest day of their lives. As awkward as it was to share a bed with him, she didn't want him to be uncomfortable. It was a strange feeling, caring about Thorne and his well-being. A couple of weeks ago, Gisela would have paid a good coin to see him in distress. The past week with him had been transformative in many ways. She was beginning to see him as a friend. A frustratingly attractive one.

He climbed into bed beside her. Lying on his back, staring at the ceiling, he assured her, "We're going to be okay tomorrow."

Gisela rolled onto her back, her gaze meeting the same spot on the ceiling. "You think so?"

"I do," he said confidently. "I'm curious to know what's inside of us."

"You mean, *who*."

They shared a short, comfortable silence.

"I'm scared," she admitted, her voice barely above a whisper.

He shifted toward her, and she turned her head to face him.

"I'll be with you. I won't let anything bad happen."

He said it with such softness that the blood stilled in her veins.

She nodded. Staring into his dark, piercing eyes, the boy she'd once dreaded disappeared, replaced by someone steady. Someone she could trust. Something came over her, and she grabbed his hand.

He widened his eyes.

She closed hers, praying to the gods sleep would find her. Her hand relaxed in his, but he didn't let go.

CHAPTER TEN

The delicious scent of porridge and sweet fruit drifted in from the kitchen. Gisela opened one eye and found Thorne's pinky finger hooked around hers. His breathing was calm, steady. She sat up, careful not to disturb him.

He blinked, sleep still clinging to him.

"I'm sorry, I tried not to wake you . . . I hardly moved."

He rubbed his eyes and ran his hand through his hair. "I'm oddly aware of your body."

Gisela's cheeks burned pink.

"Your movements. Where you are," he added quickly.

She nodded, trying to suppress a smile. "It's okay. I feel it too."

Silas's lively hum floated through the air.

Gisela glanced at Thorne, noticing his face was slightly flushed too.

"We should eat. Long day ahead."

"Yeah," she said. "Let's go."

Silas had set out bowls of steaming porridge and a platter of fruit. He was beaming as he arranged the table.

"Good morning! You two sleep well enough?"

"Better than I expected," Gisela replied, glancing at Thorne.

He hummed in agreement.

"Good. You'll need your strength," Silas said, his tone serious, yet warm.

The porridge was sweet, richer than the sparse meals they'd had on the road.

Silas kept refilling their bowls, talking between bites, his voice bright with joy.

Gisela couldn't remember the last time she laughed through a meal. And with the Trials ahead, it felt wrong to. It was strange . . . how easy it was to be here. Safe. As if she'd known Silas far longer than a day.

Her family would love him.

Maybe that's what this feeling was. A little slice of home.

"How long does it take to get through the Trials?" Thorne asked.

Silas paused, his gaze turning toward the front window. "It's different for everyone. For me and Marina, it felt like days. It's hard to measure time in there."

Gisela choked on a piece of fruit, and Thorne jumped from his seat.

She held her hands up. "I'm fine, I'm fine. Food went down wrong is all."

He sat back down, his shoulders tense and his brow furrowed.

She nodded to assure him, but inside, the weight of the Trials pressed down. *Days?*

She couldn't ignore the shift in Thorne's behavior. His glances lingered, and his voice had lost its usual gravel.

Gisela felt it too. An urge to stay close.

To protect him.

Gisela shook the thoughts from her mind. "Any last-minute advice?" she asked Silas.

Silas looked at her with earnest eyes. "Trust each other. You'll likely need to rely on one another more than you have so far. But it's much easier to do the Trials with a partner."

Thorne peered up at her from his bowl of porridge, his gaze both intense and comforting.

A jolt of reassurance hit her. Beneath it, something deeper took root. Warmth, perhaps. Or something dangerously close.

The path to the cave's hidden entrance wasn't far from Silas's home. They walked in silence, each step carrying her closer to a trial she couldn't predict or prepare for. There were no steps to follow, no ingredients to gather, no formula to guide her. Nothing like the methods she relied on to solve every other problem she had faced. The forest around them fell silent, as if it were holding its breath for what they were about to face.

They arrived and Gisela searched the area, expecting a large, ominous opening. Instead, her gaze dropped and her heart went with it. Nestled among the rocks was a crawl space leading into darkness. Her stomach turned, threatening to undo breakfast.

Thorne stepped closer. "I'll go first. I can guide you through." He placed a hand on her shoulder.

Her ears started ringing.

Silas approached, reaching for Gisela but hesitated. "What's wrong?"

"She doesn't like tight spaces," Thorne said, his hand grazing her arm.

Gisela nodded, the air scraping shallow and thin through her lungs.

Silas reached out, letting his arms hover near her shoulders, giving her a chance to step back. When she didn't, he pulled her into a firm, reassuring hug. "It's not far. I promise. You're going to be alright, darling. More than alright."

She clung to his words, tears welling in her eyes. "I didn't think I'd be facing my fears before we even started," she said, her voice trembling a bit.

Silas let her go, giving her one last look. "I'll be waiting at the house when you get back. And you *will* come back, I know it." He grabbed Thorne and pulled him in for a hug too.

Thorne stiffened, but his shoulders eased ever so slightly, as if he too found comfort in Silas's embrace.

And it was comfort they needed.

Beyond, the Trials of Kharos waited. Unknown. Her palms were slick with sweat at the thought of it. Each step toward the shadowed entrance felt heavier than the last. A gift, the gods had granted her. A prophecy, the Elder had given her.

She hadn't asked for any of it.

And yet, standing here, an ember sparked to life within her. Each choice she had made—the decision to leave her village, the trust she had placed in Thorne—led to this moment. What waited before her wasn't only the unknown. It was a choice.

One she was willing to make.

Thorne knelt at the cave entrance, peering into the small hole. Beyond five feet, darkness swallowed everything.

Gisela crouched behind him, instincts screaming to get up and run.

"Ready?" he asked.

"Not even a little bit."

They crawled through the narrow passage, inching forward as the walls closed in. The air grew cooler and denser. Every scrape of rock against their hands and knees amplified. Gisela shut her eyes in an attempt to block out her perception of the small space. What she couldn't see, her brain couldn't process.

Thorne moved steadily ahead until he stopped abruptly.

Gisela's face bumped into his backside.

"Easy there, Freckles," he teased, voice echoing. "I had a feeling you were starting to tolerate me, but I didn't know you were wanting to be that up close and personal."

Flustered, she shoved him forward. "Keep moving."

Thorne chuckled, advancing a few more feet before standing up. He guided her out of the passage into a softly lit chamber. "You made it through."

"Least of my concerns today, I'm sure," Gisela replied.

Torches flickered along the walls, their flames throwing jagged shadows across the chamber. Water dripped steadily from above with a hollow, echoing *plink*. The ceiling soared, a dark, unbroken dome of rock.

The chill settled into her lungs and slowed each inhale. Teeth chattering, she searched every shadowed corner.

"What do we do now?" she asked, inching closer to Thorne.

He glanced at the wall next to him. "*Fear.*"

"What?"

"On the wall . . . it says *fear.*"

One second, they were looking at one another, the next their vision went black.

Gisela's eyes cracked open, heavy and sluggish, as though she had been asleep for hours. She sat up, rubbing her temples, and looked over at Thorne. He was beginning to stir on the floor. She stood up and walked toward him but stopped. A strange glare shimmered in front of her. Reaching out, her fingers met a smooth resistance: a clear wall. Her breathing quickened as she ran her hands along all four sides, heart hammering. The walls enclosed her completely, the space roughly the size of a small bedroom. Her knees buckled, and panic prickled along her spine.

"Thorne! Thorne, get up!"

He rubbed his hands over his face and froze at Gisela's panicked expression. He launched to his feet and ran toward her at full speed.

"Wait!" she shouted.

He skidded to a stop, chest jerking as his forehead nearly slammed into the invisible wall.

"It's a box," Gisela said, voice cracking.

Thorne pressed his palm against the clear surface, tracing its edges. He cursed. "I'm going to get you out."

His head swiveled around the chamber, looking for something, anything he could use to break her out. A quiver of arrows and a bow lay on the ground behind him. Bullseyes were scattered around the chamber, each marked with a glowing symbol.

"Targets," he muttered. He nocked an arrow and aimed at the nearest one.

Gisela's throat nearly closed. Her chest rose and fell in rapid, shallow pulls as she pressed against the clear wall. A loud click echoed, and the wall pushed her forward, each inch sending a fresh spike of panic through her.

Thorne was ready to release the arrow when Gisela screamed. "Thorne, the walls are closing in!"

"I know what to do. Close your eyes, Gisela. Keep them closed and try to get to the middle of the box so you don't feel the walls," Thorne called back.

Gisela didn't close her eyes. She couldn't. Panic held them wide open.

Thorne drew, steady, and let the arrow fly.

It struck true. The air in front of him rippled, shimmered, and then something else stood there.

A man and a woman materialized, solid as flesh.

Thorne froze, every muscle in his body going rigid.

Cillian's harsh, ruddy features twisted into a sinister grin as he turned to Selene. His hand lashed across her face.

Selene crumbled to the floor, a pained gasp escaping her lips.

Cillian's boot struck her stomach, and an agonized cry tore from her throat as she curled inward. He yanked her up by a fistful of her long black hair.

Gisela's pulse hammered. This wasn't real. It couldn't be—but Thorne was breathing like it was.

"Stop!" he yelled, running toward them.

Gisela, still crouched in the center of the box, could only watch through the distortion as Thorne ran toward the illusion.

He ran through the figures, their forms evaporating like smoke. He grabbed another arrow, drew the bowstring, and let it fly toward the next target.

Cillian appeared directly in front of Thorne this time.

"You're a worthless excuse of a man. You're no son of mine," Cillian sneered, spitting.

Thorne recoiled, flinching as though the spit had struck him.

The taunts echoed, each one making Thorne's movements less steady.

"You're a worthless man."

"Useless coward."

"A failure."

Thorne aimed at the next target high in the chamber. His hand shook, and the arrow missed its mark.

The walls pressed in on Gisela faster now.

A wicked laugh left Cillian's lips. "See? You're useless. Pathetic. You're going to kill her." Cillian's voice was rough and distorted.

Selene's cries reverberated around the room.

Thorne crouched on the floor, hands pressed against his ears in a desperate attempt to block it out. Tears welled in his eyes, his jaw trembling.

"*You are no son of mine!*" Cillian's voice boomed, shaking the chamber.

Gisela banged on the clear walls, tears mixing with her desperate pleas. "Thorne! Listen to me. It's not real. He's an illusion!"

She scrambled to the other side of the box, but the walls were closing in fast. She hit the wall sooner than expected. The air was too thin to fill her lungs. Her hands shook as she brought them to her head and slid down the wall. She curled her knees close against her chest, making herself smaller.

She forced her eyes shut and focused on taking deep, rhythmic breaths. *Breathe.*

Four seconds in, six seconds out.

Again.

The jagged rhythm of panic eased, and her heartbeat slowed. The walls still moved, but their speed faltered. With each measured breath, they hesitated.

"Thorne, please. Please get up," she whispered, voice cracking. "You can do this. I trust you."

Thorne opened his eyes. His attention locked on Gisela, hugging her knees to her chest.

His expression smoothed as he looked at the illusion of Cillian.

"You're a shit father," he said. "You're the coward."

Nocking the final arrow, Thorne aimed at the target aligned with Cillian's head. Steadying himself, he released the arrow. It flew true and pierced the illusion. In a flash, Cillian vanished.

The sound of the walls moving ceased.

Gisela reached out, meeting nothing but cool air. Her legs wobbled as she tested weight on her feet. She had to steady herself before standing fully.

Thorne was still across the chamber, shoulders slumped, breath uneven. For a moment, neither of them moved—like stepping too fast might shatter whatever fragile calm they had just earned.

Then their eyes met.

Thorne crossed the distance first, and she met him halfway. They held each other fiercely, hearts hammering in sync.

"I'm so sorry," Thorne whispered into her ear. His arms tightened around her once—hard—before he let himself breathe.

"You did it. I'm safe, you're safe. We made it through," Gisela reassured him.

"No . . . I—I nearly got you killed," he whispered.

Gisela shook her head, pressing a hand to his chest. "You didn't. You did what you needed to. I'm proud of you."

Thorne pulled away in an instant and averted his gaze.

"Was that something that happened in the past?" she asked.

"What?"

"Cillian . . . and your mother."

He ran a hand through his hair. "I can't tell you how many times I've seen him hurt her." His voice shook as he spoke. "The older I got the more he focused on me. Better me than her."

Gisela said nothing.

His eyes were fixed somewhere beyond her. "Then I grew taller, stronger than him. That pissed him off. It didn't make things better. It just . . . made her the target again, in a way. Like punishing me for existing wasn't enough."

"At least he'll be away from her now. And he can't control you anymore."

He let out a short, humorless laugh. "Yeah, I'm something else now. Something he hates even more."

She bit her lip, thinking. Part of being an herbalist was knowing when to intervene and when to let a process run its course. With Thorne, she decided it was better to just listen.

"Now what?" he asked.

Gisela released a sigh and wandered around the cave. She searched for a hidden hallway, a separate room, anything to hint at what was next. "I faced my fear, and you faced yours . . ."

"Hardly," he said but it came out a little harsh.

Gisela looked back at him, opening her mouth to respond to his tone but decided against it. "Well, we controlled it. Our fears. When I controlled my breathing, my panic . . . the walls stopped closing in so fast."

Thorne's eyes dropped to the floor. "I just shot arrows at targets," he said, bitterness coiling around every word. "That's hardly controlled fear."

"You helped me survive," she said. "Even if you don't see it that way right now."

He clenched his fists, eyes turning wild. "I didn't do enough. You were the one who got me—" He cut himself off.

Gisela didn't try to argue. She could feel the tension radiating off him, like heat from a fire.

Instead, she let the silence linger. The cave was cold again, the dripping water echoing louder. She went back to where the word *fear* was etched into the stone, seeing *trust* underneath it.

"Thorne, look. It says *trust* now."

He moved toward her—and then a high-pitched ringing pierced the air, growing louder until it pulsed behind her eyes. They clutched their heads, teeth gritted as the sound bore down on them. One by one, the torches guttered and died, plunging the chamber into a suffocating darkness.

They dropped to their knees.

The relentless ringing pressing against their eardrums transformed into a haunting, inescapable lullaby.

CHAPTER ELEVEN

Her eyes fluttered open to a garden bathed in soft light. The unfamiliar scent of flowers and fresh greenery pulled at her senses. Tall, twisted trees arched overhead, and streaks of light speckled the ground below. Clusters of blue and violet flowers lined the cobblestone path.

Ahead, there was a colossal plant, its face a burst of deep purple petals, but it lacked a stem. Its main body was thick with black leaves and swaying thorn-studded vines.

"A Grimthorn Bramble," Gisela said as she rose to her feet.

"Like from the children's book?" Thorne asked. He stood and took a careful step forward.

"Yes." Her eyes traced the plant's hypnotic movements. "Ah, so this is what your parents named you after."

Thorne gave her a flat, bored expression but didn't respond. He continued toward the plant instead.

Gisela walked past the Grimthorn Bramble, keeping a safe distance from its menacing vines.

Past it, a mortar and pestle sat on a pedestal beside a dagger with a crystallized hilt. A hollow feeling settled in her gut as she took in the scene before her.

The fine hairs along her neck rose. Every instinct screamed that this place wasn't a real garden.

It was more like a curated stage, waiting for a performance.

Beyond the pedestal and down the winding path stood a tree so massive it was impossible to see its entirety from a single vantage point. She walked toward it, tilting her head back to see thousands of aether leaves garnished with plump dreamberries. Reaching out, her fingers grazed the rough, warm bark.

"This is a giant Guardian Tree, Thorne!" she called out.

Thorne was still mesmerized by the Grimthorn Bramble, inching his way closer to it. "Those vines are long, keep your distance."

But it was too late. Her breath hitched in her throat as one of the vines lashed out like a striking serpent. Its thorns raked across his arm. He collapsed to the ground, screaming and writhing in pain. "Thorne!" Gisela screamed, rushing over to him.

She cursed under her breath as she knelt beside him. She lifted his arm and gritted her teeth. The wound was already darkening. The poison was spreading as fast as the tale had described. As she examined his arm, she could smell the venom. It smelled like lavender but with a subtle metallic tang. Thorne's breathing became labored, his eyes rolling back as foam pooled at the corner of his mouth.

The blood drained from her face. The pulse in Thorne's neck was a fading rhythm beneath her fingers. He wouldn't die here. He couldn't.

She glanced at the Guardian Tree.

"Hylja," she whispered. She dashed to the tree, mind racing as she considered the ingredients she needed.

The tree loomed over the garden like a vulture, its branches extending into the sky.

Without wasting another moment, she scaled the tree as quickly as she could to reach the aether leaves and dreamberries. Her arms burned with fatigue, like she had been using them for hours already, but fear pushed her muscles to obey.

A gurgling sound left Thorne's lips.

"Hold on, Thorne."

She reached a branch sturdy enough to sit on, but her foot slipped, leaving her dangling by one hand. Adrenaline surged, but she forced her mind back to Thorne. He had saved her.

Now it was her turn to save him.

With a low grunt, she summoned her strength and hoisted herself up, muscles burning as she reached higher. She plucked the leaves and berries, tucking them safely into her pockets. Each pluck carried weight: his life depended on her speed and efficiency. When she had what she needed, she descended, landing lightly in the grass.

Working as fast as she could, she broke off a large piece of bark, but the sap refused to flow.

"Think, Gisela, think," she muttered, glancing at Thorne's still body. Time was slipping away; he wouldn't live much longer. Her foot tapped anxiously against the cobblestones. The pedestal caught her eye.

The dagger.

She bolted, dropping the leaves and berries into the mortar before grabbing the dagger. Sprinting back to the tree, she sliced off a piece of root from the base, sawing through its tough fibers. With a forceful jab, she drove the dagger into the tree, silver sap seeping out like liquid light. She pulled the blade free and let the sap drip into the mortar. With her feet pounding on the cobblestones, she raced back to the pedestal and ground the ingredients together.

The faint shimmer confirmed it. Perfectly combined.

Hands trembling, she hurried to Thorne. His skin was unnervingly cold. She pressed the putty onto his arm, rubbing desperately.

He didn't respond.

"Come on," Gisela urged, shaking him. "Wake up, please! Why isn't it working?"

Frantic, she sifted through her memories, like flipping through the pages of an old book, trying to recall the story of the Grimthorn Bramble and its venom.

A line from the book surfaced in her mind.

> *When venom strikes and shadows creep,*
> *Seek the tree where secrets sleep.*
> *Find the ferns with dewdrops bright,*
> *Mix with its essence to end the blight.*

"Find the ferns with dewdrops bright . . ." she whispered, her eyes scanning the garden. Clusters of ferns gleamed in the light near the Guardian Tree.

Gisela dashed over, plucking the leaves and carrying them to the mortar where the rest of the putty remained. She squeezed them, letting the dew drip into the mixture until it thinned into a glistening liquid. Clutching the mortar, she returned to Thorne and sank to the ground. She positioned him with his back against her chest and forced the liquid between his lips.

Tears streamed down her face; each one a silent plea. "Please, wake up." She pressed her face to his, her lips lightly brushing his ear. "I need you."

The world went still. The thrum of his life wavered at the edge of darkness, fragile as glass. Every ragged breath of his became an echo of fear in her.

Seconds stretched endlessly. Then Thorne gasped, drawing air into his lungs.

Her shoulders finally dropped. All the tension left her in a single, shaky exhale.

He blinked at her.

Tears slipped down her face, warm as they struck his cheeks.

"I got pricked by a thorn . . . ironic, isn't it?" he rasped.

Gisela offered a soft smile. Her hands lingered on his shoulders before she scooted back. Thorne took a few moments to gather himself and then stood, towering over her. He extended his hand, and she took it, feeling the warmth of his touch as she rose to her feet.

"Thank you," he said, his voice still rough. "It's becoming a habit of yours now."

"What is?" she asked.

"Saving me," he replied, a trace of shame in his voice. He pulled her close, holding her as though letting go might undo everything.

He still smelled like the venom, reminding her how close he had been to the edge.

Thorne drew back enough for their noses to nearly brush. He rested his forehead against hers and the world shrank to the space between them.

She peered up at him, searching for his eyes, but he kept his gaze elsewhere. "Look at me."

His eyes met hers. There was such desperation in his face that it twisted her insides.

"I trust you," she whispered.

"I—"

A low rumble surged through the garden. They pulled apart as the ground beneath them quaked. In an instant, light blurred and the enchanted garden vanished.

They were thrust back into the chamber where their trial had begun.

The rumbling persisted, growing louder as the far wall quivered. They watched, tense and wide-eyed, as chunks of rock broke loose, crashing to the ground.

"Something's coming," Gisela said.

"Of course it is," Thorne grumbled.

They turned in a slow circle with empty hands. The chamber offered nothing but stone this time.

With a deafening crash, a monstrous creature tore through the cave wall. The cavern shuddered as an eerie shadow draped over them.

The creature was enormous. Its shadowy form shifted and undulated, a nightmare made flesh. Razor-sharp claws glinted in the flickering torchlight. Its fangs dripped with a fluorescent green venom that hissed as it hit the stone. Dark tendrils pulsated with sinister energy, curling like smoke, feeding off the air around them.

Gisela paused, a strange sense of familiarity tugging at her as she stared. Drawn forward, she took a step.

"Gisela, *stop*!" Thorne's voice pierced the air.

The urgency in his tone snapped her back as the creature swung, sending her into the wall with bone-jarring force. The impact took the breath from her lungs and pain detonated through her ribs.

The chamber wavered. Shadows stretched and warped as she slid down the wall, struggling to stay upright.

"Gisela!" Thorne's desperate scream cut through the chaos as he ran toward her.

He grabbed her hands to help her stand, but she stumbled and fell into him.

The creature bellowed, the sound piercing through her, rattling her bones.

Gisela glanced to the ground and saw the bow and arrow from the first trial. Thorne followed her line of sight and grabbed it. Nocking it back, he shot at the creature, and it flew right through.

Still, he tried again.

Nock, aim, shoot.

Nock, aim, shoot.

Every attempt vanished into the shifting mass.

"How do we kill it?" Thorne yelled.

It lunged forward, swiping at Gisela again. The blow took her legs out from under her.

The creature laughed. A sound like rock grinding against bone. The vibration rolled through the floor, sending dust and rocks down from the ceiling.

She snatched a chunk of jagged stone, hurling it with all her strength. The rock shattered into dust before it reached the creature's form.

"It's not real."

The creature bellowed again, the roar slamming into her like a physical blow. Venom reeking of burned flesh spattered across the floor.

She forced herself to her feet, every movement a fight against searing pain. She leaned against the wall for balance and read the etched words in the stone. *Fear. Trust.*

And now, *Death*.

"We're not meant to kill it," Gisela said, the thought taking shape as it left her mouth. "Crag said we have to accept our fate at the end."

"And what's that?"

Thorne reached for Gisela, but the creature seized him, lifting him high into the air as its claws clamped tight. Thorne's cries, raw and strangled, pierced the chamber.

She opened her mouth to scream. Nothing came out. Her legs buckled, sending her sprawling back onto the stone floor.

The creature cocked its head, crimson eyes gleaming with malice as it stared at Thorne. With a cruel flick of its claws, it released its grip.

Thorne plummeted to the ground with a fatal thump. The sound made her stomach drop.

A sob escaped, and the air left her lungs. She searched for movement, for breath, for any sign he would rise again. There was none.

Something inside her hardened. If this was the end, then let it come.

A massive claw swept through the air again. The impact drove her back against the stone, and the world went dark.

Awareness tried to return in fragments—a sharp ache behind her eyes, the metallic taste of blood coating her tongue, the sting along her knees where skin met rock. Pain rolled through her in waves, amplified.

Consciousness was slipping away.

Even as darkness closed in, something held her—waiting.

Chapter Twelve

The frigid breath of winter whispered into Gisela's ears. The harsh reality of the chamber had faded, replaced by rolling hills blanketed in pristine snow. Snowflakes drifted down and settled on her hair and eyelashes. Her once bloodied face was now clean and unblemished.

"Where am I?"

"Your awakening," an ancient, serene voice echoed around her. "Not life, not death. The place in between."

Gisela closed her eyes and drew in the crisp air. When she opened them again, a stunning figure of ice stood towering over her, radiating power.

"I am Eira, your Primal," the figure said. "I am the extension of one whose essence you feel. Their name is not yours to call upon yet. It is a key to immense power that must be earned."

"I can't know the name of the god who gifted me?"

Eira floated closer. "Not yet. But the strength it grants you will grow with your understanding. For now, trust in what I lend you. One day, you will know when to call."

Gisela observed every detail of Eira's presence. The Primal's translucent form glowed with a fluid blue radiance, her body etched with frost patterns that looked alive, curling and twisting to the wind's rhythm. Icy tendrils extended from her fingertips. Her eyes, an ocean blue, were piercing yet kind, locking onto Gisela in a way that made the world around them fade.

"Did I die?" Gisela asked, her voice trembling slightly.

"Quite the opposite."

"What am I?"

"You are a Frostweaver," Eira explained. "It was not by chance that I chose you, Gisela. The Primals align with those whose spirits resonate with their own. You were chosen because of your strength and resilience." She paused, allowing her words to sink in. "Your heart carries the quiet strength of a snow-laden forest and the determination of a river that refuses to freeze."

Gisela couldn't look away. Her mind was a rush of questions and admiration melting together. As Eira spoke, their connection thrummed within her chest. Deep, profound, and undeniable.

"You see," Eira continued, "our bond is forged from the same essence. Together we can weave the frost and help restore the balance that has been disrupted."

At the last of her words, the chill in the air no longer stung. A cold pulse bloomed at the soles of her feet and rose, settling into her marrow—exploring, then obeying.

For a fleeting moment, there was only serenity. Clarity followed, and in its wake came the memory.

"Where is Thorne?"

Eira bowed her head and closed her eyes. A few seconds passed, and they snapped open.

"We need to return."

In a flash of blinding white light, Gisela's surroundings shifted. When the light faded, she was back in the dark chamber. The haunting image of Thorne being crushed and plummeting to the ground twisted her stomach. She scanned the room until she found him on the other side, sitting with his elbows on his knees, the heels of his palms pressed into his eyes.

Relief loosened her chest. He was alive. Whole.

She crossed the chamber with a new steadiness in her stride. Energy she had never felt before pulsed through her veins, and a faint smile touched her lips as Eira's presence stirred within her.

Gisela crouched beside him. "Hey, I was so worried," she said, placing her hand on his forearm. His skin was scorching.

"Don't touch me," Thorne snapped.

She recoiled. "What's wrong, Thorne?" she asked gently.

He looked up, eyes wild with fury and something raw underneath. "You saw what I endured. My father beating my mother half to death. Degrading me, screaming that I was a worthless coward of a son. All while trying to keep you alive. Then I nearly die by some excruciating poison. And for what? For some demon to kill us anyway? To crush me to death?"

Gisela swallowed hard. The memory of his suffering flashed vividly in her mind. "Thorne . . . we had to face this for the awakening." She paused, trying to tread lightly. When he didn't respond she asked, "Did you meet your Primal?"

Thorne scoffed. "Yeah, I met him. I reject him. I reject this entire thing."

"This isn't you," Gisela whispered.

Eira's voice echoed inside of Gisela's mind, *"It will take time. Give him grace. This anger isn't uncommon in Flamekeepers."* Eira materialized beside Gisela.

Thorne shifted his focus toward her, studying the ethereal being. His expression shifted from curiosity to distrust.

He shut his eyes—

And behind him, a figure of black fire took shape, tall and imposing. Swirling ebony flames wrapped around a broad chest and powerful arms. His eyes, set deep within the blaze, burned with a fierce intensity that locked onto Gisela's.

Her breath caught in her throat at the strength of his gaze.

"Ignitus," Eira greeted, her eyes meeting his like two storms colliding.

"Eira," he returned with a smirk.

Thorne and Gisela gawked between them.

"Do you two . . . know each other?" Gisela asked.

"You could say that," Ignitus replied.

Gisela blinked as questions she couldn't even begin to decipher came flooding in.

Ignitus turned his burning gaze to Thorne. "Reject me all you like, but fate doesn't bend for you. Accept it or be consumed by it."

Thorne's expression hardened.

Gisela's body temperature dropped. She shivered from head to toe, the searing chill biting into her bones.

Thorne, on the other hand, burned. Sweat beaded on his entire body. He tugged off every layer until only his underwear remained.

"Eira, what's happening to us?" Gisela managed through chattering teeth.

Eira's expression softened. "Your bodies are adjusting to your elements. It is . . . unpleasant, but necessary."

Thorne snorted. "Of course, more suffering."

Eira glanced at Ignitus, whispering, "He's moody, that one."

"I expected as much," Ignitus said, before vanishing into Thorne in a burst of dark flame.

Eira turned to Gisela. "You will survive this. It will be uncomfortable, but you would do well to find comfort in each other."

Before Gisela could ask what she meant, Eira faded into mist.

Gisela sighed and looked over at Thorne. He refused to look her way. Feeling too cold to argue, she curled up on the stone floor, clinging to what little warmth remained in her body.

Thorne lay sprawled, his body pulsing with heat, trapped in a fever that refused to break. He had awoken with Ignitus in a volcanic expanse, beside a small red-orange flame that burned nothing like his own black fire. Anger trembled through him, leaving him hollow. It blazed through his mind, distorting everything it touched. The trial hadn't truly ended. It lived under his skin now—in his blood, and in the Primal fused to him.

Gisela's soft, uneven breaths reached him. The sound of her teeth chattering and her body trembling tugged at something in his chest.

He gave in and inched toward her.

His burning skin met her icy chill, and the relief sank deeper than temperature alone. He pressed his chest to her back, curling himself to the shape of her body, his head settling beside her silky brown hair.

She inhaled sharply. Her body stiffened at the contact before a soft sound escaped her lips, and Thorne sighed as his warmth eased her trembling. For the first time since the trials began, peace settled. Together, they drifted into a deep, much-needed sleep.

Chapter Thirteen

That night, Gisela dreamt of a dance of ice and fire. A dance to a melody so enchanting, it made her question everything.

Gisela awoke to the familiar darkness of the chamber once more. Thorne's arms were wrapped tightly around her in a protective embrace. Her body was warm again, and her mind was clear.

"Eira, how long have we been asleep?" she whispered inside her own mind.

"Two days."

"That dream . . . was that you and Ignitus?"

"It was not. We do not meddle with your dreams," Eira responded.

Gisela wriggled free from Thorne's arms, rousing him.

He stretched, extending his limbs like a waking lion shaking off sleep. He rolled his neck, and as his eyes fluttered open, they shared a knowing look.

"How do you feel?" Gisela asked.

"Fine. I want to leave," Thorne said curtly. He stood up and made his way toward the cave's exit tunnel.

A cold weight settled in her gut.

She had hoped Thorne would wake up lighter than he had fallen asleep—less angry, less consumed. After the way he had held her through the night, she thought the anger might loosen its grip.

But he hadn't. It was there in the brief twitch of his jaw, the tight line of his shoulders, broader and stronger than before.

The walk back was quiet and rigid, with Thorne staying a few paces ahead of her.

When they crested the steep pathway to Silas's home, a gasp left Gisela's lips. The area surrounding his home was destroyed. The crops looked trampled over, trees were uprooted, and the ground was scarred by deep gashes. The destruction was stark against the untouched house.

Gisela hurried through the rubble and burst through the front door. "Silas!" she called out.

Silas emerged from his bedroom, his face a mixture of relief and concern. He swept Gisela up into a hug. "This is not how I wanted to celebrate your return," Silas said, setting her down before leading her to the kitchen table.

Thorne lingered in the open doorway, his expression unreadable. "What happened here?" Thorne asked.

"Come, sit. We have a lot to talk about," Silas responded. He moved to the kitchen to fetch two cups of water and some fruit. He placed the food and water on the table, gesturing Thorne over.

Thorne stepped forward, glancing at the empty seat next to Gisela, and chose to sit in the living room instead.

Gisela's hands curled into fists on her lap.

Silas gave Thorne an apprehensive look but continued to speak. "I was attacked yesterday. By a nasty beast," Silas said, settling into the chair opposite Gisela.

"A beast?" Gisela echoed.

"No ordinary beast. Nothing I could possibly compare it to." Silas shrugged. "The ground started rumbling while I was asleep. I went outside to find it had ravaged my crops and tore up the land. It charged me with claws the size of machetes. I struck it with my sword, but it was relentless. Crag crushed it. It won't be coming back."

"What's happening?" Gisela asked.

"Dunno." Silas leaned back in his chair. "But it's important you two harness your power quickly. I'm afraid we're up against much worse than we feared."

Eira appeared next to Gisela, and Silas gaped. "Fascinating . . . you're a Frostweaver."

Gisela smiled. "I am. This is Eira," she said, introducing her Primal.

Eira bowed her head in acknowledgment.

Silas turned his attention to Thorne, waiting for him to introduce his.

Ignitus materialized next to him before Thorne surged to his feet, the wooden chair scraping against the floor. He strode toward the empty bedroom and slammed the door behind him. The sound reverberated through the room, making Gisela jump in her seat.

"He's struggling," she said, watching the door. "He's been like this since the awakening."

Silas nodded. "He's rejecting his Primal?"

"Something happened during the Trial . . . illusions. He saw his father hurting his mother and . . ." Gisela paused, feeling it wasn't her place to explain further.

Silas looked to the floor, fingers tightening on the edge of the table. "The same thing happened with my Marina. She saw something that made her hate me so deeply, she left."

Her eyes softened in empathy as the slump of his shoulders deepened.

"She blames me for her mother's death."

"I'm so sorry, Silas," Gisela said, reaching across the table to hold his hand.

"I'll talk to Thorne. He needs to open his mind and heart. We need him," Silas said.

Gisela knew they would need every ounce of support they could muster, and with unshakeable certainty, she would need Thorne—not only for the journey, but for reasons far deeper and more personal.

Gisela glanced at the devastated land through the window. "Why haven't you revived the crops?"

Silas shook his head in defeat. "I can't. They won't grow. We'll need to leave here soon."

The closed bedroom drew her in, the echo of the slammed door lingered long after Thorne disappeared behind it.

Gisela and Silas ate dinner together that evening, discussing their plans for the journey ahead. They would leave for Rockridge in a few days, as Silas's food wouldn't last beyond that. She was thankful Silas had decided to join them. His presence was a lifeline, a warmth she hadn't realized she'd been missing. She felt relaxed in his company, the tension of the trials easing with each passing moment.

"It'll be safer there," Silas said, putting his fork to his mouth.

"I'm not so sure. They don't have their Stone either," she said. "Aren't you afraid someone will turn you in?"

Silas leaned back, rubbing his jaw. "Normally, maybe. But it's been long enough. The people in Rockridge know and trust me. I didn't want to put anyone there in a bind before, but now? No one's looking for me anymore."

The sun dipped low enough that shadows stretched across the room. The golden light turned thin and gray, stealing the warmth from the kitchen.

Gisela's fingers absently traced the edge of her cup. "I'm worried about my family. It was getting bad when we left."

Silas nodded, the wrinkles on his forehead deepening. "I worry for Marina too." He reached out to hold her hand. The gesture was small, but it grounded her.

As the evening ended, Gisela entered the bedroom and froze at the sight of Thorne asleep on the floor. She tried to swallow the lump in her throat, but it stubbornly remained. After all they had endured together, his distance felt like a knife twisting inside her heart. Her body ached—not from the cold or pain, but from the desire to be near him.

She wanted to shake him. She wanted to hold him. She did neither.

The soft yellow light of dawn filtered through the window the next morning.

Gisela peered out.

Thorne was sitting on the edge of the cliff, staring off into the horizon. His silhouette was dark against the first morning light, his shoulders hunched.

Silas joined him and she could see a slight perk in Thorne's posture.

"Silas will be good for Thorne," Eira whispered into Gisela's mind.

Gisela nodded, keeping her eyes on the scene through the window. "He's shut me out," Gisela said.

"He's angry," Eira replied. *"Not everyone finds it easy to put their feelings into words. Think about his upbringing."*

"And you know about his upbringing how?"

Eira offered no response.

She watched him for a minute longer, noting the subtle shift in his demeanor, before moving to the kitchen to prepare her breakfast.

Chapter Fourteen

Thorne wasn't sure what to say when another man looked at him without judgment, offering patience and understanding instead.

"I can see the turmoil in your eyes. The Trials were meant to test you, to push you to your limits. Feeling angry and confused afterward is normal," Silas said.

Thorne let out a ragged breath. Talking about his feelings felt like stepping into a trap, one he learned to avoid. At home, weakness was an invitation for ridicule and punishment. Cillian's laughter echoed in his mind, loud enough to make the idea of confiding in a man feel dangerous.

"Opening up is a sign of strength, not weakness," Silas said.

"I've learned to keep things to myself. It's safer that way."

"Safer?" Silas tilted his head. "Carrying everything inside doesn't lighten the load. It only makes the burden heavier."

Thorne's shoulders sagged under an invisible weight. He'd told Gisela he wanted to be better. He needed to believe it himself—that Cillian hadn't broken him. That whatever had been carved into him by years of cruelty wasn't permanent. That it hadn't hollowed him out beyond repair.

"I'm not just angry and confused," he said. "I . . . I was weak. I almost—damn it, I almost killed her because I lost control. Then I got poisoned, and she had to save me. I should have protected her. Not the other way around."

"No, Thorne. Enduring the Trials proved your strength. Ignitus is proof of that. You didn't fail. You survived. Now, you grow."

Thorne's eyes flared. "I don't know how to accept something that has made me feel this inadequate."

"Most Mystics go their whole lives without their awakening," Silas said. "You've already done what so many never will."

A gust of wind swept across the cliff, ruffling Thorne's hair. "What if I fail?"

The word was bitter as it left his lips. Failure wasn't abstract to him. It had a face.

Or a fist.

"Then you rise again. Don't allow your fear of failure to define you. Use it to drive you forward."

Thorne's fist unclenched slightly, though the tremor of tension remained. "My anger will destroy me."

"It won't. Ignitus chose you because you have the strength to control it. Trust yourself and trust him. He's no ordinary Primal."

"I gathered that," Thorne grumbled. A shadow of a smirk lifted the corner of his mouth.

Silas chuckled, easy and warm. "You're a good kid." He wrapped his arm around Thorne's shoulder and gave him a light squeeze. "You'll figure it out, and when you do, you'll be glad you did."

Thorne leaned back, soaking in the soft hues of the horizon. The crisp scent of pine and damp earth drifted over him, grounding his thoughts.

For the first time since the Trials, a thread of clarity surfaced—frayed, but real.

Thorne stood at the window as a shield of ice erupted from Gisela's hands, but it wasn't quite large enough.

Silas was outside with her, kneeling in the dirt as he tried to salvage the damaged crops one last time. Each attempt was as futile as the last.

Thorne's eyes were back on Gisela, noting the strain in her shoulders, the tremor in her hands as she practiced. Part of him wanted to go out there with her and do the same. But he was only beginning to understand this new part of himself—or Ignitus, now inseparable from him. He wasn't sure how to come to terms with it after the awakening.

"Concentrate," he heard Silas call out. "Allow your body to feel the ice building from the tips of your toes to your hands."

Gisela's chest rose and she extended her hands, summoning a massive block of ice that shot out with shocking force. It tumbled, soaring straight off the cliff. She turned to Silas, her eyes wide. "Oops."

Silas laughed heartily. "Hope nothing was down there."

Gisela hurried to the ledge and peered down, then walked back and sank beside Silas with a slump. "Are your powers working at all?"

Silas shook his head, brushing the dirt from his hands. "They are, but creating life, even in plant form, demands something more—"

Thorne swung the front door open and stood in the doorway, arms crossed, one foot resting casually on the frame. Despite the tension between him and Gisela, her face softened. His chest clenched unexpectedly. That split-second look meant everything.

Silas looked back and forth between them and stood up with a loud clap of his hands. "Let's practice together, shall we?" he declared.

"What?" Gisela stammered.

"If we're heading to Rockridge, we need to get you guys used to your new bodies. You and Thorne—face each other."

Warmth crept up Thorne's neck, and it wasn't from Ignitus. They still hadn't spoken since they were in the cave. His mind inevitably circled back to her, rehearsing words he was afraid to say. One wrong word, one wrong glance, and the fragile balance between them could snap.

"I don't think this is a good idea," Thorne said. "I haven't tried anything yet."

"That's okay," Silas said. "Try conjuring a small ball of fire in your hand. And I mean small, Thorne. For all our sakes."

Thorne hesitated as Ignitus stirred within him. He focused, willing the black fire to obey, but at first it sputtered, weak and uneven. His teeth ground. He steadied his hands, coaxing the fire until a small ball danced between his fingers.

He waited for the heat to burn him, but it only hummed against his skin, harmless.

It moved through his veins, answering a hunger he hadn't known was there. The weight in his chest, which had pressed like lead all morning, was lighter now.

His eyes shimmered, and a slight smile tugged at his lips.

Gisela scoffed.

"Now, Gisela, make a wall of ice," Silas prompted. "Keep it steady now and imagine it as a shield."

Gisela held out her hands. Her eyes were focused, reining in the icy energy as it slowly released from her fingers. A thick wall of ice formed in front of her, its surface gleaming and solidifying.

She stood on the other side, like a figure through a fogged mirror. He stared at her, his lips slightly parted.

Silas nodded. "Good, good. You see this wall between you two?"

Thorne knew exactly where he was going with this.

Gisela flipped her hair with clear irritation. She narrowed her eyes to glare at Silas.

"Thorne, melt it down," Silas said.

Thorne crossed his arms and tilted his head. "You want me to just—?"

"Do it," Silas interrupted, his tone leaving no room for argument.

Thorne shook his head. "I don't want to hurt her, Silas."

"Oh? You don't?" Gisela snapped.

Thorne stiffened at her tone and looked away.

"You won't," Silas said.

Ignitus whispered into Thorne's mind, *"You will not cause her physical harm. Not ever."*

Thorne startled at Ignitus's voice but steadied himself. He lifted his hands, and the air shimmered with heat. Black flames sputtered from his fingers until he clenched his hand shut, crushing the sparks in his palm.

He grunted, shaking his head.

"Try again," Silas said. "Slow and controlled."

Thorne's eyes narrowed. He opened his hands deliberately this time. Ignitus hummed through him, a steady pulse of heat and presence, and with it came a bigger slice of clarity. His hand no longer shook, and the fire bent to his will. The flames swirled, wrapping around the ice shield in a fierce but gentle bind. Moisture beaded on the surface, trickling down.

Gisela studied his unusual dark flames.

Within moments he could see her through the ice. She stood there, unharmed, her ice shield becoming a puddle on the ground. They locked eyes and everything else receded. Nothing existed but her, the girl he had known for years. The girl with quiet defiance in her gaze.

Gisela blinked and then walked to Silas's front door, closing it behind her.

Thorne hesitated, his foot hovering before taking a step forward.

Silas cleared his throat to catch his attention and nodded toward the door.

Thorne squared his shoulders, let the steady pulse of Ignitus anchor him, and followed her into the house.

Crag appeared next to Silas, a bemused look on his face. "That was quite meddlesome of you."

"They'll thank me for it eventually," Silas said with a grin.

The heat still hummed in Thorne's palms as he approached the bedroom door. His fingers met the handle, icy against his skin. He jerked his hand back and laughed, pressing his forehead against the door. "Freckles . . . did you freeze the door handle?" His voice was a mix of mockery and playfulness.

No answer.

"Don't worry," he said. "I can fix that." He held out his hand, focusing as heat left his palm and melted the ice. Water dripped from the handle, creating a small puddle on the wooden floor.

He opened the door and Gisela stood there, her eyes flashing with irritation.

"Oh, now you want to talk?" she said.

He stretched his neck out and walked into the room. "That's fair. I get it."

"Now that you got a little taste of your power, you feel better?" Gisela's stance was rigid, hand on her hip. "You shut me out after the hardest experience of our lives. I know you saw some horrible things, Thorne, but I suffered too."

She took a step towards the door.

"Please. Listen."

Gisela waved her hand, signaling him to start talking.

Thorne walked over to the bed and settled onto the edge, elbows digging into his knees as he stared at the floor.

"I was angry and confused," he began, then faltered.

Gisela interjected, "And I was scared and lonely."

Thorne's face tightened. "I'm sorry. I—" he stopped, choking on his words.

Gisela tapped her foot, eyes locked on him.

"I'm not used to talking about my—" Thorne forced himself to stand, then pushed the words out. "I felt humiliated. Embarrassed."

"Embarrassed? About what?"

"That I almost got you killed. That you had to save me. That . . . I died and you watched." His words tumbled out, raw and vulnerable. "I spent years learning not to feel. And then *you* came along."

Gisela's face softened . . . then hardened. "What do you think I am? Some monster who would laugh at you? Ridicule you? That was *you*, remember?"

She moved to leave again, but Thorne crossed the room and pressed his hand against the door.

She crossed her arms and glared at him.

"Let me leave. You're playing with fire," she warned.

He leaned in, the scent of smoke clinging to him. "I *am* fire," he said. "And it turns out, I don't hate it."

Her face flushed as she turned her head away.

He lifted her chin with a single finger, guiding her face back to his.

For a moment, neither of them moved.

His eyes dipped to her mouth and stayed there.

Gisela shivered under his touch, drew a shaky breath, and twisted away again. "I forgive you, Thorne," she said, before stepping out of the room.

Thorne slowed when he found Gisela kneeling outside that evening, surrounded by gathered twigs. She struck the flint against the steel, the sparks catching but quickly dying out. Her brow furrowed as she blew on the pile of kindling, trying to coax life into the small flames. The twigs smoked but remained stubbornly cold.

She wiped a bead of sweat off her forehead, her fingers stained with ash from her failed attempts. Striking the flint harder, her face flushed, and she coughed as smoke curled around her.

Thorne approached, the ash smeared across her forehead drawing a smile as he sat beside her.

"You know, I could do this for you," Thorne said. "Fire in my hands, flames at your disposal."

She pursed her lips. "I want to learn still. What if you're not around to help?"

"I'm not going anywhere."

He watched as she swallowed hard.

"I'm going to get this," she declared.

"Can I help?" he asked, scooting closer.

"I suppose."

He crouched beside her, guiding her hands with a gentle touch. After a few adjustments, the kindling caught fire.

Gisela's face lit up with a triumphant smile as the flames danced to life.

Thorne flicked his hand, and a black flame joined the orange ones.

Gisela grinned and thrust her hand out, sending out a burst of frost to snuff it all.

His expression flattened.

"Just reminding you," she said. "I can put you out whenever I want." She giggled, light and familiar.

He held the sound of her laughter close, committing it to memory. It loosened something inside him, and he understood then how easily he could be undone by her.

And how little he wanted to stop it.

"Let me get the last one," Thorne said.

"The cook gets the final bite," Silas retorted.

Gisela snatched the last Crumble Cluster from the plate, her cheeks puffed as she chewed.

Both Thorne and Silas narrowed their eyes at her.

"What?" she said around the bite. "I was tired of you two bickering."

Thorne smiled and Silas nudged him playfully.

"Did you figure out how to start a fire, Gisela?" Silas asked, taking a sip of his drink.

"I think so."

"Good. But don't you think enough things are smoldering around here already?" Silas's gaze flicked between her and Thorne, a grin tugging at the corners of his mouth.

Gisela widened her eyes, but a small smile slipped past her lips.

Something warm bloomed deep in Thorne's chest.

Gisela turned toward Eira. "How do you and Ignitus know each other?"

Thorne's hand froze mid-grip on his glass as Eira and Ignitus exchanged a quick glance. "Our previous Mystics were Soulbound," Eira said.

"Previous Mystics?" he asked, lowering his cup.

Eira looked to Ignitus, who remained silent.

Silas rested his hand thoughtfully on his cheek, waiting for them to explain.

"We were bound to them for decades. Thousands of years ago," Eira said.

"Thousands?!" Gisela asked, leaning forward.

Ignitus's voice was firm. "We are eternal. We have been here since the birth of these lands by the gods."

"What happened to them?" Thorne asked.

Eira and Ignitus shared a soft, nostalgic smile. "They died of old age. Together," Eira said.

The table fell quiet.

"Soulbound?" Gisela's voice was quiet. "What does that mean exactly?"

"It is a deep bond of the mind and body," Eira said. "It is not something to take lightly. The connection is only broken by death. When it snaps into place, it slowly changes the very essence of both Mystics."

Thorne's pulse ticked a little faster. He searched Gisela's face, wondering if the mere idea of a tether made her want to run.

Her fingers found the pulse at her neck.

He held his breath, watching her, waiting for her next words.

"Do they get a choice?" she asked.

"It isn't forced," Ignitus said. "It's a choice. It happens when two Mystics are in tune, their minds and bodies aligned. Some bonds take years to form. Some, in rare instances, come suddenly. But if the bond forms, it is because they both let it."

Thorne lay awake in bed, next to Gisela, listening to the soft rhythm of her breathing. Amidst the storm in his mind, it was a small comfort, an anchor keeping him grounded. He stared at the ceiling, grappling with the knowledge they had gained from Eira and Ignitus.

The conversation looped through his mind. He recalled the shift in Gisela's demeanor, the subtle change in her expression when she learned about the bond. He wondered if she felt what he did, or if the weight of the revelation burdened her.

Thorne stared at Gisela, her face serene in sleep.

He imagined what dreams might be playing in her mind—if she, too, saw ice and fire, as he had every night since their awakening. Brushing a strand of hair from her face, he had an overwhelming urge to protect her.

He had always been drawn to her. Stolen glances in the village classroom became subtle maneuvers to be near her, lingering by the same market stall, taking longer paths just to cross hers.

He didn't fully understand then that every cold word, every sneer, was his own warped way of masking what he truly felt. He had always worn a mask—nonchalance, confidence, sometimes cruelty—sculpted by his father.

Thorne whispered into his own mind. *"Ignitus?"*

A low hum echoed back.

He wanted to ask the relentless question that had burned holes in his mind, the one he wondered why no one else had asked yet. *"Our flames . . . why are they dark?"*

Silence lingered before Ignitus's voice cut through with a deep, steady calm.

"You are descended from evil."

"And you?" Thorne asked. *"Are you evil?"*

"I am not," Ignitus replied. *"I am only the reflection of what you inherit. The shadows of your lineage are not mine, though I bear their mark with you."*

Thorne fell silent, the gravity of Ignitus's words sinking in. Cillian's cruel, fleeting approval felt even more sinister now.

But Thorne wasn't surprised.

It was a relief to learn that the true source of evil in his blood did not come from Ignitus, as he'd feared, but from his own father.

"Go to sleep, Thorne. A challenging journey lies ahead."

Chapter Fifteen

Rounding a bend in the mountain, the rocky trail stretched ahead, twisting and narrowing between jagged cliffs.

Thorne wiped sweat from his brow, glaring at the deep descent below.

Gisela adjusted her pack with a grin. "You look like you've been caught in a blacksmith's forge. Are you going to make it?"

Thorne raised his brow. "That depends. Are you going to blow some frost my way?" A wink and a smirk followed his words.

Despite the chill in her veins, heat rose to her cheeks.

Eira's voice whispered in her mind, *"We can certainly deliver that. Hold out your hand."*

Gisela could hear her mischievous tone as she followed Eira's instruction, forming a swirling ball of frost in her palm. She blew, sending it toward Thorne's face, coating his eyebrows and the short beard he had grown over the past couple weeks with a layer of ice.

Silas glanced over, and a full-bellied laugh echoed around them. "Care to send some my way too?"

Gisela happily obliged.

Silas let out a satisfied breath, brushing frost from his beard. "Easy now," he said. "This path gets mean on the way down."

The rest of the descent took another hour. There was a newfound strength in her body that wasn't there when she had ascended that same mountain not so long ago.

The rocky heights gave way to a field of scattered boulders at the base. Overhead, a flock of birds broke from the clouds, flying hard for the mountain. Gisela, Thorne, and Silas peered up at them, noting their strange, unnatural formation.

One of the birds abruptly veered away from the group, its head swiveling in their direction. Diving at an alarming speed, a horrific caw tore from its beak. Before it crashed into Gisela, Thorne moved swiftly in front of her, projecting a blast of flames.

The roar of his fire swallowed the bird's cry.

The bird disintegrated, leaving nothing but scattered ash on the ground.

Gisela blinked at Thorne's back, heat still rippling through the air.

Smoke lingered, and a tense silence followed as the rest of the flock disappeared out of view.

"Did you see its eyes?" Silas asked.

Thorne and Gisela shared a look.

Crag appeared next to Silas. "Mystralos will continue to decline if we don't get the Life Stones back into the pedestals."

"The King doesn't even care, does he?" Gisela shook her head.

"He must be after something. Some advantage or power he believes will come from all of this," Silas said.

Muffled voices drifted toward them through the rustling leaves and Crag pressed his palms to the ground, raising a boulder to hide them.

The trio huddled in silence as the group approached. From behind the boulder, they watched members of the King's guard heading toward the mountain.

The guards dismounted their horses, tethering them to a nearby tree before beginning their ascent.

"Trail's too damn narrow," one guard said. "Last thing I need is my horse tumbling off that cliff."

"And you along with it," another said, laughing.

Gisela looked up at Thorne, her expression tense. "The guards . . . from the letter your father received?"

Thorne nodded as he processed her words. "I'd bet they're going to the cave. Stay here, Freckles," he said, throwing a smirk over his shoulder as he followed the men.

"Don't!" Gisela demanded through clenched teeth.

Silas put a gentle hand on her shoulder. "Let him go. We're right down here. He might overhear something of value."

Gisela hesitated, her frustration simmering beneath the surface. Then, a thought struck her. "I think we *all* just got something of value," she said as her gaze flicked to the tied-up horses. Mischief sparked in her eyes and Silas caught it instantly. His grin mirrored her own.

Thorne kept his footing as quiet as possible, avoiding crunching leaves and loose rocks. He crept from tree to tree like a shadow, muscles coiled, senses straining.

"Patrollin' a cave no one even knows about. What a joke," one guard muttered, kicking at a loose rock.

"Beats the villages. At least we get a view," another said.

"I swear, ever since Zaro showed up, everything's . . . off," a third guard said, scratching his head. "Weird posts lately. He's got his own agenda with all this. I don't trust him."

The first snorted. "Ravenor's too stupid to see it."

"Power-hungry more like it."

"And that potion they're usin' on the Mystics now?" The first guard shivered. "Fuckin' scary, man."

"Oh, I've heard the screams from Zaro's lab."

"The executions were mercy."

They all chuckled, jumping over a fallen tree.

"It's all taking too long. Whole realm's gonna be in shit soon. Got family in Thunderpeak, and it's gettin' bad over there," the first guard muttered.

"You hear about the scribes . . ." the second guard's voice trailed off.

Thorne pressed himself closer to the tree, chest tight.

Elysande.

The thought of her being caught up in whatever the King and this Zaro person were planning made his stomach knot.

When Thorne reached the base of the mountain, Gisela and Silas were mounted on the guards' horses, looking far too pleased with their theft.

"Our journey just got a little easier," Gisela said, tossing her hair back playfully. Noticing Thorne's grave expression, her smile melted away. "Did you hear something?"

Thorne sighed, shoulders heavy. He approached the third horse, patting its side before swinging himself up.

"They're patrolling the cave like we thought." He swallowed, running a hand over his face. "But they said someone named Zaro is close to the King. And Mystics . . . they're using some sort of potion on them. Sounds like it's making them suffer."

Silas dropped the reins.

Thorne's face softened at Gisela. "And something's going on with the scribes."

The blood drained from her face. "Elysande."

Thorne shook his head. "Your father won't let anything happen to her."

"No . . . she was summoned . . . she—"

The wrinkles around Silas's eyes deepened as he grabbed the reins of his horse. "We move fast. Let's get to Rockridge. Then we'll figure out the rest."

They set off on their new mounts, the sound of hooves thudding against dirt.

Gisela's thoughts spiraled. The potion was barbaric, and involving the scribes meant targeting knowledge itself. They were keepers of truth, not warriors or threats. Without them, the history of Mystralos would become a twist of rumor and lies, rewritten by whoever held the crown. Every attempt at a deep breath was stifled by a phantom grip closing around her ribs.

King Ravenor was seizing more power and erasing the past.

Elysande's gentle laugh echoed in her memory. Her ink-stained fingers. Her patience. Ely had never hurt anyone. She didn't deserve to be dragged into the King's plans.

The day passed as they rode, the landscape gradually shifting beneath them.

Gisela's grip on the reins tightened until her knuckles ached, the fire in her thighs spreading into a stiff, dull throb along her back.

Ahead, the rugged outline of Rockridge's village emerged. The smell of smoke and stone filled her nose.

Gisela stole a glance at Thorne, deep in thought, his eyes sweeping over the horizon.

He turned his head, his eyes steady and unblinking before his mouth curved into a slow, sly smile.

Her breath hitched, toes curling against the soles of her boots.

The King's guards flooded the entrance to Rockridge. They typically didn't visit the villages unless there was an inspection. It didn't make sense. The last inspection was only a month ago.

Silas hesitated and pulled back on the reins. "That's strange."

"The guards did say they were patrolling villages now," Thorne said.

Gisela squinted through the haze of the commotion. They were loading two young villagers into a carriage, their faces frozen with fright.

"Did they do another check?" she asked.

Silas shook his head, his expression grim. "I know a better way in."

He led them to a secluded spot where the rugged terrain met a line of trees. Silas dismounted and gestured for them to do the same.

Crag crouched and slammed his hands onto the ground. A low rumble vibrated through the earth as it shifted, forming a narrow tunnel that led beneath the village's perimeter. The earth parted in a dark, winding passage.

Gisela stared in awe. Then, her intrigued smile quickly faded. "Any chance you can make that passage wider, Crag?"

"I am afraid not. This was risky enough."

Gisela nodded as Thorne moved in front of her, the tunnel forcing them into single file.

"I've got you," he murmured, swinging his hand back until she found it.

She exhaled, a small measure of reassurance settling as their fingers laced.

"This should take us directly under the village," Silas said. "It'll be safer than trying to get past the guards."

Cool, damp air greeted them as they moved forward. The soft glow of the Primals illuminated their path—save for Ignitus, whose dark flames did little to lighten the tunnel's shadows.

"You alright?" Thorne whispered to Gisela.

She nodded, squeezing his hand. His thumb brushed over her knuckles, and the frantic rhythm of her heart steadied.

He glanced back over his shoulder.

She searched his eyes, admiring the unexpected gray within them, before her attention drifted to his mouth. It was a cruel sort of perfection—the kind that made her forget they were hiding in the dirt beneath a village.

They stopped beneath a large grate in the ceiling.

"Where does this lead to?" Thorne asked.

Silas smiled. "The tavern."

CHAPTER SIXTEEN

The tavern's weathered frame blended with Rockridge's rugged charm, stone and timber darkened by years of smoke and rain. Men lounged on the steps outside, laughing loudly, their words slurred, mugs clinking as they swayed where they sat.

One called to another, "Haven't had a fish shipment from the east in a week. Guess we'll be rationin' what we got!"

"We won't be sendin' much ore either. Can't give em' what we don't have."

A third man, leaning back on the steps, squinted at Gisela. "Well, well . . . looks like we finally got some fresh meat. Bet that chest ain't the only thing worth oglin'."

"Heh, I'd trade all our fish shipments for a night with her, no lie," said the other.

Thorne's jaw clenched, his entire body coiled, ready to strike. Without a word, he closed the distance in one smooth motion. His hands shot out, gripping the man by the collar, lifting him slightly off his feet.

The laughter died on his lips.

"Careful," Thorne murmured, voice low and dangerous. "You like those eyes of yours? For oglin'," he mocked. "I'll pluck them out of your godsdamned—"

"Now, now, that's no way to speak to a lady," Silas said to the men, pulling Thorne back.

Thorne's eyes stayed narrowed on the man before he released his grip, letting him stumble back.

"Silas Donolo! I didn't know that was you," the man stammered, eyes wide in shame.

Silas shook his head. "Better eat some barley to soak up that ale, Ed. And mind your tongue."

Ed nodded quickly. "Apologies . . . my lady."

Gisela said nothing to the man, not sparing him so much as a glance.

Thorne's attention settled on her, soft enough to reassure her.

She took his arm and guided him inside.

Heat and clamor rushed over her. The air was thick with the smell of roasted meat and the sour-sweet sting of ale. The low murmur of conversation and occasional bursts of laughter filled the room. After days of quiet and watchful travel, the noise and warmth were unreal, a glimpse into life that had no idea the rest of the world was breaking.

Thorne led her through the crush of bodies to a table tucked near the back.

"Finally, some proper tavern ale," Silas said.

As Gisela relaxed in her seat, Thorne remained tense.

"You okay?"

A low hum escaped him, though his eyes darted around the room.

At a table nearby, a woman sat with her brown hood pulled low, obscuring her face in shadow. Despite the covering, the woman's attention snagged on their table.

Gisela didn't need to confirm it with a look. She could feel the prickle of those hidden eyes tracking her every move. She forced her thoughts back to the menu. "I want an order of the Crumble Clu—"

"Silas!" A vibrant voice sliced through the tavern's roar. A beautiful barkeeper sauntered over to their table, her steps confident and graceful as she swung her hips. She dropped her hands onto Silas's shoulders and leaned in, pressing a kiss to his cheek. Her red hair spilled over him like a silk curtain. The low-cut line of her bodice struggled to contain her. "How long has it been now?"

"About a year," Silas replied. "Have you seen Marina?"

"Oh, no. She left again—was here for a short while but moved to Aquamere. I figured you would've known," the woman replied, her tone casual but edged with gossip.

Silas's shoulders tensed, and his features fell. "Ale, please, Sabrina."

"O' course. And what about you two?" Sabrina's gaze shifted to Thorne. She fluttered her eyelashes and leaned closer. "Aren't you handsome," she purred.

Thorne remained unmoved, his expression stoic.

Gisela shifted uncomfortably at the bold approach.

"Ale as well," Thorne said flatly.

Sabrina glanced at Gisela. "And you?" she asked, her voice lower than before.

"Ale," Gisela replied. She was so caught off guard that she didn't even order her Crumble Clusters.

Sabrina shot a quick, disappointed look before turning back to Thorne. "If you change your mind, I'll be in room two tonight."

Thorne reached out, sliding his hand along Gisela's thigh. He found her hand and laced their fingers together, his gaze never leaving Sabrina's.

She lingered a moment longer before striding away, her steps heavy on the wooden floor.

"She's quite forward, that one," Silas said. "Rockridge is all a bit . . . blunt."

Gisela barely registered the comment; her attention was drawn to the woman at the adjacent table.

She was watching them intently, eyes moving between each of them.

Gisela tilted her head at her, trying to make out any recognizable features beneath the hood.

Over drained mugs of ale and the comfort of a warm meal, they mapped out their next steps.

"Do you want to find Marina?" Gisela asked, leaning back in her chair.

"I do," Silas said, voice low. "I need to make sure she's safe, especially now that they're taking Mystics from the villages."

A fierce urge to return to Frosthaven gnawed at her, rivaled by the anxiousness in her gut. Thoughts of her family and Elysande circled her mind, leaving a trail of unanswered questions that only deepened her restlessness.

As the tavern thinned out and yawns became frequent, Silas stood to secure them rooms to sleep in for the night. He left, and the mysterious woman rose from her seat and dropped herself into Silas's vacated spot.

Gisela and Thorne instinctively scooted back.

The woman pulled back her hood.

"Ely!" Gisela's voice rang.

"Hush, child," Elysande whispered. "I'm not safe here. I'm not safe anywhere anymore. No one can know who I am."

Thorne leaned on his elbows over the table.

Ely glanced at him, before she turned back to Gisela with a questioning look.

"It's a long story," Gisela said.

Ely smiled with a twinkle, and a question, in her eye.

"No, no, we're just . . ." Gisela stammered, looking over to Thorne.

He leaned back, crossing his arms over his chest. His black tunic stretched across his biceps. Gisela's attention lingered on his arms, noting the muscles and veins as he moved.

Thorne raised a brow.

Gisela's face flushed a deep red before returning her gaze to Elysande.

Elysande gave a knowing glance and shot a warning look at Thorne, as if to say, *if you hurt her, you die.*

Thorne met her stare with a calm but resolute expression. "Never," he said, acknowledging the warning without flinching.

"What are you doing here?" Gisela whispered, reaching out to touch Elysande's arm.

"I came to retrieve ancient scrolls from the scribe here, Ellis. But he's gone," her voice heavy with sorrow. "They killed him."

The hair on Gisela's arms stood on end. "Then why are you still here? They could find you."

"Better that they believe the scribe here is gone than to find me in Frosthaven. Your father has done all he can to protect me and the village, but it isn't enough."

"What do you mean?"

"The villagers are angry. It's much worse there than here. Animals are coming in from the forest and attacking, food is becoming scarce. A wave of evil is spreading from the north."

Her face paled as she rushed to ask, "What about Noah, Vivi? My mother?"

"They're all safe. Tristan, though, was among those attacked. He's been in the care of your mother. He will survive, but he may never use his right arm again."

A cold jolt of shock left her breathless and still. Her anger with Tristan was a living thing, but she would never wish him harm.

Thorne let out a light scoff, earning a sharp scowl from Gisela.

"It's not safe for you here either," Elysande said, her hand resting on Gisela's.

"Why do you say that?"

A soft smile lifted Elysande's lips. "I've always known, child."

"I don't know what you're talking about."

Ely brushed a lock of hair from Gisela's ear.

Gisela jerked away, her heart hammering against her ribs, the sound of it filling her head.

Ely didn't pull back. Instead, she rested a steady hand on her shoulder. "It's okay. You've completed the Trials?"

It didn't quite sound like a question.

Too afraid to give the truth voice, Gisela simply nodded.

Ely's smile widened, warm and knowing.

Under the table, Gisela formed a tiny snowflake in her palm and sent it into Ely's hand. A faint light shone in Ely's gaze as she closed her hand around the frost. She held the tiny flake until it turned to water in her palm. "I'm so proud of you, Gisela."

Ely glanced at Thorne. He extended his hand, black flames twisting and curling like ink in water around his fingers.

She pressed a hand to her chest, a gasp catching in her throat. Suspicion hardened her features, then faded.

Thorne missed the shift, but Gisela caught the way her mask slipped.

"Who is that man with you?" Ely asked, chin tilting toward Silas at the counter.

"That's Silas. He has taken good care of us," Gisela said.

Ely's posture relaxed, the tension bleeding out of her. "Good. But please, do not linger here."

"What were you looking for exactly? Before you found out Ellis was gone?"

"A certain scroll from decades ago. But they've taken everything. I have suspicions about the King's intent."

Thorne and Gisela went quiet.

Elysande sighed. "Remember the day of the inspection? I spoke of a prophecy."

"You did. But you wouldn't tell me then."

"I believe that Ravenor thinks that if he unites the Stones, he will—"

"Wrapping up here?" Sabrina's voice cut in. She draped a hand on Thorne's shoulder.

Under the table, Gisela gripped the edge of her chair until her knuckles turned white.

"Allow me to show you to your room?"

"No, I think we'll find it on our own, thanks," Thorne replied, and a sharp flick of his shoulder sent her hand into empty air.

Elysande caught Gisela's eye and winked before rising. As she stood, she squeezed Gisela's hand, the rough edge of a parchment scrap sliding into her palm.

The dry texture grazed her skin before she swept it into her pocket.

A knot formed in her stomach, a cold pang of dread. She was reluctant to let Ely leave her sight.

"Be vigilant and wise, you two. Your courage will see you through."

Thorne and Gisela entered their room upstairs in the tavern. The musky smell had her wrinkling her nose. A single candle flickered on the wooden nightstand, its weak light barely reaching the corners. Beyond it, the room lay sparsely furnished, with little more than the essentials and a narrow bed at its center.

"One bed again," Gisela said, staring into the room.

"I can crawl into bed with Silas. I'm sure he wouldn't mind," Thorne said sarcastically.

She rolled her eyes. "That's not what I'm saying."

"Then what are you saying?"

"Nothing. An observation, is all." Gisela tossed her bag aside and collapsed onto the bed with a sigh. "Oh, I know. You could go to room two. I'm sure Sabrina would love to have your company."

Thorne's expression darkened. He stepped closer, the dim candlelight flickering over his face.

Gisela was suddenly aware of how vulnerable she looked lying there. She sat up.

He extended a hand toward her face, stopping just short of touching her. "Do you actually think I want anything to do with her?" His voice was low, rough. "Or anyone else?"

Gisela hesitated, looking away. "Thorne, I didn't mean—"

"Look at me," he said, not a command, but a plea.

She did.

His hand found her chin then, gently tilting her gaze up.

"I know the kind of man people think I am."

She forgot how to breathe, her focus solely on his words and his calloused fingers on her chin.

"And I know why you wouldn't want that," he continued. "Why you shouldn't."

His eyes didn't waver from hers. "But I don't care what they think they know. I just want *you* to know me," he said, his thumb shifting across her jawline. "I don't want anyone else. Not Sabrina, not Ruby, not anyone. Only you."

Gisela held herself perfectly still, fearing any movement would shatter the fragile confession. She took a shallow breath. "Thorne . . ."

"I know you feel it too," he murmured. "The dreams after the awakening. The chill down your spine. The burn down mine. The awareness of each other. It's always been there."

Gisela swallowed hard, tears prickling her eyes. She *had* felt it—the pull of a tide she couldn't fight, flooding her veins whenever he was near.

He let his hand fall. "If you don't feel it, if you don't want it," he said. "Tell me."

Every instinct told her to protect herself. Another part of her refused to let him go.

"I do," she said, her voice barely a whisper. "I feel it too. But it scares me."

"I don't want you to be scared of me."

"I'm not scared of you," she said, gathering air that trembled in her chest. "I'm afraid of losing you."

As the words slipped out, she wished she could take them back. Not because they weren't true, because they were. That was what terrified her the most. This was Thorne Alderose. He was the boy she once avoided, the one who made trouble everywhere he went. But now, she feared he was the man she couldn't be apart from.

He didn't move at first, as if giving her time to change her mind. When she didn't pull away—when her hand gripped his shirt instead—he exhaled.

Only then did he climb onto the bed, guiding her back beneath him. His hand slid through her hair and grasped the back of her head.

She drew a sharp breath as he lowered his body over hers. The last of the air between them vanished as she arched into him.

Thorne searched her eyes. "Being with you . . . it makes me feel like I'm finally where I'm supposed to be." He swallowed hard. "You make me want to be a better man, Gisela. But I—I don't know if there's anything left to build from." He drew a slow breath. "I care about you more than I've ever cared about anyone. It's as simple and as complicated as that. Every part of me is drawn to you." His lips brushed her ear, sending a shiver through her body.

She reached her hand to the back of his head and stroked her fingers through the soft black strands.

He groaned, closing his eyes, savoring the touch. He pressed his forehead lightly against hers. Their noses barely grazed. They opened their eyes together, like two people lost in the same dark room, hands outstretched, suddenly colliding with the light.

And realizing they were never alone in it.

The world outside vanished, and there was only them.

"You're beautiful." He swept his lips against hers, only the slightest touch, waiting for her to close the distance between them.

She pressed her lips to his, softly at first, then the subtle chill of her touch mingled with the heat of his. A current of energy flowed between them.

His hands roamed her body, studying every dip and curve.

She tugged his tunic off and let it fall to the ground. Her fingers outlined every ripple of his muscles, feeling the heat radiating from his skin.

He lifted her tunic over her head and tossed it aside, her chest bare for him to see.

She instinctively covered herself.

Thorne caught her wrists and guided them above her head. "No," he said. "Don't hide from me. You're perfect."

He leaned closer, kissing her collarbone before trailing up her neck.

She drew in a breath, arching, responding to his touch.

The sudden rap of knuckles against wood shattered it all.

Thorne stilled over her, their breaths tangled, neither of them willing to be the first to pull away.

The knocking continued and he cursed softly under his breath and pushed back.

They reached for their discarded clothes, the air between them gone cold.

"Gisela? Thorne?" Silas's voice called out from the hallway.

"Uh, yeah, just a minute," Thorne stammered as he dressed. He ran a hand through his disheveled hair, opening the door to see Silas's eyes widen.

The awkward silence stretched, and Silas averted his gaze.

"We have to go. Now."

Chapter Seventeen

Thorne secured his sword to his back in a swift motion. His breath was still uneven as he looked at Silas. "What happened?"

"Someone noticed the guards' horses. They're looking for a group of three that arrived here today. Apparently, someone gave our description and tipped them off."

"How do you know this?" Gisela asked. "Weren't you asleep?"

"I overheard them talking right outside my window. Crag could hear every word. There's a man, asking for you by name, Thorne."

The commotion from downstairs grew louder, boots stomping and angry voices echoing through the tavern.

Thorne stilled. "Why are they after me?"

"Less wondering, more running. Grab your things," Silas urged. "We're going out the window." He led them to the small window at the far end of the room. He threw it open and peered down, assessing the distance to the ground below. "It's a bit of a drop," he said. "But we have no choice."

The uproar from the hallway intensified as doors rattled under pounding fists.

Silas slipped through the window first, expertly lowering himself to the ledge before dropping down to the ground below.

Thorne followed, making the descent look effortless.

Gisela climbed onto the windowsill.

Thorne stood below with his arms outstretched, ready to catch her as she made the jump.

"Jump, Gisela," he called, his eyes focused on hers. "I've got you."

"This jump is child's play," she said. Gisela glanced back at the bed they shared only minutes ago. The door burst open behind her, and she let herself drop.

The three of them crouched low, moving swiftly through the shadows.

The sounds of the guards tearing through their room drifted through the night air. A man leaned out of the window, observing the ground below.

"It's my father," Thorne said, his voice tight.

"Let's keep moving," Gisela whispered.

They slipped into the night, heading back to the grate they used to enter the village.

As Thorne lifted it, Sabrina appeared a few feet away with her hand on her hip. She glanced over and her gaze sharpened.

Silas held his finger to his lips, eyes pleading for her to stay quiet.

Sabrina mirrored him, bringing her own finger to her lips, and then shouted, "Guards! They're over here!"

Panic surged through Thorne. He dropped the grate to the side. "Go! Now!"

Gisela jumped down first, Silas following.

Thorne took one last glance at Sabrina, whose expression was smug and triumphant.

"You'll regret that," he spat.

Sabrina's smirk only widened. "Not as much as you will, Thorne."

Then his father rounded the corner. "Thorne!" Cillian bellowed, his voice reverberating off the cold stone walls. "Son, wait!"

Thorne gave a short, humorless laugh. "Son? Since when do you call me that?"

Cillian's usual stern expression softened, strained with effort. "Your mother . . . she worries. You will return to Frosthaven."

His father had always wielded her like a sword to manipulate him. Thorne's expression hardened. "Oh, yes, because you suddenly give a shit about anyone but yourself. You're a changed man."

Cillian shifted uneasily, gripping the hilt of his sword. "I *am* a changed man. I'm captain of the guard now." He stood in the vibrant red uniform of the King's guard, the fabric crisp.

"He wants you close to him because you're his loyal lapdog," Thorne said. "You're a fool if you think the King cares for you or Mystralos."

Cillian laughed, dark and menacing. "The King knows what Mystics truly are. What they can give him. Their suffering will build his power, and when he's done . . . the realm will be cleansed of them once and for all."

"You have no idea what you're up against."

Cillian cocked his head, his nostrils flaring. "You dare threaten me? Be a man. Return to your mother and your betrothed."

"Ruby is not my betrothed. I'm with Gisela Valor," Thorne said.

Cillian's expression twisted with rage. "That wretched little bitch? You'd bind yourself to someone like her?"

"Don't you dare speak about her that way," Thorne shot back. "I'd sooner bind myself to her than ever call you father again." Every pain his father inflicted upon him, every lie he had ever fed him transformed into fury.

Thorne called Ignitus, who appeared behind him.

Cillian's mouth fell open, eyes wide with terror.

Thorne unleashed a burst of dark flames from his hands, striking Cillian with a force that sent him crashing to the ground.

Cillian's scream was pure pain and rage, a guttural sound that poured from him as he writhed on the floor, clutching the side of his face. Blackened burns marred his skin where the flames had struck. The air reeked of burned flesh, the surrounding stone walls shimmering with heat.

Thorne leapt down the grate, disappearing into the shadows below. His father's cries echoed after him, then faded into silence.

Gisela and Silas stood frozen, watching him.

The heat radiating from Thorne's skin slowly ebbed as he lifted his head. He reached for Gisela, his hand trembling when it found her.

The kiss he pressed to her lips was fierce, desperate—proof that something in the world was still good. And Gisela was good in every way he knew. She was all that made sense, all that felt safe, and he couldn't shake the thought that he didn't deserve her. But still, he couldn't let go.

Wouldn't.

Shouting and the thunderous pounding of boots flowed through the grate. With a powerful motion, Silas manipulated the earth. The ground trembled as stones and soil responded to his will. The hole above them closed and the muffled sounds from above became distant and faint, swallowed by the newly formed barrier.

"Let's move," Silas said, the corner of his mouth lifting.

Thorne's gaze lingered on Gisela, her wide eyes reflecting the heat and terror of the night. She was already moving toward him. Her hand closed around his arm, grip tight.

He saw the truth in her expression: fear, not of him, but *for* him.

He had publicly revealed himself.

As they exited the passage, the cool, fresh air of the night hit them once more.

"The nerve of that woman," Gisela said.

Silas's reply was somber. "I can't believe she did that."

"I can," Thorne said flatly.

Gisela turned to Silas. His face carried that familiar ache, the one he tried to hide.

"Let's go to Aquamere," she said. "For Marina."

Silas nodded. "If nothing else, I only need to see her. That means going through the Stone Rifts."

"I was really looking forward to having horses," Thorne grumbled.

Chapter Eighteen

The days of travel through the Stone Rifts were a labyrinth of craggy cliffs and towering boulders. Rocks jutted out like giant teeth, their sharp edges cutting into the night sky. Deep ravines and narrow chasms carved the land. The shadows stretched across the paths, forcing them to tread carefully.

A crisp breeze carried the scent of moss and soil. Each step sent a faint tremor through the earth, as if the land itself were breathing beneath them. Muscles ached and sleep was fleeting.

"We'll set up camp here," Thorne said, running his hand through his hair. "Gisela, you need rest."

"Says who, pretty boy? I'm doing just fine."

Thorne's mouth curled into a grin. "You think I'm pretty?"

She rolled her eyes, but her smile betrayed her.

Silas chuckled as he rummaged through his bag searching for the small tents. "I'm tired too. It's been a long day."

Gisela moved to help him. "How long until we reach Aquamere?"

"Probably two more days. One, if we stay on the trade route but it's probably not safe," Silas said, glancing at Thorne.

In their tent, Gisela rested her head against Thorne's chest, her arm draped across his waist. The warmth of his skin grounded her, but her mind wouldn't stop turning over everything that could go wrong.

"I'm worried," Gisela said.

"About what?" His fingers traced slow, gentle patterns on her back.

"They know you're a Mystic now. There's no going back from that."

He pressed a soft kiss to her temple. "I'll be safe in Aquamere. At least for a little while."

"And then what?"

"Then we'll have Marina. Four awakened Mystics. Whatever the King and that Zaro guy are planning, we have the power to stop it."

Gisela sat up, reaching into her bag for the piece of parchment Elysande had given her at the tavern. She unfolded it, scanning the familiar writing.

"What's that?" Thorne asked.

She glanced at him, then back to the page. It was a fragment torn from Elysande's book. She read it again. "A prophecy . . . I completely forgot about this." She handed it to him.

Thorne squinted at the words inked on the page, reading aloud:

> "Through veils of time, a Mystic King shall awaken,
> With fiery passion, the kingdom's fate is taken.
> When fire stands witness beneath the sun's churn,
> In the ember's glow, new paths shall burn."

Thorne looked over at Gisela. "I don't understand."

"Elysande alluded to this after the last inspection. She must've been searching for evidence in Rockridge. She handed this to me in the tavern."

Thorne shook his head. "A *Mystic* King though?"

"Yes. I think this prophecy is why King Thraxus started the executions."

"It was because of the Mystic in Thunderpeak. The one who lost control. An Elding."

"I think it was the perfect incident to justify his ruling . . . don't you?"

"You think he started them because of a threat to his throne?"

Gisela lifted a shoulder. "That's what it sounds like."

"But why is that relevant now? King Ravenor isn't a Mystic."

"You're right, he's not."

They sat in a comfortable silence, their thoughts racing as they tried to piece together the meaning of the old prophecy.

Thorne set the parchment aside. He tilted her chin to meet his gaze and softly kissed her lips. The kiss deepened, and heat pooled low in her stomach.

"As much as I'd like to continue where we left off, I think we need as much sleep as we can get," she whispered against his lips.

Thorne sighed. "Fine. But as soon as we get a room to ourselves . . ."

Gisela pursed her lips, a hint of mischief dancing in her eyes. "I don't think you'll do anything."

"What?"

"You heard me."

"Is that a challenge?" he asked, his voice low and teasing. He flipped her underneath him, pinning her wrists above her head. He leaned in, his breath warm against her neck, lightly teasing her senses.

A soft whimper escaped her lips.

"I wonder what other sounds I can coax out of you," he said.

A faint shuffle came from the other tent.

"He's still awake. We have to be quiet," Gisela said, giggling.

"We can't do quiet," Thorne said. "So, go to sleep, Freckles."

"You just won't let that nickname go, will you?" she said through a yawn.

"It's because I love them so much."

Thorne eased his weight off her and drew Gisela against his side, one arm settling around her. His fingers traced through her hair. She pressed closer, seeking the heat of his chest.

The prophecy, the King, the Stones—they could face all of that tomorrow. Tonight, they had each other.

Her mind slowed as she drifted toward sleep, but she could have sworn she heard him whisper, "And I love you even more."

Gisela woke up alone to the light of the morning sun. She blinked against the brightness and peeked her head out of the tent's opening, where Silas was already packing their gear.

She sighed, running her hands through her tangled hair, longing for a bath. As she braided it back, a familiar pulse of magic thrummed beneath her fingers.

Eira stirred inside her.

"Anyone hungry?" Thorne's deep voice cut through her thoughts.

She pushed her way out of the tent and stopped.

Thorne stood a few paces away with a boar slung over his shoulder. Its coarse fur glinted in the morning light.

"Nice job, Thorne," Silas said, wiping dirt off of his hands.

With a burst of flames, Thorne started a fire. Smoke curled up in lazy spirals.

Silas conjured fruit and vegetables from the ground to have with their breakfast.

"You're able to conjure food here but weren't able to on the mountain," Gisela observed.

Silas nodded. "Seems that way. But it feels weaker than it should be."

"None of the animals looked rabid while I hunted this morning, though. No white eyes," Thorne added, tossing a small branch into the fire.

"Were your parents Mystics?" Gisela asked, settling onto a moss-covered stone that Silas had grown for her.

"My mother. She was an Earthshaper too," he said, flexing his fingers absently.

Thorne took a bite of meat. "Any siblings?"

"A brother. My father was worried we would become Mystics. Luckily, I met Helena, and she helped me when I found my mark. My brother wasn't a Mystic, and he never knew I was. It's random, you know. Just because you have a Mystic parent doesn't mean you're guaranteed the gift." He paused, his gaze dropping to the fire. "I couldn't tell them. Knowing would've put them in danger. And they never had to worry about me dying the same way my mother did—at the hands of the Kingdom." He blinked, swallowing whatever emotion threatened to escape.

"I can't imagine having to worry about my parents that way," Gisela said.

Silas tilted his head. "One of your parents has to be a Mystic."

"I don't have lineage. Neither does Thorne."

Crag appeared next to Silas, arms crossed. "There is always lineage. It is in the blood," Crag said, firmly.

"Maybe I'm an anomaly."

"A grandmother? Grandfather?" Crag pressed.

"None."

"We have not been in close range to your parents, Gisela, so I am unsure. But I did not sense an awakened Primal in Thorne's father," Ignitus said, appearing next to Thorne.

"My father isn't a Mystic. He despises them. He would've never married my mother if she were one either," Thorne said pointedly. He adjusted the fire, eyes distant.

Silence fell and it wasn't the comfortable kind. Tension was thick, like a secret hung in the air that she wasn't privy to. Gisela had always been secure in who she was. A daughter. A sister. A friend. A healer. When she found the mark on her birthday, it hadn't changed who she was inside. It had shocked her, yes—a cruel mistake she once believed. But now, listening to the others, she realized she didn't know enough. She didn't know nearly enough about the world she was part of, or the powers that might shape it.

"What type of Mystic was Helena?" Gisela asked, breaking the silence.

"She was an Aquamancer. Marina is too," Silas said, chin high. "Helena named her, you know. An act of defiance, naming her after water. Something she did to shove it in the kingdom's face." A warm smile crossed his face, but there was a hint of pain in his eyes. "She was a feisty one. You would've loved her, Gisela. Marina is a lot like her mother." Silas's face sank as he said the words. "But I'm not sure she'll ever speak to me again."

"I'll talk to her," Gisela reassured. "Once she knows what's at stake, she'll join us."

"My knees aren't what they used to be," Silas said, swinging a leg over the ridge and landing on loose gravel.

Gisela landed beside him with far more grace than she felt.

Thorne hopped down last, the crunch of his boots loud in the stillness. "You're not even that old."

"In my forties and wise enough to know joints age faster when you spend weeks following the courtship of two people who swore they were 'just friends'."

Thorne blinked, and Gisela laughed.

"So," Silas continued, tone maddeningly casual, "how long?"

Gisela nearly tripped on a stone. "You mean how long we've known each other? Since we were kids."

"Mm." Silas adjusted the strap of his pack. "Right. *Known.*"

"Believe me, I couldn't stand the sight of him until—well . . ." Her gaze flicked to Thorne.

He stayed silent, a faint curl of a smile tugging at his lips.

Silas glanced back at him. "Not the same story for you, huh?"

"Well . . . I think I always—"

Silas raised a finger, cutting him off. "Voices."

Up ahead, muffled footsteps and murmurs reached them.

"They're off the trade route," Silas whispered, ducking into a narrow crevice between the rocks.

Thorne grasped Gisela's arm, guiding her into the shadowed opening.

It was hard to breathe but the feel of Thorne's hands running up and down her arms slowed her pulse.

". . . turn back before dusk," one guard's voice carried. "Lands unstable. I'm not staying for another rock avalanche."

Silas pressed his back to the stone, eyes wide.

Another guard spat. "If he burned Cillian that bad, you really wanna be the one dragging him home anyway?"

A low whistle answered. "Not me. He's probably long gone now. I say we turn back."

Gravel crunched as their footsteps faded.

Silas waited until they were out of sight before stepping out. "I don't know what's worse, being hunted, or a rock avalanche."

The mountain answered him with a sharp *crack*.

Silas spun first. "Move—"

Loose stones tumbled from the ridge above. A deep groan of shifting weight followed, and cold, absolute fear shot through Gisela's veins.

The slope was collapsing.

A boulder broke free, smashing into the path in a spray of dust and shards.

Gisela coughed, grit stinging her eyes.

Silas thrust his hands upward, the earth trembling in response, but the mass was too heavy. His knees buckled under the strain.

Crag appeared alongside him, pushing at smaller rocks as the cascade continued.

Thorne lunged to shield Gisela as she began to fall backward.

Dust filled the air, blurring her vision. Her hands shot out beneath his arms, fingers splaying. A rush of cold surged from her fingertips, obedient to her will.

Ice burst skyward, forming a thick, sturdy wall between their bodies and the shattered slope. Rocks pounded against it, but it held.

Thorne landed on top of her with his arms braced on both sides of her head. Neither of them moved, the world reduced to the roar of stones pelting ice.

Gisela blinked up at him, chest rising and falling with adrenaline.

Silas coughed through the settling dust. "By the Six."

She stared at her hands.

Eira appeared next to her, smiling. "Well controlled, Gisela."

Thorne's gaze lifted to the frozen barricade. "Impressive," he murmured.

Silas dusted himself off. "Looks like my knees won't be the death of me after all."

Thorne shot him a look, half amused, half exasperated.

Together, the three of them scrambled to their feet and pressed on. The echo of the avalanche faded behind them, leaving a foreboding sense that the land, and the gods who watched it, were far from pleased.

CHAPTER NINETEEN

Another day and night passed without incident, and after hours of navigating the rugged terrain, the ground finally leveled. Jagged cliffs and rocky outcrops gradually gave way to rolling hills, the air shifting with them—thick with moisture, carrying the faint scent of salt from the sea.

They arrived at Aquamere's gates, and Gisela stopped short.

Crystalline waters sparkled under the sun, and lakes and rivers wove through the land like threads of liquid sapphire. Homes with stone foundations were nestled among flower-filled gardens. Children's laughter rang out as they splashed in the shallows, their joy mingling with the chirps of birds flitting through willow trees. Merchants called out to one another, their voices easy and unguarded, as if nothing had ever threatened this place.

For a moment, she let herself believe this could last.

"Are we still in Mystralos?" Gisela whispered. "It's beautiful."

Thorne grabbed her hand as they strolled through the village center. "Yes. Sure is," he said, his gaze fixed on her rather than the village before them.

"Where would she be, Silas?" Gisela asked.

"I'd guess a pub," he said, tight lipped. "You two go on ahead. I don't want her to see me right away. It might give us a better chance."

"Are you sure?"

Silas nodded. "I'm going to enjoy the water."

His attention drifted to a woman loading a cart nearby. She looked up and caught his eye. Her smile lingered for a heartbeat longer than expected.

Gisela and Thorne stepped into the pub, and it was nothing like the one in Rockridge. The polished wooden floors gleamed in the soft light of oil lamps. Cascading vines and potted plants adorned the white stone walls, giving the space the feel of an indoor garden. Patrons dressed in neatly tailored garments spoke in hushed tones.

At the far end of the room, a fire crackled in the hearth, illuminating the woman seated beside it. Her white-blonde hair was pulled into a high ponytail with braids woven into it. She wore beige breeches and high black boots, paired with a loose, billowy linen shirt. Leaning back with her legs propped on the table, she radiated an unbothered confidence that drew every eye in the room, including Gisela's.

Eira whispered into Gisela's mind, *"That's Marina. Do you feel it?"*

She did. She hadn't noticed before that she could detect Silas's and Thorne's power. Everything had been new then, a thousand sensations at once after her awakening. But now, meeting a new Mystic, the feeling was clear—a flutter deep in her core, like butterflies anticipating their release.

Marina looked up from her glass, head tilting as a smirk tugged at the corner of her mouth. Thorne and Gisela crossed the room toward her table, noting the group of men around her, each with the weathered look of a man who belonged to the sea.

Marina tracked their approach.

"Are you Marina Donolo?" Gisela asked.

"Who's asking?" Marina replied, twirling a knife between her fingers.

Gisela glanced around the room, feigning thought. "Can you see anyone else asking? Or did you miss the part where I'm standing right in front of you?"

Thorne shot Gisela a look. "What are you doing?" he muttered.

Marina's grin widened. "I like you." With a wave of her hand, she signaled to the men at the table. They pushed back from the table and filed out of the pub without a word.

Thorne and Gisela took the empty seats across from her.

Marina went on twirling the knife, watching them with lazy interest.

Gisela didn't flinch. She'd seen this kind of test before—dominance disguised as ease. The only way to pass it was to play along without blinking.

Thorne looked between them, confused. "What's happening?"

"Are you here for my help?" Marina asked, her feet still propped up on the table.

"How did you know?" Gisela asked.

Marina studied her. "I know you're a Mystic. You want to sail to Mystic Isle."

"Mystic what?"

Marina tucked the blade away at her hip before leaning closer. "Mystic Isle. Are you looking to leave Mystralos?"

Thorne and Gisela exchanged puzzled glances. "No," Thorne said. "We want your help in saving Mystralos."

Marina's brow furrowed. "Then how do you know who I am?"

"We have a mutual . . . friend," Gisela said, careful to keep her tone measured.

"Why would I help you? I don't know you. This realm is hopeless. Your best bet is to go to Mystic Isle. Leave this place."

"Whatever is happening in the northern villages will spread south. I'm sure of it. This beautiful village won't stay like this for long," Gisela said.

Thorne leaned forward, elbows on the table. "Why are you still here if it's hopeless?"

"I transfer awakened Mystics to Mystic Isle," Marina revealed. "By ship."

Gisela whispered to Thorne, "Do you think he knew about this?"

"Who?" Marina asked.

Silas walked through the door, answering the question before Gisela had a chance to respond. His eyes locked onto Marina, and hers snapped up to meet his.

"Oh, absolutely *not*."

"Wait. Please, hear us out," Gisela pleaded, her voice tense but measured.

Marina's anger flared, her voice cutting sharp. "How dare you ambush me like this? I should drown you both from the inside."

Silas stepped closer to the table, careful not to provoke her further. "Marina, please."

"You all need to leave. Now," she demanded.

"Can we talk somewhere private?" Gisela asked. "Give us a few minutes to explain."

Marina's gaze, burning with rage, locked onto her father. "Five," she said, rising abruptly. She strolled out of the pub, fluid and assured. Her slender, muscular frame cut through the crowd with ease.

Gisela, Thorne, and Silas followed, weaving quickly to keep pace behind her.

They were rounding the corner of the council building when the sight of a red uniform brought Gisela to a dead halt.

Thorne stopped beside her, eyeing the man.

Gisela marched forward. "Vaughn?"

He looked down at her, pale and trembling. "Gisela Valor. Nice . . . to see you," he said, swallowing hard.

Marina stopped ahead, arms crossed, watching with a measured stare.

"What're you doing here?" Gisela asked. "They took you away. That day in the village center . . . You work for the King now?"

"Uh, yes. I—" Vaughn's words faltered.

"Wait a minute," she said, stepping closer.

Eira's certainty settled, cold and sure, in Gisela's chest.

"Back up," Vaughn said, his voice unsteady.

Thorne positioned himself protectively in front of Gisela.

She scoffed and stepped around him. "You're not a Mystic."

"No . . . I'm not."

"Explain," she said through gritted teeth.

Vaughn sighed, his shoulders sagging. "I was supposed to set an example . . . encourage Mystics to step forward." He stared at the ground before continuing. "It was wrong. I see that now. After what I've witnessed with the potion . . . my sister would be ashamed of me. But they said if I did it, they wouldn't punish my family for hiding her, and they would be paid in coin. Lots of it. I just can't return to Frosthaven. They offered me a position, so I—I took it. Please, don't tell them I spoke to you."

"What potion?" Marina interjected, advancing with a cutlass that must have been well hidden.

Vaughn crumpled at her feet. "Please don't hurt me."

Gisela stepped forward. "Tell us what you saw."

Vaughn shook his head. "If I tell you, will you leave me alone?"

The four of them looked at each other and nodded in agreement.

His shoulders were curled in, eyes glistening with unshed tears. "They get the potion . . . and . . . the screams. It's so loud. Like they're trapped in a nightmare." His face crumpled. "Afterwards. . . they're husks of themselves. Please don't make me relive this."

He vomited on the ground and the group recoiled.

"You can, and you will," Marina gritted out, looking down at him.

Vaughn wiped his mouth. "They're forcing awakenings."

"Forcing awakenings?" she asked.

Vaughn coughed, and Marina took a step back, her lip curling in disgust.

"Awakenings are when a Mystic comes into their true power."

"I know what an awakening is, you stupid little rodent," Marina snapped. "Why are they doing it?"

"I think it has to do with the Stones. They want a Mystic from each element. But I only know what I overheard . . . I'm not a high-ranking guard!"

"Are they making progress?" Silas asked.

"Some, but not much. It's not working as they expected. They don't come back as they once were." He shook his head. "Please . . . can you leave me alone now?"

"You're disgusting," Marina spat.

The group moved away but Gisela stayed, watching Vaughn shrink against the shame of his own actions. She almost felt sorry for him. Not for what he'd done, but for the desperation that forced him to betray his own conscience. She considered the lengths one might go to protect those they love and shuddered at the cost such choices demanded.

They continued down the main walkway, following Marina. "This is more than I bargained for today," she grumbled, keeping a few paces ahead.

"Eira, do you know anything about forced awakenings? Has this been done before?"

"No. But forcing an awakening cannot result in a true Primal bond. I fear the potion may be turning them into something else entirely."

They entered an alley that sloped downward to a wider path. At the end, a flight of stairs descended to a beach where a wooden house, much like Silas's on Mount Kharos, stood.

In front of the house, a cozy seating area offered a view of the vast expanse of sand and water. A large ship was docked further down the beach, partially concealed by dunes and rocky outcrops. The same men who were with Marina at the pub moved about the ship, their activities hidden from plain view.

Silas spotted the ship and snapped his gaze to his daughter. "Is that your mother's ship? What do you think you're doing?"

The old tension coiled in the air.

Thorne grabbed Gisela's hand.

Marina whirled around. "Doing what she always did. Saving our people."

"Marina, please. You misunderstand me."

"Do I? Is what I saw during the Trials a lie?"

"It's not. But I was worried about your safety. If I would've known—"

"Known what, Father? That the kingdom would execute her?" Marina's voice rose with anger. "I saw your whole conversation. She tried to get us out of here. You said *no*."

"Completing the awakening wasn't easy. You know that now. I didn't think you were ready at the time."

"That wasn't your decision to make!"

Gisela and Thorne watched, eyes darting between the two.

"Have you seen Mother's journal?" Marina asked, her voice low and burning. "She knew this land would die. They told her in Mystic Isle. She tried to *spare* us."

"Marina . . . I'll regret my choice for the rest of my life. I know I chose wrong. I'm sorry," Silas said, defeated.

"You didn't even tell your new friends about what Mother did? About the lives she saved?"

"I was ashamed," Silas cried, chin trembling. "I didn't listen to her." He sank into the sand, burying his face in his hands as sobs shook him.

Gisela understood then. Silas waited too long—and Helena had paid for it.

Marina's face softened. Her hand twitched at her side as if she wanted to reach out, but she clenched it into a fist instead. She turned away, her posture stiffening as she put on a mask of indifference. "There's no point in dwelling on it now, Father. But I'm doing what Mother would've wanted. I'm saving lives."

Silas looked up at her, eyes swollen and red. "How many?"

"Does that matter?"

"How many awakened Mystics have you taken there since you started?"

"Five. Even if it was one it would be worth it. It'd be more if the damn Trials weren't so far," she said, flicking her hand. "I can only sense the older ones who've passed inspection age."

"That's honorable," Gisela cut in. "But we need your help. We have a lot of lives to save here too."

"And what do you suppose we do?" Marina asked, hand on her hip. "Walk through the castle gates and ask Ravenor for his head?"

"Watch your tone when speaking to her," Thorne warned.

Marina's grin turned predatory. "How about I waterboard you? Let's see how long you can hold your breath underwater."

Black fire hissed in Thorne's palm. He flicked his wrist, sending a lash of heat snapping toward her.

Marina didn't flinch. She leaned away with fluid grace, answering with a surging wall of water that rose, poised to strike.

Thorne's hand lifted again, the air around him beginning to warp—but Gisela was faster.

She stepped between them, frost shooting outward, snuffing the flame. Ice climbed the wave, sealing it into a jagged frozen sculpture suspended in the air. Gisela glared at them. "Get a grip." She sighed and squared her shoulders. "We need to restore balance to Mystralos."

The air grew slick with sudden humidity.

Above Marina, moisture coiled into a feminine form. Fluid and translucent, she shimmered in shades of turquoise. Waves undulated across her body like cascading silk. Her eyes were a deep blue, exuding a sense of serenity and power. Droplets of water glistened around her, echoing the ebb and flow of the tides.

Marina's face was a mask of pride. "Meet Ondine."

Ondine bowed her head gracefully toward Gisela and Thorne.

Eira and Ignitus appeared beside them, bowing in silent acknowledgment.

Marina admired Eira and Ignitus, her expression lighting up with awe.

Crag appeared behind Silas, his presence assertive. "Marina."

Marina turned to look at Crag. She rolled her eyes. "I forgive my father, so you can cut the protective uncle act."

The tension lightened for the first time that day.

Silas glanced at Marina, the weight easing from his shoulders. He stood and pulled her into his arms.

She closed her eyes, hesitating before returning the embrace.

He held her close, and the etched lines of worry on his face smoothed.

"It's going to take time," she mumbled.

"I understand," Silas replied.

"I'm happy you two are mending your relationship," Thorne said. "But I'm going to need to hear about Mystic Isle."

Marina smiled. "Take a seat, flamebrain."

CHAPTER TWENTY

The crackling of fire and crashing of waves created a soothing backdrop as the four Mystics gathered around the flames, all eyes fixed on Marina. Years in Frosthaven, spent among herbs, bandages, and healing hands, had sheltered Gisela. The salt in the air here was a constant reminder of how far she'd traveled from the sterile mountain wind. Until now, the world beyond Frosthaven was distant, half-imagined. Every word Marina spoke pulled back another corner of that hidden life.

"My mother was a sailor, a beacon of light for Mystics on the run," Marina began.

Silas traced the rim of his cup with a finger, nodding.

"She made many trips to Mystic Isle, helping any Mystic who wanted to leave. But after one of her journeys . . ." Marina glanced at her father. "A Seer there told her that our land was doomed. She wanted my father and me to complete the Trials so we could gain entry to Mystic Isle and leave this place for good."

Silas shifted in his seat, mouth twitching.

"Why wait until after the Trials? Why not get on the boat and go?" Thorne asked.

"The land won't appear to those who aren't awakened. My men can't see it when we travel there."

Gisela tilted her head, frowning.

"Their realm isn't open to just anyone," she clarified. "My mother was executed shortly after learning the fate of Mystralos." Marina flexed her fingers at her sides.

The fire popped, sending a spray of sparks into the air.

"Maybe one of the sailors betrayed her," Thorne suggested.

Marina's eyes sharpened. "I trust my men. They've been properly questioned and vetted."

Thorne let out a low laugh. "What did you do? Waterboard them for information?"

Marina smirked and leaned back, crossing a leg.

Thorne's amusement drained.

Silas rubbed his temples. "Marina, you can't keep sailing over there. How do you know the kingdom doesn't have eyes on this?"

"Because I'm prepared," she replied, voice steady. "We're vigilant. I make sure none of the Mystics are seen getting on the ship. We're fishing. That's all."

Silas's shoulders curled in.

"We're due to go out again. You can see it for yourself. Maybe even find the Seer my mother spoke to."

Gisela's pulse kicked. The idea of leaving Mystralos now—truly leaving—made her hands go numb. She glanced at Eira. "Did you know about Mystic Isle?"

Eira hovered closer. "There are many realms, Gisela. Some more favorable than others."

Silas cut in. "I don't know if that's a good idea."

"Why not?" Thorne asked.

"They probably blame me for Helena's death too," he said. "She was very loved there."

"No," Marina said. "They don't blame you."

Silas's shoulders eased a fraction.

"Then we're going," Gisela said, even as the numbness persisted. "We have to."

Marina clapped. "It's settled." She tipped her chin, considering them. "Isn't it funny how the four of us, each with a different element, found our way to each other?"

Gisela's head snapped to Thorne, who met her gaze, puzzled. The mention of the four elements united made her pause and remember Elder Aldric. She spoke aloud:

"In times of dire, the balance shall break,
Six elements lost, a world at stake.
To mend the divide, the willing must find,
The six who unite, in heart and mind."

The group stared at her.

"What the hell does that mean?" Marina asked.

Four, Gisela realized. Two still missing.

"Are there Mystics with air and storm on Mystic Isle? Would they help?"

Marina thought for a moment, then smiled. "Maybe. But we're not ignoring what you just said."

Gisela didn't respond right away. Her thoughts drifted back to the villages, to the suffering of her people.

What was Frosthaven like now?

Helena had risked her life to save Mystics and paid the ultimate price.

Gisela clenched her fists in her lap. Helena had been brave, tough—qualities Gisela never really needed until now. She had been raised to heal; it came easier to her than anything else. Gisela anchored herself, trying to push back the shadow of doubt creeping in.

Silas and Thorne went inside the house to play darts, their cheers and laughter drifting out the windows.

A smile spread across Gisela's face as she listened.

Thorne's silhouette moved past the glass, his posture more relaxed than she'd ever seen. He was finding companionship with Silas—a figure who offered the support his own father never had. It warmed something inside of her.

"My father really likes Thorne," Marina said, jerking her head toward the house. "I can tell."

"Yeah, he's alright," Gisela said jokingly.

"He loves you."

"Your father? I love him too."

Marina chuckled. "No, I meant Thorne."

Gisela fidgeted with the hem of her sleeve, heat prickling at the back of her neck.

"He's protective of you. I ruffled his handsome feathers by my tone alone," Marina teased.

Gisela gave Marina a sidelong glance, feeling a pang of unfamiliar jealousy.

"Oh, don't worry. I'm not into the likes of him," Marina laughed. "I can see that he's handsome. But I prefer them a little more . . . burly."

Gisela picked at her nails. "Do you have someone of your own?"

"I do. But he's in Mystic Isle," Marina said, pursing her lips. "I don't get to see him often."

"That's got to be hard. Aquamancer too?"

"He's a Flamekeeper. So, I know how to push their buttons," Marina said with a grin.

They giggled together, their laughter mingling with the sounds of the game inside.

"Although, his flames aren't black," Marina added, raising a brow. "What's that all about?"

Thorne's flames were unique, that much was obvious. Fire was usually a blend of oranges, yellows, and occasionally blues, but never black.

Gisela hesitated, wincing. "I never asked."

Marina's fingers drummed against her thigh. "Why not?"

"I'm afraid to."

His flames had to have a deeper meaning, yet she hadn't found the courage to ask him about it. Thorne had been through a lot over the last few weeks. She didn't want to undermine his hard-won strength.

Eira could sense her curiosity, but Gisela refrained from asking her.

"Well, you should," Marina said. "It could strengthen whatever connection you two have . . . seems intense."

Gisela tilted her head thoughtfully.

"I've always been intuitive," Marina said.

A knot of nerves twisted in Gisela's stomach. "Have you heard of being Soulbound?"

"Ondine told me about it. Are you two Soulbound?"

"I don't know."

"Have you guys . . .?" Marina wiggled her eyebrows.

Gisela blushed, averting her gaze. "Not yet."

"*Yet*," Marina repeated, as they burst into giggles again. "I've never had many girlfriends," she admitted. "I'm glad you showed up."

"I am too," Gisela said, giving her a soft smile. "I was a bit of a bookworm before all of this. I spent my spare time studying my mother's herbalism journals and my best friend is a sixty-year-old scribe."

"A sixty-year-old best friend is better than no best friend."

"True. Except now her life is at risk."

"A King who wants to erase history sounds like a King who wants to change the story," Marina said. "Erase what's been done."

Gisela's thoughts pulled to Zaro, the man the guards spoke of on the mountain. "When we left the mountain, Thorne heard guards talking about someone named Zaro. That he's involved with everything going on," Gisela said.

"Is that the Ancient Elder Ravenor keeps invoking?"

"Ravenor never named him."

"Well, if it is, maybe they're trying to bury the past together? If no one remembers the true history, they can rewrite it however they want."

Gisela nodded, watching the flames of the fire curl and collapse. "I wonder why Aquamere hasn't experienced any negative effects from the Stones being gone yet?"

Marina's voice was quiet. "We have."

Gisela glanced at Marina, narrowing her gaze. She could sense the worry in Marina's voice.

"I've been filling the lakes. Late at night," Marina said. "The fish are dwindling as well. But it sounds worse in the north."

A chill ran down Gisela's spine, and not the kind that reminded her of Thorne.

CHAPTER TWENTY-ONE

D *rip. Drip. Drip.*

A slow trickle of water landed on Thorne's face. He blinked hard before squinting up at Marina's fingers hovering above him.

"Marina, for fuck's sake!" he yelled.

Marina's cackle echoed through the small wooden house, light and carefree.

Gisela tried—and failed—to stifle a giggle.

"You think this is funny?" he asked Gisela.

She nodded. "Yeah. A little bit."

He pinned her with the gentle weight of his body, his hands finding the sensitive skin at her waist until she broke, a breathless laugh catching in her throat. The playfulness faded as he stilled. He leaned down, his forehead brushing hers, his breath a warm ghost against her skin.

He drifted closer, gaze dropping to her lips, the space between them thinning—

"Sorry to break up the tender display, but the pub is open, and we need to get our asses there before all the good food gets taken," Marina said, strapping her cutlass onto her breeches.

Silas emerged from the second bedroom, his steps lighter than usual. "Good morning," he said heartily.

Marina smiled at her father, and this time, she didn't turn away from him.

Breakfast at the pub was warm. Not just the food or the air, but the people of Aquamere too. Smiles followed them through the village. Laughter carried through the morning air like a breeze as children darted between stalls.

Silas was already swept into their games.

Gisela and Thorne settled onto a bench, content to watch.

Marina had already gone ahead to the docks, preparing the ship for their voyage.

From the corner of the square, two councilmen stepped out of the building, their voices carrying as they leaned against the stone railing.

"Vaughn still hasn't reported in," one said. "The King ensured he was prepared for this job."

"I'll post a notice for the position today," the other said. "Might as well get someone more reliable."

Thorne smirked, nudging Gisela. "We probably scared the shit out of him."

Gisela huffed and leaned back, letting the thought drift with the wind.

"When all this is over," Thorne said, wrapping his arm around Gisela's shoulder, "we're moving here."

Gisela turned to him, surprised. "*We* are?"

Thorne shrugged. "If you'll come with me."

Warmth spread through her body. "Where you go, I go."

Thorne pulled her closer, his lips lingering against her temple.

Their hands found each other without thinking.

Easy.

As if things had always been this way. Whatever lay ahead, it had to be worth this.

He traced slow circles on the back of her hand, fire gathering beneath his thumb.

Gisela answered with a gentle squeeze, her touch cooling into a fine mist of ice. The two elements didn't clash. Instead, they wove together.

"It's strange," she murmured, watching the play of heat and frost. "How our powers blend like this, when they're meant to be opposites."

Thorne nodded, his gaze fixed on their entwined hands. "It feels right. Like we're meant to balance each other out."

Her fingers brushed his palm, sending a chill through him, and he answered with steady warmth curling around her hand. A quiet conversation.

Thorne tucked a loose strand of hair behind her ear. "Where you go, I go," he echoed.

"Hey, you two!" Silas called out.

They turned to face him.

"Let's head to the ship."

Reluctantly, they stood and followed him down the path toward the beach, their hands brushing once more before they finally let go.

"Ronan!" Marina's voice carried through the ship. "Ensure the ship is balanced and ready to set sail for tomorrow."

"Yes ma'am," he replied with a crooked smirk as he tugged the rope tight against the mast.

Her boots struck the deck in sharp, confident steps. "And Eamon." She paused, wrinkling her nose at the floorboards. "Clean this shit up."

Eamon muttered something under his breath but couldn't hide the faint smile that crept across his face. "Aye, aye, captain."

Gisela stepped onto the deck, watching the crew move in a productive rhythm around Marina's commands. They listened, really listened. No hesitation or scoffing from any of them.

Just respect that was earned.

"Ah! Gisela, Thorne," Marina called, spreading her arms wide. "Welcome aboard the Cascadia."

Pride radiated through her voice and Gisela understood why.

The ship wasn't beautiful in any polished sense—but it had a soul. Its hull was dark oak, weathered and scarred, iron bands cinched around its sides like armor. The sails were patched yet steady in the wind. The air carried oil, sea brine, and sun-baked wood. The last thing she noticed was the dragon figurehead with its jaws open in a silent snarl at the prow.

"The Cascadia?" Gisela asked.

"Renamed after my mother's Primal."

Silas blinked back tears, smiling at his daughter. "I'm going to look around myself, Marina. It's been a while."

Marina nodded.

"I've never been on a ship before," Gisela said.

Marina grinned. "It's amazing. I've never felt more at peace than when I sail."

Thorne's eyes landed at the dragon head. "Why a dragon?"

"Oh, that? My mother loved dragon stories. Said they represented strength, resilience . . . stubbornness," Marina said, shooting him a pointed look. "Figured it suited the ship."

She led them below deck, showing where they'd sleep and introduced them to the rest of the crew, who were ecstatic to meet other Mystics. It was strange to see the crew living so easily among one. They laughed easily with Marina, no fear or tension in their faces.

Hope took root in Gisela.

"There you are! I've been lookin' for ya everywhere," a man called.

Marina waved him over. "I want you to meet my second, Larz. Larz, this is Gisela."

Her second-in-command looked like a classic seasoned sailor. A long, neatly trimmed beard framed his wavy red hair, which fell just past his shoulders. His skin was tanned and weathered, his face marked with scars that looked less like damage and more like a life lived hard. Piercing blue eyes bore into Gisela's, examining her as if she were some intricate piece of architecture.

He held out his hand to Gisela.

She extended hers, and he grasped it, guiding it to his lips.

"Aren't you a pretty little thing," he said with a grin, his voice deep and smooth.

Gisela smiled, caught off guard by his flirtation.

Thorne went rigid beside her, something tight pulling along his jaw. "Isn't she?"

Larz appeared unfazed by Thorne's blatant distaste for him, releasing Gisela's hand with a slight bow. "And who's this fine gentleman?" Larz asked, turning his attention to Thorne.

"Thorne," he said, stepping in front of Gisela.

Larz's grin widened, revealing a row of slightly crooked teeth. "Pleasure to meet you, Thorne. Any friend of Marina's is a friend of mine." He glanced at Marina with a smirk, eyes twinkling with mischief.

Marina threw a hand on her hip and shot him a warning glare.

Larz extended his hand to shake Thorne's, but Thorne kept his arms crossed.

"Behave, Larz," she said, her tone light but firm. "Thorne can get quite heated, so to speak."

Thorne lifted a hand in a sarcastic wave, flames curling along his fingers.

Larz's confident demeanor faltered.

Gisela gave Thorne an exasperated look. "Thank you for the warm welcome, Larz."

"Ah, the pleasure is mine," Larz said, winking. "Or at least, I hope it will be," he added before walking away.

Thorne glared at Marina. "This isn't going to work. I'll hurt him."

"You will do no such thing, flamebrain," Marina warned. "He's harmless. Ignore his antics."

Gisela wrapped her arms around Thorne's neck, rose onto her tiptoes, and pressed a kiss on his lips.

As they parted, the storm in his eyes stilled, and his shoulders finally dropped.

"You're jealous." She smiled. "Let it go. We need their help."

"I'm not worried. He's just pushing his luck."

"Pub tonight, boys?" Marina called. "Before we set off tomorrow?"

Ronan rubbed the back of his neck, eyes turning toward land. "I have to make sure my grandmother's all set until we get back."

Gisela saw the fleeting look of regret flit across his face. She understood all too well what it was like to leave home.

"Liana will kill me if I don't spend time with her and Isla before I leave, you know that," Eamon called out from the front deck. "Woman is violent," he grumbled.

"Fair enough," Marina said, turning toward Gisela and Thorne. "One last hoorah?"

Chapter Twenty-Two

Sailing on rough seas for the first time wasn't sitting well with Gisela at all. The sunrise, yellows and oranges bleeding across the sky like watercolor, and the birds gliding above did nothing to calm her stomach. It wasn't from the ale last night. It was the relentless rocking of the ship that had her gut churning. She'd managed a small breakfast, but a strong wave sent it back overboard.

She didn't want to complain, but she wasn't sure how she'd survive the rest of the journey.

"Shit, Gisela. Are you alright?" Marina asked, striding over to where Gisela leaned over the railing.

"Never better."

Marina raised an eyebrow. "Are you seasick? Why didn't you say something?" She closed her eyes, murmured to Ondine, and the waters smoothed. "There. Better?"

"With all due respect, Marina, why the hell didn't you do that sooner?"

"Oh, the rough seas bring out the fire in you," Marina laughed.

Gisela glared at her but was thankful for the Aquamancer all the same.

On the top deck, Thorne and Silas were deep in a sword training session.

Silas demonstrated a series of intricate techniques. He guided Thorne through drills, their blades clashing rhythmically as steel sang through the air. The red-gemmed hilt of Thorne's sword reflected the light of the rising sun. After a particularly demanding sequence, they paused and grinned at one another. Silas pulled Thorne into a hearty bear hug, lifting him clean off the deck.

Gisela and Marina laughed from below, watching the bond between Thorne and Silas grow deeper.

"I think I may come back from all of this with a new brother," Marina said.

"Then maybe I'll be your sister one day," Gisela said, only realizing the weight of her words as soon as they left her mouth.

Marina raised an eyebrow, a teasing smirk forming. "Ah, so it's that serious, huh?"

"No, I don't know about that. I didn't mean—"

Marina twirled her cutlass with a playful flourish. She turned and walked away and called over her shoulder, "Yes you did."

Gisela sat at the bow, admiring the vast expanse of the open sea. The air was cool against her skin, nourishing the frost that flowed through her veins.

She sensed someone approaching from behind.

Larz.

He stopped at her side, keeping his gaze on the horizon. "Mind if I sit?" he asked.

Gisela shook her head, patting the spot next to her.

"Nothin' like it, eh?" Larz said, bending his knees to sit down.

"I don't have the words."

It almost fooled her. The serenity of it, when the world was burning, stirred something shameful in her chest. How could she feel this peace when pain ravaged Mystralos? Allowing herself this moment, while her family and her village suffered . . . felt selfish.

"When Helena first brought me aboard," Larz said, his voice pulling her from her thoughts, "I was grateful. Her loss has been devastatin' to me—to all of us."

"Why weren't you afraid of her?"

Larz let out a deep sigh, his gaze fixed on the sea. "I never bought into the 'Mystics are dangerous' nonsense. Helena saved me from a bad place." His eyes darkened. "No one ever cared for me the way she did. When Marina came back and wanted to take over, I didn't hesitate."

"Marina was born for this."

Larz chuckled, stroking his beard. "Marina questioned us all *thoroughly* when she came back." He shook his head. "Crazy bitch, but you gotta love her."

Gisela raised her eyebrows and laughed. She'd only just met Marina and already knew mercy wasn't her strong suit. A moment passed before Gisela spoke again. "Maybe someone found out Helena was a Mystic, and they didn't know what she was actually doing."

"Dunno. She always wore that stuff to cover her mark. She was cautious."

Gisela let the cool air fill her lungs and let it out slowly. "Silas told us an herbalist taught her how to make it. Is that person still in Aquamere?"

Larz shook his head. "No. I never met 'em. Figured they were executed since we've had the same herbalist for, I don't know, twenty years now. Give or take a few."

Gisela's grip tightened on the railing. Another lead, gone.

"So," Larz said, eyes trailing along her, "where's yours?"

She tucked her hair behind her ear, revealing where her mark showed through the fading hylja.

Larz leaned close, curious, when a tiny flame nicked the side of his cheek. He flinched, pulling back to see Thorne standing a few paces away, arms crossed over his bare chest.

"Loosen up there, Thorne. Your arms might get stuck like that," he said, standing and striding away. "Brooding buffoon." Larz disappeared toward the stern.

Gisela turned to Thorne, who was watching her intently.

"I haven't even seen it yet," he said, sitting down where Larz had been. "The hylja faded?"

She gave him a look as he swept her hair away from her ear and leaned close.

His breath brushed her skin as he found the faint outline of a mark patterned like frost on glass. He nibbled her ear playfully, sending goose-bumps trailing down her arms.

She laughed and swatted him away, unable to hide her smile. "Now show me yours," she said, her eyes bright.

Thorne bit his lip, a teasing glint in his eye. "Oh, you'll see it soon," he promised with a wink.

Gisela turned back toward the sea. She leaned her head on Thorne's shoulder and the steady sound of waves filled the silence between them.

"I saw you and Silas training earlier."

"Yeah, he has a lot of experience. He's a good teacher. And an even better man."

"I'm happy you have him," Gisela said, tilting her head to study him.

A shadow of pain passed through his eyes.

She reached up, cupping his cheek with her hand. "I'm proud of how you handled your father back in Rockridge. I never told you that. Everything happened so fast."

"You don't have to—" Thorne started, but the sharp sound of raised voices cut him off.

They turned toward the deck. A cluster of crew members had gathered, shouting over a split crate, shoving each other as supplies spilled across the deck.

Thorne exhaled. "I'll handle it." He pressed a brief kiss to her temple before standing.

Gisela huffed and leaned on the railing. With a quiet sigh, she conjured small snowballs in her hands and cast them to the deep sea below, watching them vanish with soft, soundless splashes.

As dusk settled, a light breeze tugged at Gisela's hair, turning it into loose, wavy tendrils that swayed in the salty air. The Mystics and sailors gathered on the deck, sitting on crates and barrels while Marina and Ondine's magic kept the waters calm.

Laughter rolled across the ship.

Gisela glanced at Thorne beside her as he watched the crew with a grin.

Ronan absently polished the hilt of his sword. His shaggy brown hair hung over his eyes, though his gaze kept flicking to Marina, only to slip away whenever she looked at him.

"You know," Ronan said at last, "when I was a boy, I thought I could talk to the ocean. My grandmother always said I had saltwater in my veins."

"Oh yeah? Did it ever respond?" Marina teased.

Ronan met her gaze. "It sang of freedom, danger . . . and sometimes, secrets."

Eamon, rolling lazily on his crate, added with a sly grin, "Sounds like my Liana back home. The freedom and danger part, not the secrets. That woman doesn't know how to keep a thought to herself."

"Ain't that right," Larz said.

"Fiercest woman in Aquamere. Met her at the fish market, and before I knew it, she had me in a headlock for taking the last cod. Married her a month later." Eamon's eyes gleamed as he continued. "And our little girl, Isla. She's got her mother's temper. The other day, she tried to swing at some poor kid for sittin' in her spot near the fountains." He shook his head with a fond smile. "Silas knows a thing or two about fierce women, don't you?"

Silas's smile was small but sincere. "I'd say so. Daughters inherit that from their mothers."

Marina glanced at her father, a faint smile on her lips, but her eyes betrayed a deeper pain.

"My girls didn't want me to leave," Eamon said.

Ronan nodded. "We'll be back soon. Then you can go back to gettin' handled by your woman."

"Aye," Eamon chuckled, glancing at the horizon. "If the gods are so kind."

Larz leaned forward, raising a thick red brow as he looked at Ronan. "When are you getting yourself a wife?"

Ronan hesitated. "It's not in the cards for me right now. My grandmother's sick. I'm all she's got."

Larz gave a thoughtful nod. "Honorable, lad, but even a man like you needs a woman to share his burdens."

Ronan's eyes flicked away from Marina. "It's complicated."

Larz tilted his head, sensing there was more. "Complicated, eh? What, she's spoken for?"

"Somethin' like that."

Gisela leaned into Thorne's side, his arm resting protectively around her.

"So, Thorne," Eamon drawled. "I reckon we'll be seeing a wedding soon, eh?"

The group chuckled lightly, but Gisela's face warmed at the unexpected question.

Before she could speak, Thorne pulled her flush against him. His gaze, intense and steady, locked onto hers, and the teasing mood among them dimmed.

"When the time's right, Eamon," he said, his fingers brushing against Gisela's cheek. "I'll marry her the second she says the word."

She bit her lip, fighting the smile tugging at her mouth.

The group fell quiet for a beat.

Eamon gave a low whistle. "Well, seems I hit the mark. Didn't mean to turn the deck into a chapel."

Thorne's lips curved, though his eyes were set on Gisela. "No harm done, Eamon."

Chapter Twenty-Three

The low, resonant sound of a horn cut through the dense morning mist that enshrouded the ship, nudging Gisela and Thorne from their sleep.

Thorne stretched, arms reaching above his head. "I think we're here."

Gisela groaned and turned away, burrowing deeper under the blankets, savoring the last few minutes of rest.

Thorne let out a soft, amused laugh. "Rise and shine, Freckles." He leaned over to press a quick kiss to her forehead.

She squirmed, half-smiling, half-grumbling.

Reluctantly, they dressed.

The chill of the fog nipped at their skin as they stepped onto the top deck, moisture clinging to their hair and clothes. A thick, swirling mist obscured the view beyond the ship. Beyond the rails, the world faded into ghostly gray. Ropes creaked under the wind, and the slap of water against the hull sounded louder in the quiet morning.

The crew had gathered near the bow, their attention focused intently on Marina as her voice cut through the haze. "Give us a couple of days."

Silas approached from behind them. "I can't see a thing," he said, squinting into the haze.

Marina's grin didn't waver. "Move it, Mystics." Her boots thumped against the deck.

Gisela and Thorne made their way to the bow, where a small dock came into view through the fog.

"Say your goodbyes to the crew," Marina said. "They can't go beyond the dock."

Gisela raised an eyebrow. "What happens if they do?"

The crew chuckled.

"We'd fall into the sea," Larz said. "You can cross over, but we can't see what's past it."

Gisela and Thorne exchanged bewildered looks.

Ronan stood tense, staring after Marina as she leapt onto the platform.

"We'll see you all soon," Gisela said, hopping off the boat with a rush of excitement. Her boots—which were actually Marina's—landed lightly on the dock.

Thorne and Silas exchanged firm nods with the men, shaking their hands with silent gratitude.

Thorne lingered a moment longer with Larz, wrapping his hand in an unbearable heat.

Larz yanked his hand away with a snarl, only for Thorne to flash him a teasing wink in response.

Gisela and Marina led the way down the wooden dock, which was shrouded in thick mist. At the far end, a small stretch of land held a swirling vortex, like an isolated tornado frozen in place.

Marina stepped through and disappeared.

"Marina!" Gisela threw her hands up, scoffing. "Typical."

"Where'd she go?" Thorne asked.

Silas walked up from behind him. "It's the entry. You just have to step through."

Gisela hesitated but stepped forward. It was like being pulled into a dream. The air shimmered and hummed against her body, a weightless pressure pressing from every direction. Colors stretched and twisted around her, light bending in ways that made her woozy. Her stomach fluttered. She grasped at nothing, trying to find something solid to steady herself.

Then she did.

As quickly as it began, the experience ended, and she landed on all fours on solid ground.

Her breath came hard as the mist peeled away.

Thorne and Silas were right behind her.

Thorne landed as if he had done this all his life, steady and sure as usual.

Silas stumbled briefly but regained his balance.

Marina was already ahead, a mischievous smile on her lips. She jerked her head toward the land below.

Gisela was struck silent, her eyes consuming the sight like they had been starved for it.

The early morning sun spilled over Mystic Isle, casting golden light across the landscape. From their perch atop a colossal waterfall, the water roared and crashed into a crystalline pool, sending clouds of mist into the air. The spray on Gisela's skin was cool and fine.

The land was divided by element, yet each region bled seamlessly into the next.

To the south, a dense forest sprawled, swallowing the cottages beneath its trees. Beyond it rose a vast mountain, its cliffs carved into stone dwellings.

She shifted her gaze to the next region, where pools of water glimmered, linked by narrow stone bridges. Tiny figures crossed them, entering houses reminiscent of Aquamere.

Farther east, fields of bright flowers and crops stretched wide. Stone homes lined the pathways that wound through them.

She marveled at the order of it all.

Northward, white-peaked mountains loomed over frozen lakes where figures glided on the ice.

Beside them, a small region raged with storm. Thunder rolled, lightning cracked through dark clouds, and wind tore through trees. A dead zone.

At the heart of it all stood the palace, built from stone and crystal that reflected a spectrum of colors. Grand columns, each representing an element, framed its entrance, and the land around it held fragments of each region.

Marina smiled. "Welcome to Mystic Isle."

Gisela was already aware of her own ignorance, and this place only proved it more. A realm where weather and elements merged in ways that shouldn't be possible.

Gisela swallowed, finally tearing her gaze away from the view. "Um, Marina? How do we actually get down to the land? We're really high up."

Marina twirled her long ponytail. "Well, you see . . . I may have left out a very small, teeny-tiny detail."

Thorne's glare was sharp. "Marina . . ."

A nervous laugh escaped her, and she raised her fingers to her mouth. A loud whistle pierced the air.

Above them, the slow, heavy beat of wings churned the clouds. Two black dragons descended from the swirling mists.

Gisela's jaw dropped, caught between the instinct to flee and a desperate, rising wonder.

Their obsidian scales gleamed, muscles rippling with each powerful stroke. Wide wings stretched overhead, blotting out the sun. Their fiery eyes glowed. Rows of teeth, sharp enough to crush stone, sent a shiver through her.

Long tails flicked behind them, jagged spikes running down their backs. Each dragon bore a saddle, large enough for two riders, securely positioned between their shoulder blades.

Gisela pressed herself closer to Thorne as the dragons' rumbling breaths rattled her bones.

"By the Six," Silas said in a hushed voice.

Marina grinned. "Aren't they gorgeous?"

Thorne's awe was immediate.

Gisela's hand closed around his, a reflex. "Did you drug us?"

"No," Marina said lightly. "But there's a place for that here too."

Silas snapped his gaze to hers and Marina gave him an innocent smile.

Thorne carefully walked up to the dragon closest to him. It puffed a small cloud of air, nostrils flaring, and he extended his hand. The dragon leaned forward, nuzzling his palm.

"We'll ride this one," Thorne said with a confident grin as he started climbing up the dragon.

"Thorne!" Gisela hissed.

"Come on, he's friendly," he called back, already halfway up the dragon's side.

"Marina, I'm going to kill you for this," Gisela snapped.

The dragon gave a low, rumbling snort as Gisela stepped closer. She jumped back before catching herself and climbed aboard.

Silas hesitated. The dragon bowed its head slightly, inviting him. He exhaled before climbing up.

As they descended, Marina whooped with joy, and Thorne followed suit.

The wind rushed past, cool and electric through Gisela's hair. The landscape—the shimmering waters, flowering fields, and distant mountains—were utterly surreal.

She gripped Thorne's waist, heart pounding, but not with fear. All her life she hated confinement, tight spaces. She was beginning to realize that Frosthaven was a tight space of its own. Here, on this dragon, she had never felt freer.

The dragons descended, lowering themselves gracefully to the ground, obsidian scales catching the light as their massive wings folded in.

One by one, they slid off their mounts.

The air was different here, quieter.

At the palace stairs stood a broad, burly man, with long blonde hair and a thick beard framing his face. His kind, blue eyes watched them with interest.

Marina picked up her pace, breaking into a run before leaping into the man's arms, wrapping herself tightly around him.

He responded with a deep rumble of laughter, holding her tight against him.

Silas strode over, his expression serious.

The man's eyes widened in surprise as he set Marina down.

Crag appeared beside Silas, comfortable here in Mystic Isle and Ignitus and Eira joined him.

Gisela couldn't help but smile at Eira, happy to see her freer here.

"And who might you be?" Silas asked.

"Oh, Father, this is Bjorn," Marina replied cheerfully.

"I'm asking this young man here," Silas said, his tone calmer.

Bjorn bowed. "I'm Bjorn, sir, it's an honor to finally meet you. I'm in love with your daughter. She is my sun and moon."

Gisela pouted and nudged Silas with a grin. "That's so sweet," she cooed.

"I'm very grateful for the opportunity to meet you, sir," Bjorn added earnestly.

Silas nodded, his features softening slightly. "I'd like to speak with you later. In private."

"Of course, sir, any time."

Thorne smirked at Bjorn and extended his hand. "I'm Thorne, and this is Gisela. She's my sun and moon too."

Gisela laughed and nudged Thorne, shaking her head. "It's nice to meet you, Bjorn."

Bjorn's Primal appeared beside him, a striking figure of orange and red flames. It shared the same impressive structure as Ignitus but had its own distinct fiery presence. "This is Pyraxis."

Pyraxis bowed and the other Primals followed in a gesture of respect. Pyraxis lingered a moment longer, studying Ignitus with curiosity.

"The Sovereign will see you now," Bjorn said, leading the way inside.

The palace gleamed in pristine white, the glare stabbing at Gisela's eyes. Whimsical spires climbed toward the ceiling, and the air smelled faintly of flowers. Light, airy corridors and open courtyards blurred the lines between inside and out, inviting gentle breezes and sunlight to stream through.

White stone and vaulted ceilings opened around them as they stepped into the throne room. At the center of the dais, a regal woman sat poised upon a seat of carved gold.

There was something about her presence that made Gisela's pulse slow, as if time itself had stilled.

She wore a flowing white gown and a small silver crown, woven with flowers. Behind her stood a towering ivory Primal who radiated pure light.

"Thank you, Bjorn," the woman said in a silky voice.

Bjorn bowed his head, winked at Marina and left the room.

"Welcome to Mystic Isle," the woman said, scanning her guests. "Marina, nice to see you again," she added with a warm smile.

"Likewise," Marina replied.

"You all may call me Seraphina," the woman said with a smile that met her eyes.

Gisela maintained steady eye contact. "I'm Gisela, and this is Thorne and Silas."

Seraphina inclined her head toward them, gaze lingering on Thorne and Ignitus before settling on Silas. "Helena's husband," she said. "I am terribly sorry for your loss."

Silas inhaled deeply, his shoulders sagging. "Thank you." His fingers twitched at his sides.

"You are all welcome here for as long as you need," Seraphina said. Her gown trailed behind her as she stepped from the dais. "But I suspect you are here for more than a mere visit."

"We are," Gisela responded. "We were hoping for some insight on what's going on in Mystralos. We wanted to find the person who warned Helena about our land."

"Our Seer?" Seraphina clasped her hands in front of her. "He glimpses the future. Omens. The threads that bind our world."

"You know what's happening in Mystralos?" Thorne asked.

Seraphina lifted her chin. "I am aware the land is in peril and that your tyrant King continues to harm Mystics under the guise of duty."

"He's also taken the Life Stones from our villages. He's been targeting our scribes and forcing awakenings," Thorne said.

Seraphina looked taken aback. "Forcing awakenings?"

"A potion of some sort," Gisela explained. "He's using it on the Mystics they find. To awaken them."

"That's an abomination. Corruption."

"That's part of why we came too. Can we speak to your Seer?"

"Of course. He gathers at the Guardian Tree here in Mystic Isle to deliver his prophecies."

Gisela blinked, caught off guard. "You have one?"

"Yes, of course," she said with a smile. "But your Life Stones . . . they must be returned to their pedestals. They, along with the Guardian Trees, are essential for maintaining a thick veil between your realm and Noxis."

Gisela frowned.

Noxis.

The name soured the air. She reached into her bag, fingers grazing the edge of the old map she'd stolen from the Village Lord's study, but let it go.

The map had marked Noxis clearly. It wasn't simply a forbidden place, a secret.

The realm itself was a threat to Mystralos.

"Noxis?" Silas asked.

"Yes, the realm to the north," Seraphina said gravely. "There is great evil there. Terrible beasts will enter Mystralos through that veil."

Gisela pictured the northern expanse on the map. Frosthaven just south of it, unaware and unprotected. Tension knotted her fingers.

"They already have. There have been attacks. We have families over there. They aren't Mystics. They won't stand a chance."

Seraphina studied Gisela, eyes narrowing. "You certainly have lineage."

Eira spoke up, sensing Gisela's rising frustration at the repeated inquiry. "We have not been able to establish who that is yet."

"It isn't anyone," Gisela said. "Don't you think I know my own family?"

"You hid *your* mark from them, did you not?" Crag interjected.

Gisela shot him a glare, letting her silence speak for her.

"When can we see him?" Thorne asked Seraphina, diverting the conversation.

"Tomorrow evening, although, I cannot guarantee he will speak."

"Understood," Thorne replied.

"We didn't even know about Mystic Isle until recently," Gisela said. "Why is it that you have to be awakened to see it?"

"Mystic Isle is the original land of the gods," Seraphina explained. "They created the outer lands as testing grounds—places where one must prove their worth to earn passage back to the isle."

"Prove themselves worthy? So, completing the Trials?"

Seraphina nodded. "It is why we have Mystic children here, and the other realms do not. The children born here are granted with the Six gods' gifts. Their powers manifest slowly, giving them time to learn and adapt."

"I'll be damned . . ." Silas whispered.

Seraphina smiled. "I will help you in any way I can. You can use any of the open palace bedrooms. I can take you to the Seer tomorrow."

The breeze was refreshing as Gisela stepped outside of the palace. In the quiet of the courtyards, the air drifted past her, so light it seemed to lift the weight of Seraphina's words from her shoulders.

Marina guided them to the garden gates. "I'm going to find Bjorn. Feel free to explore, it's completely safe here. Just don't piss off the dragons."

As Marina disappeared down a path lined with flowers, Gisela took in the gardens around her. The air was light, the land thriving—so unlike home. For the first time in a while, she felt safe.

Chapter Twenty-Four

The sounds of children playing drew Gisela northward, beyond the palace gates. They reached a large pond that sparkled in the sunlight. At the edge of the water, three children dipped their fingers in, trying to freeze the surface, but the ice melted, and their smiles faded with it. Their shoulders slouched and their lower lips pouted as they continued their attempts.

Gisela's smile softened. Persistence like that deserved to be rewarded.

Thorne, already guessing her intent, watched her with quiet amusement.

She bent to their level, speaking in gentle tones, and nodding encouragingly. Her hand skimmed the water, and a thick sheet of ice spread across the surface, freezing the pond solid. The children's faces lit up with joy as they jumped and cheered, playfully sliding across the newly formed glaze.

A warm smile on Thorne's face greeted her as she walked back over to him and Silas.

"Classic Gisela," Thorne said.

"I like kids," she replied with a shrug.

"Mystic children," Silas said, narrowing his eyes as he watched them conjure tiny snowballs. "Never imagined I'd see that." He clapped

Thorne on the shoulder. "I need a drink." And with that, he disappeared down a rocky path.

"Where to first?" Gisela asked Thorne.

"I have a suspicion," he said, grabbing her hand. "Come on."

They headed west, passing friendly Mystics helping one another with their powers. A man dressed in earthy tones moved his hands with precision, causing the ground to rise beneath a struggling cart, lifting it effortlessly onto the road. The grateful merchant nodded in thanks as the earth receded back into place.

Nearby, a woman gracefully waved her hand over a garden bed. She sprinkled water over thirsty plants, and the blooms burst brighter than before.

Her heart all but stopped. She craved a world where this was possible in Mystralos—a world where powers were a gift, not a curse—where unity thrived over fear. The way the people of Mystic Isle openly used their abilities to aid one another made her realize how much her own land was missing.

Gisela let out a quiet sigh, shaking herself free from her thoughts.

They walked stone pathways that wound through the isle, leading to well-built homes and storefronts painted in pastel hues, draped with greenery. Birds sang overhead, and further up, the two dragons that had brought them down soared through the sky. Lampposts lined the main roads, containing sparkling lights that had a life of their own.

Gisela stopped at one of them, pausing to examine it. She had never seen anything like it back home.

"A gift from Seraphina," a rough voice said.

Gisela spun around to find an old man sitting on a wooden bench, his presence as jarring as his words.

She cocked her head at him, and her stomach churned. His eyes were a deep blue, his hair white as snow, yet his skin bore only faint lines, as if time had barely touched him.

"Her Primal is rare, a force of light," he explained, straining to stand from the bench. He approached her, cautiously, and Thorne stepped beside her and squared his shoulders.

The man chuckled. "It's alright, young man, no harm will come to her here. Mystic Isle is a peaceful place. But I applaud your vigilance." The man lowered his head in respect and Thorne relaxed a bit.

Gisela looked up at him with a glare before turning her attention back to the old man. "I'm Gisela," she said, extending her hand.

"Darian," he replied, offering his own.

As their hands met, a cold shock ran up Gisela's arm. She snatched her hand away.

Darian's smile widened as he studied her face.

"You're a Frostweaver too?" Gisela asked.

"I am."

"I've never met another one."

"Is that right?" He winked before turning away, his slight limp barely slowing him.

"That was strange," Thorne whispered.

"Yeah. It was," she said, her mind still racing with questions as Darian disappeared into the distance.

Thorne kept hold of her hand, steering Gisela away from the bright streets and toward the western ridge.

The earth transformed into a moon-like terrain. Large craters scarred the ground, and smoke rose from the fissures. Lightning cracked across the sky, thunder rumbling overhead.

"What are we doing here?" Gisela yelled over the thunder. "With all the beauty that is Mystic Isle, you choose to come here. Why?"

"Would you quit complaining and come look at this?" Thorne said, throwing a smirk over his shoulder and nodding toward a particularly large crater.

Gisela approached the edge and peered down.

At the bottom of the crater lay a large egg. Its surface was dark and mottled with an iridescent sheen that glistened in the flashes of lightning. Before they could examine it further, the two dragons they had ridden landed in front of them. The impact shook the ground.

Gisela stumbled backward in surprise, but Thorne stood his ground, staring into the dragon's eyes.

The dragon returned his stare, its head tilting curiously back and forth.

Thorne cautiously approached the dragon, extending his hand as he did when they first met.

The dragon lowered its head and pressed its nose into Thorne's palm.

"How the hell do you do that?" Gisela asked, watching in disbelief.

He was a natural, as if he'd seen a dragon before. But of course, that couldn't be it.

Thorne shrugged. "It likes me." He slid his hand along the dragon's scales.

The second dragon descended into the crater, curling around the egg in a protective coil.

"Is that your baby?" Thorne asked.

"It doesn't speak, Thorne, I think we can assume—" Gisela began, but the dragon huffed a low rumble through its chest.

"See," Thorne said with a grin. "We mean it no harm."

"How did you know to come here?" Gisela whispered.

"I had suspicions that they lived in this part of the land since no one has built homes here."

Gisela walked toward the dragon and extended her palm as well.

The dragon huffed, but she stood steady. It swerved its head into her palm, nuzzling it. A smile spread across her lips. "How can something be so terrifying, yet exhilarating at the same time?"

Thorne glanced at her, his gaze softening. "I know the feeling."

He reached out, tucking a stray strand of her hair behind her ear. The gentle touch sent shivers down her body.

Their connection felt unusually strong here, a palpable tether that was thick and sturdy.

He closed the gap between them, his firm abdomen pressing against her. He placed his hands on both sides of her jaw, cradling her face, and lowered his mouth to hers. With only an agonizingly soft brush of his lips, he pulled away, earning a scowl from Gisela.

He smirked. "Let's head back."

Gisela could only stare, her mouth agape, as he retreated.

The dragon softly nudged her forward, a silent push to follow him.

She raised a brow as it spread its wide wings and ascended into the sky once more. The sudden blast of air sent her hair whipping behind her.

By the time they reached the pub, night had settled over Mystic Isle, painting the streets in silver light. For the first time today, they could just be—no trials to endure, no beast to slay, no tension in the air. A dream of what life could be like with him.

She wanted more of it.

Inside was thrumming with voices. Laughter and clinking glasses filled every corner. As Gisela and Thorne walked in, they spotted Marina, Silas, and two other Mystics at a large table in the back.

Marina caught Gisela's eye and waved them over.

They weaved their way between tables before sitting down in the two empty seats.

"Gisela, Thorne, this is Eva and Adrian Hale. Eva's a Stormcaller and Adrian's a Windbinder," Marina said.

"Pleasure to meet you both," Adrian said. He rose to greet them, his movements precise, each one measured like a dance. His auburn hair caught the light as his green eyes settled on Gisela.

Eva, shorter and nimble, mirrored his poise. She inclined her head, her sharp eyes softening as her Primal appeared in a shimmer beside her.

"I am Tempest," the Primal said, her voice soft and crackling with electric energy. Her translucent violet form shimmered with streams of white light that flickered around her. Tempest was lithe and agile, a living storm captured in humanoid form. Tiny bolts of lightning sparked at her fingertips, her deep purple eyes glowing with raw power.

Above them, Adrian's Primal hovered lazily, draped like a hammock in the air. With a slender form like Adrian's, he appeared as a swirling vortex of mist. His eyes were clear and calm as the sky itself. He glanced down at them with an expression of indifference. "Aerion," he said, giving a casual wave of his hand.

Gisela peered up at Aerion with amusement. "I like him already."

He looked down at her and gave a playful wink.

"My sister, Eva, doesn't speak. So, I can translate, if need be," Adrian said. "We're twins."

Marina toyed with the rim of her glass. "Eva is the only Stormcaller on the isle."

"The only?" Gisela asked. "Where are the others?"

"As you can see, Mystic Isle isn't crowded," Adrian chuckled. "But Stormcallers are rare. They aren't quite like the other elements. My mother was one, my father a Windbinder."

"Was?" Thorne asked carefully.

"They're dead," he said, picking his nails. His shoulders lifted in a careless shrug that fooled no one. "What's up with the black flames?"

The chatter dimmed, as though the pub itself had paused to listen.

Thorne inhaled sharply, his eyes meeting Adrian's with a steady gaze. Ignitus opened his mouth to speak but Thorne held up his hand. A silent exchange passed between them, and Ignitus fell quiet.

"My father's an evil bastard," Thorne said simply, his voice even. "So, I bear that mark. But I'm not him. I'm nothing like him."

Gisela gave his leg a gentle squeeze under the table.

He intertwined his fingers with hers.

Silas leaned back with his ale. "I can attest to that."

Adrian raised a brow and shrugged. "Hm. Okay."

"Which brings us to why we're here," Gisela cut in. "My Village Elder spoke of a prophecy . . . he said that the 'willing' could unite the six to save our realm. I—I believe that includes us, Mystics with each of the six elements."

The group exchanged glances, each acknowledging their unique abilities. Eva, being the last Stormcaller, made the situation even more dire.

Silas nodded, fingers drumming on the table.

"Our realm, Mystralos, is in danger," Gisela began, her voice barely rising above the noise of the pub.

A burst of laughter erupted from the far corner, jarring against her words.

She envied how easily these people could laugh. "Our land is dying, and our people will die if we don't act soon." As Gisela recounted their journey from Frosthaven to Seraphina's palace that day, the light in the room dimmed.

Adrian and Eva listened intently, their expressions reflecting the gravity of her words.

Adrian finally exhaled, setting his drink down a little too hard. "We knew about executions. But . . . everything else? It's a lot to take in. Marina, you know we love you, but Eva and I need some time to talk it over. How long are you planning to stay?"

Marina and Gisela exchanged glances. "Not long," Marina said. "We can't afford to."

"We know it's a huge ask," Gisela added. "I know it might seem like we're going on a hunch by asking you to join us, but . . ."

Eva grabbed Adrian's hand, her eyes widening.

Adrian looked at her with curiosity as she moved her hands in a series of quick, fluid gestures. Eva's expression was intense, her brows furrowing as she communicated with her brother.

Adrian's eyes shifted from Eva to Gisela. "Eva says," he interpreted, "that it's not a hunch."

Marina raised an eyebrow. "She clearly said more than that, Adrian."

Adrian smirked. "Nothing gets past you, pirate queen."

Eva gave her brother a nudge before signing again.

Adrian's expression softened as he continued, "Eva also says that she feels a deep connection to the cause." He glanced at Eva. "Give us a couple of days to prepare, if you don't mind. I have some things to tie up here."

"Of course," Gisela said.

"Thank you," Silas added, shaking Adrian's hand before rising.

They all left the pub, and Adrian tossed an arm over Gisela's shoulders as they walked. "I think we'll make great friends."

Thorne cleared his throat behind them.

Adrian scoffed. "Oh, don't fret. She's not my type," he said playfully. "You, on the other hand . . ." He winked before striding down the pathway into the night.

Thorne's mouth twitched, and he swallowed hard.

Gisela laughed. "Now *that*, I didn't see coming."

Thorne stifled his own amusement, shaking his head as Gisela continued to find the exchange hilarious. With a sudden grin, he scooped her into his arms and carried her back toward the palace, her laughter ringing through the night.

As she tossed her head back with a sigh, she glanced toward the pub and spotted Darian sitting outside.

A knowing smile played on his lips, then he gave a slight nod before melting into the shadows.

CHAPTER TWENTY-FIVE

Their palace room was as spacious as Gisela's first home in Frosthaven. Subtle notes of rose and sandalwood lingered in the air, instantly invigorating. Light glinted off pale stone floors, veins of obsidian threading through them.

At the center, a grand four-poster bed draped in luxurious black silk dominated the room. An elegant writing desk held neatly arranged stationery and an inkpot, while a plush seating area by the large window offered a view of the palace gardens.

The massive double doors swung closed behind them, and Thorne's gaze roamed the room like a predator surveying his territory, then softened as it landed on her.

"Not bad," he said. "Remember when I said we'd move to Aquamere after all this?"

Gisela laughed, a little breathless. "I don't think we can move into this palace even if we wanted to leave Mystralos."

Thorne took a step closer, then another, until the space between them vanished and the air went taut.

She couldn't breathe, couldn't think.

"You deserve every luxury every realm has to offer," he said, voice low and rich, breath warm against her ear. His hands grazed her waist and the small of her back with just enough pressure to make her shiver. He guided her backward until the edge of the bed met the back of her knees.

"You deserve to be cherished," he whispered, pressing a tender kiss to her cheek. "Worshipped." His lips trailed along her jaw. "Satisfied." He kissed down her neck, slow and claiming.

She tilted her head back, a soft moan escaping before she could stop it.

The sound did him in. Thorne hooked his hands under her thighs, lifting her legs to wrap around his waist as he lowered her onto the silk. He hovered over her, his eyes dark, studying, memorizing every inch.

Gisela traced her fingers along his chest, over his broad shoulders, and gripped him tightly. The touch unraveled him, warmth spreading as his fingers threaded through her hair.

Their eyes met, and they smiled—their elements intertwining, her coolness mingling with his heat.

He rolled her on top of him, positioning her on his hips. His hands traveled up her back, then down to her sides, igniting a fire in her that had nothing to do with the room's warmth.

She lifted her top over her head and tossed it aside, abandoning every ounce of restraint.

He did the same, removing the barrier between them.

She leaned forward and bit his lower lip.

With a swift motion, he rolled her back beneath him, bracing himself above her.

Gisela's eyes met his. An overwhelming surge of desire and longing swelled in her chest until she could barely breathe.

When Thorne lowered his lips to hers, the kiss was tender at first, then deepened into a fervent heat he'd held at bay far too long.

Her hands tangled in his black hair, pulling him closer.

He broke the kiss just long enough to work the fabric of her pants over her hips, discarding them along with his own in a reckless heap. Then he was over her once more, his bare chest hovering a fraction of an inch from hers.

"Wait," she said suddenly.

Thorne froze, concern etched in his features.

Gisela smirked. "Your mark."

He chuckled and lifted himself a little higher.

In the groove of his hip was a small, flame-shaped mark. Its tendrils curled upward toward his hip bone.

She reached down, tracing it with her fingertips.

He laced his fingers through hers, leaning down to press a soft, lingering kiss to her lips.

Their bodies entwined, and everything else fell away.

Thorne ran his hand down her stomach until it reached the center of her thighs, drawing a low hum of approval.

"Perfect," he murmured into her ear, lips brushing her neck and collarbone.

She gasped as his fingers entered her, and he groaned a deep, vibrating sound that made her muscles clench.

Her hand drifted down his stomach.

He grabbed her wrist. "No," he rasped, the word vibrating against her skin. "You first."

He lowered himself, his mouth settling between her thighs. He circled her with precise, teasing movements—a slow torturous rhythm that stripped away everything but the feel of him.

Never in her life had she experienced anything like this.

It was a focused, relentless adoration that made her world narrow down to the point of his tongue.

She writhed under him, her fingers digging into the sheets as she arched her back, a broken high sound escaping her as she met her release. It crashed over her in waves, leaving her heart hammering against her ribs.

Thorne didn't pull away immediately. He lingered, savoring the tremors that raced through her before slowly rising. He captured her wrists, guiding them above her head. He pinned them gently to the pillow, his body solid and grounding over her.

"Eyes on me," he whispered. He waited until her hazy eyes found his. "I need to see the look in them when you realize no one else is ever going to make you feel like this."

She could only offer a small, breathless smile, because the gods' honest truth was that she already knew it.

He kissed her—slow, deep, and tasting of her—until the world stopped spinning and her body finally stilled beneath his.

"Fuck, you're beautiful," he murmured, sliding against her. His lips met hers again, slow and soft, his hips pressing into hers with steady insistence.

"Please," she whispered.

He smiled against her lips. "I've been waiting too long for this, Freckles, I don't want to rush." At the sound of her nickname, she balked, but his low, deep laugh sent a shudder through her.

He leaned down, teeth grazing her nipple.

Gisela arched. "Thorne."

His tongue drew lazy circles around it until she was squirming in anticipation. He trailed his fingers down her stomach until he reached her center once more, circling lightly, the touch only intended to tease her further.

Gisela reached down and grasped him in her hand.

His eyes snapped to hers.

"Please," she repeated.

He swept her hair from her face, grazing her temple with his thumb. "As you wish," he murmured.

He pushed himself into her, a low groan caught in his throat as he paused to kiss her until the tension in her hips melted and she adjusted to him.

A stifled sound escaped him, his body trembling above her. "Gisela," he said, a plea and a promise.

Their lips crashed together as he moved inside her, his thrusts deepening.

Gisela cried out his name, her fingers dragging down his back as they moved together, her body drawing close to release once more.

Thorne clutched her tightly as though she might slip away.

He broke away from their kiss. His breath was ragged, his voice barely a whisper when he said, "I love you."

"I love *you*," she responded.

They both reached their peak, and time stood still. A blast of their elements, the fire of him, the ice of her, merged, wrapping them in a cocoon of searing heat and chilling frost.

Exhausted and trembling, they collapsed into each other, chests rising and falling in sync. Thorne buried his face in her neck and shoulder, arms tight around her.

Gisela's tears traced her cheeks.

He lifted his head and brushed them away.

A pulse of fire surged through her mind, faint but undeniable. The air around them shimmered, and a subtle warmth and frost threaded through the space as their elements danced with one another.

It was the connection—the Soulbinding—but not in the way she'd feared. It didn't take her will, it enhanced it, mirrored it, made the choice feel mutual and alive.

Thorne jolted, eyes widening.

"Do you feel—" Gisela started.

"I do." He lifted himself slightly off her. His mouth opened and closed, hesitant. "Do you want this?"

Her pulse quickened. Normally, she would never have chosen to bind herself to anyone in this way. Her purpose—her duty—had always been to help her people, to heal them. She was needed.

And she needed Thorne more than air.

Maybe this was too much.

But her duty hadn't vanished. It had only changed, widening into something new. Being a Frostweaver was in her blood, embedded into her very being.

And this connection with Thorne, whatever divine intervention had brought it, meant something profound.

She would choose him.

"I do."

In that instant their elements merged—not completely, just a touch, but undeniable—and with them, their thoughts.

Soulbound.

Gisela tugged on the thread of fire within her mind, and she felt a tug back.

"Thorne," she projected.

Thorne smiled. *"Yes, beautiful?"*

"We can hear each other in our minds."

"Yes, we can."

A slow smile spread across her face. She reached for his hand, entwining her fingers with his, feeling the warmth of their bond deepen.

"Ignitus?" Thorne called.

"Eira?" Gisela echoed.

A hum of acknowledgment came through their minds, and they shared a knowing smile.

Thorne rolled onto his side, propping himself up on one elbow.

"Maybe that's why we could always feel each other's presence," Gisela said.

"Maybe," Thorne replied, eyes never leaving hers.

She reflected on those moments when the sudden chill ran down her spine—her trips to the Snowdrifts, his occasional glimpses as he passed her parents' shop while she worked, their shared encounters in the village center. Each of these instances had hinted at something more.

As thoughts of Frosthaven swirled in her mind, the connection between them tugged something else loose—her family.

Nerves stirred in her core. She traced the line of his collarbone, the steady beat of his heart echoing the rhythm of hers.

"Do you ever wonder what our families will think?"

Thorne hesitated. "My mother . . . she always wanted the best for me. When my father agreed to the betrothal to Ruby, it was for political gain. The Blackwells are in the King's good graces, and they support him fully. I knew my mother was against it but standing up to my father wasn't something she was ever comfortable doing."

His shoulders tensed and Gisela reached out, cupping his jaw. The tension melted from him like snow under the sun.

Thorne leaned into her touch, eyes closing briefly in quiet relief.

"I've tried to push thoughts of my family out of my mind since we left Frosthaven . . ." she began, voice trembling as tears brimmed. "But the longer we have been gone, the worse I feel. There is so much they don't know, and it feels like I'm lying to them, you know? I mean, I guess I am. But I had to. Everything has changed since we left, and I worry about what it will be like when I finally go home."

"They'll welcome you with open arms," Thorne reassured her, wiping her tears from her cheek. "They love you unconditionally."

"I know," she sighed, staring up at the ceiling. "And Elysande. I worry for her too."

"She did the right thing hiding in Rockridge," Thorne said, tracing light circles along her stomach. "They won't be looking for scribes there anymore."

"I don't think it'll be safe anywhere, not with beasts pouring in from Noxis," Gisela said, shaking her head. "I wish I could talk to her again."

Thorne pulled Gisela onto his chest and wrapped his arms around her. "We'll find her," he said. "We'll keep them all safe."

Gisela's worry tightened its grip. It had been too long since she'd last seen Elysande, and the realm was unraveling more with each passing day.

Chapter Twenty-Six
King Ravenor

The King's private alchemy lab was dimly lit by flickering torches mounted on the walls. Vials and beakers bubbled across two long tables, strange ingredients simmering beneath Zaro's hands. Rusted chains hung from the walls, clinking with every movement, occasionally scraping against the stone. The room bore scars of old stains and scratches, and the air was potent with the harsh scent of chemicals mingling with a hint of copper.

Zaro sat in a wooden chair between the tables, his head bowed over his notebook. Sweat beaded along his brow as he worked, the torchlight catching the precise movements of his fingers as they danced between vials and flame.

King Ravenor followed his every motion—each adjustment, each note scribbled with unnerving patience.

The potions hissed softly.

The King paced, his eyes now fixed on the Life Stones perched on a smaller table in the corner of the room. His footsteps echoed on the stone floor, reverberating through the chamber as his robe flowed and twisted with each stride. "You said we would be ready by now. The Stones are in our grasp yet we're still one Mystic short of claiming them all. What's taking so long?" The King's voice sharpened.

Zaro glanced up from his notebook. Something tightened in his expression—gone as quickly as it appeared. "Stormcallers are hard to find, My King. Rushing this process would be as foolish as trying to wield a blade without mastering its edge."

King Ravenor scoffed, doing little to conceal his impatience. "I don't need a lecture, Zaro. I need a Stormcaller before the entire realm collapses. How close are we?"

Zaro tilted his head, locking eyes with the King. His gaze was steady, but his shoulders were locked. "It would be quicker if we had the boy, the dark Flamekeeper."

King Ravenor halted mid-stride. "Why is he necessary? He doesn't wield the storm. We already found a Flamekeeper."

A saccharine smile spread across Zaro's face. "Because his blood is special. Unique. It would grant you more power than you could possibly imagine. He will make a stronger conduit. You wouldn't need the storm."

"I want all six."

Zaro's jaw tightened before quickly loosening. "As do I, my King, but then we may be waiting generations. We can proceed without it."

The King scoffed. "Then we should kill the spares. They are little more than empty vessels anyway."

Zaro didn't flinch. "Once you become a Mystic, you will be able to control them as your conduits. They must remain alive, My King. It will please the gods. You've already angered them with the executions," Zaro replied, his tone carrying an underlying warning.

King Ravenor curled his lip but managed to maintain his composure. "The executions never happened, Zaro. Just ask the scribes."

A loud knock on the chamber door interrupted them.

"Enter," the King bellowed, his voice echoing through the stone chamber.

A frail guard scurried in, his uniform rumpled, his hands trembling as he carried a piece of folded parchment.

"Shut the door, you fool!"

"Apologies, Your Majesty," the guard mumbled, shutting the door and bowing deeply.

"Lower," the King snapped.

The guard lowered himself until he was nearly folded in half.

The King smirked. "What is your purpose?"

The guard stood straight and handed the King the piece of parchment. "A raven, Your Majesty. From Aquamere."

The King unfolded the parchment with deliberate hands, his focus fixed on the words on the page. A sinister smirk curled his lips as he read.

"What is it, My King?" Zaro asked.

"The dark Flamekeeper," he said. "It won't be long now."

CHAPTER TWENTY-SEVEN

Thorne slept beside her, his breathing slow and steady, the tension that usually lived in his body nowhere to be found.

Gisela watched his chest rise and fall, the faint crease between his brows smoothing away in sleep. Pale morning light slipped through the sheer curtains, casting gentle shadows across his features like it didn't want to wake him.

She leaned in and kissed him softly.

Without opening his eyes, Thorne wrapped his arms around her, holding her tightly. There was an echo of his contentment through the bond as he kissed her back, slow and unhurried. *"I need you again,"* he said into her mind.

Heat spread through her. She didn't resist it. She never wanted to. She hummed against his lips, meeting his heat with her own as they gave in to each other once more.

Afterward, he curled his body around her in a protective embrace, and she rested against him, listening to the steady rhythm of his heart. The world outside the room was distant, almost irrelevant.

Almost.

"I could stay like this forever," she said.

His mouth brushed her temple. "I could lose myself in you for an eternity," he whispered. "And it still wouldn't be enough."

A soft knock at their door brought them back to reality.

"Just a minute!" Gisela called out. She slipped into one of the silk robes hanging on a hook, the fabric a cool whisper against her skin, and she went to crack open the door.

"The light stirs, and so must we—Oh . . ." Adrian sang, pausing mid-step. His gaze flicked past her to where Thorne was pulling his tunic over his head. Adrian raised a brow, eyes twinkling with amusement. "Lucky girl," he mumbled with a teasing grin.

"You have no idea," she said as she opened the door wider to allow him in.

"You two have a good night?" he asked, his gaze flicking between Gisela and Thorne.

"We did," Thorne said, his focus settling onto Gisela.

"More than good," Gisela said into Thorne's mind.

Thorne's smirk widened as he ran his hands through his disheveled hair.

Adrian's eyes darted between them. "Seraphina would like us all in the dining room for breakfast." He gestured for them to follow him. "I'll walk you. You can get lost in this place easily."

They walked through the corridor, their footsteps echoing beneath the vaulted ceiling. The space was vast and cool, the stone carrying every sound.

Gisela slowed. She had never seen a place like this, so open, so unburdened. A world away from Frosthaven. "Why are you here in the palace?" Gisela asked.

Adrian lifted his head as he walked, shooting her a sideways glance. "You're not the only one who had a good time last night."

Gisela giggled and linked arms with him. "Oh, tell me more."

Thorne walked beside them, shaking his head, though he couldn't hide his amusement.

They entered the dining hall, light streaming through tall arched windows that stretched nearly to the ceiling. The room was too bright, the kind of brightness that pressed against her eyes. Light glinted off plates and caught on silver. Every sound scraped—dishes clinking, voices echoing, chairs shifting. She squeezed her eyelids shut, shaking her head.

Eira stirred inside her. A faint pulse, like a ripple beneath her skin. *"Your senses are heightened."*

Something inside her was different. Her senses had sharpened last night with Thorne, every touch magnified until it felt unreal—overwhelming in the best way.

This was something else.

Too harsh.

She steeled herself and approached the long table running down the center, set with a spread that could have fed a small village—eggs, pastries, fruit, pitchers of juice. Butter and sugar perfumed the air, and the fireplace crackled through the open space. She faltered before sitting, wondering how many people in Frosthaven had gone hungry that morning.

Seraphina was already seated at the head of the table with Eva, Silas, Marina, and Bjorn. She looked up with a welcoming smile. "Good morning," Seraphina greeted. "I trust your accommodations were pleasing?"

"The pleasure was copious, Seraphina, thank you," Adrian said, dropping into a seat beside Eva. His eyes flicked to a guard standing stoically at the door, and the man shifted slightly but remained impassive.

Above him, Aerion drifted lazily in his suspended perch, relaxed, a small smirk ghosting his lips as if he were in on some private joke.

Thorne and Gisela exchanged a glance before Gisela replied, "Yes, thank you."

Seraphina's smile widened as she gestured for them to sit.

Eva gave Gisela a knowing look, her smile soft and amused. She inclined her head in a wordless greeting before returning her focus to her plate.

Gisela took a seat beside Marina and nudged her. "How was last night?" she whispered.

"The pleasure was copious," Marina mimicked, earning a quiet giggle from Gisela. Then Marina's expression softened. "I missed him."

Gisela's smile warmed. "I'm glad you had time together."

Marina reached for her hand beneath the table, giving it a squeeze. "Me too." Her gaze drifted to Bjorn, whose relaxed posture and faint grin said everything about their reunion.

"Seraphina," Marina began hesitantly. "I wondered if I could borrow one of the dragons today. Take me up to the dock. I'd love to bring the crew some of the Mystic Isle delicacies."

Seraphina inclined her head. "Granted. We appreciate all you do. Take Terranox."

Silas bit into a pastry, his eyes widening. "Which one is that?"

"The one I took down here with Gisela," Thorne said easily.

A few surprised looks passed around the table.

Seraphina paused mid-sip, her head tilting slightly.

"How'd you know that?" Silas asked.

"Lucky guess." Thorne shrugged and reached for another pastry.

The clatter of silverware resumed, filling the room with the familiar sound, but Gisela's attention had already shifted. The laughter, the hum of conversation, the smell of food—it all blurred into something distant. Too loud and too far away at once.

Marina leaned closer to Gisela. "Bjorn and my father did a lot of talking last night. He didn't come to the room until midnight."

"Looks like it went well," Gisela said, her voice thin.

Silas and Bjorn shared fruit, both smiling easily.

"Thank The Six for that."

"And you and your father . . .?"

Marina exhaled and took a sip of juice. "We're working on things. As angry as I was, I did miss him. I need him still."

The words hit deeper than Marina could know. Gisela tried to smile, but it didn't reach her eyes. The ache that had been building finally broke open. She thought of her father's voice, firm and steady. Her mother's quiet humming while she blended herbs. Her brother's teasing grin. Her little sister's laughter. Each image slipped, like sand pouring through her fingers.

She needed them too.

Needed them in a way she hadn't let herself think about.

Then Thorne's presence touched her mind, gentle and worried, but even that soft contact landed too heavily. The brightness, the noise, the longing—it all collapsed inward at once.

The room tilted slightly.

Her chair scraped as she pushed back from the table. A tightness seized her throat.

"Are you okay?" Thorne's voice slipped into her mind.

"I need some air," she said aloud, and before anyone could stop her, she slipped from the room.

The air was too thin. Her heartbeat slammed against her ribs. She pressed a hand to her chest, dizziness flooding through her. The palace, for all its vastness, closed around her anyway.

You can't fall apart here. Not now.

Eira sent a wave of cold through her veins, trying to steady her.

Marina was on her heels. "Gisela! Wait!"

Gisela's legs gave out. She sank to her knees, the world collapsing into noise and pressure.

Marina knelt beside her, gripping her shoulder. "I'm sorry—I didn't mean to—"

Gisela shook her head. "No," she managed, the word breaking on her tongue.

Thorne's footsteps came fast behind them. "I've got her," he said.

Marina's shoulders slumped and her gaze fell to the floor. She hesitated before retreating, turning her head back once before disappearing down the hall.

Thorne knelt and cupped Gisela's face in his hands. "Hey," he whispered, his voice steady and calming. "Focus on me." He brushed his thumbs across her cheeks, wiping her tears.

She tried. Slowly, the storm inside her quieted beneath his touch. "I'm sorry."

"Don't be. Never apologize for this."

"I . . ." she started, choking on her words. "I need to see them. Before anything else, I need to see them."

Thorne nodded. "We'll find a way."

Footsteps approached, soft and sure. Seraphina appeared with that impossible grace, as though she was floating. "Gisela," she said. "There's something I want to show you." She extended her hand.

Gisela hesitated, then took it.

Seraphina led her down a side corridor with Thorne close behind. She paused and glanced back at him. "She's safe here. I promise you. This will help her."

He nodded reluctantly. Thorne's fingers twitched at his sides as he watched them go. *"I'm here,"* he whispered into her mind.

"I know," she responded back, giving him a soft smile before turning her attention back to Seraphina.

They strolled down the corridor, the air growing warmer and infused with the scent of lavender and lemon. At the end of the hall stood a large wooden door with intricate carvings of vines and flowers.

Seraphina rested one hand on the handle, her other hand lightly brushing the carvings.

The door opened, revealing a room unlike anything Gisela had ever seen.

Soft, enchanting light filled the sanctuary. Smooth stone floors sparkled underfoot and a giant pool of rippling water rested in the center. The sound of a cascading waterfall filled the space, wrapping Gisela in an instantaneous sense of calm.

"Do you have a favorite color?" Seraphina asked.

Gisela considered the question. "Violet."

With a graceful wave of her hand, Seraphina cast the room in a violet glow. Mist curled above the pool, tinted purple.

Seraphina led Gisela to the water's edge, where a cotton robe was draped over a smooth stone bench. "The waters here are special," she explained. "They're infused with the natural magic of the isle. They have a way of calming the mind and healing the spirit. Mystics find clarity here when their magic strains against them. Take your time." She left Gisela at the water's edge and slipped out, closing the door behind her.

Gisela admired the room before undressing and placing her clothes neatly on the stone bench. She stepped into the pool, carefully lowering herself into the warm, soothing waters.

It reached her neck, and a deep sense of peace flooded her.

Eira stretched within her, no longer bracing or tense.

The current around Gisela shifted, syncing with her pulse.

She submerged and let the water carry her. It swirled around, responding to her touch, acknowledging her presence.

When she surfaced, the tension in her chest had loosened. She leaned back and floated, letting the water guide her. Her heart steadied. Her breaths deepened. For a few precious moments, there was no fear, no guilt—only stillness.

The mysterious waters fueled Eira, and Gisela's power strengthened and refined with every ripple.

She stayed there for a time, savoring the quiet inside and out. The ache in her heart hadn't vanished, but it was no longer overwhelming or all-consuming.

She swam to the stairs and stepped out and found her skin completely dry. She looked back at the pool, pausing to examine it. The water stilled, then rippled in small acknowledgment. Gisela smiled and pulled on the robe.

Seraphina reentered, her face bright. "Do you feel better?"

"I do," Gisela replied. "I've never felt anything like that before." She glanced at the violet light dancing over the surface.

Seraphina waved her hand, returning the room to its natural state. "We must care for ourselves. It's easier to face our troubles with a clear mind. Clarity lets us see the road ahead, even when the path is uncertain."

Gisela softened at Seraphina's kindness.

The benevolence was foreign to her, having grown up amidst the rule of King Ravenor. Despite not knowing who they were, Seraphina had welcomed them warmly, offering a place to rest and food to eat. She hadn't realized how much she'd longed for that kind of generosity from a ruler.

"Come. Your friends are waiting," Seraphina said, leading her out of the sanctuary and to the palace gardens.

Chapter Twenty-Eight

They approached the gardens, and Gisela took a slow breath, find-ing it easier to fill her lungs now that the weight of the morning had been washed away in the pool. The air smelled of damp earth and roses. Stone paths wound between low hedges, and a fountain splashed steadily in the sun.

They rounded a corner to find Marina, Thorne, and Silas next to Terranox. The dragon's black scales gleamed in the light. Even lying down, he was massive compared to the three of them.

"I'll never get used to seeing a dragon," Silas said. "Helena never mentioned them."

Marina chuckled. "Yeah, probably because you would've freaked out knowing she was riding them to get here."

Silas's shoulders sagged slightly, and he rubbed the back of his neck. "She didn't tell me much about this place at all . . ."

Seraphina offered him a compassionate smile. "I'll leave you all to it," she said, bowing her head before walking back to the palace doors. Before she entered, she threw over her shoulder, "Be quick with Terranox."

"Will do," Marina called, packing her bag.

Thorne approached Gisela and tilted her chin up to kiss her. "How are you holding up?"

Gisela met his stare and kissed him again. "Better now."

"You look beautiful," he said as he pulled her into his chest. "Refreshed."

"Want to join me, Gisela? I'm sure Larz would love to see you," Marina teased, flinging her bag over her shoulder.

Thorne shot Marina a sharp glance, and flame leapt from his palm.

She doused it with a stream of water, smirking in triumph.

"You're insufferable," he grumbled.

"Thorne, want to grab a drink while they're gone?" Silas offered.

Thorne hesitated, looking down at Gisela. "You'll be all right?"

"I'll be fine," she said. "I'll bond with Terranox. Maybe I'll win his favor before you do."

Thorne tapped her nose. "Too late for that."

Terranox huffed but dipped his head.

Thorne sighed, shifting his weight. "All right. A drink might be good." He lowered his face to Gisela's as he kissed her one more time. "I love you," he said against her lips. "More than I can bear."

"Well, bear it. Because I love you too."

"Oh, relax, I'll take good care of her," Marina joked. "It's not like we're leaving for days."

With that, Marina and Gisela climbed onto Terranox and settled within the saddle.

Silas and Thorne waved as Terranox launched into the sky with a force that took the breath out of Gisela's lungs.

They soared above Mystic Isle, the surreal view never failing to amaze her.

Gisela eyed the satchel. "Do you have what you need for them?" she yelled over the roar of the wind, bracing herself against Terranox's steadying sway.

"Yep, in this bag," Marina replied, patting the satchel slung over her shoulder. "Larz loves the pastries here. Plus, some other goodies too." She raised an eyebrow with a hint of mischief, and Gisela chose not to ask.

As they reached the cliff's peak, Terranox lowered himself to land, but reared back.

Marina grasped the reins and guided him toward the dock, coaxing his heavy talons to meet the ground.

Terranox recoiled again, this time with a guttural, uneasy growl.

Marina's eyes darted to Gisela. "Something's wrong."

They dismounted quickly, sliding off his shifting back before he could take flight again. Terranox huffed, thrashing his massive head, nostrils flaring.

Gisela pressed a calming hand to his snout. "We'll be right back, Terranox."

Eira and Ondine materialized beside them.

"Stop," Eira commanded, voice like steel.

"Marina . . ." Ondine warned.

Marina's frown deepened. "If my men are in danger, I can't wait."

Eira and Ondine exchanged a tense glance, but Marina pushed past and strode down the dock, mist swirling thick around her.

Terranox roared after her and Gisela staggered back at the force of the sound. She hurried after Marina, slipping through the vortex and back to Mystralos.

Gisela stumbled out, this time landing on her feet, but the triumph was short lived.

Rain hammered down. Thunder rolled like drums across the sea. And before them . . . devastation.

The ship, once whole, floated in splintered pieces. Giant teeth marks gouged the deck.

Marina choked on a gasp and sprinted to the end of the dock.

Gisela followed, stomach twisting. Dark shapes bobbed in the water. Limbs. Clothing. Bodies torn apart by something far stronger than any storm.

A blood-curdling scream tore from Marina's lips. "Ondine!"

Ondine was already behind her, face carved in grief.

Marina knelt over the dock, plunging her hands into the choppy water. "Make it still!" she ordered, voice breaking.

Nothing changed. The waves tossed the bodies, mocking her helplessness.

Marina let out a strangled sob, tears competing with rain drops, streaking down her face.

Gisela rushed to her side and slipped an arm around Marina's waist to keep her from collapsing, her own tears blurring her vision.

"It's supposed to be safe out here . . . how did—what could possibly—" Marina's voice fractured. She dropped to her knees and thrust her trembling hands into the water again, willing the ocean to respond. "Ondine, why isn't it working!?" she screamed, her fists crashing down against the waves. Each strike was more frantic.

Behind them, Ondine and Eira were motionless, eyes dim, their silence heavy with what could not be undone.

"My men . . . my mother's ship," Marina choked out. "I made them sail out here."

Gisela reached for Thorne through her mind. *"Thorne,"* she called, but there was no response. The thought that they might be unable to communicate across realms unsettled her.

"Marina," Gisela whispered. "We need to go back."

"This is all my fault," Marina rasped.

"No, don't say that. This isn't on you. It's on King Ravenor's greed."

A deep rumble vibrated under the water.

Marina's head snapped up, grief burning away into something sharper—anger.

"Eira, what is that?" Gisela asked, her pulse kicking up.

"Beasts from Noxis," Eira replied. "We need to go back. Now."

The surface burst open as a massive eel-like creature launched skyward.

Marina thrust her hands out, trying to wrap it in water, but her magic sputtered.

The beast vanished beneath the waves with a hiss.

"Ondine!" she yelled.

Ondine only shook her head. Lost. Hollow.

The creature surged up again. Closer.

Gisela acted before fear had time to take root. Ice blasted from her palms, encasing the monster mid-air. It froze in perfect, horrifying stillness.

The rain slowed, but thunder still rumbled.

Gisela studied the suspended beast. Its face was twisted in a menacing snarl, rows of sharp, rotted teeth jutting out. Dark green scales covered its body, and spikes lined its back like jagged armor.

"If those creatures are all the way out here already . . ." Gisela's voice trailed off as she noticed Eira and Ondine exchanging worried glances.

"Why did your powers work and not mine?" Marina asked weakly.

Gisela shrugged. "It's odd," she responded. "But we need to leave. I can't get through to Thorne."

"What do you mean get through to him?"

Gisela pressed her lips together. "We can speak to each other in our minds."

Marina stared at her. Grief gave way to shock. "Since when?"

"Since last night."

Marina's mouth dropped. "So, you *are* Soulbound?"

"We need to go back and tell them what happened. I'm so sorry, Marina. But it isn't safe here. There could be more of them."

Marina wiped her face. "How are we going to get back to Aquamere now?"

Gisela's heart sank.

The answer came with slow, heavy wingbeats.

Through the swirling mist, Terranox emerged, his massive form cutting a path through the haze. He looked around, examining the unfamiliar place.

"I didn't know they could cross realms," Marina whispered. She approached Terranox, eyes darting back to the ruined ship. She clutched at her hair as the sobs returned.

Ondine vanished into her as Marina climbed into the saddle, hiding her face in her hands.

Gisela stood by the edge of the dock, staring at the wreckage.

The men who had waited for them . . . gone. The ship that had carried their hopes . . . gone. The weight of it hollowed her.

She turned to Terranox.

And the sea exploded.

A second eel shot upward, striking faster than Terranox could react.

Gisela had only half a breath to scream before it slammed into her, knocking her off the dock.

The ocean closed over her head, dragging her down in a dizzying rush of bubbles and darkness. She pushed upward, lungs burning as she broke the surface with a gasp.

"Gisela!" Marina screamed.

The creature, massive and vicious, surged toward her from the depths.

Eira unleashed a sheet of ice, freezing the beast beneath the surface—but its momentum rocked the water violently.

Gisela kicked hard, fighting the current. The dock was impossibly far. Another surge churned the sea.

A third beast leapt from the water, jaws wide.

She barely had time to inhale before it came crashing down toward her.

Terranox's roar split the storm. He lunged forward, seizing the creature by its neck. Bone cracked beneath his jaws and blood misted the air as he thrashed it, hurling the body back into the sea.

He dove for Gisela, lowering a wing toward her. She grabbed hold with shaking hands as he lifted her to the saddle.

"Go, Terranox!" Gisela commanded.

The dragon responded with a powerful beat of his wings, lifting from the dock and soaring back into the realm of Mystic Isle.

Gisela reached for Thorne through their mental link. *"Thorne!"* she cried.

His panic slammed into her like a second heartbeat. *"What happened!? Are you hurt!?"*

"Get back to the palace gardens. Now."

Chapter Twenty-Nine

Terranox soared through the misty skies, carrying them farther from the ruin behind—yet not far enough.

There was silence between them, broken only by Marina's muffled sobs and the steady rhythm of the dragon's wings.

As the palace gardens came into view, Thorne and Silas were already sprinting through the gates. Terranox landed, lowering himself so Gisela and Marina could disembark.

"What happened!?" Silas dropped to his knees as Marina collapsed into him, shaking with grief.

Thorne swept Gisela into a desperate hug, his hands running instinctively over her wet hair, her soaked clothes. "Why are you wet? What happened?" His arms locked around her with a desperation she hadn't felt from him before.

Gisela's throat tightened painfully. "They're gone. The ship . . . it's destroyed."

Silas looked up from where he held Marina, his jaw slack with disbelief.

Thorne stepped back, dragging a hand over his face as he shook his head.

Gisela moved to Marina's side, kneeling beside her as Eira and Ondine appeared.

"Beasts from Noxis," Eira explained. "Three more came for us."

Gisela tensed, the image of the beast's jagged teeth flashing behind her eyes—the violent drag downward.

The air warped with sudden pressure as Ondine described the attack on Gisela.

Thorne's fists clenched, breath sharp, fury barely leashed. At the mention of her being knocked into the water, his control nearly snapped.

"Get Bjorn," Gisela said.

Silas nodded, let go of Marina, and hurried from the garden.

"I'm okay," Gisela said, reassuring Thorne. "Terranox saved my life."

Terranox nudged Thorne's side with a low, grounding rumble.

Thorne bowed his head gratefully and moved to kneel beside Marina. "I'm sorry," he murmured. "Those men loved you."

Marina's sobs slowed enough for her to wipe her eyes with trembling fingers. Her stare was unfocused. It was chilling—the look of someone untethered, drifting somewhere grief had swallowed whole.

Gisela rested a hand on Thorne's back, their eyes meeting in a brief, solemn look as his muscles tensed beneath her touch.

They stepped back, giving Marina the space she needed.

"How are we getting back to Mystralos?" Thorne asked.

"Terranox crossed the veil," Gisela said. "If Seraphina allows it, the dragons might be able to take us home."

"What about Adrian and Eva? Can they fit?"

"Let's talk to Seraphina first."

Gisela returned to Marina and took her hand. "There's a pool here that helped me earlier. Seraphina will let you use it. Come on." She pulled Marina to her feet, walking her toward the entrance to the palace.

A guard stood there in an all-white uniform, his blonde hair visible beneath the edge of his gleaming silver helmet. "I sent word to Seraphina," he said sympathetically.

"Thank you," Gisela guided Marina through the palace doors.

Thorne followed with a tight nod toward the guard.

Inside the grand foyer of the palace, cool air swept over her, carrying the faint scent of lavender and stone.

Seraphina appeared at the top of the staircase, her usual composed demeanor now replaced by alarm. She descended the stairs, her white gown sweeping behind her as she moved. "What's happened?"

Gisela, body still trembling, recounted the events. Every detail drained more color from Seraphina's face.

Without a word, Seraphina grasped Marina into her arms and guided her toward the pool room. "Meet me in my study," she called over her shoulder. "One of the guards will escort you there."

Seraphina's study was exactly what Gisela had imagined—white and serene, with touches of pale gold. A massive porcelain desk dominated the center of the room, with plush ivory chairs in front of it. Floor-to-ceiling windows framed a vast view of Mystic Isle.

Gisela and Thorne took their seats. They glanced at one another, neither finding words to say.

Moments later, Silas entered, eyebrows lifting as he took in the immaculate room. Adrian and Eva followed close behind, their faces reflecting the collective grief.

"I told them what happened," Silas said, taking a seat next to Thorne.

Gisela wrung her hands in her lap. "Marina's magic failed in Mystralos."

Silas's head lifted. "Failed?"

"It was weak. Something's really wrong."

Before anyone could respond, Seraphina swept into the room, composure restored. "Marina is in the waters, resting," she informed them. Her gaze shifted to Silas as she offered him a reassuring nod. "Bjorn is waiting for her there." Her expression fell. "I am deeply sorry for what happened to Marina's crew. It's an absolute tragedy. How are we able to assist?"

"Well, to be plain, we have no way home," Gisela said. "Conditions in Mystralos have escalated fast."

Seraphina nodded.

"Could the dragons take us back to Aquamere?" Thorne asked.

Seraphina sighed. "I'm not sure that is feasible."

"Terranox crossed the veil," Thorne added.

"Yes," Seraphina admitted, a rare look of uncertainty crossing her face. "But they have an egg to protect. Instinct may prevent them from leaving the isle."

Gisela exchanged a glance with Thorne as he rubbed his jaw. "Is there any other way?" she asked.

Seraphina rubbed her temples.

A firm knock at the door averted her attention. "Come in."

The door swung open and Darian, the Frostweaver they'd met the day before, strolled in.

Gisela's expression froze, her body tensing instinctively.

Seraphina waved her hand, granting him permission to speak.

Darian dropped into a chair. "Word travels fast here," he said. "Sound like you kids have no way back to Mystralos? Can't imagine why you'd want to go back."

"Kids?" Silas echoed.

"You're a kid to me. I'm much older than I look," Darian replied with a wink.

"Our land is dying. Our people are in danger," Gisela snapped. "We won't abandon them."

Seraphina interlaced her fingers. "Darian, why are you here? Shouldn't you be tending to the palace's matters in your *own* study?"

"I suspect you already know, Sovereign." He crossed his leg. "They'll have a way home. Gisela and the twins. Not the Flamekeeper." His gaze settled on Thorne. "He may find the paths . . . unwelcoming."

Adrian and Eva exchanged a look.

"What are you talking about?" Thorne interjected. "She goes where I go."

"That would be unwise," Darian said, face neutral. "The trees won't answer to corruption. Or to those whose blood isn't bound."

Corruption. The word twisted her stomach.

Darian stood, shooting a quick glance toward Gisela. "I'll dismiss myself, Sovereign." He left the study, shutting the door softly behind him.

"Are you going to explain that?" Thorne demanded, snapping his gaze to Seraphina.

"It's not completely safe now."

"*What* isn't?" Thorne retorted, his anger flaring once more.

Gisela put her hand on his forearm and glared at him. "Relax," she hissed under her breath, but her pulse quickened all the same. His emotions were pouring through the bond, unsettling her—frustration, aggravation . . . and something else.

A pressure built behind her eyes, and without meaning to, she pushed back. The connection between them thinned, the strength of his emotions in her mind muting as if someone had closed a door.

Thorne stared at her, tension faltering, eyes narrowing.

Seraphina shifted in her chair and cleared her throat. "Using the Guardian Trees to travel between realms . . . your villages."

A hush fell over the room.

Silas sat back in his chair, crossing his arms.

"No," Gisela said. "I've always been drawn to Frosthaven's Guardian Tree. I've never felt that I could see other realms through it."

"Were you awakened?" Seraphina asked.

Gisela said nothing.

Thorne leaned forward, dark flames crawling along his knuckles. "With all due respect, Seraphina, that's not enough. We need more answers."

"The Guardian Trees," Seraphina said. "They bind the realms of the Six together. Descendants of the First Mystics can travel between them. The trees' roots are bound to that bloodline. But the paths are unstable now. Step through the wrong one, and you may not end up where you intend to be."

Silas frowned. "That's it? A bloodline decides who gets stranded and who doesn't?"

Seraphina inclined her head. "It is not fairness that governs the trees, only the magic that shaped them. The paths were meant for those whose ancestors first heard the Six speak their names."

Thorne's voice rose. "How does that explain Gisela being able to do that when she doesn't have Mystic lineage at all? And Adrian and Eva?"

Adrian cut in. "We've never—"

Seraphina lifted her hand to quiet them. "I will leave it up to Adrian and Eva to explain their heritage on their own time. As for Gisela . . ." She hesitated. "Darian suspects—"

"And who is Darian!?" Thorne interrupted. "Some courtier? We met him yesterday. He doesn't know Gisela. He doesn't know anything about us."

Gisela's thoughts spiraled as she recalled the chill that ran through her when she first met Darian. His cryptic words unsettled her more than she wanted to admit.

Seraphina rose from her seat. She turned toward the window, watching as the fading sunlight gave way to the shadows of night. "Follow me."

"To where?" Thorne demanded.

"To the heart of the isle."

CHAPTER THIRTY

They exited the study, and Seraphina led them into a dim corridor. At the end stood a large black stone door, veined with faint silver light.

Seraphina placed her palm flat against it. A deep, grinding rumble rolled through the hallway as the door unlocked and swung inward.

Gisela flinched at the sound, but she forced herself to steady.

A spiral staircase twisted downward into darkness.

Gisela hesitated, her fingers brushing the smooth stone railing.

Seraphina glanced back, offering a reassuring smile. "It's safe, I assure you," she said.

The air grew colder with each step, carrying a faint hum that vibrated through the stone walls.

Each twist of the staircase pulled them closer into what felt like an ancient secret.

Eva shivered, and Adrian draped his cloak over her shoulders.

The stairs ended in a tunnel system. Seraphina guided them until they reached a great arched door. She pressed her hand to its surface, and it groaned open.

The room beyond was archaic. Walls were lined with ancient, twisted roots that glimmered faintly with an ethereal light. At the center of the chamber stood a massive tree, reminiscent of the one they had seen in the garden during the Trials of Kharos. Its wide, gnarled trunk looked as though it had weathered centuries, and its sprawling branches stretched toward a ceiling lost in shadow. A thick scent of rich earth and sweet dreamberries filled the air while aether leaves glimmered among the branches like stars in the night.

"This is one of the Great Guardian Trees," Seraphina said. "You have one in Mystralos too. I suspect it lies beneath your king's castle."

Gisela slowed to a halt as the towering tree filled her vision.

And the tree stirred.

A ripple of light ran across its bark, as though something beneath it woke at her presence. A soft golden pulse traveled up the trunk and into its branches. The air warmed around her, humming in tune with her heartbeat.

Before her fingers could reach the bark, a man cloaked in midnight blue entered through a side door and moved silently into the chamber.

Gisela jerked back, but Thorne's firm grip on her arm was swift and steady, anchoring her.

"Our Seer, Byron," Seraphina said.

Byron came to a stop in front of Gisela and Thorne. His head tilted slightly as his focus shifted between the two. "Two souls. Bound by fate and love yet caught in the currents of a dying world."

Gisela took a single step forward. "You once told a woman named Helena Donolo that Mystralos would die."

Byron did not blink. "Mystralos will die. It will die as you know it to be."

Thorne's voice sharpened. "What does that mean?"

Gisela took another step forward, ignoring Thorne's interjection. "We're here to understand why and we want to know how to fix it," Gisela said. "I believe I was given a prophecy—"

Byron's voice filled the room, clear and imposing:

"In times of dire, the balance shall break,

Six elements lost, a world at stake.

To mend the divide, the willing must find,

The six who unite, in heart and mind.

By trials endured and elements' might,

The Great Guardian Tree shall rise in sight.

When darkness looms and hope is thin,

The power within shall new life begin."

Gisela swallowed, the words a familiar echo in her mind.

The room fell silent. The others behind them listened intently.

"The six are here, in this palace. Five in this very room," Byron said. "Yet you . . ." His attention shifted to Thorne.

A muscle twitched in Thorne's jaw. "Yet I what?"

Byron's expression remained neutral. "You do not yet know your role, nor of the path you must take. Your journey will reveal more than you expect."

Byron's eyes settled onto Gisela. "You have the willingness to act. A helper. A descendant of the First-born Mystics."

Gisela went rigid. "I—that's a mistake."

"It is not," Byron said simply.

An uncomfortable sort of dread settled in her bones.

He continued, voice growing strained. "Your land will die without its life source. The six must return that power and revive the Great

Guardian Tree, when it is on the brink of demise. Only then will you restore balance *for good*."

With that, the Seer turned on his heel, his movements slow, as if the weight of their exchange had exhausted him.

Gisela's hands itched to move. She wanted to demand answers, to touch him, to pull him back into explanation. "Please, I have more questions," she called out, her hand reaching to stop him. But before she could make contact, Seraphina caught her arm.

"You cannot touch him. He will rest now. There is nothing you can do."

In a trance-like state, the Seer disappeared behind the door he entered through, leaving them with more questions than answers.

Silas's voice broke the heavy silence that had settled in the room. "Well, now what?"

Adrian and Eva moved closer to the tree, awe widening their eyes. The roots pulsed faintly, responding to their closeness.

"No time like the present. Am I right?" Adrian said, his tone jarring.

Gisela shot him a faint glare, her jaw aching from tension, but she allowed herself a small nod.

"You must be extremely careful. Do not enter another realm," Seraphina warned. "Touching the tree with intention allows you to connect with it, but stepping through to another realm can be perilous. Focus solely on your destination, and do not let the tree's energy pull you beyond that."

Thorne's hands flexed at his sides. "Wait."

"I'm right here." Gisela said, placing her hands on his chest. "I'm just going to look."

"I'll try it first," he insisted.

"Do not," Seraphina said sternly. "Your magic is corrupt. The tree will reject it."

"Corrupt?" he said. "I'm not corrupt."

"*You* may not be. But your power is," Seraphina said, regret flitting along her features.

Gisela put her hand on Thorne's arm. "We will figure out how to fix it. But right now, we have to try this."

Seraphina nodded in agreement. "As long as they don't step through, they won't leave our sight."

Gisela, Silas, Eva, and Adrian approached the massive tree.

Thorne took a step forward, but stopped.

Each of them pressed their palms against the bark, and a warm, tingling pulse of energy thrummed beneath their fingers.

But when Silas reached out, nothing happened.

"All I feel is rough bark," he muttered, frustration wrinkling his brow. He stepped back, joining Thorne.

Gisela closed her eyes and the world around her fell silent. Images of distant realms shifted behind her lids, faint and elusive.

Seraphina's voice cut through, muffled from the shifting reality. "Focus on Mystralos. To the village you want to see."

Gisela drew a deep breath and pictured Frosthaven clearly in her mind. When she opened her eyes, the scene before her twisted her heart. The familiar landscape lay skeletal. Mist clung thick and heavy. Wolves prowled, fangs sinking into dying animals. The Guardian Tree was losing its essence. Its branches drooped, and aether leaves lay scattered on the ground.

A sharp pang of sorrow ripped through her, and she gasped. She stumbled back into Thorne, and he caught her without hesitation.

"What is it?" he asked.

Gisela shook her head. "The forest . . . it's dead."

Adrian and Eva staggered back from the tree, Adrian catching his sister. "I don't know what Aquamere looked like before, but the woods are swallowed in mist," Adrian said, hands on his knees, gasping.

Eva widened her eyes, unsteady on her feet.

"What did you see?" Gisela asked.

Her hands moved swiftly, and Adrian followed. "She saw Thunderpeak . . . there's nothing left."

"What do you mean nothing?" Silas asked.

Eva's movements continued.

Adrian interpreted, voice tense. "The tree's still there . . . but everything else is burned to the ground."

Sweat beaded on Gisela's forehead. "I need to go to Frosthaven."

"No," Thorne said. "It won't be safe. I can't get there fast enough if you need me, Gisela."

Silas wiped a hand down his face. "We go back to Aquamere. Quickest route. Maybe Terranox will carry Thorne, Marina and me. Adrian, Eva, and Gisela can use the tree. We meet at Marina's house on the beach."

Seraphina exhaled, her expression troubled. "Terranox may suffice. Vespera can stay with her egg, but he must return soon after. You must promise me."

"No," Thorne said immediately. "I'm not going anywhere without Gisela."

Gisela met his gaze, sorrow and resolve entwined. "It's the only way. I'll have Adrian and Eva with me. I won't be alone. You all go first. We'll meet you there."

Thorne rolled his neck, the fight in his stance softening into reluctant acceptance. "Fine. We leave in the morning."

CHAPTER THIRTY-ONE

"How did Marina take the news?" Gisela asked as Thorne stepped into their palace room. He gave her a weak smile, closing the door behind him with a soft click that echoed through the quiet chamber.

"Silas explained as best he could," Thorne said. "She's upset. Leaving Bjorn again too. But the pool helped. She sprayed me with water as soon as I walked into her room. Very Marina of her."

She let out a quiet laugh. "Maybe I should've gone with Silas instead. I'll go talk to her."

"No, you need rest. You should already be sleeping."

Sleep. How could she close her eyes when all she would see was Mystralos teetering on the brink of ruin? People were dying. Magic was weakening. And in the midst of it all, her own identity had begun to unravel. Had her parents hidden the truth from her? Were Noah and Vivi her siblings? Was she living a complete lie?

The question anchored itself in her chest, heavy and jagged. Impossible to shake.

Turmoil etched in her face and Thorne crawled across the bed, placing his hands on her shoulders. "Whatever you're feeling, Gisela, we'll face it together. You don't have to carry this alone."

She looked up at him, searching for some reassurance in his eyes but the weight of everything was too much. "I don't know who I am anymore, Thorne. If everything I believed about myself was a lie, then who am I?"

"You're Gisela," he said. "No prophecy or hidden bloodline changes who you've been. Even if it changes what you are."

A brief solace warmed her chest. She reached up, touching his cheek, letting her fingers linger.

This troublesome boy, the one who tested her patience at every turn, who had taken a strange pleasure in getting under her skin, now a man she couldn't bear to lose.

"You're everything to me," he said. "Ever since the awakening . . . I physically ache for you, Gisela. I don't know where I stop, and you begin."

She felt it too. A tether stretched thin whenever they were apart. The further they were from each other, the more it tugged at her heart, a constant reminder that they were bound together in ways neither of them fully understood yet.

"I feel it," she whispered. "I don't want to be away from you either. For any amount of time. But it's the only way."

"I know you'll be tempted to go to Frosthaven," Thorne said.

Gisela averted her gaze. The pull of her home was a quiet ache. "I would never lie to you. It's hard not to think about going back and seeing it for myself."

"You can't risk it, Gisela, promise me," he begged, taking her hands in his and holding them. "If something happened to you . . ." He kissed her knuckles. "I know your strength, but I couldn't bear it. It would destroy me."

She leaned forward, kissing him softly, letting her hands trail along the back of his head. When she pulled away, shadows of pain reflected in his eyes, as if he had already imagined losing her and couldn't shake the thought.

"I promise," she said, her voice firm. "I'll go straight to Aquamere. No detours. No risks."

Gisela surrendered to the pull of sleep, sinking deeper into its hold until her dreams became memories. She was back in the familiar warmth of her childhood home, the one before her father became Village Lord. Candlelight flickered across the low beams, casting the hanging dried herbs in golden halos.

She was ten years old again, sitting cross-legged on the earthy floor, her knees dusted brown. In front of her lay an old, leather-bound journal, its spine cracked from use, its pages filled with meticulous handwriting.

She ran her small fingers over the yellowed parchment, her eyes drawn to a word that leapt off the page: *Guardian Tree.* Beneath it, a list of ingredients she knew too well—bark, root, aether leaf, silver sap, dreamberries.

The herbs above her stirred.

A cold breeze swept the room, snuffing out the candles. Darkness rushed in and the dream twisted abruptly.

She was even younger now. A mere infant—*too young to remember this, yet the certainty of it was undeniable*—crying in a small cot, swaddled in a thin blanket. Fever raged through her tiny body. The world around her was a blur of light and shadow.

Then the cold came.

Frost unfurled around her in careful layers, cocooning her tiny form. The fever broke beneath it, soothed by the chill, her frantic cries softening.

A figure stood nearby, hidden in the shadows. Before she could make out any details, the figure turned and rushed out of the door.

The dream twisted again, pulling her forward through her memories like pages turning too fast to read.

She was much older now, walking home from work on the cobblestone streets of Frosthaven as dusk fell. The cold bit at her nose as she drew her cloak tighter. Her breath fogged the air.

A memory she knew well.

Then and now, folded together.

The past carried a weight she hadn't felt at the time.

Her mother, Ivy, stood outside their home, speaking in hushed tones with a woman she didn't recognize. The stranger's face was obscured under a hood, her posture tight and her hands clasped at her sides.

Gisela drew nearer and the woman glanced up. Panic flashed across her features before she could hide it. She grabbed Ivy's hand, gave it a brief squeeze, and hurried away, disappearing into the fog that crept along the street.

Gisela's sight was fixed on the retreating figure, until her attention was pulled to someone else. Across the street, Selene Alderose stood at the corner, bags of fruit hanging from her hands. She was watching them with intensity, and the weight of her stare made Gisela's stomach churn.

Gisela bolted upright, scanning the palace room, reorienting herself. Her fingers twisted through her tangled hair. The phantom sting of frost in her cradle, the prickling sense of being watched by Selene . . . she couldn't shake it.

Thorne stirred, eyes still heavy with sleep. "Bad dream?" he murmured, sitting up beside her.

Gisela managed to put on a soft smile. "I'm okay. Go back to sleep." Her hands trembled.

There was a quiet reach from him in her mind, concern bleeding through the bond—and without thinking, she pulled back, shielding him from her emotions.

He gave a small nod and went back to sleep.

But Gisela's mind refused to rest.

The dream replayed in a relentless loop.

Her dreams had never been directed before. This one followed a will beyond her own.

It wasn't imagination. The pieces fit too cleanly for that. The truth lay scattered, revealed out of order.

Whatever waited for her in Frosthaven, she knew one thing—she couldn't keep herself from knowing much longer.

Were they safe?

Were they even alive?

The thoughts of empty streets, of her village stripped bare like Thunderpeak, kept sleep at bay.

Chapter Thirty-Two

Mystic Isle had been kind to them.

Gisela stood in the garden, taking in its order—the Primals at ease, the absence of fear, the way magic was allowed to exist without persecution. Nothing here demanded vigilance.

She hadn't expected how much that would matter. How easy it would be to stay.

But Mystralos was dying. And peace, however real it was here, would not travel with them.

They were leaving with more questions than answers, and she would have to carry that uncertainty with her.

Thorne held Gisela in the palace garden, his chin resting on her head.

A light breeze stirred the flowers around them.

"I don't want to leave you," he said.

Gisela nuzzled into his chest. "It won't be for long."

The eel's attack hadn't left her, reminding her how unstable the realm had become, how easily everything could go wrong.

She wished he could stay with her, use the tree to get back to Aquamere.

But it wouldn't allow him, and the reason weighed heavily in her chest.

Silas slung his bag over his shoulder and turned to Seraphina. "About how long until they use the tree?"

"Terranox is fast," Seraphina answered. "You could be in Aquamere by tonight, but he'll need to return soon after resting."

"Where exactly is Aquamere's tree, Adrian? What did you see around it?" Gisela asked.

"It looked like it was in a small forest," he replied, relaxed with his arms crossed. "You can hear the ocean from it."

Marina gave a firm nod. "I bet it's on the forested cliff above my house. Tidelwood. Perfect."

Bjorn swung her around and kissed her.

Silas averted his gaze.

Their Primals gathered around Seraphina. The air shimmered faintly as their magic rippled across the garden.

Gisela could sense Eira's sadness, a deep, aching sorrow as if she were leaving a place she truly belonged. Mystic Isle had been a sanctuary for them, a place where their essence was alive and free. Aerion, however, floated above them in his usual hammock-like position, casually examining his nails. His nonchalance stood in stark contrast to the others—Ignitus, smoldering with intensity; Crag, silent and watchful; Ondine, radiating a calm readiness for whatever lay ahead; Tempest, whose concern had sharpened.

Thorne glanced over at the Primals then back to Gisela. "Ignitus doesn't want to be away from Eira either. I can sense it."

"I can sense it too."

Terranox roared, his massive body shifting as he lowered himself to the ground, ready for his riders. The vibrations from his movements hummed faintly beneath their feet.

Gisela's stomach flipped as the time had arrived. "Until tonight," she said, nodding to Marina, Silas, and Thorne.

Adrian draped his arm around Gisela's shoulder. "I'll take care of the ice princess," he said with a grin.

Gisela smiled, giving him a gentle nudge.

"Of course you will," Thorne added. "Because if you don't . . ."

"You'd burn the world down," Adrian finished, waving a hand in the air. "We know, we know."

Thorne shot him a pointed look, but his eyes betrayed a smile. He brushed a quick kiss across Gisela's forehead before turning to mount Terranox.

Marina hugged Gisela briefly. "See you tonight."

Gisela walked over to Silas, planting a kiss on Silas's cheek. "Get there safely."

"Of course."

Eira joined Gisela as they watched Terranox launch into the air, the wind whipping strands of hair across her face.

"They will be fine with Thorne and Ignitus," Eira whispered.

Gisela turned to her. "How do you know?"

Eira didn't respond.

Adrian approached Gisela's side, tilting his head to watch as Terranox disappeared into the clouds.

"Where's Eva?" Gisela asked.

"She doesn't do well with goodbyes, but she'll be here soon. I'll be back down in a bit. I have a stop to make before we leave tonight," Adrian said, winking, and disappeared through the palace doors.

Gisela shook her head with a smile and sat down on a stone bench in the garden, alone.

"Approaching the veil," Thorne's voice echoed in her mind.

"I love you," Gisela said.

"I love you. I'll see you tonight," he responded, his voice growing fainter as he crossed into Mystralos.

Gisela exhaled and ran her hands through her hair. Cool wind brushed her cheeks, and she hugged her knees as the garden's emptiness settled in.

A faint prickle crept up the back of her neck.

She turned to find Darian leaning against the garden gates, his white hair tousled by the wind.

She rolled her eyes. "You."

"Me," he said, opening his arms wide with a grin. He sat beside her on the bench.

"I don't remember inviting you to sit here," Gisela said.

Darian laughed. "Why the hostility toward me, Gisela?"

She shot him a look. "You seem . . . meddlesome."

He cocked his head, his lips curving into a wry smile. "That's likely true. You remind me so much of someone—someone I never got to truly know but observed from afar."

Gisela shook her head. "Why are you like this?"

"Like what?"

"Cryptic. Elusive . . . Annoying."

Darian's smile widened. "Ah, but mystery adds flavor, don't you think, young Frostweaver? You love solving problems."

Gisela scoffed. "You don't know a damn thing about me."

"I know enough," he said.

"Enough to drop the whole 'you might be a descendant' thing and walk away?" she shot back.

"Might?" Darian studied her. "You wouldn't be wrestling with it if you didn't already feel the truth of it."

"What does it *mean* though?"

Darian's smile faded slightly. "Family secrets can be quite burdensome."

"I don't need vague hints," Gisela said, frustration rising. "I need clear answers."

"You will get them," he said, rising to leave. "Just not today."

He walked away, and Gisela was left staring after him, her hands curling at her sides. She wanted clarity, not riddles or prophecies.

She was sick of them.

Eva entered through the gates and crossed the garden. She sat where Darian had been, close but not crowding her.

Gisela offered a small, grateful smile.

Eva returned it, gentle and steady.

The tension in Gisela's shoulders eased. She reached out without thinking, her fingers brushing Eva's hand. "Were you ever able to speak?" Gisela asked hesitantly.

Eva nodded.

Tempest appeared beside her, the air stirring faintly.

Eva's hands moved in quick, precise motions as she signed.

"Eva and Adrian are descendants of the first-born children of Mystralos," Tempest said.

Gisela blinked. "Mystralos?"

"Yes," Tempest said. She glanced at Eva who flicked her hand to say *go ahead.* "When their parents died, the loss fractured something in Eva. Her power surged in ways neither of us could steady. The silence came after." Tempest glanced at Eva, waiting for her to gesture to continue. "Eva has not drawn deeply from her power since that day," she added. "When she does, it does not return to rest easily."

Gisela looked at Eva, who traced idle patterns in the dirt with the toe of her shoe. "I'm sorry."

Eva met her gaze and nodded once.

"How did they die?"

"Her parents, Lyra and Tyvor, fled Mystralos once Lyra became pregnant. Eva and Adrian were born here, imbued with the Isle's magic."

Gisela leaned forward, her posture a plea for more information.

"Lyra and Tyvor returned to Mystralos with Helena. The guards were waiting."

The words landed hard.

Gisela dug her fingernails into the stone. "That's how Marina knows them."

Tempest nodded. "Yes."

Wind stirred the garden, the scent of the flowers brushing Gisela's nose. Leaves drifted down around them. She thought of Helena—of all the choices that had led here.

Then she looked at Eva again. Still here. Still standing.

"Can you teach me some signs?" Gisela asked.

Eva's expression brightened at the request. She nodded and lifted her hands.

"This means *thank you*," Tempest translated.

Gisela mirrored the movement, awkward at first.

Eva corrected her gently, tapping her wrist.

Gisela laughed under her breath and tried again.

Tempest continued to provide translations, guiding Gisela through each sign. "That one means *friend*," she explained. "And this one is *help*."

Gisela looked at Eva, full of gratitude as she signed, "*Thank you*."

As Eva moved, Gisela noticed the Mystic mark below her collarbone, small, jagged lines like lightning. Gisela gestured to it, then turned to reveal her own mark behind her ear, now clearly visible. Reaching into her bag, she pulled out the small container of putty and showed it to Eva.

"This hides it." She scooped a small amount of it into her hands and pressed it over her mark. "It's made from the Guardian Trees."

Eva leaned closer, studying it.

"Do you want me to cover yours for the journey?"

Eva shook her head, then signed, her hands moving too fast for Gisela to follow.

"She says she will not hide who she is," Tempest translated.

Eva's expression turned serious as she nodded in agreement.

Gisela smiled, something warm and proud blooming in her chest. "And you shouldn't have to."

Chapter Thirty-Three

The anticipation of reaching Aquamere created a lump in Gisela's throat that wouldn't budge. As they walked down the corridors toward the Great Guardian Tree of Mystic Isle, her footsteps echoed, each one heavier than the last. Her lungs constricted as the pull toward Frosthaven tugged at her like a relentless current. Each pace toward the tree felt like a battle between her heart's desire and the urgency of the mission ahead.

The cool, crisp air in the chamber soothed her as they stepped through the door and stood before the grand tree.

Seraphina approached Gisela with a look of concern, taking both of her hands in her own.

Gisela inclined her head. "Thank you for everything, Seraphina."

"You are always welcome here and if there is anything I can do, you know where to find me." Seraphina let go of her hands and walked over to Adrian and Eva, ensuring they had everything they needed for the journey.

Eira appeared next to Gisela, her face tense.

"What's wrong?"

"We need to leave, *now.*"

Gisela's heart pounded harder. "What's wrong?"

Eira hesitated, looking over at Ondine and Tempest. The brief silence was more alarming than words could ever be.

"Eira!" Gisela's voice rose, panic threatening to suffocate her as she rushed toward the Tree. The hairs on the back of her neck prickled as Eira's emotions flooded through her.

"Wait!" Adrian called out, grabbing Eva's hand and rushing toward the tree.

"What happened?" Seraphina asked.

"Something is wrong in Aquamere." Gisela pressed her palm onto the surface of the tree.

Adrian and Eva followed her lead.

The moment Gisela's hand touched the ancient bark, a tingling warmth flowed through her palm, spreading up her arm like wildfire. The rough texture of the tree softened, as if it were melting away. The air around her thickened, vibrating with energy that hummed through her body.

Her heartbeat synchronized with the pulse of the tree, each beat pumping in her veins. She closed her eyes. The sensation was both exhilarating and terrifying, like standing on the edge of a cliff, knowing you were about to fall, but trusting the plunge would deliver you safely to the other side.

Focusing intently on Aquamere, a sudden rush of cool air brushed against her skin. She opened her eyes and found her footing as the last traces of disorientation faded. They were standing on solid ground again, no longer in the Great Guardian Tree's chamber in Mystic Isle.

Gisela looked up at Aquamere's Guardian Tree. It was alive but not as vibrant as it should be.

Chilling screams and cries rose above the violent, crashing waves from the shore. A roar sounded from outside the small, forested area.

They exchanged worried glances and without a second to waste, rushed toward the village center of Aquamere.

Emerging from the Tidelwood forest line, chaos hit all at once. Villagers sprinted for shelter, their terrified screams tearing through the commotion as twisted, shadowy beasts with glowing crimson eyes and jagged fangs rampaged through the streets. Stone cracked, wood splintered, and Aquamere's beauty unraveled in front of her.

Terranox roared a mighty bellow from the center of the village, his flames scorching the earth, incinerating any creature that dared approach. His colossal form loomed like a dark sentinel, each roar making the ground quake.

Nearby, Marina and Ondine fought fiercely, drawing upon the diminishing power of Aquamere's waters. Although Marina's connection to the land of Aquamere should have strengthened her, Gisela saw the strain. A spray of water arced too far, smashing a nearby crate into splinters, narrowly missing a panicked villager hiding behind it. The water wavered as Marina fought to keep it under control.

Ondine, summoning water from the earth itself, twisted her arms in precise rhythm, hurling torrents into the beasts' lungs. Each splash silenced their cries, leaving eerie quiet in the spaces they left behind.

Silas stood firm in the village center, his palms pressed to the ground as the earth shook with his fury. Yet he struggled to summon the power he once commanded so easily. Gisela saw it in the way the earth answered him—boulders breaking apart instead of rising whole.

Crag hurled these small boulders with lethal precision, smashing them into the beasts. Each impact sent shockwaves through the battlefield, and for a brief heartbeat, pride slipped through Silas's exhaustion.

Gisela's veins surged with frantic adrenaline as she scanned the mayhem, desperately searching for Thorne.

Adrian sprinted past her as a vortex of air blasted from his hands, sweeping through the village. The cyclone locked onto the beasts, draining the very air from their bodies.

Behind him, Aerion casually twirled a finger, sending a cluster of shadowed creatures spinning into a chaotic whirlwind, his calmness striking against the frantic scene.

Eva stood paralyzed, her hands trembling at her sides. A smaller beast lunged at her, and she stumbled back, narrowly avoiding its fangs.

"Thorne!" Gisela yelled, her voice cutting through the cries of battle. She charged into the fray, shards of ice exploding from her hands in every direction.

Eira moved with her, ice rising and shifting at her sides to deflect incoming threats.

A familiar chill ran down her spine and she spun around. *"I'm here,"* she projected through their connection.

There he was—surrounded by snarling, red-eyed beasts, with Ignitus at his side. The creatures circled them, closing in.

Ignitus summoned flames from the ground, engulfing the beasts in a searing blaze of fire.

Thorne ran his hand along the blade of his sword, igniting it with flames that flickered along the steel. He spun with precision, slashing through the beasts with fluid, deadly movements. The dark fire consumed the creatures as they screeched in agony. Thorne's shirt hung in tatters, a deep gash across his chest bleeding through the fabric.

Their eyes finally met. "Gisela!" he bellowed.

A beast lunged at her from behind. She ducked and drove ice upward beneath it, sending the creature crashing to the ground as shards pierced its body.

In a wave of frost, Eira and Gisela froze the remaining beasts circling Thorne, encasing them as statues of snarling faces and glaring eyes.

Gisela and Thorne ran for each other, their bodies crashing together in a frantic hold. When they broke apart, Thorne examined Gisela's body, checking for injuries.

"I'm fine," she panted. "But your chest—"

Thorne brought his hand to it, wincing. "I'll be okay. It's not as bad as it looks."

A scream split the air, drawing their attention to Marina. A beast lunged at her with outstretched claws. Her foot slipped on the bloody ground and the creature's claw grazed her shoulder.

Adrian sprang to her side, summoning a powerful gust of wind that blasted the beast back, its neck snapping from the force. He exchanged a quick, reassuring glance with Marina. Two more beasts jumped in its place, jaws snapping.

Gisela sprinted toward them, with Thorne right behind her. She hurled ice shards through the air, impaling them before they reached her friends.

Terranox landed beside them with a thunderous roar, his fire consuming the remaining cluster of creatures.

Silas staggered over, his chest heaving with exhaustion. The group shared a momentary look of relief—but the devastation around them reminded them that victory came at a cost.

A massive shadow fell over them. A giant creature materialized from thin air. Its dark, shadowy form and razor-sharp claws were unmistakable. It was the same entity Gisela and Thorne had encountered during the Trials of Kharos.

Eva stood frozen to the side, trembling. The creature's gaze locked onto her, feeding on her fear, twisting it into a weapon. Its claw swiped toward her, and she scrambled toward the group.

The beast hovered above them, its venomous fangs dripping with fluorescent green.

It lunged.

Thorne stepped forward, his bond with Ignitus surging to life as he unleashed a torrent of black flames. The fire roared and wrapped around the creature, but instead of burning it, the flames sank into its shadowy form, feeding it—deepening the darkness until the creature loomed larger and more menacing than before.

Gisela gritted her teeth and hurled shards of ice in a desperate attempt to slow the beast.

It only snarled, shaking off the ice as if it were nothing more than dust. The beast shrieked, a sound that shook them to their cores, before releasing a blast of green smoke that seared their skin.

Eira launched an icy blast to clear the smoke before it could cause further harm.

Understanding struck Gisela all at once, as the prophecy she heard—the spark that had ignited this journey—echoed in her mind.

"Together!" Gisela yelled.

The creature's roar sent shockwaves through the square, toppling what little remained of the market stalls. Stones cracked beneath its weight, and the tremor rattled through Gisela's bones.

Gisela, Marina, Silas, and Adrian unleashed their elements in a relentless, unified assault. Marina's waters surged. Adrian's winds howled. Silas's earth trembled. Gisela's ice pierced the air.

The ground quaked—but the beast only grew darker, thicker, its roar swallowing their magic.

"It's not working!" Adrian shouted.

Gisela looked at Thorne as he stood motionless.

He looked down at his hands. "I'm feeding it," he whispered.

The fear, the shame of what his power had done, reflected in his eyes.

She reached for his hand anyway. "I trust you," she said. "You and me."

They each extended their other hand and attacked the creature.

Thorne's flames spilled out in a dark current until they struck the creature. Red and orange bloomed through his black fire, burning away the shadows that clung to the beast's form.

She looked at him from the corner of her eye, but persisted, focusing her ice on the predator.

Eva hesitated, watching the others' power converge on the beast.

Tempest moved closer to Eva, the air around her shimmering as if bracing against a coming strike.

Eva's shoulders tensed, light flickering faintly beneath her skin.

"Eva, now!" Gisela shouted. "We need you too!"

Eva hesitantly extended her hands. Lightning erupted from her, so bright it nearly blinded them all. The lightning crackled and arced through the beast, joining the combined force of the others' attacks.

Gisela's full strength tore loose as they struck together—ice, wind, earth, water, storm, and fire crashing into one blinding surge.

Elements of the gods converged in a blinding torrent of power, consuming the beast. Tendrils of shadow lashed out, but their power held firm.

The creature let out an ear-splitting screech, thrashing wildly as the light consumed it. With one final, collective push, the creature exploded into a cloud of black smoke, which dissipated into the night.

The Mystics collapsed to their knees, bodies trembling.

Eva swayed unsteadily, eyes glassy.

Tempest cried out—a loud, agonizing sound—as Eva's knees buckled.

"Eva?!" Adrian reached for her.

Her gaze drifted. Before he could get to her, her eyes rolled back, and she collapsed to the ground.

CHAPTER THIRTY-FOUR

"Eva!" Gisela yelled, scrambling over to her side. "Eva, stay with me."

Adrian stepped forward and knelt beside them, taking hold of Eva's hand.

Gisela found Eva's pulse beneath her fingers—faint, but there. "I can help her."

Adrian shook his head. "An herbalist won't be able to help with this. Not even one as good as you."

"Why not?" Marina asked, nursing her shoulder.

"This is how it happened last time." He exhaled deeply. "She needs rest."

"Tempest?" Gisela said, trying to summon her.

"It won't work," Acrion said, his usual nonchalance replaced by gravity. "Tempest is deep within her, anchoring her here. It's better this way."

Gisela brushed a hand over her friend's forehead. They couldn't risk another attack.

Not like this.

"We need to protect the village," Gisela said, her voice steady despite the fear bubbling beneath the surface. Around them, the streets were littered with debris and claw marks carved deep into the walls of homes.

A faint haze still hung in the air, carrying the scent of damp stone and blood. "Create a barrier around the perimeter."

Adrian nodded, a thoughtful crease forming on his forehead. "I can use the wind to detect anything approaching. It'll give us an early warning, maybe even slow them down."

"Good," Gisela rose to her feet. "I'll add a layer of ice. It'll freeze and weaken anything that gets too close. If they try to cross, they'll be trapped."

Marina glanced at Silas, who was staring at the ground in defeat. "My power is weakened and his . . ." She trailed off, her voice fading in resignation. "Why aren't you guys affected by this?"

Gisela shrugged, but Adrian offered an explanation. "Maybe it's a descendant thing?"

"Yeah? Then what about Thorne?" Marina asked, her attention shifting toward him.

Thorne clenched his fists, black flames sparking to life around his hands. He ignored Marina's question. "I'll set up a ring of fire."

Marina drew in a slow breath. "My father and I will bring Eva back to my house."

Silas, still silent and visibly shaken, lifted Eva and carried her down the pathway toward Marina's home.

"Let's go," Thorne said, heading toward the village's outskirts.

Adrian was the first to act, raising his hands to the sky. The wind answered his call with a powerful gust, swirling in a protective current that encircled the village.

Gisela stepped forward, ice crawling over the barricade in jagged ribs, cold enough to bite through bone.

Thorne summoned his flames, sealing it. They roared to life, coiling around the ice barrier like a serpent. The black fire hissed and crackled, emitting an eerie glow across the village.

The heat was intense, but the ice held firm, the two elements existing in a delicate balance.

The flames rose higher, the smoke curling into the sky, creating a thick veil of protection.

Gisela stood back, watching as their combined powers fused into a formidable barrier.

When the roar of the fire quieted, the sounds of the village rushed back in. Distant weeping drifted through the smoke.

Someone's home had collapsed. Someone else called a name that would never answer.

"I hope this works. We've bought some time, at least," Gisela said.

Thorne nodded, his focus still fixed on his flames. "It will."

Adrian placed a hand on Gisela's shoulder, giving it a reassuring squeeze.

Together, they turned back toward the village, where people cautiously peeked from their homes, surveying the damage done to their once peaceful land.

An older man stepped out of his house, the front door falling off its hinges, and approached them. "You're Mystics," he said as others gathered around him.

The battle had left no room for secrets, and a coil of dread settled in Gisela's chest. She had kept this secret since her mark first appeared, and it felt strange to admit it to a stranger.

"We are," Gisela said.

"And we just kept this village breathing," Thorne said roughly. "If any of you have a problem with that, you can fuck off."

The man raised his hands in surprise, taken aback by Thorne's aggression.

Gisela stiffened at his tone, shooting Thorne a disapproving glare. The man hadn't approached them with hostility.

"I'm not here to turn you all in," the man said. "I simply wanted to thank you. As the Village Lord of Aquamere."

Adrian puffed his cheeks, shaking his head. "Such a hothead, aren't you?" he said, walking toward the pathway to Marina's home.

Thorne's jaw tightened.

"There's no need to thank us," Gisela said.

"We don't know what's going on. It's clear that Mystralos is falling apart. We've had no word from the King about the Stones," he said, throwing his hands in the air. "Without you Mystics here tonight, we'd all be dead. So, thank you."

Thorne's anger deflated as he rubbed a hand over his face. "I apologize, sir. We're a little on edge."

The man nodded. "I understand, young man. Not everyone supports what's been done to your kind. You've got more allies here than you think. War is coming, and the people are ready to fight back."

Gisela went still at his words. She wasn't used to hearing them without a sword waiting after.

Thorne gave a low bow, a subtle gesture of gratitude as they turned to leave.

"Before you go," the man said. "If it helps any, the King's guard showed up here. They were looking for a Mystic named Thorne. They threatened to punish anyone aiding him."

Gisela's muscles stiffened. "What did you say?"

"Well, I don't know anyone named Thorne, so I said I didn't know where he was."

"Do not confirm it's you. It will put them at risk," Gisela said into Thorne's mind.

"Thanks for the warning, sir," Thorne said.

They left the Village Lord behind, the barrier's glow wavering at their backs.

Thorne didn't speak as they headed toward the beach.

Gisela almost reached for the bond, but it was so new. His emotions bled too easily into hers to touch without consequence.

"What's going on with you?" Gisela asked.

He didn't look at her. His jaw was flexed, tight and silent.

"Hey," she pressed, stopping before they reached the steps leading down to the beach. "You've been snapping at everyone. They're trying to help us, and you're just—"

Thorne whipped around so abruptly she startled. "I'm just what? A hotheaded asshole?" His voice came out like scraped steel, catching Gisela off guard.

"Thorne, that's not what I meant. Adrian was only—"

"I know," Thorne bit out. Then winced, dragging a hand through his hair. "When we got to shore, we could see the beasts pouring through the village. I knew you'd show up at the tree and I wouldn't be there. I had to fight, had to keep everyone alive. I was godsdamned terrified you'd—" He stopped himself, inhaling hard.

Gisela frowned. "I can handle myself. You don't need to protect me from everything."

He scoffed, heat radiating off him as his temper flared. He ran his hands down his face before locking eyes with her. "Of course I do! For fuck's sake, Gisela, you're my entire life now. You're a part of me." Pain reflected in his eyes, and silence stretched between them. "You blocked me out in Seraphina's office yesterday. I felt it."

She stiffened. "I didn't *block* you out."

"You did," he said quietly. "And fine. Maybe it's better that way. Get the corruption out of your head."

"What? No." Her expression softened enough for him to misinterpret it.

"Don't look at me like that. Like you pity me."

"I don't pity you," she said, voice firm. "I know you're tormented. I can feel it. But you can't treat people this way. People who are trying to help."

Thorne inhaled slowly through his nose. He turned away from her. When he finally looked back, his expression hardened. "You know what, Gisela? Since I'm such a problem, why don't you stay away from me tonight? Or hell, turn me in, since apparently there's a bounty on my head. Make yourself some coin."

His words stung like a slap to the face.

She shot him a long, pained look before breaking eye contact. "How could you even say that?" she whispered. "This isn't you."

Something in his face cracked—not anger, but despair. "Maybe it is. Maybe it's who I've always been."

Gisela shook her head. "You told me not to pity you but look at you, Thorne. You're pitying yourself." She shoved her bag into his hands. "Give the hylja to Marina for her shoulder and put it on your damn chest." She backed away, shaking her head.

Thorne threw his head back to the night sky. "Gisela, wait."

She turned and quickened her pace. As she approached Marina's house, she veered off down the shore, past Terranox's sleeping figure in the sand.

Thorne's brows knitted as Gisela retreated. The depth of his mistake and the harshness of his words hit him like a physical blow.

Ignitus's voice struck Thorne's mind. *"You need to control yourself, Thorne. You're pushing away the one person who would do anything for you."*

"I know," Thorne muttered. *"I'm a fucking idiot."* He ran a hand through his hair.

"You're angry at your power."

Thorne's spine straightened. *"It fed the damn thing."*

"Your fire was absorbed. That, I am sure," Ignitus said. *"And that frightened you."*

Thorne swallowed hard. *"I was making it stronger . . . of course there was fear. Fear of what I could be capable of."*

Ignitus's voice remained steady. *"Do not let your fear of failure sabotage you. Control your emotions."* Heat traveled through Thorne's veins. *"Gisela is not your father. She thinks the world of you."*

Thorne let out a long sigh. The ache in his chest was a wound that had never truly healed, reopening with every breath he took. His father's influence still clung to him. Cruelty, bitterness, anger—the poisoned gifts of Cillian Alderose left scars too deep to ignore.

He longed to sever the chains of his father's hold, to uncover the person he was meant to be—someone free from that legacy. Yet the fire inside him, relentless and unquenchable, remained tethered to his core, waiting for the right moment to erupt.

For now, Thorne forced himself to focus. Gisela needed him, and he had to face the consequences of his actions and words.

Sorting through his emotions would have to wait.

Ignitus's voice broke through his train of thought. *"Not to mention, pushing Gisela away puts distance between me and Eira. I shouldn't have to suffer because of your outbursts."*

Thorne scoffed but understood as he walked down the steps to Marina's home.

"Gisela . . ." he said, trying to reach her through their mental bond. But all he heard was the violent crashing of waves against the shore.

CHAPTER THIRTY-FIVE

Thorne entered Marina's house, and the silence assaulted him like a wave of mourning crashing through the room despite their victory.

It didn't feel like a win.

Silas slumped on the couch, his gaze lost and distant.

At the table, Marina carefully dabbed a wet rag on her shoulder.

The bedroom door stood ajar, candlelight flickering across the hall. Adrian's voice murmured softly inside.

Marina glanced up as Thorne entered the kitchen. "Where's Gisela?"

"We had a fight." Thorne took his sword off his back, laying it on the table.

Marina's nod of understanding was almost imperceptible. "You should tend to that," she said, gesturing to the gash on his chest. "It'll fester."

Thorne twisted open the jar of hylja and pressed it over the wound. Cool spread beneath his palm. He handed the jar to Marina. "Use this for your shoulder. Gisela's orders."

Marina arched a brow but took it.

Footsteps sounded in the hall. Adrian stepped into the room, eyes tired, shoulders tight. He didn't sit—only paused long enough to glance toward the door behind him.

"She still out?" Marina asked, wiping her hands on a towel.

Adrian nodded once. "Yeah. Breathing's steady."

"Good." Thorne lowered himself into a chair. "Is Silas okay?" he whispered.

"I think the fight drained him," she said quietly. "His weakened power is taking a toll . . . he feels like he failed us."

Adrian finally sat, his body angled toward the hall. "No one failed." His hands pulled at his trousers. "We weren't ready for that."

Marina studied him. "Is she going to be okay?"

Adrian exhaled. "She has to be."

Marina opened her mouth, then stopped.

"I shouldn't have brought her," he said. "She hasn't pushed her power like that in a long time. I told myself we'd be careful." He glanced toward the hall again.

Thorne watched him closely. "You didn't know what we'd face."

"No," Adrian said. "But I knew the risk. She's not like the rest of us. If something happens to her—" He stopped, swallowing hard. "There's no replacing what she is."

Silas shifted on the couch, his attention sharpening.

"She made her own choice," Marina said.

Adrian nodded, but the tension didn't leave him. "I know, but that doesn't make it easier to live with." He pushed to his feet. "I'm going back in." He didn't wait for a response before heading down the hall.

"Look, we've all been through a lot over the past few days. We need rest and then we need to figure out where to go from here," Marina said, scooting back from her chair. "I'm going to find Gisela." She stood and walked out the front door, leaving Silas and Thorne alone.

Thorne moved to sit beside Silas. Silas had been there for him when he needed it most, the least he could do was return the favor.

"You know, a wise man once told me that you shouldn't let your fear of failure define you. You should use it to drive you forward," Thorne said.

Silas met Thorne's gaze, his heavy eyes lightening. "I'm tired. Not having my full power . . . it's not right."

"I understand."

"Do you?" Silas asked, skepticism in his voice.

Thorne leaned back on the couch, resting his head against the cushion. "Not exactly," he said. "But I know what it's like to feel inadequate. We couldn't have done what we did without you."

Silas nodded. "I really needed to hear that."

"We all do sometimes."

"What happened between you and Gisela?"

Thorne sighed. "I let my anger talk first."

Silas gave him a pat on the shoulder. "You've come so far. You two will work it out. You're allowed to make mistakes. Be aware and fix them."

"I think she wants space right now."

"Then give her that," Silas rose from the couch, stretching his back. "I'm going to get some rest and recharge."

Thorne watched as Silas headed toward the bedroom. When the door shut behind him, Thorne was left alone in the quiet of the house. Despite his effort to stay awake for Gisela, exhaustion took hold of him, and he drifted into a restless sleep.

Gisela sat by the water, leaning against Terranox's warm side, her fingers digging into the damp sand.

Marina scanned the shoreline. When she spotted Gisela, she walked over, her footsteps barely making a sound on the cold, wet shore. Marina settled beside her, the two of them staring out at the ocean.

They sat in comfortable silence, listening to the sounds of waves pulling in and out, leaving seaweed and shells in their wake.

"I don't know if I'll ever look at the ocean the same way again," Marina said. "I know my men are out there . . ." She shook her head, her voice breaking. "It's not fair."

"No," Gisela said. "It isn't."

"We'll have to find someone to check in on Eamon's grandmother. Maybe Liana and Isla can help."

Gisela nodded, saying nothing.

"Do you think they hated me for it?" Marina asked. "Before they died?"

Gisela turned to her, resting a hand on Marina's knee. "No. They would never blame you for what happened. They followed you because they believed in you and they believed in your mother."

"I wish she were here," Marina whispered.

"I would've loved to meet her."

Marina let out a weak breath that resembled a laugh. "You two would've talked about plants and shit for hours. She wasn't an herbalist, but she always made sure we had jars of that stuff to cover our marks." She glanced at her shoulder. "Which healed me, by the way."

Gisela laughed, shaking her head. "Oh, the *stuff* that's kept us alive all this time?"

"I don't have much of her stash left," Marina said. "But I don't think it's going to matter anymore. They'll find out about us soon enough."

"You never learned how to make it?"

"No. But she kept the ingredients in a notebook."

Gisela sat a little straighter. The memory of her dream flashed—the ingredients listed neatly in a notebook. "Can I see it?"

"The notebook?"

"Yes. Do you still have it?"

"I took a lot of our things from Rockridge before I moved here. It's at the house."

Gisela pressed her fingers to her chin. It couldn't possibly be the same notebook . . . but she wanted to see it anyway. Helena's trusted herbalist. The one who had taught her to make the hylja. Larz had said they were likely executed.

"So, when are you going to patch things up with flamebrain?" Marina asked hesitantly. "He's all worked up over your fight."

Gisela shook the lingering thoughts from her mind. "He's struggling. We all are. He lashed out at me but I'm not angry with him. I wanted to clear my head."

Marina exhaled, long and slow. "Thank The Six. The last thing we need is a moodier Thorne."

Chapter Thirty-Six

The sun was already high, spilling warm light through the windows by the time Thorne woke. He rubbed his eyes, ran his hands through his tousled hair, and shuffled to the window. Outside, rough waves pounded against the shore, and the campfire's smoke curled into the wind, carrying the briny tang of salt and fish. He pushed open the door and stepped into the cool sea breeze.

Adrian crouched by the flames, flipping a fish using his wind. He glanced up briefly, his eyes still shadowed by the previous night, though his tone remained light. "Good afternoon, sunshine."

Thorne blinked against the light. "How long was I out?"

Adrian straightened, wiping his hands on his pants with a hint of tension in his shoulders. "It's mid-afternoon," he said pointedly.

"Where's Gisela?"

A slight smirk tugged at the corner of Adrian's lips. "She's cleaning up with the villagers. Figured you needed the extra rest." He shot Thorne a sidelong glance. "I briefly considered launching your bedroll into the sea. Decided against it."

Thorne chuckled, rubbing the back of his neck. "Probably wise."

Adrian leaned back, one eyebrow raised. "Careful. I could take the breath right out of your lungs. And I'm fairly certain I already do. Good looks can have that effect."

"You wish," Thorne replied with a laugh and shook his head. "How's Eva?"

Adrian's grin faded, his posture stiffening as he glanced away from the fire. "She's been moving around more. I think she'll be up soon."

Thorne climbed the stairs and stepped into the streets of Aquamere. The village stirred with life—not the usual bustle, but a quieter kind of purpose. Villagers cleared debris from the battle that had ravaged their home the night before. Despite the wreckage, a warmth lingered in the air, not from Thorne's protective flames but from the collective effort of the people. He watched as neighbors lent each other a helping hand. A woman, her face lined with exhaustion, offered bread to a neighbor, who accepted it with a grateful bow. An older man tended to the wounds of a younger one with gentle, steady hands. Even the children ran errands with determined little faces, bringing water and supplies to where they were needed.

Then Thorne saw her.

Gisela was at the fountain, surrounded by a group of children. Her sleeves were rolled up as she worked to clean the area. With a casual wave of her hand, the fountain froze over, and the children squealed as they slid across the ice. One small girl clung to Gisela's side, her tiny hands gripping her tunic as if she were afraid to let go.

"You're so beautiful," Thorne whispered into her mind.

Gisela's gaze lifted, finding him. Something in her eyes sent a rush of heat through him. She bent to whisper to the little girl, who burst into a wide, toothy grin. The child released her grip and skipped off to join the others.

As Gisela approached, Thorne's posture relaxed. There was something about the way she moved—so calm, so effortlessly graceful, like the weight of the world couldn't touch her. She was a far cry from the girl she had been before they left Frosthaven. Back then, there was an edge to her, as if she had to be ready to defend herself at a moment's notice. The memory twisted inside him. He had been part of the reason for that edge. But seeing her now, poised and self-assured, left him aching with regret and admiration all at once.

"Hey," she said softly.

"Hi." He reached out, brushing his thumb along her cheek. "I'm sorry, Gisela. I was angry, and I took it out on you. You're the last person I'd ever want to hurt. I'll understand if you don't want to talk to me."

Her eyes narrowed. "You think I'd give up on you that easily? Now I'm really insulted," she said playfully.

They held each other's gaze. He tried to smile, but it faltered. "You don't understand. Every time you look at me like that, it feels like forgiveness I don't deserve."

She reached up, her hands trembling slightly as she cupped his face and kissed him, soft and certain.

All the noise in his head went quiet. The guilt, the fear—gone. All that was left was her, and the way she made him believe he could still be worthy of love.

"Aw, the love birds made up," Marina called out, her tone light and teasing. "Thank the Six." She approached and handed them steaming bowls of soup before they settled on the cobblestones together. "And for our dessert-loving lady, Aquamere's finest treat," she added, presenting Gisela with a small plate that held a miniature cake shaped like coral branches, glazed in ocean blue and topped with tiny edible flowers and shards of candied seaweed. "Coral Cakes."

Gisela's eyes brightened as she ate it all in one bite, a quiet hum of approval escaping her.

Thorne feigned a pout. "You couldn't have let me have some?"

"Oops," she responded through their mental link.

He nudged her playfully, grinning.

Gisela blew gently across her soup. A thin mist of frost escaped her mouth, cooling the broth instantly. She took a sip, then nodded. "Everyone did great today."

"Yeah, Thorne did a really great job sleeping," Marina said, but winked at him.

He shot her a look.

"I wonder what's happening in the other villages." Marina stirred her soup.

Gisela's smile waned and Thorne noticed the subtle hitch in her breath. Her gaze drifted away, and she pressed her lips together as if steadying herself.

"Oh, I almost forgot!" Marina said. She rummaged through her bag. "My mother's notebook."

Gisela stilled before taking it. Her fingers tightened around the worn cover. As she flipped through the pages, hope touched her features and then vanished.

Thorne watched her skim faster, then slowly. She leaned closer to the page, tracing the faded ink with her eyes. At the bottom, her thumb paused over a small signature—two letters and a scratchy heart.

"Can I borrow this?" Gisela asked.

"You can have it," Marina replied with a mouth full of soup.

Thorne tilted his head, studying Gisela. "What is it?"

Gisela looked up, her voice steady but filled with urgency. "I want to go to Frosthaven. Today."

His frown deepened. "You can't. Not alone."

"You said Frosthaven was already unstable before you left. Worse than here," Marina said. "It could be much worse now."

"All the more reason I need to check on my family. I can't handle not knowing. It's eating me alive."

"Then we'll go together," he said. "We'll take Terranox."

Marina shook her head. "No. We can't do that either. He has to return to Mystic Isle once he wakes up from his rest. You're not burning that bridge, Thorne. I won't let you."

"I agree," Gisela said. Her jaw was set, and her fingers curled around the book's spine. "We need all the allies we can get."

Thorne exhaled through his nose and pushed to his feet. "I hear you," he said. "And I know Frosthaven matters. But getting the Stones back will stabilize the realm faster than anything else we can do right now." Thorne's gaze dropped to the floor before lifting to Gisela. "Once we're done here, we go straight to the castle and get the Stones back. We don't have time to waste anymore." His expression hardened. "No more delays."

Evening fell, and Gisela knew what she had to do—*what she was going to do.* She couldn't ignore the persistent tug inside her, pulling her toward her family. With the Guardian Tree, the journey to Frosthaven would be quick. *Just a brief trip,* she told herself. She'd check on her family and return before they even realized she was gone.

They gathered around the campfire on the beach. The air was lighter tonight, touched by laughter and the faint scent of salt and smoke. For the first time since they arrived back in Aquamere, they let themselves breathe. They drank ale and savored the fleeting taste of normalcy in the middle of chaos.

Gisela nestled in Thorne's lap with her head resting on his shoulder. His fingers wove through hers, and he stole gentle kisses against her temple and cheek. The warmth of his touch should have soothed her, but anxiety was ravaging her insides. It made what she had to do tonight all the more painful.

When the fire dimmed and they all turned in for the night, Thorne and Gisela settled on their bedroll in the living room.

Gisela stilled herself, pretending to sleep so Thorne would finally allow himself to rest. Each breath she took grew heavier, the ache in her chest burrowing deeper.

"I hope you know what you are doing," Eira's voice murmured in her mind.

"I don't have a choice, Eira."

Thorne shifted beside her, and guilt lashed at her like a whip. She froze, then carefully rolled onto her side, facing away. When he settled again, the space between them felt wider than the room.

Gisela carefully slipped out of their bed and crept to the door, the floor cool beneath her feet. Her pulse hammered in her ears. She turned back to look at Thorne.

He'd be angry.

But she couldn't wait a moment longer. It would only take an hour or so.

She thinned the bond.

Easing the door open, the hinges groaned, making her wince. She waited long enough to ensure he stayed asleep, then shut it.

Outside, she grabbed her boots and pulled them on. The beach stretched out before her, silent except for the gentle lap of the waves.

Terranox still slept soundly in the sand, his massive form rising and falling with each breath. She smiled faintly before her gaze lifted toward the forest line.

"Shit." She'd forgotten about the barrier.

Her eyes were drawn to the cliff above Marina's house. Determination settled inside her as she turned toward it. With each step, she prepared herself for what she was about to do.

CHAPTER THIRTY-SEVEN

"Wha—what?" Marina mumbled, stirring groggily from sleep. Her eyes fluttered open to find Eva hovering over her, her face pale and frantic. Startled, Marina yelped, tumbling out of her bed in a heap of blankets.

Eva bent down, putting a finger to her lip before her hands flew through signs.

Marina blinked, still shaking off the haze of sleep, struggling to follow her movements. "You're awake!" Marina exclaimed, wrapping her arms around Eva.

But Eva pushed her away, shaking her head vigorously.

"What's wrong?" Marina asked, suddenly fully awake.

Tempest appeared beside Eva. "She says Gisela is heading into danger."

Marina jumped up from the floor and dashed into the main room. Her face fell. Thorne was alone on the bedroll, Gisela nowhere in sight. Marina hurried out the front door and sprinted down the beach, her eyes frantically sweeping the darkened shoreline.

As she looked up in frustration, something caught her eye. Something was glinting in the moonlight, halfway up the cliff.

Gisela was embedding shards of ice in the rock to pull herself higher.

"Gisela! What the hell are you doing!? Are you insane?" Marina's voice rang out, panic surging as she watched the dangerous ascent.

She didn't even think.

Marina rushed into the churning sea, the aggressive waves battering her as she fought for balance. "Ondine, I need you to get me up there."

A hint of hesitation came from Ondine, but the Primal obeyed anyway, lifting Marina in a powerful surge of water toward the top of the cliff.

At the top, she stood with her arms crossed, her stern expression fixed on Gisela as she climbed the final few feet. "What are you *doing*?"

"I'm going to Frosthaven. I had to go around the barrier somehow," Gisela responded with a wave of her hand.

"You have lost your damn mind," Marina shot back. "You can't go alone. Not now. Thorne will have a fit!"

"I need to see my family."

"You saw how bad it was here! If the same thing is happening over there, you won't survive it."

Gisela scoffed, her expression hardening. "You sound like Thorne. I don't need protection. My family does."

"Gisela, please," Marina implored, throwing her arms out. "I can't let you go alone, and we can't leave here yet. Eva just woke up. Throwing her into more chaos right away isn't an option." Marina caught the briefest easing in Gisela's face at the mention of Eva waking, but it passed quickly.

"You have your father here with you. You know he's safe," Gisela said, her voice quiet but cutting. "How do you think I feel? Not knowing if my family is even alive."

Marina swallowed a knot in her throat as the image of her crew flashed through her mind. The faces of those she couldn't save haunted her, and she understood Gisela's desperation all too well. "Nothing I say will make you change your mind?"

Gisela shook her head.

"What about Thorne? I can't keep this from him. He'll burn me alive."

"By the time he finds out, I'll already be in Frosthaven. He'll be angry, but it doesn't matter."

"Easy for you to say, you won't be here," Marina muttered. She had no desire to deal with that. "Fine," Marina sighed. "I'll walk with you."

A few small animals with swirling white eyes emerged from the shadows. Gisela froze them instantly. Her steps were confident as they walked to Aquamere's Guardian Tree.

"Gisela, I feel sick to my stomach. Please, don't do this," Marina pleaded, her voice trembling. "I can't handle losing you too."

"If there's immediate danger, I'll come right back. I promise you," Gisela replied.

Marina's stomach churned as they approached the base of the tree. She gripped her own elbows, her fingers digging into her skin through her sleeves. She had never been so conflicted. The reality of the danger Gisela could be walking into was a weight on her chest, made heavier by the thought of Thorne. To help Gisela was to betray his trust; to stop her was to abandon her friend. But if it were her own family, she wouldn't hesitate either. She knew she couldn't deny Gisela this chance, no matter how much it scared her.

"What happened to the fearless Marina I've come to know?" Gisela asked, glancing at her as they drew closer to the tree.

"That was before I lost everything," Marina whispered.

Gisela's expression softened. "You haven't lost everything. You still have us."

Marina nodded but the knot in her throat held. "I'll wait here for a few minutes. If you don't come back right away, I'll assume you're okay. And you *are* going to be okay . . . right?"

Gisela pulled her close. "I'm sorry for putting you through this."

Marina wanted to hold on, to stop her. But she knew better than to try. She blinked back tears, her voice cracking. "I get it. But when you get back, you're in big trouble."

A soft laugh escaped Gisela's lips as she pulled away, locking eyes with Marina one last time. She turned and placed her hand on the trunk of the tree.

The forest stilled. The leaves on the Guardian Tree shuddered, though there was no wind.

Gisela went rigid.

Marina watched her grip tighten against the bark, watched the color drain from her face. For a heartbeat, Gisela didn't move at all—just stared at something Marina couldn't see.

Then Gisela looked back at her. There was no explanation in her eyes. Only urgency. Fear.

A decision already made.

"Gisela, wait—don't!" she called out.

Gisela vanished, leaving Marina to drop to her knees.

"Damn it!"

Marina had said she would wait. She'd told herself she would trust Gisela's promise to come back if something was wrong. Scrambling to her feet instead, she sprinted back toward the house.

Marina barreled through the door, jolting Thorne awake. Breathless and flushed, she paced the room.

"What?" Thorne asked, rising on one elbow, scanning the empty space where Gisela had been. "Where's Gisela?"

Marina flinched, running a hand through her hair.

"Marina . . . *where is she*?" Thorne scanned the empty room. He closed his eyes, focused, before disappointment was etched in his features.

Marina exhaled shakily. "She went to Frosthaven, Thorne."

Thorne's anger surged, flames erupting at his fingertips as a wave of heat enveloped the space, stealing the oxygen from the room. Without another word, he stormed outside and unleashed his fire, the blast sending the ocean recoiling in a hiss of steam.

Marina rushed after him as Adrian, Eva, and Silas followed close behind.

Thorne looked to where Terranox slept.

He was gone.

"Where is Terranox?" he demanded. "Terranox!"

Adrian approached Thorne cautiously. "You can't take him. He has to go back to Mystic Isle. He probably already left."

Thorne's eyes were wild as he turned to Adrian. "Adrian, go after her. Please."

Adrian shook his head. "I can't. I won't leave Eva. She needs me here, especially now that she's awake."

Thorne's frustration boiled over. "Gisela!" He dropped to the ground. "Why won't she answer me?"

Marina watched his face shift.

"The bond is still there," he said. "But she's distant."

"She hesitated," Marina said. "I think she saw something but she went anyway. I tried to stop her."

Thorne's head snapped up, anger igniting in his eyes. "You were *there*?" he growled. "How could you let her do this, Marina?"

Marina narrowed her gaze. "Don't you dare blame me. She wasn't changing her mind. What was I supposed to do, hold her down? She's not a child."

Thorne's face softened, but before anyone could respond, a powerful rush of wind swept across the beach.

Terranox descended from the sky, landing hard in the sand, his wings stirring the waves into froth.

"Thorne, please, think this through," Silas said, taking slow steps toward him. "Let her do what she needs to do. Gisela is strong. You know that."

"She went alone," Thorne said. "Into something already unstable."

Silas frowned, his concern deepening. "Rushing in without a plan could make things worse. She might come back before you even get there."

Thorne closed his eyes, bringing his hands to his temples.

For a second, Marina thought he might actually listen.

"Ignitus," he called. "Can you sense Eira?"

"I can feel her," Ignitus said. "Gisela can't hear you from this far away. They're using enormous power."

The ground felt less solid under Marina's feet.

Thorne's eyes snapped open. He was already moving toward Terranox as he spoke. "If that much power is being used, waiting isn't safer. It's worse."

"But we have no plan!" Marina shouted.

He settled into the saddle, hand gripping the leather strap. "I'm bringing her back. That's the plan. If I stay here and something happens to her—" His voice broke off. "I won't forgive myself."

Terranox launched into the air.

Adrian sighed and Aerion appeared next to him, shaking his head. "Well, this is a disaster." Adrian muttered a curse and turned back to the house with Eva in tow.

Marina watched in frustration as Thorne and Terranox disappeared into the night, the dragon's silhouette blending with the darkness.

He always acts first, thinks later.

Marina let out a ragged sigh. Her hands wouldn't stop trembling as she tried to grasp how quickly everything had splintered.

Silas placed a hand on Marina's shoulder. "He's acting out of fear. And love."

Marina nodded. "I know. How long until we go after them?"

Silas's gaze was distant. "First, we need to make sure Eva is stable."

"I agree," Marina said solemnly, following him into the house.

With a final glance at the night sky, Silas closed the door.

Chapter Thirty-Eight

The Guardian Tree of Frosthaven was dying. The sight of it emptied Gisela's lungs.

Its leaves had turned the color of ash, the trunk bending as if crushed by its own grief. Around it, dark creatures prowled the ruins of what had once been a haven.

She reached out, her fingertips brushing the tree's surface. The bark was cold—too cold for something still alive. The tree still clung to enough strength to bring her here, but not for much longer.

The creatures scented her distress and advanced, circling closer. She stilled, though every instinct screamed to move. She reached inward, summoning her power, only to find it slipping away.

"Eira, what's going on?"

Eira materialized next to her. "I feel weak here. It's the tree . . . the land."

Gisela pushed, digging deeper and deeper inside to find a scrap of power.

Power flickered beneath her skin, weak and scattered.

Eira dropped to the ground, her glow dimming. "You're pulling from a dying source," she rasped.

"Then we need a new source," Gisela said through clenched teeth.

The power inside her was slipping. She shut her eyes, reaching past Eira's fading glow, past the dying hum of the Guardian Tree.

Please, she thought, though she didn't know who she was pleading with—the gods, the land, or whatever still listened.

A pulse answered, faint and ancient. It wasn't a word she heard, but a resonant hum vibrating in her marrow.

Frost crept up her arms, burning cold. The air trembled. Eira's light flared again, stronger, drawn to whatever force Gisela had tapped into.

The beasts charged and a thick sheet of ice exploded from her hands. The barrier held them back and froze two of their snarling forms mid-leap.

She didn't see the third one.

It lunged from the side, claws flashing.

Gisela stumbled back, tripped over a gnarled root, but caught herself.

With a hoarse cry, she forced another surge of power. Frost exploded outward and the last creature stilled, encased in ice.

Their guttural roars reverberated through the clearing as they thrashed against their icy prisons.

She ran.

She fired blasts of ice whenever a beast lunged toward her. Each surge pushed them back, their snarls muffled as frost locked around them.

The plants she once collected were withered and lifeless, their vibrant colors replaced by a muted gray. The devastation only deepened as Gisela advanced out of the forest. Trees that had once stood tall and proud were now twisted and blackened. Every step sounded too loud in the silence of what had once been alive.

From the forest's edge, she looked out over the field and into the village of Frosthaven. A makeshift wall was being hastily erected around the perimeter. Jagged and uneven, it stood like a fragile promise of safety—but it held.

Snow fell, dusting her hair and eyelashes. Gisela tilted her head to the sky, her chest swelling with a small, cautious hope. She was home.

She darted across the field, as she had done countless times before, boots punching through crusted snow. The cool air swept across her face, biting and exhilarating. She was more alive than ever. Remnants of the power she tapped into vibrated under her skin.

Once she reached the wall, she conjured blocks of ice to climb up and over.

She landed on the other side and scanned the empty streets. The village was eerily quiet, its usually vibrant streets now deserted. Every shadow too still, every window too dark.

She moved swiftly through the shadows, knowing every turn and narrow cut. Her heart skipped in her chest as she turned onto her street. Her house came into view, and a hollow ache opened beneath her ribs. The exterior was a patchwork of scars—scuffs and structural repairs that hadn't been there before.

Curiosity surfaced, but she pushed it aside and focused on what mattered now.

She reached for the door, her hand hovering inches from the wood. She almost knocked, then remembered. This was still her home.

Inside, Noah, Vivi, Ivy, and Orion were gathered in the living area. Their faces went slack, shock and disbelief etched into every line.

Ivy brought her hands to her mouth, a sob slipping through her fingers.

Orion looked exhausted, dark circles shadowing his warm brown eyes. His face appeared sunken, and his clothes hung loosely on his frame.

Vivi tilted her head at Gisela, a smile breaking through the tension. "Sissy?"

Gisela's heart soared. "I'm home." Gisela shut the door behind her, and as she turned around, Noah was there, pulling her in close.

He stepped back, brushing snowflakes from her shoulders, searching her eyes. "I don't even know what to say."

"You can say you missed me." She hugged him again, inhaling his familiar scent. "Because I missed you." She glanced over his shoulder at their parents, where Ivy clung to Orion, her face pale.

"We woke up and you were gone," Orion said stiffly. "Why?"

"I—" Gisela's thoughts flashed back to the night she left. She thought someone had watched her leave. "Didn't you see me leave?"

Ivy rushed over, tears streaming, and buried her face in Gisela's neck. "I missed you, terribly." She grabbed Gisela by the shoulders, as if afraid she might vanish again. A shock ran through Gisela's body, and her sense of balance shifted.

"Aren't you freezing?" Vivi asked from the table.

Gisela hesitated, feeling like she was in a dream. The warm scent of herbs drifted from the kitchen.

She couldn't believe she was really looking at her family.

"Tea. I'll make tea," Ivy said, hurrying toward the kitchen.

Orion approached Gisela and hugged her. "Where did you go?"

Gisela hadn't decided how much of her journey she would share. The state of the villages made her feel she could reveal some truths, but the fear of putting them in danger still weighed heavily.

"I saw the plants you put in my room," Noah said, breaking the silence. "You went to figure out what was happening, right?"

Gisela nodded, strangely at a loss for words.

Noah looked back and forth between her eyes. The room was filled with a heavy silence, broken only by the distant clinking of dishes and the soft murmur of Ivy preparing tea.

They all walked to the table.

Orion's chair scraped against the floor and the sound pierced Gisela's ears.

"Eira, tell me . . . tell me I don't sense what I think I sense."

Eira hesitated, feeling like she was betraying the other Primal in the room. *"Your mother."*

Something in Gisela fractured.

Orion's eyes locked onto hers, worry deepening. "Gisela, can you please say something?"

"Mother," Gisela whispered, still holding her father's gaze.

Ivy returned, her teacup clattering in her trembling hands. Her eyes were wide with fear as she looked at Gisela.

"What in the hell is going on?" Orion demanded, shifting his gaze between his wife and daughter.

Gisela reached into her pack and pulled out Helena's journal.

"What is this?" Orion asked, scratching the back of his head.

Gisela opened the notebook to the page with the ingredients for hylja and slid it across the table.

Ivy looked at the page with tears welling.

"It was you. You taught Helena how to make hylja," Gisela said.

"What is hylja?" Noah asked.

"You knew Helena," Gisela pressed, ignoring her father and brother. The wind whipped against the windows, rattling the panes in the silence.

Ivy wiped the tears from her cheeks as she sank into a chair. "She was my best friend."

Gisela slowly sat down beside her mother, putting a hand on Ivy's arm.

"I'm going to need someone to tell me what's happening!" Orion yelled, slamming his hands onto the table.

Gisela took a deep breath and said aloud, "Eira."

"Who's Eira?" Noah asked.

Eira appeared beside Gisela, her presence elegant and regal.

Noah stumbled back, crashing into the table while Orion gasped.

Ivy pressed a hand to her forehead.

"How—how did you . . ." Orion stammered.

"I'm a Mystic, Father," Gisela said.

Orion vehemently shook his head. "No. The inspections. They would have seen—"

"I used hylja," she explained. "A putty I made from a tree in the forest to cover it up." Ivy closed her eyes, tears streaming silently down her cheeks.

"We have no lineage. This doesn't make sense," Orion said, shaking his head.

Gisela turned to her mother as a surge of unfamiliar anger bubbled inside of her. "I could have been better prepared."

Noah, Orion, and Vivi all turned to Ivy, waiting for her to respond.

"I wasn't sure," Ivy said, her voice trembling.

"Ivy?" Orion said, his face wrinkled with pain.

"Come, Glacia," Ivy said, her voice barely above a whisper.

A Primal emerged from within her.

Glacia was a vision of icy splendor, resembling Eira in form but surrounded by a shimmering aura of frost. Delicate crystals of ice adorned her body, reflecting light in intricate patterns. A wave of ancient frost swept the room, turning their breath to mist and raising goosebumps along Gisela's arms.

Noah recoiled.

Orion clenched his fists.

The room fell silent, the fire snapping loudly in the hearth.

"What a relief," Glacia moaned, stretching.

"Why didn't you tell me?" Gisela asked. "What if I never figured out how to make hylja? I would have been slaughtered."

"The same reason you didn't tell us about you," Ivy said, her words tumbling out in a rush. "I didn't want to put any of you at risk. I had a feeling, but I couldn't be sure. And the moment I said it out loud, it would have made it real." Ivy hurried down the hall and returned with a black notebook.

Gisela knew it in her bones. This was the notebook from her dream.

"I made sure the knowledge was there," Ivy said, setting it on the table. "The Guardian Tree. The hylja. Everything you could have needed." Her voice wavered. "I hoped you'd never have to use it."

Gisela swallowed. "It was you," she whispered. "You saw me leave that night."

Ivy nodded, pride shining through her tears. "I did. And you are *awakened*. By the Six, Gisela."

Orion's face was slack, glancing back and forth between them. "How could you hide this from me? I'm your husband."

"Please, Orion. You must understand the danger I would have put you in. Especially as Village Lord—"

"How long?" he asked, pain in his voice. "How long have you been a Mystic?"

Ivy met his gaze, her heart heavy with the truth.

"I met you when we were twenty," he said slowly. "Were you already a Mystic then?"

Ivy nodded, tears welling up. "I'm sorry, Orion. I loved you and I couldn't risk—"

"What about me?" Noah interrupted. "Is this going to happen to me?"

"Not necessarily," Gisela replied.

Vivi sat silently, absorbing the revelations.

Orion paced, dragging his hands down his face.

"There are more pressing matters," Gisela said. "The King is letting everything fall apart, and these beasts . . . something bigger is at work. We can't keep pretending he's going to bring the Stones back."

Ivy sipped her tea, gathering her thoughts. "Helena . . . she knew this would happen. She came to warn me. I didn't believe her."

Gisela nodded. She had seen that warning.

In her dream.

"I know her husband and daughter. They've been helping me."

"Helena was my best friend. I learned herbalism there, eventually taking over before meeting your father. Helena was engaged at the same time, and we went our separate ways. But she came here to warn me about what she had learned. I couldn't leave. I hoped she was wrong."

Gisela's mind raced.

"Helena had been trying to grant Mystics safe passage to Mystic Isle," Gisela said. "But the King has been forcing awakenings. He's corrupting the bond entirely."

Ivy's hands were shaking, seemingly communicating with Glacia.

"I've had no communication with the King aside from his men searching for Thorne Alderose," Orion said, still pacing. "Every raven, every messenger I've sent has gone unanswered."

"Do you know where Thorne is?" Ivy asked.

"He's been with me," Gisela said.

Noah scrunched his face in disgust. "Thorne? Gisela, he's been nothing but trouble our whole lives."

"You don't know him, Noah," Gisela snapped.

Noah recoiled but didn't push back.

Ivy studied her daughter, her eyes narrowing. "You're in love with him."

"We're Soulbound."

Ivy gasped.

Orion finally halted, fingers rubbing his temples. "What does that mean?"

"It means we're . . . tied together. Mind and body. We can speak to each other through our minds when we're close by."

Gisela's family was stunned into silence.

"I know this is a lot," Gisela continued. "But I needed to come here. I needed to make sure you were all okay."

Gisela told her family everything.

Orion listened with care, his fingers absently drumming against the wooden armrest of his chair. All his life, he had been fed lies about Mystics, believing them to be dangerous and a risk to humanity. One had lived under his roof for years. Now the burden of that truth rested with his daughter as well.

Ivy, who had worn a careful mask for decades, was visibly relieved. Her hand rested lightly on Orion's, a simple yet genuine reminder of the bond they have.

Gisela's heart warmed at the sight. Her father loved his family unconditionally, and seeing it now grounded her.

Noah, her brother and best friend, leaned forward, eyes bright, absorbing every word. She could sense his pride in the woman she had become, but she also felt the weight of his concern.

The conversation stretched into hours. The soft crackle of the fireplace filled the room as Gisela described Mystic Isle.

Ivy's posture stiffened with every mention.

Once Vivi had drifted off to sleep in Orion's arms, Gisela pressed a gentle kiss to her little sister's forehead, feeling the warmth of her soft hair against her lips before Orion left to put her to bed.

Noah hugged Gisela fiercely, and she could feel the unspoken understanding that she would need to return to Aquamere that night—or risk not going back at all.

Before going to sleep, Orion pulled Gisela into his chest and rubbed her head. "I hope you know I love you, no matter what. We'll figure this out. I won't let them hurt another Mystic again. Not in my village."

Gisela's relief swelled, a bright, fierce light inside her. She had the push she needed, the motivation to fight for the people she loved and the world they deserved.

Ivy was the last to leave, and Gisela seized the opportunity to speak with her mother in private.

"I told you I came here through the Guardian Tree. Do you know how I'm able to do that?"

Ivy shook her head, curiosity sparking in her eyes.

"It's because I'm descended from the First-born Mystics. Which means you are too."

"I didn't know that. My father left my mother when she was pregnant. He was a Mystic. When he found out, he left shortly after."

Gisela pulled her mother close, feeling the tremor in her frame. She held her for a moment longer than usual, then pulled back to meet her eyes.

"I'm scared for you," Ivy whispered.

"I'm scared too," Gisela admitted. "But I have the best people on my side. When this is all over, I can't wait for you to meet them."

"Can I walk you to the tree?"

"No. It's dangerous out there. I froze a lot of the beasts, but there could be more."

Ivy laughed, raising a brow. "Do you think I don't know how to use my power? It's been far too long since I have, but it was formidable, thank you very much."

"The power is weak here though."

"Gisela, I have decades of power lying dormant in my body. It's time it came out."

The crunch of snow beneath their boots echoed in the silent night. Gisela's heart ached with every step she took to the tree. She didn't want to leave her family. Not yet.

But she could go back to Aquamere with a renewed sense of relief.

They reached the clearing.

Ivy saw the bodies of the creatures, scattered around. "You've outdone yourself, my girl."

Gisela let out a breathy laugh.

Ivy lifted her gaze to the Guardian Tree. Her lips pressed tight, holding back the swell of sadness.

"I love you," Gisela said, pulling her mother in for one last hug.

Ivy clung to her, her fingers digging into the fabric of Gisela's cloak.

She asked her mother one final question. "Where did he go?"

"Who?" Ivy said, tilting her head.

"Your father. Where did he go when he left? Do you know?"

"Mystic Isle."

Gisela's face paled. The thought that had lived in the back of her mind surged forward. "Do you know his name?" she asked, hesitantly, but she feared she already knew the answer.

"Darian."

Gisela clenched her teeth so hard she thought they would break. Before she could process the revelation, a rustling sound came from the bushes behind Ivy.

A daunting figure stepped into view, silhouetted against the moonlit clearing.

His face was a disturbing sight—half of it was burnt beyond recognition, the charred skin twisted into a grotesque mask. The other half retained the harsh, familiar features of someone she knew, the remnants of long black hair hanging in uneven strands.

"Gisela and Ivy Valor. What a lovely surprise," Cillian Alderose said, his tone dripping with malice.

"Cillian," Ivy nodded, keeping her tone steady though her fingers trembled. "We were out here seeing if there were any plants to salvage for the shop."

"At this hour?" He stepped closer, boots crunching on the frosty ground, one hand resting on the hilt at his side.

"Well, you're out here Cillian," Gisela shot back. "Why is that?"

"I came to collect Selene. Seems my wife's gone missing," he said, his tone clipped. "It's fortunate I'm here. Had these beasts not frozen to death, they might've killed you." A ghost of something like regret flickered in his one good eye, though his scarred side remained a frozen mask. "But now that you're here, you're under arrest for aiding and hiding a Mystic. Who just so happens to be my son."

"He's not here. I don't know what you're talking about."

"Do not reveal yourself," Eira's voice whispered in Gisela's mind, icy and calm. *"There is opportunity."*

She took a step closer to Ivy and leaned close to her ear. "If he takes me, you have to let me go. Don't reveal yourself."

Ivy's lips pressed together, and she gave a faint shake of her head.

Gisela gave her a firm nod, grounding herself in the certainty of the plan.

"Do you think you haven't been seen with him? You were in Aquamere together," Cillian pressed, stepping so close that the shadow of his figure merged with hers.

Gisela hesitated, not knowing how much Cillian truly knew.

"Well, I doubt it was you who saw me. It doesn't look like you can see much at all," Gisela taunted.

Cillian's fury twisted his scarred face. "Vaughn," he spat. "Such a weak excuse for a man. He gave you away with very little effort."

"Little shit," Gisela muttered. She attempted to reach Thorne through their bond, but the connection felt impossibly distant.

"Eira, I can't reach Thorne."

"He is too far away, but he is coming. They know you are here," Eira responded.

"Come quietly," Cillian said, restraining his anger. "And I won't have to hurt you too badly."

"You touch my daughter, Cillian, and I will hurt you myself," Ivy threatened.

"Threatening the King's guard, Ivy? *Tsk tsk.* You know better than that," Cillian mocked.

A group of armed men emerged from the shadows, the glint of their weapons catching the dim moonlight.

"It's okay, Mother," Gisela whispered and took a cautious step toward him.

Cillian lunged. The iron hilt struck the base of her skull. Pain flared, stars exploded in her vision, and she crumpled to the ground, barely conscious.

"Gisela!" Ivy screamed, the sound cracking the still night air. She staggered back as the guards formed a barricade around Gisela.

"Ivy, go home to your pathetic husband." Cillian hoisted Gisela's limp form over his shoulder. The winter wind whipped through the clearing as he hauled her toward the iron-bound carriage, the door slamming shut with a final, echoing thud.

Chapter Thirty-Nine

High above the darkened coast, the night narrowed to the roar in Thorne's ears and the fire burning beneath his skin. His voice was strained as he clung to Terranox's saddle. "Why didn't you tell me they were leaving?"

"It is not my place to intrude on the minds of others without their permission. Primals respect the boundaries of individual will. You would do well to honor the same for Gisela."

"I've never tried to read her thoughts. I don't even think I can."

"Yet."

Thorne stiffened, not knowing what that meant, but pushing it aside. "You could have warned me. You know how dangerous this is."

"There is a delicate balance we must maintain," Ignitus replied. *"To intrude upon their thoughts without consent would breach the trust we have with them. Primals are bound by our own code of respect. We guide and support, but we do not dictate or invade. Eira would not have broken that trust with Gisela."*

Thorne exhaled, settling into the saddle. The fire in his hands dimmed.

"I don't know why she shut me out."

Ignitus chuckled. *"Don't you? You wouldn't have let her go. You've been adamant about her not going. Trust that she can handle this. She is more powerful than she knows."*

"I hope she didn't make a mistake."

"She hasn't," Ignitus said. *"And she has you to rely on, even from afar. Trust in her strength, as she trusts in yours."*

Thorne and Terranox soared through the night and into the morning, keeping high above the clouds as the first pale light of dawn bled into the sky. They had pressed on through the frigid winds with relentless speed. Despite the dropping temperatures as they entered the northern region, Thorne's body remained perfectly warm. The Snowdrifts stretched beneath them in a stark, desolate expanse of white.

The Guardian Tree came into view and dread sank into Thorne like an icy blade. The sight was worse than he'd imagined.

Terranox descended slowly, his massive wings cutting through the air before he struck the earth beside the once majestic tree, the impact sending a tremor through the clearing.

Thorne slid off the dragon's back. His boots sank into the slushy earth as his eyes locked onto the trunk. It stood half-dead, its leaves wilting and falling, the vibrant energy it once radiated now reduced to a faint, failing pulse.

"By the Six," he muttered. He approached the tree and reached out to stroke his fingertips along the bark. It crumbled beneath his touch, becoming dust on his gloves. His thoughts stumbled, clashing with the reality before him—the tree was dying, and with it, the path back.

"Can she even travel back this way?"

Inside him, Ignitus stirred, a restless ripple answering his fear.

The bodies of the beasts lay scattered around the clearing, their fur matted with dark blood and slick with half-melted ice. Their lifeless forms were grim evidence of the battle from the night before.

Thorne knelt beside one of the fallen creatures when he saw it—drops of blood staining the snow and dead grass. His fingers brushed the ground, trembling.

"That's not animal blood," he gritted out. "That's Gisela's blood. I can feel it."

A cold, numbing fear clawed at Thorne's insides. His breathing quickened, becoming ragged gasps.

The crunch of footsteps broke through the silence, snapping Thorne out of his spiraling thoughts. His hand instinctively went to his sword. Unsheathing it with a metallic ring, he turned toward the sound. His muscles tensed, ready to face whatever threat might emerge from the brush.

He almost wished for an attack.

A flash of blonde hair caught his eye. He squinted, tilting his head as a familiar woman stepped out from behind a tree.

"Hi, Thorne," Ivy said, her voice somber.

Thorne blinked, taken aback. "Ivy?"

She spotted Terranox curled at the base of the Guardian Tree and jerked back. Before she could speak, Thorne's voice cut through the clearing. "Is she here?"

Ivy's shoulders slumped as she cautiously drew nearer. Redness ringed her eyes, swollen from hours of crying.

"They took her," Ivy said, her voice trembling. "She's gone."

Thorne's face paled, his nostrils flaring. "What do you mean they took her?"

"The guards . . . your father." She grimaced. "They took her away. I couldn't do anything. She told me not to." Ivy swallowed. "I came back . . . I thought maybe the tree could answer me—help me find you. And here you are."

The words were like lead, anchoring him in a suffocating stillness. Thorne's grip locked around the hilt of his sword, his knuckles straining white. "Why?" he asked through clenched teeth. "Did they hurt her?"

Ivy swallowed hard, fresh tears welling in her eyes. "They arrested her for aiding you. Cillian hit her on the back of the head with his sword. Knocked her out."

White-hot rage surged through Thorne, fiercer than anything he had ever felt. His fists clenched, nails digging into his palms, and then something inside him snapped.

Thorne tilted his head back.

The sound that tore from him wasn't human.

Black flames burst from his body, surging outward in a violent wave. The ground ignited beneath him, slush turning to steam, grass to ash.

He roared again, and again, each cry ripping through the still morning air, releasing every ounce of his fear, rage, and desperation.

"Thorne, *stop*!" Ivy's voice cut through the roaring flames. She thrust her hands forward, and a storm of frost exploded from her fingertips, snuffing out the fire.

Glacia materialized beside her, reinforcing the frosty winds. They swirled through the clearing, extinguishing the last of the flames.

The fire died, leaving behind only a shroud of mist and smoke.

Thorne's eyes were wild and unfocused, until they snapped to Ivy. "You're a Mystic?" he rasped.

"Control yourself," Ivy said. "Don't destroy the place Gisela loves the most any more than it already is."

Thorne's anger and fear gave way to desperate sorrow. "I need to go to her." Hot tears burned behind his eyes. He couldn't bear the thought of Gisela alone, hurt, in his father's hands.

Ivy stepped closer, cautiously but firmly. "You can't rush in without a plan. You're going to need your friends' help, Thorne. You can't do this alone."

"Listen to the Frostweaver," Ignitus said, his tone soft but steady.

The storm in Thorne's mind settled, clearing the way for rational thought. Charging in blindly could make things worse—for Gisela, and everyone else. Yet the pull to destroy everything and everyone standing in his way still simmered beneath the surface.

"Come to the house," Ivy urged. "Before the villagers wake up."

They left the woods in silence. The trees loomed behind them, stripped down and broken. The smell of char and frost clung to the air and Thorne's mind drifted to the clearing again. The dying Guardian Tree, the scattered animals, the bloodied snow—it all sent a rage through him.

They cleared the makeshift wall along the perimeter and the village unfolded before him.

Frosthaven lay still. Broken doors swung from their hinges. Stone walls were cracked, windows shattered. No villagers moved through the streets, no chatter, no market calls—just silence. Everything looked dull, like the missing Ice Stone stripped the village bare, leaving loss in its wake. Thorne slowed, taking it all in.

He followed Ivy into their home. The mingling scent of herbs and a faint trace of Gisela tugged at him.

Ivy moved to the kitchen and pulled a pot from the shelf.

His eyes roamed the room, lingering on spots where Gisela left traces of herself. There was a cup on the table, a blanket draped over a chair.

Somehow, he knew they were hers. He traced the rim of her cup and his hand clenched. Reluctantly, he sank into her chair, his posture stiff and uncomfortable, letting the faint trace of her presence press against him.

They sat in the pressurized silence of the kitchen for a while before Thorne spoke. "Is Orion going to be okay with me being here?"

Ivy offered a soft smile as she stirred honey into her tea. "Yes. Gisela told us everything. You don't have to worry . . . not at all."

Thorne's shoulders eased a fraction, though the ache in his heart remained. This isn't how he imagined reconnecting with Gisela's family. Maybe they'd have declared their love, hand in hand, with a hint of surprise from her family—perhaps more than a hint.

Ivy slid Thorne's cup of tea closer to him. "I've been hiding it from my family for as long as I've known Orion," she admitted, her gaze falling to the floor. "I only wanted to protect them."

"It was beginning to torment her . . . not knowing where her lineage came from."

Ivy's face crumpled. "That was never my intention. I always knew she was special. When she was born, I had this . . . intuition—" She broke off, swallowing.

Thorne watched her, a thought catching and quickening his pulse. He chose his words carefully. "You're awakened," he began. "So, you might know . . . is my mother a Mystic?"

Ivy frowned, thinking. "I don't think so. But maybe she never awakened."

Thorne's hope unraveled. "Have you seen her? Is she home?"

Ivy ran a hand through her hair. "She left right after your father did."

"To go where?"

"No one knows." Ivy lifted her cup and took a small sip.

Maybe Cillian's service to the King had been his mother's way out, a chance to escape the abuse she had endured for years. The thought of where she might have gone was impossible to guess.

"You need to go back to your friends and make a plan to get Gisela back," Ivy said. "I can help in any way you need, but I don't want you barging into the castle alone. Do you understand, Thorne? My daughter's life is at risk. I know you love her. I felt it back at the clearing. But I won't let you put her in even more danger by acting recklessly."

Ignitus appeared behind Thorne, locking eyes with Ivy. "Intuitive, you are."

Thorne rolled his eyes at the truth behind Ignitus's words. This was his moment to prove he had the self-control, the restraint to do this right. He couldn't let his rage steer him. Not anymore.

Noah and Orion came from the hall, their faces shadowed with worry. They froze at the sight of Ivy, Thorne, and Ignitus at the table.

Orion approached slowly and sat down, while keeping his eyes on Ignitus. "I've already sent a raven asking for my daughter's immediate release."

Noah dropped into the chair beside him with a bitter snort. "A worthless effort."

"It's me they want," Thorne said. "I won't let her suffer because of that."

"She already is," Noah snapped, frustration barely contained.

Ivy shot him a glare. "This is not Thorne's fault."

"It's okay," Thorne said, nodding at Noah. "I understand. I'll do whatever it takes to get her back. Trust me on that."

Orion leaned forward, eyes sharp. "You need to be smart about it."

"I'll go with you," Noah offered, rising from his seat with determination.

Ivy and Thorne shook their heads. "No," they said in unison.

"We're dealing with much worse than the average King's guards," Ivy warned. "This is beyond what you're prepared for."

"I don't want to waste any more time," Thorne said, pushing his chair back with a loud scrape as he stood abruptly. "I need to fly back to Aquamere."

Noah perked up. "Fly? The dragon is here? The one Gisela told us about?"

Ivy stood, her hands gripping Thorne's shoulders as she looked him in the eye. "They knew you were in Aquamere. That's how they knew Gisela was with you. It was Vaughn. He gave you up."

Thorne rolled his neck, anger lacing through his restraint. "I'll fucking kill him."

He moved toward the door and Orion stepped forward, blocking his exit. "Bring my daughter back home first."

Thorne met Orion's gaze and didn't flinch. "I will."

Chapter Forty

Gisela jolted awake as the King's guard carriage lurched over rocky ground, the clattering wheels hammering a rhythm into her skull. Damp timber and stale air filled the cramped space. She reached for the throbbing at the back of her head, but her hand jerked to a stop as the iron bit into her skin. She glanced down at her feet.

Shackled.

With a groan, she pushed herself up off the floor, her body aching from the rough ride. Leaning against the wall of the carriage, she closed her eyes and forced her breath to slow.

"Eira."

"I'm here," came the soft reply inside her mind. A single tear slid from the corner of Gisela's eye—one she allowed herself—before she wiped it away. She checked the small, barred window.

Daylight had come.

Muffled voices from outside drifted in. The guards rode close to the carriage, their voices barely rising above the rhythm of hooves. Cillian rode well ahead, a distant shadow leading the way.

"They're saying they saw a giant bird above the clouds," one guard said.

"A giant bird?" another scoffed. "And I have a Grimthorn Bramble in my yard."

They snickered, their laughter grating on her nerves.

"The King doesn't care about birds. He cares about Cillian's boy."

Gisela stilled.

"Right," another responded. "Fire like that doesn't come from nowhere. If the King gets his hands on that kind of power—"

The rhythm of the lead horse shifted. The conversation died instantly as Cillian doubled back.

Leather creaked.

"We could freeze the shackles off," Eira offered.

Gisela shook her head, her expression hardening. *"I don't want them to know. Not yet."*

The carriage halted, gravel crunching beneath the wheels. The door flew open and bright morning light slammed into her, stinging her eyes.

Cillian stood there, silhouetted against the sun, the scarred half of his face looking even more ghoulish in the daylight. "Get up," Cillian barked.

Gisela stood, legs weak but her chin high. She met his gaze, revulsion turning in her stomach. She forced a smirk. "Aren't you a sight for sore eyes."

Cillian leapt into the carriage. His hand snapped out, knotting in her hair. With a brutal yank, he hauled her to the door and threw her out.

She landed hard. Pain flared through her throbbing skull. Still, she looked up at him with a smile.

"Go take a piss. The King doesn't want his carriage full of waste. A guard will escort you."

"You've always known how to care for a woman, haven't you, Cillian?" she said with a jagged sweetness.

"You've got a smart mouth for such a stupid girl," he said. "Running around with my son? You're as foolish as he is. For that, your life is over."

She obeyed and walked off to the side near a bush, fighting back the humiliation that rose like bile. Her jaw clenched. She refused to let Cillian see her break. As she bent down to relieve herself, the escorting guard kept his eyes averted.

When she returned, Cillian was waiting with a malicious grin on his face.

She climbed back into the carriage and a stale piece of bread struck her shoulder and bounced off the dirty floorboards.

"Hungry?" Cillian slammed the door shut behind her with a satisfied grunt.

Gisela reluctantly picked up the bread, her stomach growling in response. She chewed it slowly, tasting grit and anger. She would need every scrap of strength for what came next.

She didn't know how much time had passed, but the stiffness in her wrists and legs told her it had been a while. Peeking through the small window of the carriage, Gisela took in the hum of life in Tevrin. Laughter, shouting, and the clatter of hooves and wheels reached her ears. She realized how different it was from the villages. Here life moved boldly, full of energy, almost daring her to notice it.

The King's castle rose above it all, massive and gray, its stone walls streaked by centuries of weathering. Tall spires cut into the sky, and the stained-glass windows, deep crimson and sapphire, caught the sunlight, scattering splashes of color across the bustling grounds. A wide moat shimmered between the fortress and the town.

Heavy chains groaned as the drawbridge descended. With a jolt, the carriage rolled forward, wheels clattering over the wooden planks. The door swung open, and sunlight blasted in, forcing her to blink. Even the air smelled fresher here.

Cillian jumped off his horse, barking, "Move."

She shuffled her way out and leapt down with a smirk. Right where she wanted to be—if everything went according to plan.

But plans had a way of breaking.

Gisela's feet stumbled as she was dragged down a dark corridor in the King's castle, the stone walls narrowing with every step. They stopped at an iron door at the end, where Cillian pulled out a ring of keys, the metallic jingle echoing. With a twist, the door clicked open, shooting out a blast of cold air. Cillian's malicious smile suggested he thought the chill would be unbearable for her. He was wrong. The cold sang to her.

The stairs descended, winding deeper into the castle's depths, where light and warmth dared not venture. Each step sent a shiver down her spine, not from the cold but from the weight of where she was headed. They came to a stop at yet another door. Cillian unlocked it to reveal a long hallway lined with prison cells, their iron bars coated in rust. The air was stale, smelling like metal and mildew. A dim, flickering light lit up the grim path, while the slow drop of water echoed in the silence.

They reached a small cell at the back of the hall. Calling it a cell was generous—it was more like a narrow gap in the wall, barely wide enough to fit a person.

Gisela clenched her jaw at the sight. Her heartbeat kicked hard against her ribs at the thought of being confined in such a tight space.

Eira stirred uneasily inside, her restless energy flooding through her veins.

Cillian's smirk widened. "I picked the one I thought you might like best."

Gisela steeled herself, staring at Cillian with unyielding defiance. She refused to let him see the fear creeping up her spine.

"Or," he said, leaning closer, "you could tell us where Thorne is, and you won't have to go in there at all."

"I don't know where he is," Gisela said, her voice steady. She leaned in closer as well. "And even if I did, I would never tell you."

Cillian's expression darkened. He grabbed Gisela by the hair, yanking her forward. Pain flared in her scalp, but she refused to utter a sound. She wouldn't give him the satisfaction. He shoved her into the cramped space. The echo of the slamming door rang in her ears.

She watched him walk away, nostrils flaring.

"What are you planning to do?" Eira asked.

Gisela's lips curved into a determined smile. *"I'm in the castle. As close to the Stones as I can get. Once everyone's asleep, I'll break out and find them. The Ice Stone has always called to me. I can find it."*

As the reality of her confinement sank in, her breathing quickened. The tight space was oppressive, suffocating. She closed her eyes, imagining herself in the wide-open field near the Snowdrifts. There was no room for fear—not now, not when she was so close to the Stones.

"They will come for us," Eira said with concern. *"Thorne won't wait."*

"Then I have to be quicker than him."

Gisela waited. She kept her eyes closed as much as possible and focused on the steady rise and fall of her chest. Eira's soothing voice guided her through the moments when the walls tightened around her, urging her to stay calm. The silence pressed against her ears. There was no sign of movement or life in the hallway, but she suspected that prisoners didn't survive long down here.

Once she was sure that no one would come for her tonight, Gisela focused her energy on her shackles, channeling a frigid cold that grew more intense. They weakened and the sudden slam of a door echoed down the hall. She froze, cursing under her breath as the footsteps of two—no, three men—approached.

The whites of the King's eyes were stark in the dim corridor as he strode forward, his robes trailing behind him. He had come all this way, through every locked door, to see her himself.

Cillian followed closely, but it was the third figure, cloaked in a long black robe with a hood pulled low, that drew her attention. His features were hidden, but something about his presence made the air feel colder. A slight flutter in her chest made her stiffen.

"Thank you, Cillian," the King said stiffly. "You're dismissed."

Cillian recoiled, his expression soured. "Your Majesty, I thought it would be wise if—"

"Are you implying I lack wisdom?" the King's voice rose, cold and cutting.

"N—No, I'm merely suggesting, since it's my son—"

"I did not ask for your suggestions, Cillian, nor do I require your assistance any longer. You are *dismissed*."

Gisela smirked behind the bars of her cell, flashing Cillian a quick, mocking wink.

His jaw clenched, lips curling in barely restrained rage as he spun on his heel and stormed down the hallway. The door slammed shut behind him.

"He will become a problem, my King," the robed figure said.

"I am well aware, Zaro," the King replied curtly.

Gisela's expression shifted slightly as something strange flooded through her body, a sensation both unsettling and familiar.

"Gisela Valor," the King began, his voice smooth yet cold. "The herbalist. What a disappointment it is to see you here."

"I agree, Your Majesty," Gisela replied, her eyes sweeping around her cramped cell with a touch of sarcasm. "These arrangements are quite disappointing."

The King chuckled, though she couldn't tell whether it was genuine or a cruel façade. "I don't wish you harm. You will be moved to a larger cell. This was Cillian's doing."

Gisela's eyes narrowed with suspicion.

"Or you can be released right now. If you tell us where Thorne Alderose is."

"What do you want with him?" she asked.

The King studied her with a calculating stare, weighing his words. "You two were never close before. What has changed?"

"And how would you even know that?"

"Cillian sings like a canary. About many things," the King said, his tone darkening. "So much so, he's informed me of his son's power, which appears to be quite unique."

"And why hasn't Cillian been punished for hiding that from you as I am now?"

"He has earned his place here. If he'd truly known, he would have turned him in immediately. His hatred for his own son has oddly outshone his hatred for Mystics."

Gisela blinked. "Why do you want to hurt Thorne? He hasn't done anything wrong."

The King cocked his head, smirking. "Hasn't he? Have you seen Cillian's face?" He gave Gisela a pointed look before his expression shifted, the smirk lingering. "But my intention is not to harm him. Or any Mystic, for that matter."

"You're doing that now. Forcing awakenings. It may not seem like harm to you . . . but it is."

The King's smile widened into something sinister. "Intervening with their awakening is surely better than slitting their throats, don't you think?"

Gisela flinched. "Why do you need to—"

"You're a smart girl, aren't you, Gisela?" the King said, turning away from her cell. "I'll have you moved, but I expect to be given Thorne's location," he called over his shoulder.

"You feel that right?" Eira whispered into her mind.

Zaro stepped forward, allowing a nearby torch to illuminate his face. A strange, eerie light sharpened his eyes, as though they held a power beyond this world. His features were precise, his face unnaturally symmetrical—as though he had been carved from the gods themselves. Or something else.

"Who are you?" Gisela asked, her voice cutting through the tense silence.

Zaro's lips curled into a wide, unsettling smile. "The Ancient Elder, of course."

Gisela let out a soft, mocking laugh. "They actually believe that, don't they?" She leaned against the bars of her cell, her tone lowering with challenge. "You've been keeping a different secret, haven't you Zaro?"

"Ah, but you're harboring the same secret, Frostweaver," Zaro replied, his tone laced with a knowing edge.

Gisela's mask slipped, but she caught it, her eyes narrowing.

Zaro's gaze never left hers as he lowered his head slightly, his stare penetrating.

"What are you?" she asked.

Zaro's face became a mask of neutrality. "I am many things."

Gisela's frustration flared. "You're a Mystic, working under a tyrant King, helping to kill your own kind. Aren't you ashamed of yourself?"

Zaro's brow lifted ever so slightly. "You think they're dying?" For a moment, genuine concern crossed his face.

"They might as well be. You're forcing awakenings. It's barbaric."

"The King is an impatient man," Zaro said.

The way he said the word "king" made Gisela pause. "Speak plainly," Gisela demanded through gritted teeth.

Zaro let out a soft chuckle. "We're going to have to build some trust first, Gisela. We hardly know each other."

"What makes you think I'd ever want to trust you?"

Leaning close to the bars of her cell, Zaro's voice dropped to a whisper. "Because, for now, our goals align."

He turned to leave, but Gisela's voice stopped him in his tracks. "What do you want me to do? I'm a little stuck in here, if you haven't noticed."

"I want you to stop trying to freeze your shackles off," he said, "and wait to be moved."

Chapter Forty-One

Gisela's absence pressed on Thorne so deeply that he thought his ribs would cave in.

Aquamere spread out beneath Terranox's wings, the shoreline quiet, Marina's house dark and still. No movement outside. No figures waiting in the sand.

Terranox landed.

Thorne slid from the saddle, boots striking the ground hard. He stood there. Alone.

The door opened.

Marina stepped out, her posture rigid.

Silas followed, then Adrian and Eva.

None of them spoke. They didn't rush forward. They only stared at him, as if bracing for the truth they already sensed—but didn't want confirmed.

"Where is Gisela?" she asked.

Thorne's shoulders slumped as he looked at the sand. "I was too late," he said. "She was taken by the King's guard. By my father."

Eva gasped.

Adrian cursed.

Silas stepped forward. "But you came back here . . . ?"

Thorne nodded, his expression pained. "Because rushing in blind could get her killed. I won't be the reason that happens."

Silas clasped Thorne's shoulder. "Then we plan."

Thorne lifted his head.

A plan meant restraint. It meant swallowing the fire clawing inside, the instinct screaming at him to burn everything down until she was safe in his arms again.

He was willing to choose her over his rage.

Maps and scrolls littered the kitchen table, borrowed from Aquamere's Village Lord, like a puzzle waiting to be solved.

"So," Adrian said, rubbing the back of his neck. "What do we do?"

Thorne didn't answer right away. The castle rose in his mind as fragments—dark stone corridors from obligatory visits as a boy with his father. Too cold. Too large. Always echoing, no matter how low one spoke.

Eva's hands moved slowly this time.

Adrian watched her sign, shaking his head.

"What is it?" Silas asked.

"She says there might be a way in," Adrian said. "A Guardian Tree. Seraphina said there would be one beneath the castle."

Thorne's head snapped up. "No."

Eva frowned.

Adrian raised his brows. "You don't even want to hear—"

"I've seen what's happening to them," Thorne said. "At Frosthaven. The decay is advanced."

Eva bit her lip. Her hands hovered mid-sign, then lowered to her sides.

Thorne looked at her, softening his features. "Whatever path you think might work . . . it's not worth your lives."

A small, traitorous part of him hated that he knew better. The tree would be faster. Hours instead of days. Minutes, if everything went right.

But speed would come at a cost he wasn't willing to pay.

If the King threatened him, used him as leverage, as bait, if he pushed her far enough to make her reveal herself to save him . . .

Thorne closed his eyes and reached for her through his mind, knowing it was futile.

"Agreed," Marina said.

"It's too dangerous," Silas said, looking at Eva. "For anyone."

Eva didn't sign. She looked down at the table instead, fingers curling slowly into her palms.

Adrian shifted his weight, glancing at her. "She understands."

"We take Terranox. Get close. Get me inside," Thorne said.

Silas studied him for a long moment, as if weighing whether to challenge him—then gave a single nod.

Thorne turned toward Adrian, whose attention was fixed on Eva's pale face. "You stay," Thorne said. "She needs you."

Adrian's jaw worked. "I don't want to be a sitting duck."

"You're not," Marina said, placing a reassuring hand on Adrian's shoulder. "We're going to get the Stones back, no matter what. But first, we need to get Gisela, and it's best if you two stay here." She lowered her voice so Eva wouldn't overhear. "I don't think she's ready."

Thorne started packing his bag, his movements swift and urgent. "We can't delay anymore. Every moment we wait—"

"I know," Silas said.

Thorne felt sick.

Gisela was in his father's hands. No matter how hard he tried to escape the man, his shadow hovered over him like a recurring nightmare. It was his fault Gisela was in danger—his recklessness at Rockridge that had exposed him for who he truly was.

He'd dragged them into the open and handed his father the blade.

He wouldn't make that mistake again.

Whatever the cost, it would be his, and his alone.

CHAPTER FORTY-TWO

A sharp clinking echoed through the dark as keys rattled in the lock, pulling Gisela from her restless haze.

A guard with trembling hands unlocked the door and opened it with a reluctant creak. "You're being moved," he said timidly.

Gisela rose slowly, blinking away the remnants of sleep. She stretched her stiff limbs after a night spent on the stone floor.

She had toyed with the idea of ignoring Zaro's offer and using her powers to freeze her shackles off. But learning that he was a Mystic had complicated things.

"Zaro is no ordinary Mystic, Gisela, you must be careful," Eira warned inside her mind.

"What do you know about him?"

"Nothing. I can't even sense his Primal. It feels . . . wrong."

The guard led her up a winding staircase, back into the grand expanse of the main castle. The change in the air struck her first. Less damp, scented faintly with oil and metal polish.

They entered a side corridor where wooden doors with heavy locks lined the walls.

He stopped at one door and unlocked it.

The room was modest but livable. A narrow bed stood beside a basin in the corner. No windows. The air was still and thick. Too comfortable for a prisoner. Comfort meant manipulation.

"I have to lock you in now." He closed the door, the iron latch dropping into place.

The hours bled together. Without windows, she couldn't tell what time of day it was.

She paced the small room, her mind reeling with Zaro's words. She'd come here with a plan—get inside the castle, retrieve the Stones, escape, and deal with the consequences after.

Simple.

And reckless.

She hadn't accounted for Zaro being a Mystic . . . or whatever he was.

Her thoughts drifted to Thorne, to the others. Were they already coming for her? She hoped not. She needed to end this before they did something stupid. Before *she* did something she couldn't undo. Maybe this whole plan had been a rash one. Thinking was supposed to be her strength—seeing the path no one else did. Yet now, pacing circles in a locked room, all she could see were the ways this could go wrong. All the things she still didn't know or understand could derail everything.

A knock came and her back stiffened. "Well, it's not like I can let you in," she said dryly.

Zaro's low laugh followed. He unlocked the door and entered the room. "I thought I would offer you some sort of respect, my lady," he said. "I'm pleased to see you still shackled, only for the mere fact you chose to heed my advice."

Gisela rolled her eyes. "Can you unlock them now?"

Zaro shook his head. "Afraid not. The King would have questions. We can't have that."

"You see, I'm not sure I like where this is going," she said, crossing her arms. "The least you can do is give me some transparency. I think a night in that awful cell warrants something."

"You want transparency?" His tone cut through her. "The Stones were never meant to be reunited for the good of the realm. That's a lie he fed his court so he wouldn't have to explain what he's really doing with them."

He stepped closer, and the torchlight traced the clean lines of his face as he pulled down his hood. Black hair spilled over his shoulders like ink. His features were unnervingly perfect, familiar in a way she couldn't place. Zaro's smile curved as he looked down at her. "I let him take them because I wanted the world to *see* it. To see what kind of ruler Ravenor really is."

Her pulse picked up. "You let this happen to prove a point? Do you know the damage it caused?"

He didn't answer. Instead, he reached out and brushed his fingers along her cheek. The touch was light—but wrong—sending a jolt through her chest that made her flinch.

Frost burst from her hands.

Zaro pulled his hand back, laughing low in his throat. "I get it now."

"What does that mean?"

"Relax, Gisela. I know I can be a little intense," he said, propping himself against the wall.

Her mouth went dry, senses heightened. "You've allowed corrupted awakenings. You've ruined their chance at a stable bond with their Primals. Why?"

Zaro's expression shifted, then smoothed into something unreadable. "Timing. You know how long true awakenings can take," he said. "Ravenor is impatient. He believes the awakened Mystics are conduits.

That through them, he can draw power from the Stones themselves. To become a Mystic King."

Mystic King. King Thraxus' prophecy.

"*Can* it work?"

Zaro smiled. "I let him *believe* it will."

"At what cost?"

Zaro sighed. "They are alive and well, Gisela. What's a handful of Mystics with unstable bonds? Versus the hundreds he has killed over the years?"

As sick as it made her, she understood the calculation he was making. There was something in the way he spoke, the way he moved—like he was certain the outcome justified the damage.

"What about the scribes?" she asked. "The killings?"

"That blood is not on my hands," he said, and for once, his voice softened. "He sought to eliminate the evidence of the executions."

Gisela shook her head in disbelief. His tone shifted but the calmness he wore felt wrong.

"The King wanted the scrolls, but some of the scribes defended them with their lives."

Gisela cringed at the thought. "Why would he want to do that?"

Zaro's smile turned into something sinister. "Who wants to be ruled by a hypocrite king?"

Gisela's fingers flexed at her sides.

Zaro pushed away from the wall and walked toward her.

A loud knock had their eyes darting to the door.

Cillian barged in, his lip curling in disgust at the sight of Zaro. "The King has need of you."

"Of course," Zaro said, shooting Gisela a wink before striding toward the door. "Are you coming, Cillian?"

Cillian's face twisted with hatred. "I think I'll stay with the prisoner. But is she really a prisoner Zaro? *You* had her moved *here*, yet this isn't where we keep our treasonous citizens."

The revelation that Zaro—not the King—had arranged her relocation gave rise to a fragile hope. Perhaps Zaro was, indeed, protecting her in some way. At least for now. If Zaro thought he was gaining her trust, she'd let him. That could be useful.

Zaro stepped closer to Cillian until his chest was nearly touching his. "I'd watch your tone, Cillian. The King hasn't been happy with you as of late."

Cillian scrunched his brows, defiance flaring in his eyes. "Things were fine before you sauntered your way into this kingdom. Where are you from again?"

Zaro looked down at Cillian with an expression Gisela couldn't fully make out.

Cillian's fury turned to fear, but he quickly masked it with a scowl and turned to storm out of the room. Goosebumps trailed down her arms. How easily Zaro had silenced the usually arrogant man, like a predator toying with its prey. The sight sent fear prickling beneath her skin.

"He won't bother you again," Zaro said, turning away. He stepped out, and the lock clicked into place.

Zaro was an odd contradiction. For someone who stood at the King's side, she expected arrogance, cruelty. Not this cunning defiance wrapped in charm. His words had the shape of kindness but carried something else beneath them. And then there were the small, unguarded shifts—the brief tightening of his jaw, the silent disdain in his eyes when he spoke of the King. Subtle tells.

Trust could be feigned—the truth couldn't.

CHAPTER FORTY-THREE

Gisela stared up at the stone ceiling, chains biting into her wrists. The room was stuffy, but not unbearable. Still, she was a prisoner. She could slip free, leave this room, search the castle, find the Stones, vanish. She had the skill. The power. Yet something anchored her.

Her gut had guided her through everything, even when reason rebelled. Now it wavered. Was it caution? Fear? Or a stubborn hope that something more might unfold if she lingered a little longer.

Then there was Thorne. Her thoughts inevitably circled back to him. He would never leave her here to rot. The reckless, stubborn side of him—one she both loved and feared—would surge straight into danger. Consequences be damned. She could almost see him, storming the castle, fire in his veins, willing to burn the place to ash to reach her. That terrified her more than anything. She couldn't let him risk everything for her.

She inhaled slowly, the cold air fueling her lungs. Escape had to be on her terms. No more waiting.

Rising from the bed, she focused on her shackles. There was no hesitation as she poured her power into the metal. Frost spread rapidly, creeping along the chains and freezing them solid. With a hard jerk, the frozen metal shattered and flew across the stone floor.

She moved to the door and pressed her palms against it, feeling the lock's mechanism through the wood. A burst of ice could shatter it, but that would draw attention. Instead, she let her power seep into the lock, freezing its inner workings. A faint crack, a gentle push, and the door swung open.

The corridor beyond was unnervingly quiet. She paused, listening for footsteps, shadows, any trace of movement. Slowly, she edged toward the main area of the castle. The door creaked under her touch, and she peered left and right—nothing.

Twisting through winding halls, she hugged the shadows. She rounded a corner and froze. Voices and the faint scrape of armor echoed ahead. A tug pulsed through her, familiar and insistent, pulling her gaze toward the staircase to her right. She drew back a step, but the voices were getting closer.

She pressed herself into the stone and peered around the corner.

A figure staggered into view.

One of the guards slowed, his grip tightening on the sword at his side.

The man's steps were uneven, his head jerking as if pulled by invisible strings. His eyes were glassy and unfocused.

"You're not supposed to be here," the guard said.

"I—I can't control it."

Blackened frost crawled along the man's arm, veining his skin before dissolving into smoke.

"It won't listen."

Boots thundered from the stairwell behind them. Two guards appeared, movements brisk and practiced.

"Come, Sihtric. We need to get you back to your room."

They approached hesitantly, but the man didn't resist. He let them take his arms, hauling him away as the frost sputtered and died on his skin.

Gisela's stomach turned. *This* was alive and well? Whatever this was—mercy, necessity—she had just seen the cost and didn't know if it was worth it.

Gisela darted up the stairs, heart hammering. She turned another corner, following the pull until she ended up at a large door. Placing her hand on the handle, it thrummed under her skin. The Stones were inside—she could feel it.

Before she could consider how to get in, a voice slid over her like oil.

"Oh, dear, we have found ourselves in another predicament, haven't we, Gisela Valor?" Cillian's voice slithered through the corridor, cruel and malicious. "Seize her."

Two guards closed in, spreading out as they advanced.

Gisela moved on instinct, muscles coiling as she slipped into the drills her father had taught her.

Cillian's laughter bounced off the stone walls. "It's no use, Gisela."

The first guard struck without warning, steel flashing too close.

She twisted in time, but not cleanly enough. The blade grazed her shoulder, slicing a shallow line of fire through her skin.

Pain flared, sharp and blinding. It stole her breath for one heartbeat too many.

The second guard swung.

She barely managed to twist away, the force of it rattling through her ribs as the blade whistled past. Too close. One misstep and it would have shattered bone.

"Don't kill her, you fool!" Cillian bellowed. "We need her alive!"

Gisela staggered back, eyes darting between them. She searched for weight shifts. Tension in the shoulders. A fraction of hesitation.

Keep your stance strong, focus on your opponent. Find their tell. Her father's words rang clear, but her shoulder screamed when she raised her arm again, and the memory faltered.

The first guard lunged again.

She sidestepped, letting his momentum carry him into the wall.

His blade struck stone, sparks skittering as he stumbled.

The second guard hesitated.

Gisela feigned left, then pivoted right, driving for his sword-arm. She caught his wrist and wrenched downward, forcing the blade loose in his grip.

His free fist slammed into her wounded shoulder.

Pain shot up her arm. Her fingers spasmed.

The guard's sword clattered across the floor, skidding just out of reach.

The first guard recovered fast, his blade leveled at her chest.

Blood ran down Gisela's arm, dripping from her fingers. Her shoulder throbbed with every breath, pulse roaring in her ears.

The ring of steel faded, leaving only her ragged breathing. She met his gaze anyway—and smiled.

Cold surged from her feet, racing up through her veins. Frost crept along her boots, climbed her legs and spread toward her hands in a whisper of ice.

"*Stop.*" Zaro's voice cracked through the corridor like a whip.

The two guards bolted, pale and trembling.

Cillian's anger flared. "Idiots."

Gisela let the tension drain from her shoulders. "Looks like your guards need better training."

Cillian charged as his face twisted in rage.

Reflexively, Gisela thrust her hands forward and released a wave of frost that slammed him against the wall. He crumpled to the ground, limp and unconscious.

Zaro's eyes bulged. "Are you mad?!"

"Maybe I am. That was payback for him knocking me out." She brushed her hands on her pants. "Now, if you'll excuse me, I have the Stones to take back."

"That door is not yours to open," Zaro said.

Gisela tilted her head. "Aren't we on the same side?"

Zaro's jaw worked, hands flexing and unflexing at his sides. "We are. But let me handle what happens next."

Gisela raised a brow. "That's not going to work for me."

"Whatever you think you're here to do," he said evenly, "it isn't that." He briefly looked at the door before returning his gaze to her.

Something in the sudden shift had her skin crawling. But the Stones were her priority.

He took a step closer. "I didn't get this far by improvising, Gisela. You'll get the Stones," he said. "Just not like this."

Gisela narrowed her gaze.

"We need to hide him." Zaro hauled Cillian's limp form into a small closet. "Freeze it closed."

Gisela glared at him, insulted at his order.

"Do it," Zaro said, forcing the words out. "Please."

With a resigned sigh, she extended her hand and encased the lock in ice.

"Now, listen," Zaro began. "We need to—"

"Zaro," the King's voice echoed through the hall. "What is she doing out of her room?"

Zaro pivoted smoothly. "I was escorting her to your throne room, as requested."

Gisela searched for any hint of honesty, but he wouldn't look at her.

The King's eyes glazed over for a moment. "Is it that time? Ah, yes, good," he responded, turning to walk away, then pausing. "Why is she unchained?"

"She convinced one of the guards to release her, my King," Zaro said evenly.

The King's gaze shifted to Zaro, scrutinizing him with a penetrating stare. He gave a curt nod. "Find the guard who allowed this. He will answer for it."

"Of course."

"Now bring her in."

CHAPTER FORTY-FOUR

The throne room was designed for obedience. Wide enough to expose, bare enough to leave nowhere to hide.

Blackened torches burned in iron sconces along the walls, their flames throwing jagged shadows across the stone scarred by centuries.

Each step Gisela took echoed on the dark floor, carrying the chill of the room with them. Dread coiled tighter with every stride toward the dais.

Four massive columns marked the corners of the chamber. A deep crimson rug cut a straight path to the throne. The seat itself loomed atop a low rise of stone, obsidian-backed and upholstered in blood-red fabric. Above it, portraits of King Ravenor watched from every angle, each one more grandiose than the last.

Gisela's lips curled with disdain.

Beside her, Zaro waited in silence, hands folded. He looked down at her with that same pleasant smile—too smooth to be comforting. He wore charm the way other men wore armor.

The doors behind them groaned open.

King Ravenor strode in with a determined step, boots striking the rug as he advanced to his throne. He sat with a deliberate slowness, and the room held its breath.

Guards fanned out at the base of the dais, stoic, waiting for their King to speak.

Zaro took his place at the King's right, as though he'd always stood there.

"Where is Cillian?" the King asked.

The guards below him exchanged puzzled glances, while a ghost of a smirk touched Zaro's lips.

"For someone always up my ass," the King muttered, "he picks a convenient time not to be here." His gaze snapped to Gisela. "I'm giving you another opportunity to tell me where Thorne Alderose is."

Gisela stood silent, her gaze locked with the King's. She'd rather die than betray Thorne.

But she wasn't going to die today.

The King's lips thinned. "Still won't tell me, hmm?" He snapped his fingers.

A side door opened. Two guards entered, pulling a captive between them. A burlap sack was tied over their head, and the captive's feet dragged along the floor.

Gisela's fists clenched so hard her nails bit skin.

"I'm going to ask you again," the King said, leaning forward. "Where is Thorne?"

The guards yanked the sack free, and Gisela's breath caught.

Elysande.

Her face was bruised and blood-streaked, one eye already swelling shut. But her spine remained straight despite it.

Something hot and violent surged through Gisela's body. She couldn't breathe around it.

Couldn't think past the red edge of it.

"Consider this encouragement," the King said. "I hear you two are good friends."

Zaro's jaw tightened. A muscle jumped near his temple, gone a heartbeat later.

"Gisela," Elysande rasped, her voice strained but steady. "Don't tell them anything. Please." She swallowed hard. "My life isn't worth what Thorne's is meant to do."

"I can agree with that sentiment," the King added.

Static hissed in Gisela's ears, drowning out the voices in the room. She could freeze this room. She could bury it in storm and ice.

But the cost—

Zaro's subtle shake of his head told her he knew exactly where her mind had gone.

"Tell me what you want with him," Gisela demanded. "Tell me, and I'll tell you where he is. But you can't hurt Elysande."

Elysande's head jerked toward her. "Gisela, *no*."

The King's gaze slid to Zaro. "He assures me Thorne's fire is the key."

"Key to what?"

The King stood abruptly, intensity radiating from him like heat from a forge. "Another question, and she dies."

The guards at the bottom of the dais stiffened, and those holding Elysande tightened their grip on her.

"You don't understand, Gisela," Elysande rasped. "This isn't his plan—it's—" Her words snagged on something unseen. Elysande's knees buckled, and the guards released her in surprise.

Gisela lunged instinctively.

"*Stop!*" King Ravenor demanded.

The command hit like a boulder. Gisela froze mid-step, breath ragged, eyes locked on Elysande's unmoving form. "What did you do to her?"

"I did nothing to the woman. She's weak. Mad perhaps," the King said. "Where is he?"

Gisela's power swarmed under her skin, looking for an exit. A release.

Eira stirred inside her.

"I'm right here," Thorne's voice came from the entrance, calm and steady.

Gisela turned.

He walked in flanked by guards, his features composed to a dangerous stillness. The room shrank around him. The men at his back held themselves a fraction too rigid, as if aware they were escorting something far more dangerous than a prisoner.

When fire stands witness . . .

The words echoed in Gisela's mind, a voice she didn't recognize—but the phrase she did.

Elysande's parchment. The prophecy threaded through blood and time.

The air was thick as she drew breath, as if the room itself recognized it.

"What are you doing!?" Gisela projected into his mind, but Thorne wouldn't meet her gaze.

He walked past her, as though it cost him something. His attention was fixed on the King.

King Ravenor took a cautious step back. His hand twitched—halfway to an order he didn't give.

"Let her go," Thorne said, voice steady. He glanced briefly at Elysande on the floor, a shadowed weight crossing his features before the mask returned. "Let them both go, and I will surrender myself to you."

Pain folded inward, sudden and vicious. It settled deep in her stomach as if something vital had been torn loose.

There wasn't a reality where Thorne wasn't there. No future that didn't have him standing beside her—fire and ruin and stubborn devotion woven into her fate.

He was offering himself up without hesitation, willing to burn away everything he was if it meant she could keep breathing.

The understanding of it hurt almost as much as the choice itself.

But she'd be damned if he made this choice without her.

"*No!*" The word tore out of her. "He wants your power, Thorne. He believes it will help make him a Mystic King."

Thorne's brows furrowed, then he smoothed it away.

The King's laugh cracked through the hall. "I do not 'believe', girl." His eyes flicked to Zaro. "Tell them."

"A Mystic King," Zaro mused, nodding. His eyes settled on Thorne, his expression narrowing. "Thorne is very valuable."

Thorne didn't flinch. "Take me and let them go."

The King considered him. "Give him the nullification potion."

Zaro's head lifted sharply. "Your Majesty?"

"Don't," the King snapped. "If he truly wants to surrender, I need to guarantee he will not burn my castle to ash." His gaze narrowed. "Bring it."

"It—it's not quite ready, my King," Zaro stammered.

"I'll take it," Thorne agreed. His voice was confident, yet his eyes betrayed him.

"Thorne, don't do this." Gisela's knees weakened. It took every ounce of strength she had left to stand.

Thorne wouldn't look at her. He stood unmoving, like a man who'd already made his peace with something no one else could see.

The King leaned down, whispered into a guard's ear, and the guard left the room.

A hollow quiet settled over Gisela like dust. *"Thorne, tell me you're planning something. Please."* She stepped forward, but hands closed on her arms and yanked her back.

Through the bond, searing rage flooded through, stalling Gisela's breath.

"Don't touch her," Thorne warned, his voice loud and commanding. "Or I *will* burn this place to the ground."

The guards hesitated before releasing her.

Zaro continued to stare between Thorne and Gisela.

"You lied to me," Gisela said. "You said we were on the same side."

Zaro didn't say a word. He regarded her for a quiet moment, then shifted his attention back to King Ravenor.

Thorne's head turned slightly—still not to her. Still not meeting her eyes. His focus stayed on Zaro.

Before Gisela could name the emotion building in her core, the guard returned, clutching a small vial in shaking hands. He set it on the King's outstretched palm.

King Ravenor studied it, then Thorne. "Seize him."

Thorne's voice entered her mind. *"Go to the forest clearing behind the castle. Marina and Silas are waiting."*

"No!" Gisela's voice broke.

She didn't think or weigh the consequences. She threw her anger forward and frost exploded from her hands.

Guards slammed backward. Steel skittered across stone. Torches flared, then dipped, their flames fighting the sudden chill.

Zaro's mouth thinned, his gaze lifting to the ceiling.

"Well, well," the King said, shaking his head. "Gisela Valor is a Mystic, too." Rage contorted his face. "Your family will die for this."

Thorne finally looked at her, fear sitting stark in his eyes. *"Why did you do that?"*

Gisela swallowed hard against the lump in her throat. *"Where you go, I go."*

Boots thundered again, more guards rushing into the throne room.

And then they stopped.

The guards clawed at their throats, faces reddening, lips turning blue. Their mouths opened in silent gasps. Weapons clattered uselessly to the floor.

"Tsk tsk, I don't think so," Adrian's voice purred through the hall.

Gisela and Thorne's gaze snapped to a door behind the throne.

Adrian emerged, descending the steps with the effortless grace of a man who had never doubted his place there. "See, Thorne? I told you, I could take your breath away."

Eva followed, striding steadily with confidence.

A long-awaited warmth blossomed in Gisela's chest at the sight.

"Now, King," Adrian said, "should your guards go outside? Get a little *air?"*

The King's body shook with fury. "You think you can—"

Wind snapped through the room.

Adrian propelled the choking guards out through the doors and slammed them shut, the impact rattling the hinges. Then he turned back, calm as if he'd merely cleared a table. "None of you will touch him," he said. "Or that potion."

The King's eyes darted around the room, counting bodies, measuring threat. Realizing, too late, that he had fewer hands than he needed.

And still, Zaro hadn't moved. He remained at the King's side, watching the scene with the calm patience of a man waiting for a cue.

The doors opened again.

Marina stepped in with Silas, her cheeks flushed with restrained fury, gaze locked on Thorne.

"You made us wait," she said. The calmness in her tone didn't fool Gisela. "You were going to do it," she continued. "You were going to give yourself up, and you didn't even look back."

Thorne's jaw clenched. He didn't deny it.

Marina's gaze flicked to Gisela, softened, then returned to Thorne. "Don't ever do that to us again."

Silas stepped closer. "Next time you think about sacrificing yourself, remember you're not the only one who pays for it."

Thorne nodded once. Barely.

The King's eyes darted frantically to the empty space where his guards should have been, leaving only Zaro at his side.

Zaro moved to walk off the dais, his gait graceful as he strode down the stairs. "Well," he said, a smirk turning the corner of his mouth. "This was always how it was meant to end." He chuckled.

"Do something, Zaro," King Ravenor said.

Zaro's gaze remained on Thorne.

With fiery passion, the kingdom's fate is taken.

Gisela felt it then, an invisible pressure in the air, like the world itself had been waiting for the last piece to arrive.

Zaro's voice dropped, almost gentle. "Did you actually believe it would be possible? That you could steal the gifts granted by The Six?"

The King sneered, but his eyes betrayed him.

Uncertainty.

Zaro's smile thinned. "You murdered Mystics for years, then wondered if the gods would answer you." His gaze hardened. "We do not kneel to hypocrisy."

The King's uncertainty shifted to realization and he lunged—but Zaro raised his hand. The King stopped mid-step, as if the air had hardened around his throat. His fingers clawed at his neck, breath stuttering.

"King Ravenor?" Zaro asked, feigning concern. "Are you alright?"

"I'm not doing that," Adrian whispered.

"Oh, foolish, King Ravenor," Zaro cooed, bending down to meet the King's gaze. "You were so impatient. Predictable."

The King's gasps grew frantic as his face turned blue. He collapsed to his knees, his eyes darkening in fury and disbelief.

Zaro's gaze pinned Thorne. "When fire stands witness beneath the sun's churn."

The words hung in the cool air.

"And fire stood witness today."

A broken sound tore from the King's throat as he pitched forward, scraping at the stone as if retreat were possible.

Zaro's hands remained steady, his expression neutral, casual even.

With one final, wet gasp, the light left King Ravenor's eyes, and he collapsed. His crown rolled across the stone with a hollow, metallic ring. Life drained from him as quietly as the air Zaro had refused to give back.

Zaro's gaze flicked briefly to the vial at Ravenor's feet, then away.

Marina and Eva stepped closer to Gisela, while Silas and Adrian edged toward Thorne, their eyes fixed on the body at the foot of the dais.

King Ravenor was dead.

Gisela couldn't hear anything. Couldn't see anything other than the body.

The scene before her took on the surreal edge of a lucid dream, the kind so real it makes you wonder if you're actually asleep.

A distant part of Gisela—the healer, the girl who once believed in mercy—flinched at the thought of a life lost, however deserving. The sensation scraped at her insides and vanished before she could indulge it.

All that remained was relief.

"What just happened?" Marina whispered.

Zaro regarded them with keen eyes. "I did tell you I was on your side, Gisela."

Thorne crossed the space in two strides and pulled Gisela into his chest. She winced as his arm grazed the slice on her shoulder, but she didn't care—she clung to him, breath shaking, burying her face in his scent.

Zaro's head tilted, studying them with calm curiosity.

"I'm sorry," Thorne whispered into her ear.

Silas's voice cut through the silence. "Who are you?"

Zaro bent and lifted the fallen crown. He set it upon his own head with deliberate care. "I am the Mystic King."

"No, it's not that simple," Marina shot back. "You've been planning this all along?"

"I understand how it looks," Zaro said. "But power alone doesn't crown a King." He turned to Thorne. "Witness does."

Marina's laugh came out raw. "You allowed this—this tyrant—to destroy our land, only to usurp his crown?"

Zaro's eyes cooled. "Would you prefer him alive?"

"No," Marina spat, "but my entire crew is dead because of him . . . and because of *you*."

Marina lunged at him, but Zaro halted her in mid-air with a wave of his hand. "Now, now. Let's not act in haste."

"Let. Me. Go."

With a graceful flick, Zaro released her.

She hit the stone hard enough to make her wince, then surged back to her feet, shaking with rage.

Silas stepped between them, voice controlled. "We have questions."

Zaro's smile returned. "Of course you do. But understand this, I only want the best for Mystralos. Although my methods were unconventional, the realm needed to witness the lengths Ravenor would go for his own glory."

Gisela and Thorne pulled apart, turning their focus to Zaro.

"To be fair, the same could be said for you," Adrian added.

"Where are the Mystics you awakened?" Gisela pressed.

"They're safe," he replied.

"That's not what I asked."

Zaro's smile thinned. "They live. They are no longer under Ravenor's hand. They are protected, cared for, and will serve in positions where their gifts can be refined. They will be guided, no longer hunted or tortured. Their freedom is theirs in ways they've never known."

Relief brushed Gisela's mind before something harsh settled.

Guided freedom.

A kinder cage was still a cage, but it was infinitely better than Ravenor's rule.

"This is bullshit," Marina said through clenched teeth.

Zaro's voice went quiet. "Believe me, I regret what it took. But they will be housed, healed, and taught. They will not die by Ravenor's hand."

Thorne shook his head. "This was your plan all along. Infiltrate the kingdom, slowly create your own defenses? Let the world rot?"

Zaro didn't flinch. "The executions ended. The Stones were always within reach. Ravenor exposed himself. The realm will be how it was intended." He turned to Gisela. "I'll retrieve the Stones."

The offer struck Gisela. The possibility of recovering the Stones without further bloodshed was too good to be true.

"Fuck you," Marina spat but Silas grabbed her arm, his eyes widening in a silent plea for restraint.

"Do you want them or not?"

"We do," Gisela said, turning to Marina.

"It's his plan that got my entire crew killed, that destroyed my mother's ship. How could you be so quick to forgive him? We don't even know him."

Gisela's thoughts tangled in on themselves. Zaro was a risk she could not justify, but the Stones were nearly within her grasp. He was offering the very thing she had come for, and walking away felt like a betrayal of the purpose that had carried her this far.

"We came here for the Stones. We're getting them," Gisela asserted, trying to shake off the unease gnawing at her gut. She had to focus on the goal, no matter what the cost.

Silas's expression remained neutral as he maintained a firm grip on Marina's arm. "Let's take the Stones and get out of here."

Elysande stirred on the floor and Gisela rushed to her aid. She brushed the stark white hair away from her face, relief flooding her as she stared into her friend's dazed eyes. "You're okay," she whispered, squeezing her hand.

Zaro considered Elysande before leaving the room.

Eva approached and kneeled beside Gisela. Together, they helped Elysande to her feet, steadying her as they guided her over to the rest of the group.

Elysande was still out of it, her gaze unfocused. "What happened?" she barely rasped out.

"It's okay, you're safe now," Gisela reassured her, though the words felt thin, fragile.

"Don't lie to her," Marina snapped, her eyes blazing with anger. "I can't believe you're willing to let this nobody come in and steal the throne."

"What choice do we have, Marina?"

The Stones. They needed the Stones.

Marina's face hardened as she stared at the spot where the King had fallen. She reached into her pocket and pulled out a small strip of weathered rope—frayed, salt-stiff. A piece of her ship.

A piece of them.

Her jaw trembled. Then she turned away, grabbed Silas's arm, and stormed out of the room.

Thorne slid his arm around Gisela's waist. "We'll figure it out," he said. "She'll be alright."

Gisela shook her head, tears prickling at the corners of her eyes. She didn't blame Marina for her anger. For all she knew, she could be making a deadly mistake. But the promise of the Stones—their power to restore what had been lost—outweighed her fears, at least for now.

Zaro returned with a leather bag clutched in his hand. "They're in here," he said, extending it to Gisela. "See for yourself."

Gisela peered inside. They glimmered dimly, a shadow of the radiance the Ice Stone once held upon its pedestal. Only Thunderpeak's stone remained vibrant.

"Thank you, Zaro," she said.

Adrian nodded solemnly before following Marina and Silas out of the throne room.

Eva struggled to support Elysande as she rose.

They made their way out, and Elysande glanced up at Zaro. Her face drained of color. Her lips moved, shaping words too faint to hear, her voice reduced to a rasp.

"N—ox . . ."

Gisela frowned, leaning closer.

"Bring her back home," Zaro said. "She's not well. The woman needs rest."

Elysande shook her head vehemently, repeating the same unintelligible phrase.

Eva guided her out, leaving Thorne, Gisela, and Zaro alone in the grand, echoing space.

Zaro's gaze landed on Thorne. "I knew you would come for Gisela," he said, a faint smile touching his lips. "But your timing was impeccable."

Thorne held his stare, measuring Zaro in silence.

"Gisela," Zaro continued, turning to her with a casual ease that felt deliberate, "why don't you go on ahead to your friends. Smooth things over. I'd like a word with Thorne."

"Why?"

Zaro's smile widened, disarmingly gentle. "Surely, you don't believe I'd hurt him after all of this?"

"Whatever it is you want to say to him, you can say to me."

"It's okay, Gisela. I'll be out there soon," Thorne said.

She was taken aback. *"Are you sure?"*

"I am."

CHAPTER FORTY-FIVE

"Come," Zaro said, motioning for Thorne to follow him. Without waiting for a response, he turned and led the way toward a side door in the throne room.

Thorne glanced back at Gisela, offering reassurance, but she remained rooted in place.

They disappeared behind double doors.

Her fingers fidgeted nervously at her sides. Every step he took toward that threshold felt like a step toward a place he would never return from.

Trust him.

Trust Thorne.

She stepped outside and found Marina, Silas, Eva, and Adrian waiting in the courtyard. Elysande sat on a bench, mumbling to herself. The air was fresh, and the distant bustle of Tevrin drifted to her ears. Outside these walls, life carried on, completely unaware of the shift in power that had just begun.

"It's over. We have them," she said.

"Gisela," Marina said. "You really believe this is the right choice?"

She met her gaze, hesitating. "Yes. We need to restore balance as soon as possible. King Ravenor is dead. We have the Stones. This is everything we wanted."

Marina's expression softened slightly. "Trusting him is a risk."

"I know," Gisela replied. "But if we don't do something, we'll lose everything."

Marina looked away, frustration mingling with concern. "I can't shake the feeling that there is more to it than this. What if it goes wrong?"

"Then I'll take responsibility," Gisela said, stepping closer. "I want to make this right. For all of us. For Mystralos."

Silas interjected, placing a reassuring hand on Gisela's shoulder. "We're all in this together. The Stones will set everything right again." He paused, his eyes landing on the bag of Stones. "But the Seer's words . . . they've never left me. *'Only when the Great Guardian Tree is revived will balance be restored for good'.*"

Adrian shifted on his feet, turning back toward the castle. "The castle's tree . . . it didn't look decayed."

Gisela tilted her head. "Maybe fate has shifted."

Marina sighed, the tension in her shoulders easing. "Just be careful where you put your trust, okay?"

"I will. I promise."

They started walking, and Silas fell into step beside Adrian. "You used Aquamere's tree to reach the one beneath the castle . . . Thorne said it wasn't safe."

Adrian hesitated, then nudged Eva gently. "It was her call. She saw—"

Eva's fingers closed around his wrist.

Adrian winced. "She says some dangers are worth the risk," he said. "This was one of them."

Zaro and Thorne stepped into a small study. Through the large window, he could see Tevrin sprawled out, a patchwork of rooftops and winding streets. The sun was almost completely set.

Lanterns kindled one by one across the city, hearth smoke curling from chimneys as it settled into evening.

Unaware.

Zaro moved behind the desk, gesturing for Thorne to sit in the chair in front of it.

Thorne hesitated, sweeping the room, searching for hidden threats.

"You don't have to worry, Thorne, I assure you." Zaro studied him with an unsettling calm, his fingers lightly drumming the desk. A thin crack branched through the wood beneath Zaro's hand, then sealed itself as his fingers stilled.

"You've made quite the journey. I must admit, it's no small feat to confront a King. Even with powers as unique as yours." With a wave of Zaro's hand, the door behind Thorne swung shut.

Thorne's gaze darted to the door, before slowly turning back to Zaro. "You're a Windbinder?"

Zaro looked at Thorne thoughtfully. "Among other things."

Thorne said nothing. He was used to men who wielded power as a weapon, who saw others as pieces to move on a board.

"You're probably wondering why I wanted to speak with you alone," Zaro continued. "I have a proposition for you."

Thorne remained standing, crossing his arms over his chest. "A proposition?"

"Yes. Come work for me here, at the castle. Surely you don't want to return to Frosthaven?"

Thorne was struck by Zaro's ask. "I won't leave Gisela."

Zaro's expression remained unchanged. "She's more than welcome to join us. In fact, I encourage it."

Thorne sat down, thinking for a moment, when Zaro bent to retrieve two drinking glasses.

"Thirsty?"

A dark liquid poured from his fingertip, filling the glass. It rippled once before settling.

Water.

Thorne's throat tightened as the liquid caught the light, shimmering like ink.

Zaro took a sip, a sly smile spreading across his face.

"I don't even know you," Thorne finally managed to say.

"Ah, but you will," Zaro replied. "It'll take time to establish trust. I understand that. Gisela and I already made some progress on that front."

The way he said Gisela's name didn't sit right with Thorne.

"Once the Kingdom learns of their tyrant King's demise, executions will end for good, and the realm can live in peace as it once did. You'll see the change in the tides."

"Well, it's hard to trust someone who would let beasts ravage the villages of the very realm you claim to want to protect. People died. Even more were injured. Our powers are weakened."

"Were yours?" Zaro asked, leaning forward in his chair.

Thorne tilted his head, his gaze hardening. "What do you know about me?"

Zaro regarded him. "Not nearly enough, unfortunately. But that can change. Think about my offer, Thorne. Together, we can reshape this realm. I'd like you by my side."

There was so much Zaro was saying and so much he wasn't. But one thing was clear: whatever Zaro's true intentions were, he was far from finished.

"I'll consider it." Thorne got up to leave when Zaro's voice made him stop.

"Oh, and Thorne?"

Thorne turned, waiting.

Zaro smiled, leaning back in his chair. "Tell my sweet Selene that I *will* find her. She can't hide forever."

Thorne's face paled. "How do you know my mother?"

Zaro looked amused. "Oh, Thorne. What did your *father* always say to you growing up?"

Thorne's mind raced through painful memories. Cillian had hurled many insults at him over the years. He made his aversion for Thorne evident in any way he possibly could. But one phrase stood out before all others.

"You are no son of mine."

He had known it was Cillian's way to inflict pain, to distance himself from a son who never met his impossible expectations. But now, hearing Zaro's words, the meaning twisted into something far darker. Thorne's heart pounded in his ears as he struggled to piece it all together.

"That's right. You are no son of his," Zaro said, his voice dropping to a low, steady lull. Black flames wrapped Zaro's fingers—the same dark, hungry fire that lived in Thorne's veins. "Because you're mine."

Gisela stood at the base of the castle steps as Thorne descended. He was pale, tension carving deep lines into his face. The six Mystics had gathered, their eyes fixed inside the bag containing the Stones. After all they'd been through, here they stood.

She studied Thorne as he approached. "What was that all about?"

Thorne's gaze dropped to the ground, avoiding her. "Not right now."

When Gisela reached for his arm, he stiffened beneath her touch. She searched his face, but he kept his eyes averted.

Gisela knew Thorne. She was bound to him, soul and mind alike. She knew his anger, his sadness, and the jagged edges of his torment.

But this . . . this was something else.

She brushed his mind, but couldn't read what lay there.

"They look dull," Adrian muttered, frowning as he lifted Windspire's Stone from the bag.

Gisela carefully picked up Frosthaven's Stone. It was warm, like its elemental energy had faded. She turned it over in her hands and bit the inside of her cheek.

With slow deliberation, Gisela reached into the bag and pulled out Rockridge's Stone, offering it to Silas. One by one, she matched the Stones with their corresponding Mystic. Thunderpeak's Stone stung as her hand grazed it, and she pulled back.

Eva reached in and took it, her hand stalling for a moment as her fingers closed around the Stone. She withdrew slowly, her knuckles white against its defiant glow.

When she reached Sunhold's Stone, Thorne shook his head, his hand curling away.

She held the Stone out to him. "Take it," she insisted.

His fingers closed slowly around it.

"I trust you," Gisela said.

He turned away.

She let the familiar frost flood her veins, tightening her grip on the Ice Stone. A shiver crept up her arm as its surface cooled against her skin. Around her, the others—Marina, Silas, Eva, and Adrian—followed suit, focusing their energy into their Stones.

Eva hesitated, tilting her head, inspecting hers. It glowed bright in her hands before she had done anything.

Gisela turned to Thorne.

He stood with the Stone in his hand, nostrils flaring.

"You can do this," she urged, taking his hand.

Pain crossed his face, then something steadier took hold beneath it. He exhaled and let the fire go. The Stone pulsed in his grasp, its dull glow brightening.

Around them, the other Stones flared to life, beaming with renewed energy.

Only Gisela noticed the faint black fissure running through Sunhold's Stone.

ACKNOWLEDGMENTS

Writing *Veil of Kings* as my very first piece of writing was as magical as it was grueling. This story came to me while I was driving to my ENT appointment for my relentless vertigo. I was listening to *The Last Kingdom* soundtrack, because if you know me, you know that is my favorite show of all time.

The music spoke to me so clearly that Gisela introduced herself to me and the world she was born into.

It is a dream come true to see this story come to fruition.

First and foremost, I want to thank my husband, Aaron, for being the best husband and supporter from the moment I told him I wanted to write a book. I want to thank my four children for behaving well enough to let me write this book. I love you all so, so much.

To my beta readers—Aaron, Dad, Alexis, Janine, and Keren—thank you for reading this book in its infancy and for giving me the confidence and guidance I needed to make this book stronger.

To Allison and the team at Golden Editorial, this book would not be what it is without you and your meticulous attention and advice. Your support has been unmatched.

I want to thank David Gardias for creating an amazing book cover that captured the essence of Mystralos and the Guardian Tree.

To Andrés Aguirre, for creating the map of Mystralos and for being so incredibly talented, it still blows my mind.

To my readers, thank you for taking a chance on a debut novel, and for taking a chance on Gisela and her team of Mystics. I am forever grateful.

About the Author

When Michelle Kirby isn't hallucinating her next story to music, she's juggling four kids, two dogs, and her husband (who, she assures everyone, actually helps with the juggling).

Michelle received her bachelor's degree in psychology from the University of South Florida in 2014. She is a content creator on Instagram and TikTok, where she talks about all things books and writing.

Michelle enjoys reading, gaming, and watering her plants while staying in her sweatpants for as long as she can.

Stay connected with Michelle at
www.michellekirbybooks.com/

Follow Michelle on Instagram and TikTok
@MichelleKirbyBooks

9 781972 159002